the
further
adventures of

SHERLOCK HOLMES

THE DEVIL AND THE FOUR

SAM SICILIANO

D0785033

TITAN BOOKS

THE FURTHER ADVENTURES OF SHERLOCK HOLMES:
THE DEVIL AND THE FOUR
Print edition ISBN: 9781785657023
E-book edition ISBN: 9781785657030

Published by Titan Books
A division of Titan Publishing Group Ltd
144 Southwark Street, London SE1 0UP

First Titan edition: August 2018
10 9 8 7 6 5 4 3 2 1

What did you think of this book? We love to hear from our readers. Please email us at: readerfeedback@titanemail.com, or write to Reader Feedback at the above address.

To receive advance information, news, competitions, and exclusive offers online, please sign up for the Titan newsletter on our website:
www.titanbooks.com

To all the folks at Titan Books, for resurrecting my writing career and supporting my vision of Sherlock Holmes.

Author preface

My source for many details of life in fin-de-siècle Paris and for the particulars of Satanism and the Black Mass was Joris-Karl Huysmans's bizarre 1891 novel *Là-bas*, "Down there." Most of the somewhat incoherent prayer to Satan near the end comes directly from Huysmans. Also, for those new to my Holmes series, I should perhaps warn that this novel contains major "spoilers" for the second book, *The Web Weaver*.

Part One,

Henry

Chapter One

S herlock Holmes and the lion stared at one another. The gray-white light from overhead glistened on Holmes's long sloping forehead and his swept-back black hair, and brought out the blue in his mostly gray eyes. The lion had a bushy black mane and yellowish orbs with long black slits in them. I sensed an odd sort of bond between them, a shared consciousness, an intelligent awareness, a certain dignity, and something unpredictable as well.

The lion was the first to look away, or rather he raised his head slightly as his mouth opened up in a great yawn which revealed his enormous fangs and pink tongue. Perhaps I only imagined it, but I thought I could smell his fetid breath. He raised his tawny paw, some six inches across, and began to meticulously lick it. The action was exactly like that of my cat Victoria, only on a greatly amplified scale. This cat, however, crouched upon a concrete floor rather than a carpet, with thick steel bars and a restraining fence separating us. My wife Michelle and I occasionally speculated on whether Victoria would gobble us up if we somehow shrank in size so we were only a few inches tall. I supported the affirmative case, Michelle the negative one.

We sauntered on. In the next cage a tiger was sprawled across the concrete, eyes closed, his massive head resting on his paw. I stared at the elaborate pattern of black upon yellow-orange of his face, then at the long white whiskers, the ears with their spots of black and white. The long striped yellow and black tail was the *pièce de résistance*. I shook my head. "He is a beauty. It does seem a shame to keep such magnificent animals in small cages without any trees or greenery."

Holmes nodded. His black overcoat and frock coat were both unbuttoned; he held in one hand his umbrella, his top hat and gloves in the other. Outside it might be a cold rainy November afternoon in London, but the lion house of the Regent's Park zoo was heated, uncomfortably so. It accentuated the pungent animal smell in the heavy air all about us.

"A common enough reflection, Henry, one which I share." He raised his umbrella and gestured at the bars. "All the same... a cage is a curious thing. Bars like those are certainly abundant in London."

"What are you talking about?"

His mouth rose up slightly on one side, an ironic gleam showing in his eyes. "Do not the black wrought-iron variety stand before most of the stately townhouses of our great metropolis? And they line our many parks as well. But who is the true captive, I wonder? Are the wealthy keeping the riffraff out, or locking themselves in?"

"The wealthy can leave their houses whenever they feel like it."

"True, but a native of the South Sea Islands or a visitor from another planet might appropriately assume that London was a vast collection of cages, of specimens kept in various dwellings."

"Yes, but they would be wrong."

He shrugged. "Would they? I wonder. Sometimes it seems to me... Bars are not necessary for a cage—the reptiles are behind glass. If the glass were thick enough, you could cage even a beast like our friend here. Such a cage would be almost invisible."

I stared at him. "Your point being?"

"Must there be a point? Might we sit for a moment. I think I shall indulge myself in a cigarette—if you will allow it, Doctor." His gray eyes again waxed ironic. I had been known to lecture him about his tobacco usage.

The cages were in a row all along one side of the lion house, while on the other, three concrete steps rose to a long platform with benches. Holmes and I went to the nearest bench. He set his hat, gloves and umbrella down on the wood, removed his overcoat, then withdrew his silver cigarette case from within his jacket pocket. He lit a cigarette, leaned back and exhaled a cloud of smoke. His thin pale face seemed particularly angular, almost exaggerated, as if he had become a caricature of himself. As most people acknowledged when meeting him in the flesh, he was nowhere as handsome as Sidney Paget's version illustrating Watson's stories.

In summer the lion house could be a madhouse filled with running and shrieking children, but this Thursday in November was exceptionally quiet and peaceful, the vast hall nearly empty. The row of skylights cast gray light on the concrete. The soft murmur of a couple talking as they walked echoed off the high vaulted ceiling, their words indistinguishable. A lion gave a low, coughing sort of roar, more inquisitive than ferocious.

"Perhaps I have a point, after all, Henry. Perhaps London, like most cities, is one vast cage. Most of its inhabitants are trapped here, forced to labor in factories or offices and to daily breathe the noxious winter air heavy with coal smoke and soot. No fresh air or greenery for them. Perhaps we all dwell inside a variety of cages of the plate-glass variety, cages unseen, encasing us like the layers of an onion, each cage inhibiting us, enclosing us, in its own way. What, after all, could be more secure than invisible bars? None of us is truly free. No one. We are all imprisoned within ourselves."

A soft laugh slipped from my lips. "What a cheery reflection! You have outdone yourself today."

He shrugged. "It must be the beastly weather and the idea that it is just beginning, that weeks of gray cold rain or yellow fog lie before us."

"I think it is time for you to take a winter holiday. Southern France, the Côte d'Azur, can be splendid this time of year. It may be cold, but never so dreary as London."

He only shrugged. We stared at the sleeping tiger, who stirred and shifted onto its side, the big head rolling off its paw. We had walked a long while, and it was good to rest my legs. All the same, the hot stifling atmosphere with its rank animal smell was unpleasant. Holmes finished his cigarette, then dropped the butt and crushed it underfoot. "One cannot escape oneself on a holiday, not even at the south of France before the Mediterranean Sea."

I stared closely at him. "What is wrong with you?"

He sighed and slapped his knees with his gloves. "Shall we walk? It is suffocating in here."

"Yes, let's walk. It is uncomfortable."

On the way out we passed a handsome woman wearing a sable coat and a blue hat with blue plumes. She laughed at the small boy whose hand she held. Her perfume was overdone, but it did cut through the cat smell. The cool wet air and the steady drizzle outside were actually welcome. Holmes and I both paused under the eaves to button up our coats, put on our top hats, and open our umbrellas. He gave me a brief hard stare, appeared ready to speak, but then turned and strode away. We walked round the huge edifice of the lion house back toward Regent's Park. Holmes looked briefly at me again.

"What is it?" I asked.

He lowered his eyes. "I know... that is to say... Michelle has heard nothing, has she? Nothing of Violet?—of Mrs. Wheelwright?"

I sighed wearily. Now I understood. Violet Wheelwright had been at the center of one of his most challenging cases, one which had ended in tragedy. I suspected she was also the only woman that Holmes had ever truly loved.

"You know I would tell you if she had. You will be the first to know if there is any word, I promise you."

"Yes, yes." He shook his head twice. "Of course I know that. I do know it. Only... Blast it all, Michelle is her friend! You would think she would have the common decency to..."

"Michelle worries about her too."

His gait seemed to freeze for a second, his eyes shifting again to mine. "Does she now?"

"Yes."

"It has been three years, and Michelle has not heard from her for two years."

"Yes, that is correct."

"She need not send us cheerful monthly missives with all the quotidian details of her life, but she could at least let us know..." He seemed briefly to swallow his words, even as his eyes were fixed straight ahead. "She should let us know that she is alive."

I nodded. "Yes, I agree with you. After all Michelle has done for her—and you as well—you both deserve that much, but it does little good to speculate about the worst. If anything had happened to her, I think we would have heard about it."

"But how? She has willingly disappeared. It is all the same whether she be alive or dead. People disappear without a trace all the time."

I drew in my breath, hesitating. "If she were going to harm herself, I think she would have let Michelle know."

"Would she? Would that not be a worse betrayal? Would she not feel that it would be better that Michelle was deceived, that she still thought her alive? Would that not be better than the pain of knowing that she was truly dead?" His voice revealed something of his torment.

"I shall tell you what I tell Michelle. It is no use torturing yourself. You have done all that you could for her, and when I last saw her, she seemed much better. She had begun playing the violin again. Her disastrous marriage was finished, and–"

"At the cost of her husband's life."

"He would have killed her–he would have killed you."

Holmes's shoulders rose in a sort of half-shudder.

"But as I was saying, that was finished, and so were all her crimes. She was starting a new life, and she understood that she had done wrong. She was seeking redemption. That takes time, perhaps a lifetime. When she has found it at last, then she may come into our lives again." Holmes stared ahead, his mouth fixed and tight. I grasped his arm lightly above the elbow. "We must hope for the best."

"I am not good at… My profession deals in facts and certitude, not in hope."

"All the same, there is the old saw, where there's life, there's hope."

"If only I knew there was life—if I knew that, then I could hope." He shook his head. The rain had begun in earnest, the falling drops a steady drone on the black fabric of our outstretched umbrellas. "Where is she, I wonder? She could be anywhere—a flat near Regent's Park, or even somewhere close to Baker Street, or further still, outside of London. Greenwich, perhaps, or further yet, Manchester or Liverpool. No, not Liverpool. She may have parted from this sceptered isle. I can well imagine her on the Continent. Perhaps Vienna. With her natural elegance she would fit in well there. Or maybe Paris, Rome or Berlin. But enough of this—*enough*. I have trodden this particular path far too often, worn down a deep groove.

"I hope our meeting this afternoon with Mr. Hardy will lead to an interesting case. Idleness has always made me brood, and it grows worse with her long silence. I pray that Hardy tells us something of interest, something to divert my mind, to keep that savage beast ennui—far worse than any lion or tiger—at bay!"

I smiled. "If only you could lock up ennui in one of those invisible cages."

"Yes, if only. Unfortunately, I always seem to end up sharing that innermost cage with Mr. Ennui."

"Ah, so he is a gentleman, after all, and not a beast."

"He is no gentleman." We had reached a busy street at the edge of the park. "Let us hail a cab and get out of this rain. Unless the traffic is particularly wretched, we should be there slightly before our three o'clock appointment."

Mr. Hardy's butler must have been waiting for us, for he opened the door almost at once. A tall thin man of about fifty, he wore the customary black morning coat, waistcoat and cravat. Thick graying hair puffed out over his large outspread ears, and his broad smile was unrestrained and natural, rather than stiff and polite.

"Gentlemen, do come in! You must, of course, be Mr. Holmes, and this must be..."

"*Vernier*," I said firmly. "The name is Vernier, Dr. Henry Vernier."

The butler's eyes were puzzled, even as his smile briefly faltered. "Indeed? A pleasure to meet you, Dr. Vernier. Let me take your umbrellas, your hats and overcoats. Beastly day, isn't it? Feels more like December than November, but we have a jolly fire going and some excellent brandy. This way, please."

We followed him up an ornate walnut staircase to the next floor, then down a hallway. He opened the door and waited for us to enter. Two tall windows stood on either side of a sturdy hearth constructed of red brick, and in the fireplace, yellow-orange flames flickered about a massive blackened log. A big man in a gray tweed suit quickly rose from a well-worn black leather sofa and smiled at us as he came forward. He appeared about the same age as his butler, but although his light-brown hair had no gray, most of it was missing on top. Perhaps by way of compensation, he had an enormous bushy reddish-brown mustache. His face was very full, his neck thick if not exactly flabby.

"Ah, Mr. Holmes, so good of you to come! I'm John Hardy." He clasped Holmes's lean hand in his big one, then turned to me. "And this must be..."

My mouth stiffened, but the butler spoke first. "This is Dr. Henry Vernier."

Hardy gave me a puzzled look, but Holmes spoke. "Henry is my cousin and my very good friend, Mr. Hardy."

"A pleasure to meet you, sir." Hardy's grip was as formidable as I expected. "Might I offer you something to drink, something to take the edge off, as they say?" He gestured in the direction of a sideboard of finely carved dark wood with its formidable array of decanters and bottles. "Good day for a brandy, I think, and I have quite an assortment. It's my trade, after all—wine and spirits, that is: importing French wines and brandies, to be exact, and exporting our own whiskey in the other direction. The French invented brandy, you know—God bless them!"

Holmes spread his hands apart, his fingers opening up. "I shall trust your expertise, sir."

I nodded. "So shall I."

"Very good. I have just the thing. Saunders, would you pour us some Armagnac? The eighty-one Montesquiou."

"Very good, sir."

"You prefer Armagnac to cognac?" I asked.

He gave an emphatic nod. "No question there, no question at all. Brandy was born in Gascony in the eleventh-century. Their distillation process is superior, and they never cut the product with water. Cognac has the name and nowadays industrial production, but I could give you a dozen more reasons why… But I mustn't start down that path, or I shall never stop! Brandies and clarets are my specialty, you know." The butler hovered before us with a tray holding three snifters. "Help yourself, gentlemen." After Holmes and I had our glasses, Hardy took the last one and raised it. "To your very good health!"

We raised our glasses as well, then I passed the rim under my nose. The amber liquid was marvelously fragrant. I took a slow sip. It was absolutely smooth-tasting and flavorful, far better than the brandy Michelle and I normally drank.

Holmes shook his head. "Remarkable, sir. My brother Mycroft

is also a connoisseur of brandies, but I have never tasted anything to equal this."

"A connoisseur, is he! We must have a contest sometime. He can bring two or three of his best, and I shall do the same." Hardy took a big swallow, then gave a contented sigh. He gestured toward the fire. "You must be cold. The fire also takes off the edge."

Holmes and I stepped nearer the fireplace. Hardy raised his glass, tilted it slightly, letting the red-orange firelight set the brown-gold Armagnac alight. "Nothing prettier than a good brandy, except perhaps a good red wine. One is the parent, the other its offspring. Spirits is an apt name for them: nothing better to lift human spirits." He took a sip.

I had another swallow. What was true for Holmes was true for me: I had never tasted anything better. It did set my insides all aglow, and accompanied by the warmth of the fire, I felt truly content. We shared a companionable silence for a few minutes, which Holmes finally broke.

"This is indeed the ambrosial nectar of the gods, but I fear I must return us to earth. You asked me here on a matter of business, Mr. Hardy. Something of urgence, your note said."

Hardy's amiable countenance shifted, uneasiness clearly visible in his eyes. "So I did. So I did." He sighed. "Why don't we sit down? He took one end of the black leather sofa, Holmes the other, while I sat in a matching chair. It was very comfortable. The sitting room had a sparse masculine air, with no doilies, knickknacks or china figurines. Hardy sipped the brandy, put the glass on a tile coaster, then leaned forward and set his elbows on his knees. He drew in his breath, as if readying himself to launch, then began.

"It concerns my wife, sir. I have the good fortune to have been married for thirteen years. I was forty when I married, a resigned bachelor of somewhat fixed and stodgy ways, but I have never had any regrets. To the contrary, I have been most happy. I wish I could say the same for my wife." He drew in his breath. "So much of it comes down to temperament, in the end. I think that must be it. Some are simply born more high-strung, more finely tuned, than others. Nothing much troubles me. Oh, I can become impatient or irritated, but a certain sense of life's basic absurdity soon makes me smile at circumstances. It does little good to fret and fume. That only makes matters worse.

"Marguerite, on the other hand—that is my wife's name, Marguerite, and as you might suppose, she is French—she has never, I fear, been truly happy. I have tried my best. I have always treated her kindly, given her anything she might desire, but I sometimes think nothing has truly made a difference. Can someone be born sad, Mr. Holmes?"

Holmes only shrugged, but I said, "I think not."

"You might feel differently if you knew Marguerite, Dr. Vernier. There is perhaps an explanation, a partial one, anyway. She always wanted a child, and there was… hope on two occasions, but it was not meant to be."

My brow furrowed. "Miscarriages?"

Hardy almost winced. "Exactly. She was in her thirties when we married. Yes, if we had a child, things might be different. Perhaps."

Holmes stared closely at him. "But perhaps not?"

"As I said, it seems to me some people are born sad. That, and…" He hesitated. "It seems odd to me, odd that she should somehow conceive of it as a punishment."

"A punishment?" I said.

"Yes. She is Roman Catholic, and she does have that Catholic sense of sin."

"And you are not Catholic?" Holmes asked.

"No. Plain old Church of England, although we were married in the Catholic church. I had to take some instructions and promise to raise any children as Catholic. I was willing enough to do it, willing to do almost anything as a matter of fact."

Holmes had begun to tap lightly at his knee with the outstretched fingers of his right hand. "If I could make sadness go away, Mr. Hardy, I could become a very rich man. It would also be far more rewarding than my current profession. You have still not said why you sent for me."

Hardy leaned forward, staring at him intently. "Her sadness is a fact of life we had both become accustomed to, but fear is another matter entirely. She is frightened, Mr. Holmes, badly frightened. That is why I need your assistance."

"Do you know what has frightened her?"

"Yes. I know what, but not why."

"Tell me what you know."

"I shall do better than that: I shall show you." He leaned back in the sofa and took two papers from the end table, one a sheet of fine notepaper, the other a tan rectangle of newsprint. "Before I give you these, I should perhaps explain that they are not the originals. Those I managed to briefly see, but soon after, Marguerite cast them into the fire. They had come together in the afternoon post. The letter was striking and simple. My French is somewhat limited, but I comprehended the words and wrote them down soon after. I also managed to find a copy of the newspaper article later on. I have a friend who subscribes to *Le Petit Parisien*. He remembered reading the notice and helped me find it. Perhaps you should begin with the brief article. I could attempt to translate if…?"

Holmes gave his head a brusque shake. "That will not be

necessary. I have spent some time in France and am fluent in the language. Henry was raised near Paris and speaks French like a native." He leaned forward to take the clipping, stared at it for a couple minutes, then passed it to me.

A brief entry under "Paris" was circled in pencil. The well-known artist Gaston Lupin had died of heart failure. A lady friend had left him alive and in good spirits the night before, and his valet had found him dead the following morning. He left behind a collection of artworks worth a considerable fortune.

"Was the original also circled?"

"Yes. The clipping came with this letter. Let me read it aloud. Perhaps that might somehow help make sense of it." He paused, raising and tipping his head slightly to see better. "*Quatre pour le Diable.*"

My breath came out in a confused laugh. He had a strong accent, but the words were clear enough. "Did you say '*quatre pour le Diable*?"

"Yes."

"'Four for the Devil,'" Holmes murmured.

"Exactly. Then there are—and it should come as no surprise—four lines. '*Le premier est Gaston. Le deuxième sera Angèle. Le troisième sera toi. Le quatrième sera moi.*'"

Holmes's forehead had creased. "'The first is Gaston.' Clear enough what that might suggest. 'The second will be Angèle. The third will be you.' The implied threat is obvious. 'The fourth will be me.' That is odd. Little wonder your wife is frightened. May I see the letter? Thank you. I assume it was written exactly like this, a line for each, five lines in all. And no signature?"

"None at all."

"And the envelope? Did it have a return address?"

"Marguerite burned it before I could have a look, but I did recognize the stamp. It was a French one, as you might expect for a letter written in French."

Holmes ran his fingertips along his right jawline, his eyes troubled. "'Four for the Devil.' You said your wife was Catholic? I suppose she must believe in the Devil."

"Very much so, Mr. Holmes."

"You mentioned that she has that Catholic sense of sin. Combine that with a belief in the Devil, and you have the makings of a considerable misery. Is she at home now? I must, of course, speak with her."

Hardy shook his head quickly. "No, no—she is abroad, that is. In Paris."

"When will she be back? There must be some connection between her and this murdered artist."

Hardy's cheeks rose slowly in a pained expression. "There is a problem, Mr. Holmes. It would be best, for now, if you could pursue the case on your own. Marguerite is... that is to say, when I told her I wanted to employ your services, she absolutely forbade it. This is a private matter, she said, not to be poked at by detectives. Besides, she could never discuss it with a man. But she knew of a woman, a woman who had acquired something of a reputation as an amateur detective, a woman who had helped one of her friends. She would go to Paris to meet this woman and see if she, too, might be helped."

Holmes sighed softly. "So you are acting against her wishes?"

"I certainly am—can you blame me?"

I shook my head. "I cannot."

Holmes rose to his feet, swung his left arm round back and clasped his wrist with his right hand, then took two steps toward the fireplace. He turned back toward Hardy and me. "Nor can I exactly blame you, but on the other hand, I fear I cannot take the case without her cooperation. Let this remarkable woman in Paris serve as her Sherlock Holmes." His voice was ironical.

"Please, Mr. Holmes, I beg of you—you must help her. I shall pay whatever sum you demand. I know she is being unreasonable, but she is afraid and…"

Holmes stared closely at him. "And…?"

"She has never revealed much about her past. In fact before we were married, she told me she had not always led a virtuous life. She was ashamed of what she had done. But what was done was done, she said, and she had found consolation in her faith, as well as a sense of forgiveness. All the same, I promised never to question her about her earlier years. She wanted to forget them, to put them firmly behind her. I asked her if she could promise to be true to me and live up to the vows of matrimony, and she told me she could. 'With all my heart,' she said." Hardy's voice shook slightly. "That was all that mattered to me, and we have been happy together—I swear we have. But now…" He raised the letter in his big hand. "This is something from her past come back to haunt her, written by some person who bears her ill will."

Holmes stroked his chin thoughtfully, then his eyes shifted to the sideboard. "Would you mind if I had more of your excellent Armagnac?"

Hardy rose to his feet from the depths of the sofa, which appeared something of an effort for so large a man. "Not at all! I could use another spot myself. And you, Dr. Vernier?"

"Please."

He poured some for Holmes, then came toward me with the ornate rounded bottle and added to my glass. After taking some for himself, he returned to the sofa. Holmes had already sat down and was staring thoughtfully at the brandy. The easy convivial air between us three was gone. We drank in silence. Hardy's eyes were fixed on Holmes. At last he spoke.

"If I take this case, my path must eventually cross hers. You do not expect me to try to hide the fact I am working for you?"

"No, Mr. Holmes, I do not." A mirthless smile pulled at his mouth. "I am not trying to swear you to secrecy, not at all. Eventually, too, I think she may see reason. There will come a time for a meeting. All I ask is that you delay it as long as possible. Perhaps, too, I may lay the groundwork for such a meeting. Besides, won't it take some time to investigate this Gaston's sudden death? That seems the logical starting point, or am I mistaken?"

Holmes shook his head. "No. That is where I must begin."

"And you said you speak fluent French—that is excellent! I shall be happy to pay for one of the best hotels in Paris, and of course, I shall cover all your expenses."

Holmes smiled briefly at me. "We have not been in Paris together, Henry, for a long while, not since that business of the Palais Garnier and its opera ghost."

Hardy turned to me. "I shall gladly pay for your expenses as well, Dr. Vernier."

"That is very generous of you."

"Please, Mr. Holmes—let us take things a step at a time. Go to Paris, try to find out about this artist. See if you can discover any past link with Marguerite. Given your reputation, you must have contacts in the Paris police?" Holmes nodded. "Perfect! Please, I…"

Holmes raised his hand, his thin fingers outstretched. "Very well, Mr. Hardy—you win. We shall take it a step at a time. I shall go to Paris and see what I can discover. But you must at least answer a few questions. You said your wife is French. Did you meet her here in England or in France?"

"I met her in London thirteen years ago on a fine spring day upon Westminster Bridge. It was late Sunday morning, and I had begun a long stroll. I was halfway across the bridge when I saw her. I must confess that although I was a confirmed bachelor, I always had an eye for the ladies. She certainly stood out from the ordinary London women. I knew her nationality at once. She has the dark brown hair and eyes, almost black, so typical of French women. She is quite tall, and her bearing and elegant dress marked her as a lady. She was wearing a spectacular black and burgundy silk with a matching hat. Alongside her dark hair, her face was very pale, and her hands in their gloves gripped fiercely at the railing. She was staring out at the Thames, her eyes very far away, lost. I stopped, then went to the railing myself, and looked down at the gray-blue waters. I glanced at her twice, but she did not even see me. Her face, her hands, seemed frozen.

"At last I asked her if she was well. 'What?' she asked, and that single word revealed that I had been right. I asked her the same question in French. She seemed relieved to hear her native tongue. She told me she was feeling… *un peu épuisée.*" He gave us a questioning look.

"Worn out," I said.

"Even so, or weary. I said that it must be difficult making her way in such a huge city when the language was new to her. She smiled at me, and that, gentlemen, was when I knew I was lost. She told me that was indeed the case. I suggested that perhaps she might wish to sit for a while and have a biscuit and coffee, something to revive her. We sat and chatted. She had been in London some two weeks and was completely overwhelmed by it all. She asked if she might practice her English with me. People had been brusque and unhelpful with her. I was happy to oblige. We spent the afternoon together, and I showed her some of the not quite so common sights. I suggested dinner, and then, well, you can gather where it went."

Holmes had been regarding him closely. "Did she say why she was in London?"

"One of the first things I asked her was how long she planned to be here. 'Indefinitely,' she told me. She was weary of Paris and France. She wanted to begin a new life in London. By the end of that first day, I too thought about beginning a new life. We discovered a shared passion for music and the arts. We went to a performance of Gounod's *Faust* at Covent Garden two weeks after we first met. It's our favorite. We have seen every production of the opera done at Covent Garden or the Palais Garnier in the last dozen years."

"You said she seemed sad," Holmes said. "Was it always that way, even from the beginning?"

"Well, she certainly seemed… preoccupied. She would be happy and laughing, but then she would stare off into space and her eyes would go blank. There was less of that, however, as time went on, and more signs of happiness." He smiled gently, then finished his brandy. "I had never believed in love at first sight, but she made a convert of me."

"And did she ever speak of her life in France?"

"She told me she had lived in Paris, but little else. Her reticence became rather noticeable. I would ask her questions, and she would answer, but she never volunteered any information. It was also soon obvious that she was a wealthy woman. I could not ask specific questions—that just isn't done, after all—but I would make vague inquiries, which received vague answers. After I had finally proposed to her and she had accepted, I..."

Holmes raised his hand. "Did she accept at once?"

"No. She told me she would have to think about it. I kept reminding her, but it was only after six months that she finally agreed, with some reluctance. I was—well, I was rather put out, or rather, my feelings were hurt. She realized that, and she touched my cheek and told me I was not to blame, that I was a generous and noble man, and that I mustn't doubt myself. That was when she told me she wanted to forget her past, that I must not ask her about her earlier life."

Holmes nodded. "And did you then discover the exact amount of her wealth?"

Hardy laughed once, then again. "I did indeed! I have done very well in my trade, Mr. Holmes. Even a dozen years ago, I could have lived in Grosvenor Square had I wished, although the peers and highbrows would still be unwilling to associate with a lowly chap like myself who dirties his hands in business. But Marguerite had ten times as much money as I did! She willingly gave it all over to me to invest, and I daresay I have doubled it within ten years."

"Did she say where this fortune came from?"

"She did tell me that much. It was an inheritance. She had a wealthy uncle who died without children, and he left it to her."

"And her mother, her parents, did she ever speak of them?"

Hardy's forehead creased. "She never knew her father. Her mother... They are estranged. That was clear."

"Was her mother a lady?"

"She was only a dressmaker, but she has her own shop in Paris now."

"But despite her humble origins, your wife was clearly a lady?"

"Given Marguerite's manners and elegance, there was never any doubt."

Holmes stared at him. "No?"

Hardy stared back. "Mr. Holmes, you must understand, whatever her past, Marguerite has been a good wife to me. She has made me very happy. Our life together has been a good one."

Holmes's mouth remained tightly closed, but he eased his breath out through his nostrils. "So I see. And this letter—how long ago did she receive it?"

"About three weeks ago."

"And were you with her when she opened it?"

Hardy's face formed a characteristic expression, almost wincing. He nodded.

"Tell me exactly what followed."

He drew in his breath resolutely. "We were in our sitting room. I had a letter of my own which I read and set aside. I vaguely heard her opening the letter. It was quiet with only the tick of the clock and the snapping of the fire. I glanced at her, then looked again. She was sitting very stiffly on the sofa and staring off into the distance. The two papers and the envelope lay on the floor before her. I asked if she had dropped something, and she did not respond. Her face was deathly pale.

"I stood up. 'Marguerite?' I repeated her name. I had begun to worry. I stepped closer and touched her arm. She was quivering, and her teeth were clenched. I became alarmed and said her name again. She did not even hear me. I took her arms and raised her up. I was afraid she was having some kind of fit. I begged her to speak to me. I touched her face, and finally she seemed to see me.

"I brought her some brandy, helped her sit, and told her to drink it. I had to help her. When she was finished, she sank back into the sofa, closed her eyes, and clenched her fists tightly. I asked her repeatedly what was wrong, but she would not answer. I picked up the newspaper article, looked at it, then read the odd letter twice.

"'What is this nonsense?' I said.

"The pupils in her dark eyes were huge. She looked down at the papers sitting on my lap, then snatched them and balled them up in her fist. She put them in the fire before I could stop her. 'What is wrong with you?' I asked.

"She shook her head wildly. 'Nothing. It is as you said—it is nonsense—only nonsense. Only a joke.' She made a fierce horrible laughing sound which completely contradicted her words.

"I asked her repeatedly to tell me what was the matter, but she would say nothing. I daresay she slept not a wink that night, and I was wakeful myself. The next day she made an effort to pretend all was well, but I was not deceived. After a few days of her obvious misery, I asked again what had frightened her. She was evasive as ever.

"That was when I mentioned your name, Mr. Holmes. I knew you were the best, and that if anyone could get to the bottom of this, it was you. I've already told you how she responded. She had discussed the situation with her friend Mrs. Stanton who knew of a woman in Paris who had helped a mutual friend. I could not believe my ears, but there was no budging her. She said I must trust her, that I must leave this matter to her. My pleas for some explanation of what was wrong went unanswered.

"I became almost angry, and that was when she began to weep, in a silent desperate way even as her hands shook." He shook his head. "What could I do? I did not want to cause her further pain. She left for Paris last week. Since then I have mulled things over, gone back and forth, but I finally wrote you yesterday, Mr. Holmes."

Holmes ran his slender fingers along his brow and into his black hair. He opened his mouth to speak, then closed it briefly. "Mr. Hardy, I have no doubt whatsoever that this is a serious business. You wife's reticence about her past raises obvious questions. Are you... are you absolutely certain you want me to pursue this? I may discover things which may make you regret involving me."

Hardy stared resolutely at him. "I love my wife, Mr. Holmes. I cannot bear to see her suffer. I suspect this will not simply somehow resolve itself."

Holmes laughed once, harshly. "No."

"I told her before we were married that I didn't care about her past—that what mattered was what sort of wife she would be. I have no complaints on that score—none. She has been a good wife, and we have been happy together. Whatever she has done in the past is past, irrelevant to me. Our thirteen years together are what matter. Nothing can change that."

Holmes nodded, his expression wistful. "Very good. It is just as well. I suspect she is in danger."

Hardy had raised his brandy glass, but he held it suspended in midair. "Do you think so?"

"Yes. This is most definitely not a joke. I shall look into the matter. I can leave for Paris the day after tomorrow."

"Excellent, Mr. Holmes—excellent! I wish I could accompany you. Typically in the course of a year, I travel constantly back and forth between London and France on business. We have a townhouse in Paris off the Champs-Élysées. However, I have crucial business to attend to in Scotland—the whiskey trade, you know."

"It is best I go alone." Holmes glanced at me. "Or with my usual traveling companion, one whose French is superior to mine."

I shrugged. "My practice is as anemic as ever. I can spare a few days."

Hardy nodded eagerly. "It is settled then."

"Oh, and could you provide me with the name and address of your wife's mother's shop?"

"I believe so. I shall also give you an address for myself in Scotland and that of our Paris townhouse." He gave a great sigh. "I am relieved, gentlemen, greatly relieved!"

Holmes stared down at his glass, swirling it slightly, then his gray eyes returned to Hardy, the corners of his mouth rising grimly. "That may be premature, sir." He tossed down the last of his brandy.

Being mid-November, the sun had set by around four PM. Twilight hung heavily over London, the atmosphere thick with mist, drizzle and coal smoke as we walked back toward Baker Street. Light came from the gas street lamps, the lamps of passing carriages, and the large rectangular windows of shop fronts. The cobblestones and walks were black with moisture, white highlights glistening. Cries, rumbles and clatterings formed a great din all around us: paper boys in cloth caps, street vendors of baked potatoes, emaciated girls with flowers—all hawked their goods; horses' hooves with their iron shoes clopped on the street while the vehicles' wheels groaned. Two massive draft horses pulled a two-story omnibus which went by. I felt sorry for the unlucky people seated up top exposed to the elements. An advertisement lettered on its side said something about a "scientific dress-cutting" establishment on Regency Street.

"What is scientific dress-cutting?" I mumbled.

My words seemed to take several seconds to register with Holmes. "What was that, Henry?"

"Nothing important. I suppose you must still be thinking about Mr. Hardy and his wife. A mysterious business, that."

Holmes gave a sharp laugh and shook his head. "I fear it may not be so simple as it appears."

"Simple? It hardly seemed simple to me."

"Come now, is not the lady's former profession obvious enough? She was probably a prostitute who left her trade."

"But he said she was a lady."

He laughed. "Oh, Henry! You truly are a hopeless romantic. She would not have been a common trollop, but one of the higher class, more expensive variety—a *courtisane.* Such women can make a considerable fortune and, if they have any business sense, retire early. They can then marry and lead a respectable life. However, they are an obvious target for blackmail. I have handled such cases before. The husbands, however, were hardly so understanding and sympathetic as Mr. Hardy."

"She could simply tell him the truth. She practically seems to have done so. As you say, I think he would understand and forgive."

"Yes. That is why I suspect something more serious, more complicated. Blackmailers do not generally drag the Devil into their dirty trade, and I am always suspicious when a death is attributed to 'heart failure.'"

I shook my head. "Murder. Again."

"Yes, Henry. That is my stock and trade after all." He glanced about at the street crowded with traffic and the people surrounding us, the men in their dark coats and hats, the women in their bright garments dimmed by twilight and mist. "You were raised as a Catholic, were you not, Henry?"

"Yes, Michelle and I both were, but as I have told you before, in my case it did not exactly take."

"And were you afraid of the Devil?"

An unwilled smile pulled at my mouth. "Terrified, actually. I was an agnostic at an early age, but my doubts didn't seem to restrain my fear of the Devil. I was frightened of the dark, too. I thought Old Scratch might be lurking under my bed. The priests at school didn't help matters. One told us that if you dug deep enough in the earth, ten feet or so, you would strike the fires of Hell."

Holmes laughed. "That is taking literal-mindedness to an extreme! But then we live in an age of extremes. The marvels of science and new technologies overwhelm us, triggering a reaction. Some idealize the Middle Ages while others turn to devil worship. France and Italy, in particular, are hotbeds of Satanism."

"Are you serious?"

"Oh yes. It is the dark shadow of Catholicism; the two go hand in hand. Most of it is harmless mumbo-jumbo, a blend of superstitious nonsense and perverted rituals like the Black Mass. Sexual decadence and perversion are also characteristic. But that note... Gaston was one of the four, and Marguerite, obviously, but the other two... Somehow I think a woman wrote that note. Three women, then, and a man."

Remembering exactly how frightened I had been as a boy made me uncomfortable, even after so many years. "And you, did you believe in the Devil?"

"I did, but I was not terribly afraid of him. The fear came later."

"Fear of the Devil?"

"No. Fear of evil. I too have my doubts about Old Scratch, but evil is another matter. I have seen too much of it. Many strong-willed people have a great force or power about them. In some cases that strength of character becomes warped and dark. Simply being in the presence of such people is deeply disquieting. And when they torment others and actually take pleasure in human suffering..."

I shivered. "In other words, why blame the Devil? Certain people are capable of unspeakable crimes on their own."

"Exactly, Henry. Exactly."

"And you think that is what we may be up against?"

"I hope not, Henry. But we shall see. Perhaps this will turn out to be an uneventful trip to Paris during which we enjoy the fine cuisine and take in the opera."

Another smile briefly pulled at my lips. "Somehow when we travel together it never seems to work out that way."

Holmes gave a sudden sharp laugh. "By the time we arrive, perhaps my female counterpart will have neatly wrapped up the case for us!"

Chapter Two

"Tomorrow we shall have a *petit déjeuner français*, Henry, but today we must fortify ourselves with a hardy English breakfast to prepare ourselves for a busy day."

The Meurice was one of those rare hotels in France which catered to the client's every whim. Thus instead of bread, confiture, croissants and coffee, we ate bacon, sausages and fried eggs accompanied by buttered toast. Afterwards, we sipped our strong black coffee and regarded the ornate dining room with its high ceilings and a sparkling chandelier, its elegant table settings of white linen and silver, the men in black frock coats and their ladies in colorful silks, all quietly and decorously eating.

"Where are we going today?" I asked.

"First we will visit with Mrs. Hardy's mother, Madame Delvaux."

"Her mother? But I thought they were estranged."

"Indeed, and finding out why should be most informative. Afterwards we shall meet with a genuine curiosity, one of those unique Englishmen who combines both eccentricity and genius, the Reverend Algernon Sumners."

"The reverend? A priest, then. Anglican or Roman Catholic?"

"Things are a little vague in his case. He studied at Oxford, then preached briefly as a village curate, but something happened which made him return to London. He later converted to Roman Catholicism and now wears clerical garb, but I am not certain he has actually been ordained."

"He dresses as a priest, but he may not be ordained? He does sound eccentric. And what exactly is his area of expertise?"

"The occult, Henry, and Satanism in particular. In the afternoon, I think we might go our separate ways. You can play the tourist while I visit some art galleries and see what I can discover about our friend, the late Monsieur Gaston Lupin."

Soon we strode through the big lobby and out the revolving doors to the Rue de Rivoli. Holmes whistled some tune and swung his stick rhythmically. To our left, across the street, the Jardin des Tuileries was mostly deserted, cold and desolate-looking under the gray sky, its trees bare of the foliage. It was quite a contrast to summer when the park overflowed with people and greenery on the warm days. We turned right at the first corner, the Rue de Castiglione and headed in the direction of the Opéra. This was one of the typical Paris streets which changed its name every couple blocks, becoming Place Vendôme and then Rue de la Paix just before the Opéra. This last street was home to the House of Worth, the most chic and famous temple to fashion in Paris; empresses and princesses from all over Europe went there for dresses.

Ahead of us we could see the tall column of the Place Vendôme with the statue of Napoleon up on top. I recalled that it had been taken down after the uprising of the Paris Commune in 1871, but reconstructed three or four years later. Madame Delvaux's small shop was down a side street off the Place Vendôme, not too far from the more elite Rue de la Paix. On a plate glass window was written in large letters, DELVAUX, and then smaller, *Couturière Exclusive.* Holmes opened the door, and I followed him in.

A woman seated at a large desk stared up at us from over the edge of the spectacles perched on her thin nose. Piles of magazines, obviously fashion ones, were stacked behind her on shelves, and two beautiful silk dresses were on display. Through an open doorway we could see young women in the back working with brightly colored material and paper patterns. Intermittently came the whirring sound of a sewing machine being operated by a treadle.

"*Oui, messieurs?*"

Holmes had removed his black silken top hat. "Madame Delvaux?" At her nod, he continued in French. "I wondered if you might be able to assist me. I am here on behalf of Mr. John Hardy." He paused, but the name made no impression. "Your daughter Marguerite's husband."

At this, she eased her breath out in a weary sigh, then sat back in the chair and crossed her arms. Her forehead had deep creases that appeared permanently worn in. Her dark hair was parted in the middle, shot with gray, and her black eyes were faintly hostile. A beautiful navy silk dress, no doubt one of her creations, contrasted with the pallor of her skin. "Is she in trouble?"

"Perhaps," Holmes said. "That is what I mean to find out."

"I can tell you nothing–nothing at all. I know nothing." With this last, she swung her arm and hand out from the elbow in a dismissive gesture.

"If you could only answer a few questions, that would be most helpful."

Her lips pursed briefly. "Are you from the English police?"

Holmes shook his head. "No, no, she has done nothing wrong, nothing dishonest."

"But you said she might be in trouble."

"Not in trouble with the law. Someone has threatened her. She is afraid."

Madame Delvaux shook her head emphatically. "I can't help you with that. I have not seen her for a long time."

"How long exactly?"

Forehead still creased, she reflected briefly. "Over a dozen years ago."

"You are obviously not on good terms with your daughter, madame."

She smiled bitterly. "Very perceptive, monsieur."

"When did this estrangement begin?"

"And why precisely should I answer your questions?"

"You are, after all, her mother, and I wish to help her. Besides, it hardly seems a secret."

She laughed. "No, I suppose not. When did it begin? Not exactly at birth, but it was never easy. When she was eighteen I broke with her, but the difficulties had begun a year or two earlier. I had scrimped and saved to send her to a proper school, one taught by the good sisters. I had no shop of my own then. I labored for hours a day cutting and sewing for a pittance. Even though she was poorer than the other students, you could never tell it from her clothes—I saw to that. But it was a mistake. She wanted to be rich and idle like the other girls. She was clever and intelligent, but she would not put her talents to good use. By the time she was eighteen, I was starting my shop. I wanted her to work here with me. I would have paid her well enough—far more than what I ever got!—but that was not good enough. Instead she must pretend to be a lady. She would flirt with men, and she would…" Her face had flushed, and she shook her head. "Never mind."

Holmes glanced sideways at me. "How did she live?"

Madame Delvaux gave him a savage look. "Must I say it?"

"I suppose not."

She stared down at the desk top and her hands. "She was not a cheap little… She did not have to register, thank God—no, she was better than that. She started with an infatuated young nobleman who gave her presents and money. She knew he would never marry her. She was not stupid. But she did not care. And after… I heard there were others." She glared up at Holmes. "Now do you understand our estrangement? I am a decent woman, monsieur, I go to Mass every Sunday, while she…"

"She is about forty-eight now. That was a long time ago."

She stared into the distance. "Some thirty years."

"But you said you last saw her about a dozen years ago."

"Thirteen—it was thirteen years ago."

"What did she want?"

Again the bitter smile twisted her lips. "She offered me money. Imagine! She said I had been right, that her life had been wrong, but that she was a changed woman. She would give me money to show that she was different. I could retire. I asked her where the money came from, and she made up some ridiculous story. Long and short, she would not tell me, and I told her I did not want her filthy money. Unlike her, I was not made for a life of idleness. My store was flourishing by then, and I liked my work. She could keep her dishonest money and leave me in peace."

Holmes hesitated. "She does not have a rich uncle?"

"She has no uncle at all! Only an aunt. Why do you ask?"

Holmes shrugged. "There was some mention of an uncle. I needn't keep you, madame. I have two final questions. Have you ever heard of an artist named Gaston Lupin?"

"No. Never." She had not hesitated and was obviously telling the truth.

"And did Marguerite ever have a friend named Angèle?"

"Angèle?" She laughed in earnest. "No, she would hardly be one to have a friend with such an angelic name."

"Did she have any friend at school whom you can remember?"

"Yes, one. Her name was Anne, Anne Marie."

"What was she like?"

"A stupid sort of girl who was putty in Marguerite's hands, one who also came from a poorer family, and would do whatever Marguerite commanded. In short, the worst sort of friend for a girl like my daughter. She would indulge Marguerite's worst faults—her laziness and vanity."

"I see. One last thing, madame." Holmes hesitated, his lips tightening as he stared down at her. "Did Marguerite ever know her father?"

She stared back at Holmes, then gave a brusque shake of her head. "Never. He left when she was one year old. We *were* married, monsieur." This last was said very gravely. "He was my one grand *bêtise*, my one stupidity. I wanted better for my daughter. But instead it was *bêtise* after *bêtise*." For the first time, there was almost more pain than anger in her voice.

Holmes nodded his head. "Thank you, Madame Delvaux."

She sat up very straight in her chair, folding her arms again and assuming a very businesslike posture. "Good day, monsieur."

We went to the door and stepped out into the street. I eased my breath out slowly. "Estrangement is an understatement."

Holmes had set his hat back on his head. "Indeed it is. However, nothing she told us much surprised me."

"It is sad to see a woman who so despises her own child."

"Great love can turn to great hate, Henry. The emotional intensity stays the same, but the polarity is reversed. Come, let us be off to see Algernon. He may be an expert on black magic and sorcery, but all the same, he is a most jovial sort of person."

Sumners's flat was forty minutes' walk away in the older part of the Marais. We had to trudge up a typical steep ancient circular staircase to the fourth floor. We went down the hallway, and Holmes rapped at the last door on the left. It opened inward revealing a plump man in a black soutane. His cheeks were rosy, and his graying hair was parted in the middle with a strange bob on either side, almost as if it had been deliberately curled. A golden pince-nez sat perched upon his lump of a nose, and he had a magnificent gray and black mustache and goatee which hid the fold of flesh under his jaw.

"Ah, Sherlock Holmes! We meet again at last." He took Holmes's slender hand between his massive fleshy ones, bobbed it eagerly up and down. Next he did the same with my hand. "And you, sir?" His voice was high-pitched with a very precise, rather excessive enunciation of every word.

"I am Dr. Henry Vernier, his cousin."

"Pleased to meet you, Doctor. I am Algernon Sumners. As Holmes is an old acquaintance, you too may address me as Algernon. Come in and have a seat. Move the cats if you will."

Indeed, two chairs and the sofa all had feline occupants. I lifted an enormous black cat (which given its size and weight must have been male) from one side of the burgundy velour sofa. The cat made a hoarse sort of meow of complaint. I sat down beside him and began to stroke his back. He immediately stepped up onto my lap, circled about, settled, and purred loudly. Holmes had to move an orange tabby to attain his side of the sofa. Sumners settled his bulk into a worn leather chair before a tall bookcase filled with massive tomes. Nearby was an enormous desk covered with books and papers.

"You said in your telegram you had need of my expertise, Holmes. How can I help you? By the way, do smoke if you wish." Next to his chair was a smoldering pipe which Sumners took up and drew in upon several times; at last he released a cloud of fragrant smoke.

Holmes withdrew his cigarette case from his inside jacket pocket. "Well briefly, Algernon, what can you tell me about Satanism in Paris?"

A high clarion laugh burst from Sumners's lips. He grasped his pince-nez by the curling metal which held its chain and let it plop onto his belly. One of the black buttons from the row on the soutane supported the chain. "Briefly? But that is a grand topic indeed, one worthy of many hours of discourse! Might I presume you are interested mainly in the contemporary situation? Good, good. That narrows the field considerably. Satanism today is alive and flourishing in this grand metropolis. The only European city which might have more devotees would be, naturally enough, Rome."

I stared at him in disbelief. "Are you serious?"

He laughed again. "Never more so. Why do you ask?"

"Well, there have been so many technological and scientific advances in the nineteenth century. I think of Satanism as belonging more to the Middle Ages. And Rome?–*Rome?* Why Rome?"

"Well, Rome because it is the seat of the Church, and therefore also of its antithesis. Just as the pope acts as central authority, so there also reigns an anti-pope. In general, too, the main celebrants and many devotees of Satanism come from the ranks of the religious, from priests and nuns, and where can more be found than in Rome? That explains why London is so lacking in Satanism compared to the Roman Catholic capital cities. As for your technology and science, what has that to do with anything? Indeed, science has conclusively demonstrated that invisible and unseen forces surround us; it has confirmed a mystical realm alongside the mundane world of the senses."

I shook my head. "So nuns and priests actually convert to Satanism?"

"It is not a matter of conversion, but of changing sides."

"How could they choose the Devil over God?"

"Many of them fall into a form of Manichaeism, seeing God and Satan as two roughly equal powers waging eternal war across time. They take the Devil's side and hope that he will someday be triumphant. As Satanists, they also have their own twisted rituals, symbols and ceremonies modeled after the Catholic ones, the chief of which is the so-called Black Mass."

Holmes had crossed his legs, and his right foot began to bob. "They may speak of Satan in grandiloquent terms, but their pathetic rituals show them to be perverts and little more. They are chiefly fascinated with human excrement and sexuality."

Sumners drew in on his pipe. "True. Much of it is posturing, wallowing gleefully in the mud, so to speak, and glorying in their delightful wickedness. Indeed, a good deal of it is harmless, mere play acting. Most of the stories about slaughtering infants to obtain blood for their blasphemous sacraments are apocryphal. I am afraid most items one can purchase from the Satanic herbalist are as false or adulterated as the Parisian foodstuffs you find in many markets. The same holds true of alchemic goods: generally they are just colored powders, not rare minerals or elements. However, that being said, not all of Satanism is harmless make-believe. Some of the adherents are genuinely evil. Others are mentally deranged, more or less insane. In either case, great harm can be done."

I shook my head. "For God's sake, the twentieth century is not far away—I cannot believe we are having this conversation!"

Holmes smiled sardonically. "Some things never go out of fashion."

"And these Black Masses are actually performed today in Paris?"

"Oh yes, and they are part of a tradition going back for centuries. Many believe the Black Mass originated in France. The ceremony is an inversion and desecration of the usual Catholic Mass. A naked woman acts as ornamentation for the altar, the priest holding the chalice over her backside or front. Sometimes he sets the vessel between her legs. The crucifix involves a naked Jesus whose male sex is prominent. As for the host, that is another major topic in itself. Suffice to say common ingredients include semen, human excrement, various other ordures, and baby's blood or flesh. After consuming the host, the participants are often overcome by a frenzy which culminates in a veritable orgy of deranged sexual acts."

"Lord," I murmured, "how absolutely vile."

Holmes drew in on his cigarette, then eased out the smoke. "Definitely not an edifying spectacle. As I recall, Satanists also have a lurid fascination with incubi and succubi."

Sumners smiled, then scratched at his goatee, losing his fingertips in its abundance. "Yet another topic worthy of lengthy discourse! They do indeed." He noticed my puzzled look. "Incubi and succubi are demons who take, respectively, male and female forms. They have sexual intercourse with humans, often in the middle of the night. They are tempters and temptresses. There is some debate whether the same demon can assume either female or male form. There is also some debate about whether a child, half-demonic, half-human, can be engendered."

"Now that all sounds more like fairy tales," I said.

Holmes snubbed out his cigarette in an ashtray. "Satanists also traffic in spells, do they not?"

"Absolutely. Like the old-fashioned village sorceress, they deal in love potions, but most common are bad luck or death hexes. One can have a curse put upon one's enemy that will cause misfortune or an untimely death. These spells also frequently involve various concoctions being brewed up. One slaughters white mice, for example, which have been fed consecrated hosts, and takes their blood. Likewise, various disgusting substances can be fed to fish, and the oil derived from them is so toxic, a drop or two will kill the victim within three days. As with the blasphemous hosts, favorite ingredients are human or animal blood, semen and excrement."

Holmes nodded thoughtfully. "Technically that seems more a matter of a poison than of a curse."

"A narrow line separates the two, especially since, for example, one can deliver the actual poison to the victim by means of a dead person's spirit or by a living voyant, a person of power capable of acting at a distance. Indeed, however, the history of Satanism and witchcraft is also the history of poisons. An early scandal at the court of Louis the Fourteenth involved Satanists who were making poisons and aphrodisiacs. A few of the perpetrators were actually executed. Even the king's favorite mistress was implicated. She also reputedly served as the nude altar piece at the Black Mass."

I glanced at Holmes. "Do you actually suspect someone has put a hex on Mrs–?"

"*Hssht.*" Holmes quickly raised his forefinger to his lips. "The lady's name must remain confidential." He turned to Sumners, "A client of mine," and then back to me. "That is certainly what someone wants her to think. Whether the person who wrote the note actually believes in Satanic curses is another matter."

While I stroked the cat with one hand, my other tapped nervously on the sofa arm. "Can we at least agree that such curses are superstitious mumbo-jumbo with no basis in reality?"

Sumners smiled broadly. "Sorry, old fellow, but as a religious man, I am not willing to make such a universal dismissal. I believe in the force of the dark powers."

I gave Holmes an inquisitive look.

"I too believe in the force of the dark powers," he said, "powers which are not always preternatural. And I believe in the power of suggestion. The fear that one is cursed can actually make one ill and drive one to desperate measures. You can see the truth of that in primitive societies and tribes where someone sickens and dies in the belief he has been cursed."

"Well, I for one do not believe in the Devil," I said.

"Do you believe in God?" Sumners asked.

"I am an agnostic. I don't know."

Sumners laughed. "Then you should be agnostic about the Devil, too! Surely there is as much–if not more–proof that he exists than does God. After all, evil seems much more extravagant and overblown than good."

Holmes's sardonic smile appeared. "That is certainly true. In my profession I have seen nearly every variety of human evil imaginable."

"But has it not generally been counteracted by good?" I asked.

He shrugged. "'Generally' is perhaps too strong. 'Often' might be true. Many of my cases have ended in ruin or death, and not always for those who most deserve it." He turned again to Sumners. "Are there not counter spells against these curses?"

"Ah yes, white magic as opposed to black, so to speak. Often the countermeasures are religious in nature. There is an abbé in Lyons known for his abilities to reverse the most maleficent of Satanic spells. I believe he calls upon Michael, the Archangel, or some great biblical high priest. The spell can be blocked and even turned against its maker."

Holmes nodded, even as his right hand unconsciously stroked the orange tabby curled beside him. "Are you familiar with the actual Satanic groups in Paris?"

"Yes. I have my agents, Satanic impostors who are actually practicing Catholics. They keep me informed of the various goings-on."

"You spoke of the anti-pope earlier. Is there an anti-archbishop, an anti-cardinal, for Paris?"

"Yes, although he never had any grand rank in the church. He was only an abbé, name of Durtal. He is generally acknowledged as the most powerful Satanic master in the city."

"But he is not the only one to perform the Black Mass."

"No, no—although his Masses are the most grand and spectacular. His are high Masses, so to speak. On second thought, wouldn't a high Black Mass really be a low Black Mass, since all is inverted? Regardless, Paris is full of priests of questionable virtue. It is a dumping ground for castoffs from the countryside, those accused of various sins involving ladies or altar boys, or of raiding the collection box. They are reassigned to Paris, paid a pittance, and given the dirty work upper-class priests disdain: early morning Masses in the cold church, funerals outdoors in the chill rain, visiting the poor and sick. Many of these men have already been corrupted. Satanism is the logical next step. And of course, Satanism does give license to commit the most base and disgusting sexual acts. If Catholicism idealizes chastity, Satanism idealizes lust."

Holmes's mouth briefly twisted upward on one side. "Always two sides to the human coin. Chastity and lust, light and dark, God and the Devil, good and evil."

He and Sumners chatted a while longer. One topic was familiars of the Devil, generally black animals like wolves, dogs, cats, crows or ravens. The conversation made me feel strange and unsettled. This was a side of life of which I had been completely unaware.

Finally Holmes withdrew his watch from his waistcoat pocket and glanced at it. "We have taken enough of your time, Algernon." He stood up, and I set the big black cat to one side—he protested loudly—and rose. "This has been very illuminating."

Sumners placed his pince-nez back upon his nose, then inhaled deeply as he stood. "The pleasure was mine, Holmes. Come again anytime. You must not leave Paris without another visit."

"I am certain I shall be consulting with you again in the near future."

Sumners again took my hand between both of his, grasping it tightly with his right hand. "A pleasure, Dr. Vernier. I hope we have not distressed you too much. There is always the consolation of the Church, you know."

I tried to smile politely. Holmes and I descended the four flights of stairs, passed the concierge's loge, and stepped out onto the narrow street crowded with people. A carriage went by, the horse's hooves clopping on the cobblestones.

"It's hard to believe out here in the daylight," I said, "that any of what he told us could possibly be true."

"There is always something rather unbelievable, incredulous, about evil. He is an expert in such matters."

"You said he was a priest. Does he have a parish, a congregation?"

"No."

"Then what on earth does he do for a living?"

"He has some limited family income. He is working on his magnum opus." Holmes smiled, forestalling my next question. "A grand history of witchcraft and Satanism throughout the ages."

"And you think somehow Satanism is linked to the case of Mrs. Hardy?"

"As I said: I am not certain. We do know someone is trying to frighten her, and if she is a devout Catholic, then the Devil provides a ready-made tool."

"Four for the Devil," I murmured softly. It was not that cold, but I felt a sudden shiver make my shoulders rise.

"Exactly."

Holmes and I had an excellent lunch together, and then I went back to the hotel, while he set off in a cab to visit various art galleries. I was to meet him later that afternoon in front of Notre Dame. After a brief rest, I strolled back along the Rue de Rivoli toward the Île de la Cité and the cathedral. I considered stopping at the Louvre, but the sun had broken through the clouds, flooding the broad avenue and the narrow side streets with yellow light. After so many days of dismal gray clouds or yellow fog, it seemed a shame to waste such a day indoors.

Instead I wandered through the old Jewish quarter of the Marais to the Place des Vosges. This was another spot that was often full of people in summer, but now the green lawn was deserted. I strolled through the arcades round the square and stopped for a coffee. I drank it outside, enjoying the sun on my face, but I kept on my gloves and did not dawdle long. I took my time making my way back. I crossed one bridge to the Île Saint-Louis, then soon another over to the Île de la Cité. By then, the sun was down, the great square before the Notre Dame Cathedral in twilight. I pulled out my watch, saw that I was early, and passed through the massive door into the church.

It was much cooler inside, the vaulted ceiling far above hidden in shadow. All the color seemed to have gone out of the world, only grays, blacks, muted browns and shadow remaining. As I walked down the central aisle, I could hear voices off to the side and the murmur of my footsteps echoing above. When I was halfway to the altar, I turned to sit on one of the benches with their wicker seats. Before me a row of thick pillars rose up into arches. The air was damp, heavy, with a faint hint of—what else?—incense.

I had been raised a Catholic, but when I left home as a young man, I abandoned my religion. I had always, at heart, been an agnostic, unlike Michelle who was certain that a deity existed. All the same, I felt the power of the place, the aura of centuries of tradition and prayerful meditation. Then, too, it was a welcome refuge from the incessant clamor of the modern city. I wondered if I could still remember the words of the Hail Mary in French. "*Je vous salue, Marie, pleine de grâces,*" I began, and that was enough to carry me through to the end.

I said another for my grandmother who had been a passionate devotee of the rosary. We had occasionally said it together, most often because she promised me some treat as a reward. Obviously she had hoped that eventually the prayers themselves would become their own recompense. That never happened. I remembered being terribly bored and how slowly the last decade or two of Hail Marys would go. Grandmother had died two years ago, and I still missed her greatly.

I sat for a long while, savoring the silence. I watched the tourists slowly walk down the aisle. The light at the tall windows continued to dim. You could no longer make out the colors of the stained glass. Finally I pulled out my watch. Someone had lighted the candles of a nearby chandelier, but I could barely make out the face. Time to look for Holmes at our appointed meeting spot, the nearby statue of Charlemagne.

I rose, walked down the aisle and then out through the central doorway. The sky over the distant buildings was blue-black, streaked with clouds, a star or two visible. It was almost five o'clock, and the rumble of the city was louder than ever, the square itself full of people, carriages all lined up along one side of the street. The gas street lamps were lit and burned yellow-white. I went to the statue of the mounted Charlemagne and his two companions on foot, its metal weathered to a gray-green color.

I turned to look back at the church. The two towers stood out against the fading red sky; theirs was a perfect symmetry that never existed in nature. Each had two tall windows up top, two smaller ones below. The three arches over the great doors were also symmetrical, as were the sculpted figures in relief, forming inner layers like those of some gigantic onion with a wedge cut out. The wood of the enormous doors appeared black.

A group of priests walked by, all wearing black soutanes with the ankle-length skirts and the broad-brimmed hats of country clerics. As might be expected, in the square before France's greatest cathedral, many priests and sisters came and went. One pair of sisters had odd white headgear like a bent and folded piece of paper or some half-open white blossom, while another had the more conventional black veil with white bands over her throat and across her forehead. A heavy wooden rosary hung at her side. She passed me at an angle, and I realized I had been so intent upon her habit that I had hardly noticed her face, which was, of course, the whole point of a sister's habit. She stumbled slightly, recovered, then walked very briskly.

My eyes wandered to the left, and I saw the unmistakable tall thin figure of Sherlock Holmes in his black top hat and overcoat. At first I thought he might have paused mid-stride, but he was not moving. He appeared somehow frozen, his stick raised in midair. I started toward him. The brim of his hat shadowed his eyes, but his lips, parted slightly, also appeared locked in place.

"Sherlock?" I was close enough he must have heard me, but he still had not moved. "Sherlock?" I had to say his name a third time before he responded: he drew in his breath sharply and the ferrule of his stick fell and struck the cobblestone. I drew closer, but he would not look at me. "What is it? What's the matter?"

Instead of answering, he snatched off one glove, then took off his hat and ran his bare fingers back through his black hair. His face was so pale it almost seemed to glow in the twilight. He clenched his teeth briefly, grimacing.

"Are you all right?"

"*No*," he whispered, his eyes focused in the distance. He turned abruptly. "That nun—did you see?—did you see…?"

"Which nun? There are so many."

"The one… The one who… Dear God," he whispered, then his hand shot out and gripped my arm so tightly I winced.

"What is wrong with you! Are you ill? Does anything hurt?" This last question triggered an explosive bark of a laugh. "Are you having pains in your chest?—in your head? Is it your heart?"

"My heart?" he murmured. He drew in his breath slowly, struggling for composure. At last he seemed to really see me. "Henry."

"Yes—now tell me what is wrong. Are you ill?"

"Ill? No, not ill. It is only… I have had a shock."

"What shock?"

Again his hand rose, and his fingers slipped back through his hair. "I feel almost… dizzy."

"You had better sit down. That bench there, perhaps."

"No, no—I want to walk, and I need… I need… a cognac—yes, a cognac."

"Well, there is a café just across the street, but are you sure you do not want to sit for a while?"

"No, the air will do me good—and a drink." He put on his hat, pulled on the black leather glove, then was off at a rapid pace.

I followed. I could not recall him ever acting quite so peculiarly. I still wondered if he might be sick, if it might have been some sort of fit. Inside the crowded café, Holmes went directly to the counter and removed his hat and gloves. "*Un cognac, monsieur, s'il vous plaît.*"

The bald stout older man wore a white shirt and black vest. His eyes were curious as he took the bottle and poured into a small glass. Holmes took the glass and tossed it down. He coughed sharply once. "*Un autre, s'il vous plaît.*" The bartender's brow had furrowed. He poured into the glass again.

I grasped Holmes's arm. "What are you doing?"

He slowly drew in his breath, paused, then eased it out through his nostrils. "I am all right now. It has cleared my head. Don't worry: this one I shall sip." He took a small swallow. "A very poor relation of Hardy's magnificent Armagnac indeed."

"I think it is time you explained yourself."

"I told you. I had a shock."

"What shock?"

"Something unexpected."

"What, for God's sake—what?"

He stared closely at me, his lips pressing tightly together. "I cannot say."

"Will not say, you mean."

"Yes, that is exactly what I mean."

"Does it have to do with the case?—with Mrs. Hardy?"

"No—*no.* That doesn't matter."

"What then?"

He sighed softly, then took another sip of the cognac. The bartender was still staring at him. "Would you care for a cognac yourself, Henry, or perhaps *un verre de vin?*"

"I don't want anything until you tell me what has happened to you."

"Please drink something—to humor me. Please."

"Oh, very well." I glanced at the bartender. "*Monsieur, je voudrais aussi un cognac, s'il vous plaît.*"

Holmes took another small sip. His breathing seemed to be normal now. I took a big swallow of cognac. I felt slightly shaken myself. "Now will you explain?"

Holmes stared down at the counter top. "I cannot—not now. Perhaps another time."

"You don't trust me?"

"Of course I trust you!" His voice was sharp. "It is not a matter of trust, but... some matters must remain private. Everyone must be allowed certain secrets. This is one of those."

"And it has nothing to do with the case or with Satanism?"

"No, not in the least." He took a long slow breath, then one side of his mouth rose. "Life will play its little tricks on us. Was it only fancy, I wonder? I wanted answers, but not that particular one."

"Since you will tell me nothing, I cannot comment."

"You were not meant to. I was only thinking aloud." He sipped his cognac. "Yes, either a phantasmagorical construct of the mind, or the most ironical answer ever to a prayer." He laughed again, and I shook my head. "Poor Henry! Forgive me. I did not mean to alarm you." Some color had come back into his face. "Perhaps someday I can explain—but not today." He sighed deeply. "It is too early for dinner, especially after our substantial lunch, but we might amuse ourselves after a day of travail. One can pick up a flat boat near the east end of the Île de la Cité. The night is clear and relatively warm. We shall forget the case and everything else, while we join the tourists and take in the lights of Paris from the Seine."

I looked up at him. He was staring at himself in the big plate-glass mirror which hung behind the bar above a row of bottles. His gray eyes shifted in the mirror, his reflection staring back at me. He drank down the last of his cognac.

After an enjoyable boat ride, we took a cab back to our hotel and went to our rooms to freshen up, then down to the restaurant. Soon the waiter brought a small plate of escargot for Holmes and some charcuterie for me. He skillfully opened the bottle of Bordeaux and poured a half-inch of the deep red liquid into Holmes's glass. Holmes swished the bowl, took a brief sniff, then sipped. "*Excellente. One can always rely on Saint-Émilion.*" The waiter poured him more, then gave me some. Holmes raised his glass. "Cheers." We clinked glasses. Holmes had a swallow, then took up a small fork and pried a snail from the striped multicolored shell. He glanced up at me, then smiled. "I see that gastropods are still not to your taste."

"No. Although almost anything would be edible when drowned in butter, garlic and parsley."

"Exactly."

"Did you find out much about Gaston Lupin this afternoon?"

"He is clearly a second-rate artist of little repute. None of his paintings are much in circulation. I did meet one dealer who had known him personally, and he was an admirer. He told me Lupin had extraordinary technical skill, an incredible eye, and amazing visual memory. He could walk through the Louvre, stare at a painting from any era for a few minutes, then return to his studio and produce an almost identical copy, down to the last detail of the brushwork. Originality, on the other hand, was in short supply. However, he did paint some nudes of merit which sold well."

"Nudes?"

Holmes smiled. "Female nudes, of course. And like many an artist, he knew his models well, both visually and biblically. I also stopped briefly at Lupin's home near the Champs-Élysées and spoke with the butler and valet. The butler was not very accommodating, but the valet turned out to have read all of Watson's stories. When he saw the name Sherlock Holmes on my card, he was ready to obey my every command. It was late enough I could not stay to give Lupin's room a thorough examination, but I told them I would be back tomorrow or the next day to have a look. I also sternly instructed them to disturb nothing, although, unfortunately, as might be expected, the room has been tidied up since Lupin's death."

"A shame that—and that the corpse, as well, was not left out for you, but then they did not know at the time that Sherlock Holmes was on the case."

Holmes smiled. "Very good, Henry—quite witty." He withdrew

the last of the snails, regarded it balanced upon the end of his small fork, then put it into his mouth and chewed thoughtfully. "They do have a taste, after all, a rather earthy one."

I shook my head. "Like dirt, you mean."

Holmes laughed, and I wondered briefly if I should ask him again about his odd behavior before the cathedral, but I did not want to remind him of something that had obviously shaken him, curious though I might be. His thin lips were pressed together in a rigid half-smile, but his gray eyes were suddenly lost in the distance. He seemed to stare past me, but I could tell his gaze was not fixed on anything in the dining room. Despite his good humor, he looked weary and faintly unsettled.

"Oh, I forgot to tell you," I said. "Michelle may join us at the end of the week. She has not had a holiday for some time, and I pointed out that when I travel with you, events generally take a catastrophic turn and I have to beg for her to come. Perhaps if she arrives before I send for her, that will act as insurance to prevent the worst from occurring, as when you take an umbrella along to forestall rain."

Holmes smiled. "A well-reasoned supposition."

"I hope you don't mind."

"Of course not. She has a way of making herself very useful, especially in cases which involve women. Besides, you can spend some time with her as a tourist instead of following me about in my tedious visits."

"I did not find Madame Delvaux or Algernon Sumners tedious in the least."

Holmes sipped his wine, his eyes thoughtful. "Tomorrow, though, I think we shall take the bull by the horns. I really cannot proceed with this case without calling upon the main character."

I frowned. "Mrs. Hardy, you mean?"

"Exactly, Henry. In so nebulous a business as this, meeting her would doubtlessly be most illuminating."

"But her husband told us your investigation must remain a secret from her!"

"So it shall, Henry. So it shall. Yes, perhaps in the afternoon, after I do some shopping in the morning."

"Shopping? Whatever for? You buy all your clothing in London, your tailor is first-rate, and while Paris may reign supreme for the ladies, London is superior for men."

"All the same, there are some garments I need, as well as a few little trifles and knickknacks."

Chapter Three

TRUE to his word, the next morning Holmes set out on some
mysterious shopping expedition. He met me for lunch
carrying two large paper bags, but he would not reveal the
contents. After eating he retired to his room. I relaxed with a
book in a chair next to the window which overlooked the Rue de
Rivoli and the Tuileries. Later there came a knock at my door.

When I opened it, a tall thin man stared at me. His black
soutane with its roman collar made his priestly vocation
obvious. I frowned, staring at his striking countenance, which
was somehow familiar in more ways than one. His gray hair
was parted down the middle, a golden pince-nez perched on his
lumpy nose, and his bushy goatee and mustache were salt-and-
pepper colored.

"Yes?" I asked.

"Dr. Henry Vernier?" He had a high-pitched, rather nasal
whiney voice.

"That is my name."

"Mr. Holmes has sent me to ask if you will—"

I noticed he was holding a large paper bag. I suddenly smiled. "*Ahh!* For once—*for once*—you have not fooled me! I am not completely stupid after all."

"What do you mean, sir?"

"A very good disguise, Sherlock, very good indeed."

He gave me a curious look. "I don't understand you, sir. Explain yourself."

I stared more closely. Could I possibly be mistaken? "Sherlock?"

At last his face relaxed into a smile. "Very good, Henry. Do you think it would deceive someone who was not so intimately acquainted with me as you are?"

"Yes, absolutely. That beard hides the shape of your jaw, and the mustache conceals your mouth. You have also done something to your nose. Putty, I suppose. And your voice… You were imitating Algernon Sumners, his pitch and enunciation—in fact, he was obviously the model for your facial appearance as well."

"Yes, so he was. And I shall present myself to Madame Hardy as Dr. James Sumners, the brother of Algernon Sumners."

I shook my head. "I wish I could be there to see it."

"And so you shall, Henry, so you shall, if you are willing to let me work on you as well."

"Gladly."

Holmes had a much larger soutane in the bag, as well as a black wig and false beard. First he belted a pillow round my waist to make me appear fat, then had me put on the soutane. Next he pulled the wig over my brown hair. The fake beard was more of a project. He used spirit gum to hold the beard in place, then applied some black coloring to my mustache so it would match. When he was done, he gave a nod and led me to a mirror.

I shook my head in disbelief. "I'm not sure even Michelle would recognize me."

"The beard is not so convincing as mine, but then mine took over an hour to construct. Oh, I almost forgot—this will help, too." He withdrew a pair of spectacles from the sack.

I put them on; the lenses were clear glass. "The perfect finishing touch."

"Yes, I think so. By the way, can you speak in a falsetto voice?"

"Like this?" I spoke in a high pitch.

"Excellent. I shall do most of the talking, but if you do speak, use that voice. You shall be Mr. Robert Grantly, a vicar. We are, of course, Anglican, not Roman Catholic. Our cassocks should be double-breasted with the thirty-nine buttons, but these Catholic garments, as might be expected, were all that I could find in Paris. Mrs. Hardy will surely not know the difference. I telegraphed her this morning, stating that I was a friend of her husband who hoped I might be able to offer her some spiritual consolation. I said we would call upon her around four thirty this afternoon. Our makeup is well done, but it might not stand up to close scrutiny under bright light. However, by that time of day, the more subdued lamp lighting will help conceal our disguises. The townhouse is off the Champs-Élysées not far from Lupin's. We have over an hour and a half at our disposal, and the rain has ceased, so we might stroll over there in a leisurely manner. Oh, and I have two plain black overcoats and two wide-brimmed priest's hats in my room for us to wear."

The rain had stopped, but we took our umbrellas with us. We cut through the Place de la Concorde to reach the Avenue des Champs-Élysées, then started through the park. Because of our sacerdotal attire, we often received respectful nods, especially from older ladies. The carriage traffic on the broad boulevard was brisk. Further on, many ladies and gentlemen in fine attire were gazing into the windows of the fancy shops. The sky was overcast, it was growing dark, and the gas lamps were already lit. We passed a haberdashery, a jeweler's and a dress shop, before turning down a side street. Soon we turned another corner.

On either side, the buildings formed a solid wall of worn beige stone, five stories high, with tall narrow windows on the first, second and third floors. On the second floor, stone balconies jutted out, supported by elaborate cornices, with a protective railing of floridly designed, curving black wrought-iron. There were no streetlights, and only a few lamps next to massive wooden doors were lit. It was much quieter, the street almost deserted, and the busy Champs-Élysées seemed far away indeed.

Holmes pulled out his watch, then squinted to try to make out the face. "Nearly four thirty. Their house is number nine." He raised his umbrella to point across the street. "Just there."

Two women came round the far corner across the street from us. One of them was tall and wore a purple coat with fur cuffs and collar along with a wide-brimmed plumed hat of the same color. She was obviously the mistress, while the smaller woman at her side in a plain hat and coat was the servant.

"I wonder…" Holmes murmured.

Some shadowy form swept past me, leaving a chill wind in its wake—an animal, a big black dog, that loped across the street. It halted before the two women, hunching slightly. We could hear a low growl, then loud fierce barks.

"Good Lord." I started forward, but Holmes seized my arm.

"Remember to stay in character, Vicar." He strode past me, traversing the street at a diagonal, even as he raised his umbrella. "I say—I say!" I followed him.

The two women cowered against the stone wall of the building. The mistress had dropped her handbag, and her arm was raised in a protective gesture. Her face was dead-white, her eyes and mouth opened wide. The smaller woman looked disturbed, but not so frightened. We went past the dog, who turned to snap at me. I turned round, holding my umbrella before me for protection, and Holmes stood next to me, also brandishing his umbrella.

The dog was all black except for a white smear above its eyes so he tended to blend into the shadow. His yellow-white teeth with the two sharp canines were bared, his pink tongue lolling slightly to the side. His barks were short and savage. He paused briefly to lunge for the umbrella tip, then resumed barking. Amber rings glowed round the black pupils of his fierce eyes. I had never seen an animal so angry. Given his size and black color, I could not help wonder if he were part wolf. Certainly he was wild enough. Our umbrellas seemed a feeble defense.

I glanced at Holmes. "If we can make it inside perhaps..."

The dog suddenly reared upright, raising his paws. His large pointed black ears were erect. His head turned to the side as if listening, then to us again. He bared his teeth, growled once, then with a final turn, he bounded away. I heaved a sigh of relief.

"Madame, are you all right?" Holmes asked.

The tall woman staggered a step forward, then slumped against the wall. "*Mon Dieu,*" she murmured, "*Mon Dieu.*" She might have slipped downward, but Holmes grasped her arm.

"He is gone, madame—departed." He was using the Sumners voice.

"There ought to be a law against such hellish beasts," the shorter woman said in French.

"Might this possibly be Mrs. Hardy," Holmes asked, "Mrs. Marguerite Hardy?"

"Yes, sir," said the smaller woman.

"I was just coming to call upon her. It was opportune that we arrived somewhat early. I am Dr. James Sumners, and this is my friend, the Vicar Robert Grantly." Mrs. Hardy didn't seem to hear. She was still dreadfully pale.

"How do you do, sir. I am Jeanne, Mrs. Hardy's maid." She spoke English with a very heavy accent.

"We must get her…" I started in my normal voice, but Holmes struck my ribs with his elbow. I raised the pitch of the last word. "…*inside.*"

"Robert, if you will assist me, we shall escort you indoors, madame. A frightful carnivore that. A swallow of brandy–perhaps some of your husband's ambrosial Armagnac–and you will be good as new."

A feeble, reflexive smile flickered over her lips, but she still hardly seemed to hear him. Knocked against the wall, the purple hat had slipped back and sideways, and her forehead suddenly creased, even as her eyes focused on us at last. "You saw–you saw that creature? I did not imagine…?" Her English was only slightly accented. Her dark eyes lost their focus, turned inward. "No, no, of course you did." I took her left arm and helped Holmes lead her the few steps to the doorway. She was almost as tall as Michelle and big-boned. I doubted that Holmes and I would be able to keep her on her feet if she actually fainted.

Jeanne had picked up her mistress's handbag and found the key. She used it to unlock the dark oaken door, then pulled it open for us. We guided Mrs. Hardy through the doorway. "*J'ai peur,*" she murmured to no one in particular: *I'm afraid.* A single lamp of green and blue glass illuminated the vestibule.

Jeanne used a match to light a candle, then grasped the handle of its brass holder. "This way."

We followed her down the dim hallway to a sitting room, then led Mrs. Hardy to a voluminous sofa of striped velvet. She collapsed into it, thought for a second or two, then removed her big hat and set it beside her. Her hair was dark, almost black, save for a white streak above her forehead, and it was bound up in a chignon with a silver brooch holding it in place. She still appeared ghastly.

"You look like you have seen a ghost," I said.

"Do you think...?" she began anxiously.

"That was a creature of flesh and blood," Holmes said. "Ghost dogs do not leave tooth marks in the ferrules of umbrellas." He turned to Jeanne. "Is there some brandy at hand?"

"Oh yes, sir." Holding the candle before her, Jeanne walked to a nearby side table. Holmes followed, then poured some brandy from a crystalline decanter into a glass. He returned to the sofa. "Drink this, madame." Mrs. Hardy took the glass, stared down at it dully. "Do drink. It will make you feel better." She hesitated, took a quick swallow, then grimaced slightly.

Jeanne had set down the candle, and she was lighting a nearby lamp. "I've never seen such a thing, such a *monstre* of a dog before. I can tell you it gave me quite a fright."

Holmes glanced at her, his eyes narrowing slightly. "You were quite courageous, mademoiselle, much more so than your mistress."

"Perhaps it is because I know dogs. I growed up with them."

She lit a second lamp, and more color came into the sitting room. It was well furnished with furniture of dark wood and purple and burgundy velvets. Several ornate vases were placed round the room, and framed paintings hung on the walls. High overhead was a chandelier with dangling crystals of glass.

Holmes had removed his hat. "Would you like to take off your coat, madame?" She was still wearing the purple coat with the dark sable cuffs and collar.

She shook her head. "No. I'm cold." I saw that she was trembling.

"The brandy," Holmes said. "Do finish it."

She raised the glass and swallowed it all. Her shoulders rose in a reflexive shudder.

"I could do with some myself." Holmes walked back to the side table and poured another glass of brandy. "Would you care for a spot, Robert?" I nodded, and he poured a second glass, then walked back to me.

I took a big swallow. It was obviously one of Hardy's wares, far superior to anything I usually drank. "It is very good." I was careful to pitch my voice unusually high. I gave a sigh. I felt disturbed myself. As a physician, I had treated people who had been badly mauled by dogs. That savage black animal had been the stuff of nightmares.

Holmes had taken a swallow. "Wonderful, truly wonderful. Would you care for a touch more, madame?"

She licked her lips, then shook her head. "No thank you." She stared up at us, her eyes great black circles, the swollen pupils leaving only thin rings of dark brown. For the first time she tried to smile. "Thank you, sir. If you had not been there…" A shiver also contorted her face.

"If you feel ill, perhaps we might come back another time."

"*No.*" She raised her right hand, fingers outspread, and the glass fell from her other hand, landed on the brightly colored carpet and rolled a few inches. "I mean to say… please stay. I… I don't want to be alone—not just now."

"Gladly." Holmes bent over to pick up the glass.

Mrs. Hardy looked at the maid. "You may leave us, Jeanne."

"Very good, madame, but first, may I take your coats and hats, reverend gentlemen?" She folded the coats over one arm, held the two hats in the other, then departed.

"Do sit down, Mister... or, it was Doctor, was it not? I have forgotten your names."

"I am Dr. James Sumners, and this is my very good friend, the Vicar Robert Grantly."

"Please sit down, Dr. Sumners, Vicar. Oh, and help yourself to more of the Armagnac if you wish." She had absentmindedly pulled off one glove, and now she removed the other. She had large elegant hands with long fingers. She touched the streak of white hair over her forehead lightly.

"So I shall." Holmes poured himself more, then sat at the other end of the sofa, while I took a nearby armchair. "Are you sure you are up to some company, Mrs. Hardy?"

"Yes, quite sure." She smiled again, but she looked worried, tiny creases showing at the corners of her eyes, the hollows beneath them shadowy. As the fear wore off, she appeared simply exhausted. From what we had heard, I suspected she had not been sleeping well for some time.

"I spoke to your husband recently—he is an old friend—and he mentioned that something had upset you. He was obviously worried about you. He told me about an odd note you had received in the mail. It is presumptuous, I know, but I thought perhaps I might offer some spiritual assistance in your time of need."

She eased out her breath in a sound which was a weary sort of laugh. "You have already assisted me. If you had not come when you had..." The fear showed again in her dark eyes.

"I am glad we could help." My high-pitched voice sounded ridiculous to me, but she did not seem to find it unusual.

"You are, I believe, Roman Catholic, while we are of the Anglican faith, so I can hardly serve as your confessor. All the same, I can offer you my sympathy and perhaps discuss that which troubles you."

Her forehead had creased again, even as a smile came and went. "How odd."

Holmes stared at her politely for a few seconds, then said, "Odd in what way?"

"That you should come to see me. You are the second person of the cloth to come calling, although the abbé did not know my husband."

Holmes sipped his brandy, watching her closely. "A priest came to call on you?"

"Yes. Just last week."

"And what was this priest's name?"

"Monsieur l'Abbé Jules Docre. He is one of the priests at Saint-Sulpice."

"And why exactly did he call on you?"

Her mouth slumped downward at the sides. "He too thought I might be in spiritual distress. He said... sometimes God seems to take possession of him, to guide him, and he wanders the streets of Paris until he arrives before a certain door, and he knows that someone within needs him."

"And he thought you were such a person?"

"Yes."

"Did he elaborate?"

"He said... he said he could sense my suffering, and also that..." Again she licked her lips, then clamped her mouth shut. "Must I go on?"

"Please," Holmes said. "I assure you, we are your friends."

"He sensed something evil hovering nearby, an evil presence. He suspected someone had called upon the Devil to..." She could not finish.

"Someone has cursed you, put a spell upon you?"

"*Yes*–how could you know that?"

"From that wicked note your husband told me about. *Four for the Devil.*" At his words, she shrank back into the corner of the sofa. "And do you believe the priest?"

"I don't know what to believe!" Her voice was anguished.

"My friend the vicar and I are not so inclined to credit the active involvement of the Devil in daily affairs, as was the case with our fellow clergymen in the past. Before presuming the infernal, one must absolutely rule out human maleficence. Do you have any enemies? Is there anyone in particular who might wish you ill?"

Some of her color had come back when she drank the brandy, but now she grew paler again. Holmes did not rush her, but merely stared. At last she lowered her gaze. "Yes."

"And would this person stoop to sending so hateful a note?"

Again she was a long time in answering. "She might." The words were almost a whisper.

"'She.' A woman, then." She nodded but did not speak. "Curious. One does not normally think of the gentler sex as being capable of such cruelty and vengefulness, but if it is possible... Did you discuss this with Monsieur l'Abbé Docre?" Again she nodded. "And the good father actually thought this woman might have trafficked with the Devil to revenge herself upon you?"

Mrs. Hardy compressed her lips tightly together. "Might I have a little more of the Armagnac."

"Certainly." Holmes bounded to his feet and went to the side table. I smiled at Mrs. Hardy, but she would not meet my gaze. Holmes returned with a clean glass since she had dropped the first one. He sat again opposite her on the sofa. "Would you care to tell me about this woman, who she is and what she has against you?"

Mrs. Hardy slowly shook her head. "I cannot." She took a big swallow of brandy.

"No?"

"Everyone must have their secrets, Dr. Sumners. *Everyone.*"

"Could you tell your husband about it?"

"Absolutely not! *Never.*"

"Ah." Holmes nodded. "I see." He stared closely at her. "It is something shameful, then?" She would not meet his gaze, but her dark eyes started to shine, to go liquid. "My dear lady, I am sorry—I do not wish to upset you. You must forgive me. I did not mean to pry. I shall say one last thing, which may or may not be of consolation. If you do have an enemy who harbors a grudge, that may suffice to explain matters without the involvement of diabolical forces—despite what the good father thinks. I will not criticize your faith. In the end, we Anglicans share much in common with the Roman Church, but we are more reluctant, in this day and age, to find a devil, so to speak, lurking behind every bush.

"But enough of this unpleasant topic! Your husband said you had gone to Paris to seek out the help of a woman, a sort of Sherlock Holmes of the ladies." Holmes chuckled, a sound I had never heard him make before. "Have you found her, and has she been helpful?"

Mrs. Hardy squared her shoulders and sipped the brandy before speaking. "I have found her, and yes, she has been helpful."

"Excellent! I am not one to disparage the female sex. I think it is possible for a woman to have powers of intelligence and detection.

Not the same, perhaps, as those of Sherlock Holmes, but adequate enough to aid you. Moreover, a woman would naturally have far greater compassion and sympathy for your distress than a man."

Mrs. Hardy smiled wearily. "Yes."

"Might I ask her name? Although I would understand if you wished to keep it secret."

Her forehead scrunched up again. She took a sip of brandy, then let her free hand and her forearm slump on the sofa arm. "I don't see why not. She did not ask me to keep it secret, and she is well known among ladies of a certain society in Paris. She has helped others. Her name is Rose Grace. She is a widow."

"She is English?"

"Oh yes."

"And what age is this remarkable lady?"

"A little past thirty, I believe." She covered her mouth with her long fingers, suppressing a yawn.

"How did you hear about her?"

"From a friend. She told me all about her. Madame Grace helped Madame Lacroix find a stolen necklace, and she also helped restore a kidnaped girl to her parents."

"My goodness!" Holmes exclaimed. "Formidable indeed. Perhaps she can assist you."

Mrs. Hardy's brief smile was grim. "I am not so sure. I... I don't know if I need the services of a detective—or of a priest." She sighed, then yawned.

"I see you are tired, Mrs. Hardy. We have kept you long enough, I think."

She raised her hand. "No, no—stay a little longer, please. Are you perhaps hungry? I know it is only a little past tea time in London. If you would care for tea or anything..."

"No, no, Mrs. Hardy. We have been in Paris for a week and are quite *à la française* by now. This marvelous Armagnac is the finest thing you could have offered us. No need to spoil its delicately lingering taste with tea and biscuits!" She managed a smile. "And now we must discuss more pleasant matters. We have not yet visited Mr. Hardy's wine and spirits store. I believe it is not far from here, is it?"

We talked with her for a while about the store and its various goods. The Armagnac seemed to have had its effect on her. She was also relieved that we had dropped the earlier topic. Still, her attention came and went: you could see it in her dark eyes, which would lose focus and stare past us. She struggled not to yawn. Clearly she was exhausted. At last we rose to leave. She pulled the cord to summon Jeanne and have her fetch our coats. She thanked us again profusely for rescuing her from the dog. We could see her grow frightened as she spoke.

Holmes grasped her wrist tightly, which was unusual for him, wary as he generally was of women. "My dear lady, it was nothing. I am only glad we were there to help you. Surely Providence was at work." He hesitated only an instant. "By the way, there was one other question I meant to ask you, vis-à-vis that unpleasant note. Have you ever actually known anyone by the name of Angèle?"

She lowered her eyes briefly, then stared resolutely at him. "I have never known anyone by the name of Angèle."

"I see. Very good, then. *Au revoir*, madame—and I truly hope it is *au revoir* and not *adieu*."

Holmes and I stepped outside. The street was dark now and deserted. Holmes took off like a shot in the direction of the Champs-Élysées, and I followed. "It is only five thirty," he said. "There may still be time. We shall try, at any rate. We shall fetch a cab. He may still be available. The Parisians do not eat supper until eight or nine."

"Who will be available?"

"Monsieur l'Abbé Jules Docre."

"Why do you want to see him?"

"Come now, Henry! Surely that is obvious even to you."

"I suppose it is, but what's the great hurry?"

"Well, if nothing else, it is to see him today while in the guise of the good Dr. James Sumners, rather than as Sherlock Holmes. I would prefer not to waste another couple of hours tomorrow applying a fake beard and makeup."

"But the name of Sherlock Holmes might carry more weight."

He smiled faintly. "Just now I do not want to carry more weight. Come along, Vicar."

We found a cab, but it was slow going because of the late afternoon traffic. We made our way eastward and across the Seine toward Saint-Sulpice. We stepped out at the square before the great church. A cold drizzle fell. The nearby fountain of the four bishops, each in their little alcove underneath the ornate sculpted roof, was shut off, and the plane trees were bare of leaves. I paused to stare up at the great facade with its many pillars and two mismatched towers, the slightly taller bell tower on the left, then followed Holmes. We went up some steps, passed between two columns, and he pulled open one of the massive doors.

Inside the vestibule an old man in a dark suit sat near a table with pamphlets and papers, his short plump hands folded neatly on his lap. A small lamp barely illuminated the shadowy space. Holmes asked if he knew where we might find Monsieur l'Abbé Docre. He told us the priest often spent the time after dusk atop the bell tower, which could be reached from a stairway with an entrance near the side chapel dedicated to Saint Francis Xavier.

The interior of the church was a great echoey dark cavern, distant candles at the altar and others in the chapels providing the only light. Holmes found some candles near the doorway to the tower. "Are you ready for some exercise?" he asked.

I shook my head. "He would be up in the tower! If it were day, I think I would have to let you go on alone because of my vertigo, but I suppose in the dark I cannot see any great depths."

"Exactly. Just follow me and don't look down."

We started round a winding staircase. Holmes held the candle on its holder out to one side, providing a feeble light. Up only a floor or so was a wooden landing with several doors, but we did not stop. As we climbed into the darkness, the candlelight briefly showed the rounded worn bronze of enormous bells and great crisscrossing oaken beams reinforced with iron, the bolt heads and nuts the width of a man's hand. Intermittently along the outer wall were the huge slanted slats of the sounding shutters. A wet chill wind sighed softly through the gaps.

We reached a wooden platform, and Holmes stopped briefly to catch his breath. When the wind increased, the tower seemed to hum faintly. Occasionally there was an actual whistling. We resumed our climb and soon came to the largest bell yet. Holmes shone the candle on some writing on its exterior, but I could not make it out. An intricate floral and leaf design in relief was all along the upper part of the bell.

"The great bells all have names," Holmes said, "women's names like Thérèse and Caroline. Rather corpulent dames, I fear, weighing several tons apiece. This monster here takes four men to ring." He paused to gesture with the candle. "You grasp the iron bar there with your hands, then work in tandem with your partner, pushing with your feet at those boards to move the bell. There are places for two more men on the opposite side."

"Lord, I can only imagine what it must sound like up here. I don't know how they can endure the din."

"If they are sensible, they have cotton wool stuffed in their ears. However, the old master bell-ringers all suffer from deafness to some degree."

My hand firmly grasped the iron rail, sliding along the cold curving metal as we climbed upward into the darkness. We passed more sounding shutters, and I knew we must be in the tallest section of the tower. We came to another wooden landing, a rotunda, and its center opened into the depths below. Only a rather rickety-looking rail of black iron stained with orange rust protected us from the abyss, and I instinctively stepped back toward the wall.

Holmes grasped the railing and gave it a shake. "I certainly would not rely on this for safety. It seems overdue for replacement." He stroked his chin briefly. "I'm not sure I can resist... This must go all the way to the bottom, Henry, and as I recall the tower is slightly over two-hundred feet tall."

I shook my head with a shiver. "Do not tell me how tall the tower is."

He had reached into his pocket and withdrawn something. He set down the candle on a ledge formed by an oaken beam, then held out a coin over the abyss. "No one can be below. We would have heard them. Dropping this should be harmless enough."

He opened his fingers, and I stepped a little closer. Almost immediately there was a clink of metal striking metal as the coin hit a bell below, and then nothing.

Holmes had leaned forward, but after two or three seconds, he stepped back. "Did you hear that final plop, Henry? No? You were too far away. I could hear it very distantly. Let us see if Monsieur l'Abbé is up top."

A final bit of iron stairway curved upward, and a misty rain swept in through the lighter, rectangular opening to the outside. Holmes started up the stairs. I hesitated, then followed him. I didn't step out onto the roof until I was certain there was a protecting wall. Even then, I stayed in the center grasping an iron railing. Because of the wind and the distant rumble of the city, the man in black with his back to us must have heard nothing.

"Monsieur l'Abbé Docre?" Holmes called.

He turned, and the light from the yellow-gray sky let us see him clearly. His wet black hair was plastered down, but his pale proud aristocratic face showed a curious nervous energy, especially his eyes. His nose was long and thin, his cheekbones stood out, and his mouth was narrow with full, rather petulant lips. His thin neck jutted out from the band of the white roman collar, and the black soutane with its notch at the throat was his only garment.

"*Oui?*" he asked.

"Do you speak English?" Holmes asked.

At that his lips formed almost a sneer. "*Pas de tout.*"

Holmes switched to French. "In that case, I shall try my French." I could tell that Holmes was actually playing up his English accent. He walked to the stone balustrade. "Quite a view! Robert, won't you have a look? You can see Eiffel's tower with its two beacon lights, and just there, the dome of Les Invalides."

"No, thank you," I said.

Holmes turned to the priest and pointed to the northwest. "Aren't they building a new church on that hill over in Montmartre?"

"Yes. What do you want?"

"My friend and I wished to speak with you briefly about a matter of importance."

"What is this matter of importance?" The drizzle was becoming a major downpour, but the priest didn't seem to care.

"If we might step inside… It would be easier to converse."

He shrugged. "Very well."

We all descended the iron stairway to the rotunda. Docre came last and closed the slanted door to the exterior. I shivered slightly. It was hardly much warmer inside the tower.

"Much better," Holmes said, even as he raised his pince-nez and put it in place upon his nose.

Docre eyed him closely, then me. "You are priests?"

"Of the Anglican faith."

He drew back, squaring his shoulders. "False priests, in other words."

Holmes seemed amused. "To your way of thinking, perhaps. I am Dr. James Sumners, and this is my friend, the Vicar Robert Grantly."

"*Bonsoir*," I said, mispronouncing the word horribly.

"I do not know what thing of importance two heretics would have to talk about with me."

"Briefly, we are friends of Madame Hardy," Holmes said, "Madame Marguerite Hardy."

"Friends?—or tempters, rather?"

"Tempters?" I asked incredulously.

"You would lead her from the true church to the false one of the abominable Henry."

"I assure you," Holmes said, "we are not trying to convert her. We are only worried about her."

Docre nodded. "As well you might be. As well you might be." He had folded his arms. His air of disdain was muted, but still apparent. He was of medium height, probably around five foot six.

"Is there not somewhere more agreeable than these lofty and cold heights where we might speak briefly?" Holmes asked.

"Yes, I suppose so." He looked about, then bent over to pick up a torch akin to a policeman's dark lantern. He withdrew some matches from his soutane pocket, struck one, and lit the lamp. "Come with me."

Holmes took the candle, and we started the long descent. Docre's torch was much more powerful than the candle, and its dancing beam opened up the interior of the tower, showing the complex network of beams, joists, ironwork, stone, and in the middle the massive forms of the bronze bells. I was careful not to look down, but only grasped the rail and lowered one foot after the other. When we came to the level with the doors just above the ground floor, Docre stopped and waited for us to join him.

"Where do these doors go?" I asked.

Docre pointed at a door. "There are some flats in the tower and above the church. That one there is where the chief bell-ringer, old Carhaix, and his wife live. Besides a place in the rectory, I have a room here where I go for silence and prayer. Come along."

He opened the door, and the torch revealed a walkway through what must be the attic over the church itself, a cave with beams of oak on either side, each one made up of about four slabs cut at an angle, so that the effect was like the ribs inside some enormous whale. On our left was a curving surface like a giant's skull made of splotchy bronze.

"What on earth," I murmured, but as we advanced, I saw it was only another bell, one lying on its side with a long black crack showing that it had split. Holmes stopped to swing his candle round toward the far end, and we could see the clapper lying on the side, and the spot over and under the inner rim where it had struck the metal and made gold shiny spots. In the shaft of light you could see motes dancing about; the musty air was thick with dust. Various boxes were everywhere, as well as the colored statues of saints and angels, many with missing or broken limbs, noses, hands, feet or wings.

After about twenty yards, we came to a wooden wall built up on the right side. Docre went a little further, then turned and opened a door. We followed him inside. He set down the torch, lit a couple candles, then extinguished the torch. The room was fittingly monastic: a single bed with a hard-looking mattress, a wooden prayer stool with a black volume on its single shelf and a faded purple velvet cushion which would not offer the knees much protection, a teetery-looking table and two chairs, and a small black stove which was not lit—it was still very cold.

Docre gestured at the table and chairs. "Sit down if you wish."

Holmes nodded, "Thank you," pulled out a chair and sat. I also sat. My legs were tired from the climb up and down the tower. Docre took a small towel and rubbed at his wet hair with it. Then he folded his arms and stood with his back ramrod straight, peering down at us. I felt vaguely like a school boy about to be reprimanded by the master.

Holmes set the fake pince-nez on his nose, the fastidiousness of the movement uncannily mirroring his "brother" Algernon Sumners. "Mrs. Hardy told us you sought her out," he said, "that you sensed something was wrong."

"That is true. I often wander the streets of Paris, going here and there, and on occasion, I sense something amiss. There is a sort of pricking at the back of my neck, then a feeling of apprehension, even of anxiety. I know what that means. I follow it. I let the feeling grow stronger, but as I approach the afflicted one, it abates. I know that God has sent me as his agent. With Mrs. Hardy, I felt drawn like iron toward a magnet. Never has the attraction been so strong. I knew that she was in great peril, that not only was her life threatened, but worse still, that her immortal soul was in danger. The Enemy did not want merely death, but damnation."

"What enemy?" I asked.

"The Devil, of course." He stared at us suspiciously. "You do believe in the Devil, don't you?"

Holmes nodded. "Certainly we do." I also nodded. "Mrs. Hardy said she had an actual enemy, a woman."

Docre frowned. "That is only speculation. A woman is hardly plausible."

"Regardless, this enemy has cast some sort of spell upon her?"

"The person could not have done this on their own—it is not a matter of herbs, potions, or nonsensical mumbo-jumbo. In this case, someone has truly worked with the Devil. A very powerful demon—or many demons—must be involved."

The strange energy I had noticed earlier in the priest had grown stronger, flamed in his dark eyes. His was a very handsome face. With his aristocratic bearing, his fine features, his curly black hair and pale skin, he resembled some romantic poet, another Lord Byron. I could imagine the ladies in the congregation swooning over his stern poetic sermons. The small room seemed so cold. I thrust my hands in my coat pockets, restraining a shiver.

Holmes stared closely at him. "I was under the impression that innocence could resist diabolical forces, that the Devil could not enter the house, so to speak, unless you opened the door for him."

"A confused metaphor, Dr. Sumners. Regardless, who is truly innocent? You of the heretical church often ignore the doctrine of

Original Sin. No one in this world is free from sin. Even the most innocent-looking child has wicked thoughts and desires. Only the degree of corruption varies."

"Come now," I said. "Isn't that an exaggeration?"

"If you spent as much time in the confessional as we Catholic priests do, you would know the truth of my words. Who can plumb the depths of human iniquity? However, our age has its own special blight–indifference, lassitude. Remember the words of Revelation? 'So then because thou art lukewarm, and neither cold nor hot, I will spew thee out of my mouth.' Active evil, in its own way, is better than blind idleness. During the Middle Ages, there were grand saints and sinners, the extremes of good and evil. Now we are left with only a sort of dull spiritual mediocrity. The great mass of humanity cannot rise to either goodness or maleficence."

I stared at him. "It sounds as if you would prefer to have lived in the Middle Ages."

He gave a brusque nod. "Yes."

"Well, as a…" I caught myself. "You would not have liked the medical treatments of the time. We have made great progress."

"*Progress.*" He laughed.

"Antisepsis and anesthesia have made possible…" Holmes gave me a warning look, and I stopped at once. Docre simply looked baffled.

"I too have often longed to live in a more poetic age," Holmes said, "one in which great deeds were still possible in the name of God."

"Then you understand." Docre lowered his arms, hesitated, then sat on the edge of the bed. The mattress had almost no give to it.

"Let us return to the subject of Madame Hardy. So diabolical forces assail her, assisted by some powerful enemy. What do you propose to do, Monsieur l'Abbé?"

"Do?"

"How is the Devil to be thwarted? Prayer, blessings or…?"

The priest shook his head. "Petty measures may not work in her case. Her adversary has called upon demons for assistance; we may need to call forth powerful allies of our own."

"Such as?" Holmes asked.

"The Archangel Michael and the great high priest, Melchizedek. If she has been poisoned, that is the only thing that may save her."

"Poisoned!" I exclaimed.

Holmes glanced at me. "Remember, my brother explained to us that certain deadly venoms can be concocted from vile blasphemous ingredients, then administered by voyants or spirits of the dead."

Docre jerked his head downward. "Your brother knows what he is talking about."

"So a ceremony may be necessary to save her?"

"Yes, but I cannot tell yet. I am still trying to determine the exact situation."

"If we can assist you in any way…"

Docre sat up straight. "I do not…" He paused to slowly draw in his breath. "I know you mean well, but I do not need your help. You would only be in the way. Frankly, false priests such as yourselves are useless in a situation such as this."

Holmes smiled faintly. "I see."

"Will you be in Paris long, or…?"

"No, not long. The vicar and I will be returning to England very soon. Despite our doctrinal differences, I can tell that we will be leaving Madame Hardy in good hands."

"I promise you that I will do everything possible to save her."

"Tell me, Monsieur l'Abbé, you are obviously no common priest. I am no expert, but your French is excellent, not that of a common person. You were obviously well educated. Does your family come from the aristocracy?"

Holmes's question obviously pleased the priest. "Yes. My father is a baron, and my older brother will inherit his title. My father is... His enthusiasm for the faith is somewhat remiss, but my mother is a true saint. She always encouraged my vocation and was delighted when I was ordained. We both knew from early on that I was destined for the priesthood."

"So you have always had a religious bent?" I asked.

"'Bent'?" He frowned. "It is not a mere inclination. From the earliest age I have been aware of the other world that hovers about us, the powerful agents of good and evil."

Holmes hesitated. "And have you seen demons, then?"

I opened my mouth in dismay. The priest did not hesitate. "I have."

The corners of Holmes's mouth rose briefly. "What do they look like?"

"They are foul, of course. They are black. They are twisted. There are crusted pus-filled sores on their scorched skin, and the proportions of the body and face are all wrong. They have mouths, but as you might well assume, they have no teeth or tongues."

"Why not?" I asked.

"Because they do not eat corporeal food."

I smiled awkwardly. "Oh. Yes."

He stared closely. "Do not assume that what you cannot understand is madness, Monsieur Grantly. During the long history of the true church, many have been gifted–or cursed–with the power to see angels and devils. It is true that this is rarer nowadays than in the past. I did not ask for this power. In truth, I have not always wanted it. But it was given to me and has allowed me to help those under diabolical threat."

Holmes nodded. "Well, this has been most enlightening, Monsieur l'Abbé. I think it is time for us to be on our way."

We both rose, as did Docre. "Do you know the way out? Good." He relit Holmes's candle from one of his own. "I shall remain here for prayer and meditation." Holmes grasped the candle by its holder. "You said you are leaving Paris. That is for the best. It should not be necessary to warn you, but all the same—do not interfere in this matter. It is beyond your powers or your understanding. You would only make matters worse for Madame Hardy."

"We certainly don't want that! Good evening, sir."

Holmes and I followed the walkway back toward the landing. The great ribbed expanse could hardly be made out in the flickering candlelight. We went down the winding staircase, then through the vestibule and out of the church. The rain had subsided again to a drizzle, but the wind on my face was cold and damp. I thrust my hands into my pockets. "What a lunatic," I muttered.

"That was not mere lunacy, Henry."

"You cannot believe that someone can actually see angels and devils?"

"The idea is part of Christian theology."

"All the same... Lord, I'm freezing, and I'm sick of this false beard and wig. Can we stop for a quick *apéritif* somewhere warm, and then get back to the hotel so we can take off these ridiculous clothes and have some dinner?"

"Ridiculous, Henry? Shame on you! Have you no respect for men of the cloth?"

"They don't have to have pillows belted round their waists. It's coming loose, by the way. I just hope it doesn't end up down by my ankles." We started across the street toward the square. "That was quite a surprising story he told, although your *brother...*" I gave the word ironic stress, "...helped prepare me. All the same, can we not rule out diabolical poisons concocted of excrement, fish oil, and profaned hosts?"

"Perhaps so, Henry, but there are many different kinds of poisons. He was right about one thing. Mrs. Hardy is in great danger."

Chapter Four

The next morning after a more limited French breakfast, we set out again on the Rue de Rivoli. "How long a walk did you say it was to Gaston Lupin's home?" I asked.

"Perhaps twenty minutes, certainly no more than half an hour. It is only a few blocks from the Champs-Élysées, very near the Hardys' townhouse."

I laughed softly. "How could an artist ever afford to live in such a neighborhood?"

"That, Henry, is the obvious question about Gaston Lupin. Second-rate artists do not generally live alongside the nobility and ambassadors. While his female nudes in oil were well executed, they were never sold for much. He could not have made a fortune from his work."

"Perhaps he came from a wealthy family."

"I could not find him in any of the French equivalents of Debrett's or Burke's."

"Maybe his father sold wine and spirits."

Holmes laughed. "Perhaps. Hopefully we will have some answers by suppertime."

"And who will provide these answers?"

"Mr. Barrault."

"And who is Mr. Barrault?"

"Who else? His valet. What better source for the intimate details of a man's life? And as I said, he is an admirer of mine. I also hope to obtain the name of Lupin's doctor and his lawyer. I am curious about Lupin's will."

We crossed over the invisible border between the First and Eighth Arrondissement, and found the townhouse on a quiet narrow street away from the bustle of the Champs-Élysées. The stone was beige-colored, and short black wrought-iron railings were at the bottom of each tall window with white shutters along the sides. Holmes raised the brass knocker and rapped twice.

The door swung open, revealing a short man in black, his face very pale, his long sloping forehead and balding crown all aglow from the gray light. His dark eyes stared up at us, and the corners of his mouth were lost under the enormous black mustache which seemed the biggest part of him. "*Monsieur Holmes, ah, bienvenue! Entrez, entrez, s'il vous plaît.*"

Holmes and I removed our top hats and gloves. Holmes introduced me in impeccable French. Barrault stared at me, his forehead creasing. "*Pas Docteur Vatson?*"

Holmes glanced at me, clearly amused. Watson's stories had been translated into French two or three years ago, much to Holmes's dismay. "Bad enough every Englishman thinks I am an intimate acquaintance," he had said. "Now the French can make my life miserable as well."

Barrault set our top hats on a table near the door and put

Holmes's stick in a colorful Chinese vase two feet tall. "This is a great honor for me, Mr. Holmes. I have always followed your exploits with great interest. My English is not the best, but since your adventures are available in French as well…!"

"Very good, Monsieur Barrault. This morning I want to have a thorough look at the room where you found your master. Also, should you have any doubts about confiding in me, this letter should resolve them." He withdrew an envelope from his inner jacket pocket.

"Not at all, Monsieur Holmes—not at all!"

"All the same, have a look."

He took the letter from Holmes and went to a nearby lamp. I followed and glanced over his shoulder. Written in that pompously elevated style of the most formal French, it stated that all citizens and officers of the law should assist Monsieur Sherlock Holmes in any way possible, as he had the full confidence and assurance of the French Third Republic. It was signed Monsieur Louis Lepine, *Prefet* of Police, Paris. I gave Holmes an incredulous glance. The prefect was a political appointee and the highest ranked police officer in France.

Barrault handed the letter back to Holmes. "I am not surprised, Monsieur Holmes. This letter was not really necessary, but it does clarify the matter."

"Very good. I believe it was you who found Monsieur Lupin in his bedroom?"

Barrault made a grimace. "Yes, cold and dead in the morning."

"Show me the room, if you please."

"This way, monsieur." He led us through a beautifully furnished parlor with many grand paintings to a stairway.

As we went up the stairs, Holmes asked, "Had your master been in ill health recently?"

"Not at all, Mr. Holmes. His death came as a complete surprise."

"And how were his spirits?"

"His spirits?"

"His mood. Had he seemed sad or unusually silent or self-absorbed?"

"Not at all. He had gone out with a friend and returned with her after dinner. They seemed most animated and content."

We went down a hall to the bedroom. It was even larger than the parlor, and again, paintings were hung everywhere: a country landscape with cattle and mountains, a still-life of fruits and a dead pheasant, and closest to the bed, a nude red-headed woman, almost life size, whose white flesh seemed to glow even in the dim room. However, fittingly enough, the dominant feature in the room was the bed itself, a Gothic concoction of black wood with four thick pillars topped by miniature spires, complete with crosses. Joining the pillars were four arched spans which supported the canopy, each span rising in the middle to form a broad gable. A scarlet quilt covered the mattress along with several pillows in scarlet cases.

"Good Lord," I murmured, "it looks like it belongs in a church. Or it might be a confessional which has gone terribly wrong."

"Mr. Lupin was very proud of it," Barrault said. "He found it some ten years ago."

Holmes's thin lips had formed a bemused smile. He stepped nearer, touched one tall pillar with his long fingers and let them slide slowly downward. He hesitated, then lowered his head to look up under the canopy. "Interesting. Did it originally come with the mirror?"

Barrault opened his mouth but said nothing, even as his cheeks slowly flushed. At last he shook his head. "I wouldn't know about that, sir."

"No? How many years were you with Mr. Lupin, Barrault?"

"Thirteen."

"And he must have often had female visitors to his bedroom."

Barrault was still flushed, but he said nothing.

"Need I remind you of the letter I showed you just now?"

"No, sir, of course not. It's only… we were together for many years, and he was always truly kind to me. I would not want his reputation sullied."

"Let me assure you, sir, I am no scandalmonger. I will be discreet."

Barrault nodded. "He did have many lady visitors over the years, but…" He scowled, obviously thinking hard. "Ladies only of the highest class."

"And was there a special lady, one who was a more frequent visitor? You spoke of a friend who had joined him for dinner the night before he died."

"Yes, a Mademoiselle Labelle, a red-head, older than most. She was a recent acquaintance. She was with Mr. Lupin during the day and that evening."

Holmes seemed to actually rise up on his toes for an instant. "Was she now? And did she spend the night here?"

"No, sir. As I said, I found him alone in the morning. She had left around ten the night before."

"Are you certain of that, Barrault?"

"Yes. She had sought me out to say that the master needed me before she departed."

"And what did he want?"

"He didn't want anything, sir. He said she must have been mistaken. He seemed annoyed with me at first, until I explained that she had told me I was needed."

"You said she was a frequent visitor. Did she often stay the night?"

Barrault gave a reluctant nod. "Yes, sir."

"And how long had he known her?"

"Let's see now, it was last summer, after Bastille Day, I believe. Yes, almost exactly after, so the middle of July was when she first came calling."

"About four months, then. And just how frequent were her visits? Daily even?"

"Not quite daily. Once a week at first, but three or four times of late."

Holmes nodded, even as his eyes swept about the room. He raised his long slender hand in the direction of a door at the far side of the bedroom. "Where does that door there lead?"

"That is to Mr. Lupin's private study. He was not to be disturbed in there, not unless it was something of great importance. The maid did occasionally clean the room, but only under his strict supervision."

"I shall want to have a look."

Barrault stiffened slightly, his fists clenching. "But..." He seemed to reconsider. "Very well, sir. I can unlock it for you."

"Please do so. By the way, I assume Monsieur Lupin had an address book. If so, could you fetch it for us."

"Yes, monsieur, and he kept it in the study there. I'll only be a moment." He crossed the room, unlocked the door and went into the study.

I stepped forward and looked up under the canopy of the bed. Sure enough, a large mirror ran its entire length. I laughed softly. "It hardly goes with the Gothic motif."

"No. That and this painting reveal a great deal." He approached the nude to the right of the sculpted bed headboard. "It is signed

Lupin. Notice the long curve of the back and the rounded buttocks, the warm sensuous flesh tones. Clearly he was an admirer of the female form." He gazed at it until Barrault returned frowning.

"It is very odd. I cannot find the address book. It was always in the right top desk drawer, but it was not there, or in any of the others. I cannot imagine where it might be."

"Well, if it turns up, please contact me at once at the Meurice Hotel. You may leave us now."

"Leave you?" Barrault was clearly uneasy.

"I intend to do a lengthy and thorough search. There is no reason for you to remain here."

"As you wish, Monsieur Holmes." He nodded and departed.

Holmes tossed aside one of the pillows on the bed and pulled back the red quilt. "Pity. Doubtlessly the sheets have been changed. If only I had been here that morning! Let us first have a look at this mysterious private study."

Holmes entered first. The room was again filled with art, but this time much of it was immediately recognizable. My eye went to a copy of the *Mona Lisa*, then to another much larger nude alongside it. The woman's face was partly visible in this painting, turned to the side, showing a corner of her mouth rising in a slight ironic smile. Her reddish-brown hair was pulled up in a chignon which left her long slender neck bare and showed off her small exquisite ear. Her torso was turned so that one breast was also in portrait, so to speak, curving up underneath to the nipple, while the other was more face on. The areolas were painted the faint pink of a woman who had not conceived babies and nursed, and she looked to be in her early twenties. She was slender, but voluptuously curved. My eyes swept down to the dark triangle of pubic hair, and then I looked away, mildly embarrassed at both the painting and my predictable reaction to it.

Holmes went straight to it. "Yes, another Lupin. Definitely an eye for the female form. And that ear…" He was silent for a moment, then murmured, "Yes." He turned and went to the carved walnut desk, glanced at a bookshelf alongside it, then pulled open the center drawer. "*Ah*." He took out a leather covered case about nine inches long. "If I am not mistaken… Yes. A hit, Henry–a veritable hit!" Inside lying on blue velvet was a hypodermic syringe of silver metal and glass, the barrel and plunger separate from the two needles with their fittings.

"Good Lord," I murmured softly. "Do you think…?"

"Cocaine or morphine, without a doubt. Probably morphine. It is the drug of choice nowadays in France, *très à la mode*." He hesitated, then took the barrel and plunger and held them up toward the open window. "Empty, of course." He shook his head, then gazed at me. "The syringe and hypodermic needle may have been conceived of as a medical device to help alleviate pain, but more often they are carriers of death. Sometimes the process is through gradual degradation. Other times it is swift. The Angel of Mercy becomes instead the Angel of Death."

He opened the side drawers. One of them was very deep. Holmes took out a large wooden box and set it on the desk top. Inside were several small vials in a holder and a large bottle. Holmes drew in his breath sharply through his nostrils, raised the bottle to show me the label. Alongside a pink poppy, written in black script were "Morphine" in large letters and the name of the chemist's shop at the bottom. It also said the dosage was one gram per ounce.

"Do you think he took an overdose?" I asked.

"I would give odds on it. The question would be if it was deliberate on his part or not. I suspect not. Barrault said he was in good spirits, but more significant is Madame Labelle. She may have sent up Barrault to give herself an alibi, to show that Lupin was still alive when she left."

"But why would she want to murder him?"

"That, Henry, is what we must find out—if it is the case. One thing we can do is have the contents of this bottle examined; if there is more than one gram per ounce, then it was probably modified to kill him. However, we must not presume too much too soon. All the same…" He smiled slightly, his eyes gleaming. "I must search this room and the bedroom thoroughly. I shall begin with this desk." He pulled out the center drawer again and began to take out the contents.

I walked away from the desk. Butterflies seemed to flutter in my stomach. Why should I be surprised? Murder and death followed Sherlock Holmes like his shadow. The model in the big canvas had a certain sardonic look in her eye, as if she found posing naked to be faintly comical. Or perhaps it was the artist's lust she found comical. The image made me restless. Despite her extravagant red hair, the pupil of her eye was brown. Somehow she seemed familiar. I felt uneasy for a moment, for some unknown reason, and turned away. It also reminded me I would not be seeing Michelle for a few days.

I walked around the room glancing at the other paintings. The one of the *Mona Lisa* was very well done, to my eye almost identical to the one in the Louvre. On the nearby wall was a small round painting of a Madonna and Baby Jesus, she holding an apple in her long slender hand. Probably a copy of a Botticelli, although it had no signature. Next to it was the much darker, gloomy self-portrait of the aged Rembrandt.

"He is certainly good at imitation," I murmured.

Holmes froze for a moment. "What did you say?"

"That Lupin was good at imitation."

Holmes laughed sharply. "*Yes.*"

"What is so amusing about that?"

Holmes did not reply. I went to the big overstuffed leather armchair next to the bookcase and sat down. I closed my eyes, sighed, and wished I was back home. I tended to forget until I was in the middle of things that these cases with Holmes could be quite disturbing. I opened my eyes. He had finished with the desk and was glancing about the room. He clasped his left wrist behind his back with his right hand, his white hands standing out against the black of his frock coat, and began to examine the paintings. He stopped abruptly before one.

I closed my eyes again and drew in my breath deeply. I hadn't slept well the night before. Madame Hardy and Docre were both troubling. And I always missed Michelle's presence in my bed when I traveled alone. I almost dozed, but opened my eyes at last. Holmes was standing in the same place, his back toward me, but his hands hung at his sides now, the fingers spread apart. His face was hidden, but his entire body showed the tension like a cat about to pounce.

"Is something the matter?" I asked. He said nothing. "Sherlock?"

He turned to me, revealing a triumphant smile on his thin face. "Nothing is the matter!" He turned and removed the round painting of the Madonna from the wall. He strode to the window and examined the back where the light was better. "*Worm holes.* It would make sense. Or would it?"

"What are you talking about?"

"There is a famous Botticelli painting, one discovered late in our own century—the *Madonna of the Apple*, a sort of sister version to the better-known *Madonna of the Pomegranate*. The Virgin, in offering the apple to the Baby Jesus, is purifying the fruit from the sin of Eve. The painting was hardly found before it was lost again. There was theft, murder, and scandal involved, all here in Paris, as I recall."

"But surely it is only a copy?"

"Is it? The original was never recovered. You must know Poe's story about the purloined letter. This is exactly the same: how better to hide something precious than to have it out in the open surrounded by others of its kind? The wood panel appears antique, and the tempera and colors look to be those of the late Renaissance. I dare not leave this here a moment longer. My visits to Lupin's doctor and the lawyer can wait, although I shall have their names. What if the mysterious Mademoiselle Labelle were to reclaim this in my absence?"

"But you cannot just take it."

"Can't I? I shall give Barrault a receipt. Besides, we shan't have it for long."

"No? Whom will you give it to?"

"The Sûreté nationale, Henry, the French equivalent of Scotland Yard, and more specifically to Commissaire Juvol, an old friend of mine. We shall also take him the bottle of morphine for examination."

He turned again and something fluttered slowly down to the floor. "What is that?"

"What?" Holmes asked.

I stood, stepped forward and bent over to pick it up. I turned it slowly to and fro. The feather was a dull black. "It must have been stuck to the back of the frame." I turned it again. "What kind of feather is it, I wonder?"

"That is obvious, Henry—a crow or, given the size, perhaps a raven."

My mouth pulled back in disgust. "I hate the noisy beggars. They feed on carrion, too."

Holmes smiled ever so faintly. "They are the harbingers of doom, Henry. And perhaps..." His eyes grew thoughtful. "... familiars of the Devil."

Juvol and Holmes shook hands, and then it was my turn to have my own fingers crushed in the commissaire's massive paw. Juvol was almost as tall as Holmes, but he must have outweighed him by some fifty pounds. He was broad-shouldered and barrel-chested with a thick neck, square jaw, and an exuberant red-brown mustache which seemed to almost grow outward, rather than downward. His eyes were a clear cool blue. His navy-blue suit and waistcoat were well cut, and the jacket must have taken yards of material. All in all, he looked more like some stocky Scotsman than a Gallic policeman, but he spoke elegant French. As was also the case with the English, you could tell a French person's social class from their language, and Juvol had obviously been well raised and educated.

We exchanged a few pleasantries. Juvol thought I was French, and when I told him I had lived in England for many years, he was surprised. "Monsieur Holmes speaks excellent French, but you, you have absolutely no accent!" I explained that I had spent my youth in France and learned both languages, since my English mother spoke mostly English with me.

"Ah, how I envy you!" he exclaimed. "So much easier than struggling with grammars and dictionaries." He glanced at a satchel Holmes was holding. "I suspect this is not simply a social call, Monsieur Holmes. I believe you have something there to show me."

Holmes smiled, set the satchel upright on Juvol's desktop, then with a flourish pulled away a cloth, revealing the circular painting like some shield emblazoned with the Virgin's image. Juvol's smile vanished, mouth stiffening, eyes widening. "*Mon Dieu,*" he whispered.

"Do you recognize it?"

"I certainly do. *La Madonna della Mela.* It was some twenty years ago. I had only been on the force a year or two when it was stolen. The crime was a sensational one. The newspapers were filled with it for weeks, and it was a familiar topic amongst policemen and citizens alike. Where on earth did you find it?"

"At the home of Monsieur Gaston Lupin."

"The artist?–the one who died? Ah, then perhaps it is only a copy."

"Perhaps. I am no expert, but the wood seems sufficiently aged. The colors of the tempera resemble those of the Botticelli works I have seen in the Uffizi."

"May I?" Juvol grasped the painting by the golden frame and held it up before him, his long brawny arms extended. "It is a beautiful thing." He set it down on the table. "We know a good deal more nowadays about the chemistry of paints and the nature of wood than we did twenty years ago. I shall have some of the experts in our crime laboratories examine this. Hopefully they will be able to tell if it is the original or not."

Holmes nodded thoughtfully. "Do you know if the painting was ever formally examined in the past, ever authenticated?"

"No, I do not."

"The crime was considered one of the major art thefts of the century," Holmes said. "I was about to start my career as a consulting detective when it happened. What can you tell us about the case?"

"Well, it involved the murder of the Comte de Laval, its owner.

He was found naked and stabbed to death in his bed. That first detail did not make it into the newspapers. His wife and children were away at the time. He had bought the newly discovered painting for several thousand francs three years earlier. The police received an anonymous tip by telegram and went to the apartment of a Mademoiselle Dujardin—*la belle* Mademoiselle Dujardin. She wouldn't let them in, so they burst open the door. They soon found the count's diamond ring in some hidden cranny, but she tried to tell them it was a gift from an admirer. The circular frame of the painting was discovered on top of her wardrobe." He pointed at the painting. "If that is genuine, then one of the frames is not the original. Under questioning, Mademoiselle Dujardin began with one story, then switched to another. In the end, at her trial, she said she had been taken in by a man, an evil man who had deceived and betrayed her. She claimed that he had never told her he meant to murder the count. She said she was only an innocent victim, not an accomplice. Her voice broke, and she wept.

"I was there for part of the trial, attending whenever I had a few spare moments. I fear I used my policeman's uniform to get myself in. There were not enough seats to accommodate the crowd, and like so many other male spectators, I was soon half in love with the woman. Dujardin might have gotten off lightly, but the prosecution made much of the ring. If she was not a willing participant, if she was as horrified as she claimed, then what was she doing with the count's diamond? And why had she tried to hide it, then claim it was a gift? In the end she got twenty years at *le Prison Saint-Lazare*."

Holmes's forehead was creased. "You said she changed her story. What was the earlier version?"

"I'm not sure. Some preposterous tale involving a female accomplice, I believe."

Holmes nodded slowly. "But there was never any mention of Gaston Lupin, never any question of him being involved?"

"No, I think not, but we shall find out for certain. I shall have the report pulled from our files, and we can go over it together. It cannot, of course, leave the building, but you are free to spend as much time with it as you wish. And there is another thing." His big fingers stroked the end of his bristly mustache. "The detective in charge of the case has retired, but he will doubtlessly be happy to speak with you. I can write you a letter of introduction, although the name of Sherlock Holmes would be enough in itself. Georges Tabernet was one of the Sûreté's finest, a wily and clever man with a truly first-rate intellect. He may know a thing or two which did not make it into the formal report."

"Excellent!" Holmes exclaimed. "And can you also find out if Mademoiselle Dujardin is still at Saint-Lazare?"

"Certainly. It has been around twenty years, so perhaps she has regained her liberty."

"How soon will it take to retrieve the file?"

"No more than an hour, and I can also send one of my men to Saint-Lazare to check on the woman. In the meantime, I insist you and the good doctor join me for lunch. There is an excellent restaurant two blocks away, close to Notre Dame. The escallops of veal are particularly exquisite."

Holmes nodded. "An excellent suggestion, and you shall be our guest, I insist."

"No, no."

"Please. Besides, my expenses are being covered."

"Well, we shall see. I must start the processes moving, and then we may depart."

Holmes lifted his hand. "Wait—there is one other thing." He

took the morphine bottle out of the satchel. "I found this in Lupin's room. Perhaps you could have your lab also examine the contents and see if the dosage matches what is on the label. I suspect it is considerably higher."

The policeman gave an appreciative nod. "The case grows more and more interesting, eh? Not only grand theft, but a possible murder as well."

It was a short walk. The restaurant proprietor greeted Juvol warmly and gave us a quiet table in a corner before the window. The veal was everything the commissaire had promised. As the dish was prepared with white wine, we accompanied it with a cold white Alsatian poured from a tall thin green bottle. Juvol was clearly a man with an appetite for both food and drink, and he soon ordered a second bottle, a white Bordeaux. For such a big man, he handled a knife and fork meticulously, dabbing now and then with his linen napkin at his lips and mustache. He and Holmes did most of the talking. They discussed several recent noteworthy criminal cases in the two capital cities.

After the veal, the waiter returned with a large plate upon which were a round of Camembert, a wedge of Roquefort, and a thick yellowish cheese, Morbier, with its characteristic streak of gray ash running through the middle. Juvol smiled and nodded at the waiter, then used his knife to cut off a big piece of Roquefort. He mashed it upon a slice of baguette, making a mountainous smear of blue, white and gray, then bit off half the round.

"Ah, the queen of cheeses, the Roquefort! There is nothing else like it." Holmes also took some, but I did not care for blue cheeses. I settled for the Morbier. Juvol refilled Holmes's and my glass, then his own, finishing the bottle.

I sipped some wine, then covered my mouth to stifle a yawn. "I think I shall need a nap after this wonderful meal."

"Nonsense." Juvol cut off some Morbier. "This is only fortification for our look at the file."

"Perhaps you would prefer to be a tourist again this afternoon, Henry," Holmes said. "And you could return to the hotel for a brief nap, first. There is no need for you to join us in our examination."

"I may take you up on that, especially the part about the nap."

Holmes took another bite of the Roquefort. "This is very good. The sheep's milk gives it a characteristic piquancy. We have discussed some recent events, Juvol, but not those of the past. You said you were present at Dujardin's trial. What, by the way, is her *prénom*?"

"Simone."

"Simone Dujardin. And were you really half in love with her, as you said earlier?"

Juvol shook his head, his smile bittersweet. "That was perhaps an exaggeration. All the same, she was an amazing beauty, one of those extraordinary French women a man cannot tear his eyes away from, one who makes you ache with longing. She had the face of an angel, one of those blond innocents you see alongside the Madonna in the paintings of Botticelli. Her hair was long and curly, and the plain gray prisoner's smock somehow emphasized her beauty. She had large blue eyes, and when they filled with tears, you wanted to rush to protect her."

Holmes stared thoughtfully at him. "Are you being ironic?"

He laughed. "I don't know! She made quite an impression on me. I had some experience by then with the duplicity of women, and yet I must admit that, at the time, I was quite smitten. She was only eighteen years old and small in stature, which added to that air of vulnerability. But under cross-examination about the diamond ring, she revealed another side of herself. She showed flashes of rage and made contradictory statements. The lead prosecutor had considerable experience. He knew how to get under her skin."

"Do you think she might have been the actual murderer?" Holmes asked.

"At the time, I was convinced that she was innocent and that her conviction was a dreadful miscarriage of justice. I was younger then and still somewhat naïve. Now I am not so sure. I would definitely not rule it out, but a part of me still wants to believe so beautiful a woman could not have committed so hideous a crime."

"Surely if she had a male accomplice," I said, "he must have been the murderer, not her—not a woman."

Holmes and Juvol both gave me faintly pitying looks. "Ah, Dr. Vernier, if you were in my line of work…" Juvol shook his head. "Many a prostitute would kill a client for a few gold coins, and some actually do. It is fear of the guillotine that restrains the others, not the supposed softer temperament of their sex."

I sighed. "My wife is also a physician, and she works so hard to *save* lives. It is difficult to imagine a woman who would kill."

"Come now, Henry," Holmes said. "You know better. You have seen women who kill."

I frowned. "You cannot mean Violet—that was self-defense—almost an accident."

Holmes recoiled slightly, almost as if he had been struck. "No, no—not her, but Constance, Constance Grimswell." He swallowed once. "She had her own cousin killed by that monstrous son of hers." He glanced at Juvol. "A most interesting case. I must tell you about it sometime." His cheeks had a slight flush. "But returning to the matter at hand, you said that in an earlier version of her story, there was no evil man who had led Dujardin astray. Her accomplice was a woman?"

"Yes, I believe so, but again, Tabernet would know best."

"And they were after the painting?"

"Dujardin said she knew nothing about the painting, and that, I believe, was true. When the police found the empty circular frame in her room, she apparently did not even know what it was. Unlike with the diamond ring, she did not understand its significance. I remember Tabernet saying she could not believe a mere thing of wood and paint could be worth so much."

"I suspect the prosecution must have tried to claim she was a prostitute." Holmes used the French euphemism *fille de joie*—"girl of joy."

"Well, she was definitely no common street whore registered with the police—she would have had to have been a *courtisane*, the high-class variety instead. However, her background was spotless: a respectable upbringing, education and employment. Still, the obvious question was what would a respectable young woman have been doing in the count's bedroom that evening?—especially in the absence of his wife and children. A woman's seductive silk nightgown was also found in the bedroom, one which fit Mademoiselle Dujardin perfectly."

Holmes rubbed his long thin hands together. "I am eager to see the file. Can we leave now or...?"

Juvol gave him an incredulous stare. "Without dessert? There are several superb choices. One must not rush a meal such as this."

Holmes smiled. "I suppose not."

Juvol swirled his wine in the glass, then took a sip. "By the way, perhaps I might ask a rather obvious question, one which I have politely postponed."

"Yes?"

"What brought you to Paris in the first place, my dear Holmes, and more specifically, to the home of Lupin?"

"Ah, well, I have a client who knew the artist, and she was... distraught by his death. I always mistrust a diagnosis of heart failure, so I thought I would have a first-hand look."

"And who is this client?"

The corners of Holmes's mouth slowly rose, but he did not speak.

Juvol shrugged. "Well, I had to ask."

"And I have to remain silent."

"What with the painting and all, we shall certainly have to open an investigation into Lupin's death—especially if the analysis of your bottle shows a higher dosage of morphine."

"I wish you luck. He was probably a *morphinomane*, a confirmed addict, and unless the woman confesses to murdering him, it will be hard to prove the overdose was deliberate. Chemists bungle things all the time."

"Would suicide be a possibility?" Juvol asked.

"His valet said he was in good spirits."

Juvol shook his head. "*Damnation.* You are right. One never knows with these blasted *morphinomanes* and their needles."

After dessert, I took Holmes's advice and returned in a cab to the hotel for a nap. My lunches back in London were spartan ones accompanied only by water; the large quantity of wine had made me very drowsy. When I woke up, I walked to the Louvre and spent the afternoon wandering the vast halls. As usual, I was bedazzled by the museum's sheer abundance. One could spend days there and not see everything.

Around six I met Holmes again before Notre Dame; it was only two blocks from the Prefecture of Police. This time he was his usual self. There was none of the stupefaction of two nights before. He was whistling some Gilbert and Sullivan air and twirling his stick, obviously in the best of spirits.

"It is too early for dinner," he said, "especially after our gargantuan lunch, but we might still find Miss Dujardin at home. She was released from prison about a year ago."

We walked to the Left Bank. Holmes was full of restless energy. Anyone with shorter legs than I would have had difficulty keeping up the pace. He paused before a battered-looking old building, then opened the front door. Sitting at the entrance to his *loge* was the concierge, an old man in a drab dark jacket and trousers with a folded newspaper upon his lap. He stared up at us from beneath the spectacles perched on the end of his narrow nose. Holmes asked him for the number of Mademoiselle Dujardin's room.

"Room four on the third floor."

Holmes nodded and started forward.

"Wait, wait, *monsieur*. Save yourself a climb. She is not at home. She is never at home."

"What?"

The old man shrugged. "I have not seen her for a long time."

"How long exactly?"

"Weeks, months."

"But don't you see her when she pays her rent?"

"She paid a year's rent in advance, last March it was. I think I saw her come and go once in June. She was up there for only an hour or so."

"A year's rent in advance? That is quite unusual, is it not?" The concierge laughed and nodded. "And you have no idea where else she may be staying?"

"None."

Holmes stroked his chin. "What does she look like, Mademoiselle Dujardin?"

"Small, quite small, with blond hair. She dresses well."

"Pretty?" Holmes asked.

The concierge gave him a brief, conspiratorial male smile. "Ah, *oui, monsieur.*"

"*Merçi beaucoup, monsieur.*"

We stepped back out into the cold air. "Curious," Holmes said. "I must speak with Juvol. He can have his men search her room."

We took a cab back to our hotel and went directly to the hotel restaurant. Soon the waiter set down plates with steaming aromatic *gigots* of lamb before us, and this time we accompanied our meal with a red wine from *Bourgogne.* "I could become accustomed to eating like this every night," I said, "although I would probably grow fat."

"We have Mr. Hardy to thank for our high standard of cuisine."

"That was odd that Dujardin is never at home, and yet she pays for the apartment. Did you find out much about her from the report?"

"She struck me as rather shrewd. When her first story about two female accomplices would not work for her, she changed to a second version which would garner sympathy with a jury, one involving an evil domineering man."

"So you don't think a man was involved?"

"I did not say that. We have one obvious candidate."

"Who?"

Holmes laughed. "Henry, Henry! Gaston Lupin, of course."

"But he was only an artist, not a criminal. Did his name come up in the report?"

"No—as I might have expected."

"Did you find out anything more of interest this afternoon?"

"Juvol already gave us the salient facts. The report was, as is customary with French bureaucracies of every stripe, extremely long-winded. Le Comte de Laval was stabbed twice in the chest.

A few of his wife's jewels were stolen, but she had taken the most valuable ones on her trip. There were signs on the count's wrists that he had been bound."

I frowned. "Certainly a man must have been involved then. A small woman like Dujardin could hardly tie up a grown man."

Holmes's mouth flickered briefly upward. "Not unless he was a willing participant."

I opened my mouth, then closed it. "Oh, yes, I see what you mean. It's still hard to believe a woman could have actually stabbed him in the chest."

"Come now, Henry. You know your Shakespeare, do you not? Remember Lady Macbeth goading on her husband? And she was a most willing participant with the daggers in Duncan's assassination."

"That is only a story, after all."

"Is it? It is true that women prefer poison. I still suspect that is what happened with Lupin. Easy enough to tamper with his morphine bottle and double or triple the concentration."

"Accidental overdoses with opiates are common enough. Perhaps that painting was only a copy, and there is no real connection to the theft and murder of the count."

Holmes's faint bittersweet smile returned. "Perhaps. Things are progressing nicely, Henry. I did not think this morning that we could have discovered so much in a single day. But there is one gaping hole that concerns me."

"What is that?"

"We have no clue as to the whereabouts of Angèle, no idea who she might really be, except possibly a friend of Mrs. Hardy."

"But she said she did not know her."

"Of course she did! Blast it, if only I could more directly question Mrs. Hardy, but then I would give myself away. This situation is untenable–and dangerous. I think I shall telegraph Hardy and tell him I must present myself as Sherlock Holmes to his wife."

"Well, I suspect sooner or later Angèle is bound to turn up."

His expression was grim. "Later is what I fear."

"How so?"

"Remember the note, Henry. *Le premier est Gaston. Le deuxième sera Angèle.* I would prefer to find her while she is still alive."

Chapter Five

For Thursday, Holmes had scheduled a luncheon meeting with the retired inspector Tabernet, but in the morning he and I visited two of Lupin's acquaintances.

First was Dr. Pascal Bazin. His elaborately furnished waiting room and office put those of Michelle and mine to shame. The old doctor was dressed very formally in a fine frock coat and a shirt with a faintly yellowed white collar. His watery bloodshot brown eyes blinked dully at us from behind the thick lenses of his spectacles. His ineptitude soon became obvious. He muttered stock laments about the tragic death of Lupin, struck down in his prime. He admitted that he had signed the death certificate, but when Holmes questioned him about the diagnosis of heart failure, he grew defensive.

"Of course it was heart failure! In the end, it's always heart failure, isn't it? Your heart fails, then you die."

I glanced at Holmes and rolled my eyes.

When Holmes asked if he knew that Lupin was a morphine

addict, the doctor became outraged. "Never!" he cried and demanded to know who had made such an outlandish accusation. Clearly we would learn little from the doctor, so we soon departed to visit Lupin's accountant.

Monsieur Julien Moullet's offices were just off the Champs-Élysées, and his plush black frock coat with the silken lapels was even more impressive than the doctor's. Lupin had obviously sought out the most costly and ostentatious professionals. Moullet was of medium height, thin, with the pale complexion one might expect for someone who labored daily over ledgers. His wavy brown hair was almost the same color as his eyes, and he had a rather translucent mustache with a reddish tint to the brown. Unlike the doctor, he knew of Sherlock Holmes; he stared through a thick monocle at the business card in amazement.

"Monsieur Holmes! It is an honor—a very great honor. How may I help you?"

Holmes first showed him the letter from the prefect of police. Moullet's eyes widened, making the monocle plop out. He gave a quick nod and put the monocle back in place. "Of course. It is to be expected."

"What can you tell me about Monsieur Gaston Lupin, the deceased artist?"

"Ah, *pauvre* Monsieur Lupin! *Un moment, s'il vous plaît.*" He left the room briefly and returned with a thick brown-paper file. "This has all the documents concerning the unfortunate Monsieur Lupin. Have a seat, gentlemen." He gestured with his small delicate hand at the wood and leather chairs before the vast shining expanse of his walnut desk. We all sat, and he undid some strings to open the flap of the file, then pulled out a great stack of papers.

"Did you work for Monsieur Lupin for a long time, sir?" Holmes asked.

"Indeed I did, although my senior partner, now retired, initially handled Monsieur Lupin's affairs."

"How many years was Lupin a client with your firm?"

"I believe…" He turned over the bulk of the papers, looking for the ones lowest down, then set the monocle again into his right eye. "Yes, almost nineteen years exactly."

"And what did you do for Monsieur Lupin? Why did he need an accountant?"

Moullet's right eyebrow shot upward. This time he held the monocle by its cord in his slender right hand. "It is our opinion, sir, that any gentleman of means needs an accountant."

An ironic smile pulled at Holmes's mouth. "Perhaps, but can you tell me more specifically what you did for Lupin?"

"Well, to put it briefly, we handled everything involving money for him."

"Everything?"

"Yes. He did not like to trouble himself paying bills or taxes, paying tradesmen or servants, managing his bank accounts, or investing his money. Let me see…" Again the monocle went into Moullet's eye as he regarded a paper. "At the first interview he said, 'Do not bother me with any details. I want you to take care of it all.'"

"Did you actually invest his money?"

"No, sir. It was just distributed to several banks, half here and half in Geneva, and his only gain was from the interest. Given his great wealth, he wisely saw no need to risk his capital with foolhardy investments, hence the division amongst banks."

"How much money did he have?"

"Let me see." Again the monocle went in place, and Moullet sorted through some papers, writing down some numbers, which he then proceeded to add up a column at a time.

When he told us the sum in francs, my mouth parted. It took me a while to roughly divide by twenty-five, but I knew that it was a prodigious sum. "Good Lord–that's over half a million pounds."

Holmes eyed Moullet thoughtfully. "Did anyone ever ask him how he obtained such a fortune?"

The monocle again tumbled from Moullet's eye onto his chest, restrained by its cord. "We would never ask so indiscreet a question!"

"So you took care of paying everyone in his employ and all his expenses?"

"Yes, any bills such as those for his doctor, his tailor, his cordwainer, his house upkeep, were forwarded on to us and promptly paid. One of my assistants also went to his home at the beginning of every month and gave all the servants their wages. He also gave Monsieur Lupin a few thousand francs for pocket money."

"Did he pay his servants well?"

Moullet frowned. "Well?"

"Yes, well."

"Let me see." Moullet shuffled more papers. "Here are his typical monthly expenses. Yes, I would say he paid them well, much above average."

"Might I have a look?" Moullet handed Holmes a sheet of paper, which my cousin quickly scanned. He nodded. "Yes, he was generous. And this 'pocket money'–it seems a considerable sum. Do you know what he did with it?"

Moullet shrugged. "The usual, for a gentleman, I suppose. The theater, restaurants." He hesitated for a moment.

"Women?" Holmes asked.

Moullet frowned ever so slightly. He obviously found the question distasteful. "Perhaps."

"And are there any regular monthly payments you cannot exactly explain, especially to a woman, a woman by the name of Angèle or Anne or Anne-Marie?"

Moullet lowered his gaze for a few seconds, then looked up. His forehead was creased above the monocle, and the thick lens made his right eye appear smaller than his left. "How could you possibly know that?"

Holmes drew in his breath slowly. "What exactly is the name?"

"Anne-Marie Varin."

"How much was she paid?"

"Two hundred francs a month."

Holmes laughed softly. "A pittance for Lupin. And do you have an address for Madame Varin?"

"Yes, sir. It's in the Faubourg de Saint-Antoine, near the Rue de Charonne."

"Could you write it down for me?"

Holmes stroked his chin with his long fingers while Moullet wrote, then he took the piece of paper, folded it into quarters, and slipped it into his inner coat pocket. "You have been most helpful, Monsieur Moullet. I was planning to visit Monsieur Lupin's lawyer, but you may have the answers I seek. Did Lupin have a will?"

Moullet nodded, even as his mouth pulled into a wry smile. "Yes, sir."

"And would you know who the beneficiaries of that will are?"

Moullet gave a sharp laugh and shook his head. "The beneficiary is his old mother, who must be nearly eighty. Monsieur Belvaux the lawyer and I both tried to dissuade him, since it seemed extremely unlikely she would outlive her son. However, in the end, his wish will be fulfilled, although what in heaven's name she will do with such a fortune remains a mystery."

"I see. And where does the lucky woman live?"

"Near Chartres. She was receiving some…" Again he glanced downward. "…five hundred francs a month."

"One final question, sir: would you say that Monsieur Lupin was a clever man?"

Moullet frowned. "Clever?"

"Yes, clever."

"Well, he was, no doubt, an extraordinary artist."

"But you were never struck by his great intelligence?"

Moullet's eyes were wary, his mouth carefully neutral. "No, Monsieur Holmes. I cannot say I was."

We said our farewells, then went out onto the street. Holmes paused briefly to withdraw his watch. "No time before our lunch with Tabernet. We shall have to visit her afterwards." He put back his watch and strode briskly forward.

"Visit whom?"

"Madame Varin. Anne-Marie Varin, our Angèle."

"Do you really think so?"

"Without a doubt." He stopped suddenly. "I wonder… Can it wait?" Beneath the brim of his top hat, his eyes were troubled. "We have made our appointment with Tabernet. We must keep it." He resumed his brisk walk, and I followed.

From the Champs-Élysées we took a cab which crossed Paris, then wound uphill to the Belleville neighborhood and stopped before a small brick house with a few faded pink roses still on the bushes. A short stout man with a big white mustache and a freckled bald pate answered the door. Holmes introduced us, then asked if he would like to dine with us at some nearby restaurant.

Tabernet reflexively made the sign of the cross. "I never eat at restaurants. Never."

"We hate to impose ourselves upon you," Holmes said. "Surely there must be some place..."

"*None.*" The single word announced the matter was settled. "While I was with the police, I occasionally worked with the department of health and sanitation. If you had seen the adulterated horrors I saw..." He shuddered. "The only way to be certain is to buy everything from those merchants you trust and to prepare your own food, which my wife has done. Please come in."

We were introduced to Mrs. Tabernet, a short stout woman in a plain muslin dress. She and her husband seemed a sort of matched pair like crafted salt and pepper shakers. She led us to a sturdy trestle table set for four with thick earthen crock ware. She swept away to the kitchen, then returned with a huge soup tureen and ladled out a pungent-smelling bouillon, brownish-yellow broth with glistening spots of oil floating on its surface.

Tabernet declared what an honor it was to dine with Sherlock Holmes. His wife nodded and exclaimed that she had read all of his adventures. Holmes's mouth formed a pained smile. The soup was delicious, and it was followed by a well-cooked joint of mutton accompanied by various roasted vegetables. Tabernet asked if we would mind having cider rather than wine, and when we concurred, he poured some from a big brown glass bottle. He explained that Madame Tabernet was originally from Brittany, and they had a reputable source for the best cider of the region. After a cheese course, dessert was an apple tart seasoned with cinnamon. The meal was not fancy, but it was absolutely delicious. Madame Tabernet had many questions for Holmes, and she spoke more than her husband. Afterwards the men retired to the sitting room with coffee, while Madame Tabernet returned to the kitchen.

Tabernet sagged down into a worn brown leather chair that he somehow faintly resembled. "Now that we have dined, Monsieur Holmes, we may get down to business. You have been very polite, but I know you want to hear about the case of the stolen *Madonna of the Apple.*"

Holmes smiled. "I do indeed."

"It is difficult to believe it has been twenty years. As one of my most memorable cases, I kept a copy of my report, which I reviewed yesterday afternoon. It was hardly necessary. The case remains fresh in my mind, partly because it was my first after my promotion to commissaire. Even now I can see the face of Mademoiselle Dujardin before me."

"Describe that face, if you please," Holmes said.

Tabernet held the tiny cup with his big fingers and, rather delicately, sipped the dark brew. "The first word that comes to mind, odd as it may seem, is 'angelic.' Of course, that was only an impression—and a completely misleading one, at that."

"Diabolic would be more appropriate?" Holmes asked.

"I fear so. When I first encountered her at about two in the morning, I clearly saw that other side. It is curious how great anger will make some people flush, others go pale. In my long career I have seen both phenomena, but when she realized she had been betrayed, she was a striking manifestation of the latter. Her very lips went white even as her hands trembled. With her extreme pallor and fury, as well as her great beauty, she reminded me of the ice queen from a fairy story. She was a ravishing woman, and despite her young age, only eighteen, she already knew how to wield that beauty. As a policeman and a married man, I was immune to her charms, but I could feel their pull. The prosecutor at the trial was clever and managed to reveal something of the real woman. I say woman, because she was old and hardened beyond her years. She was no girl, despite her age."

"Can you describe her physically? There was a faded photograph in the file at the Prefecture, but obviously it was made before the late eighties when Monsieur Bertillon standardized the photographing of suspects. It is faintly blurry, and she looks rather plain."

"I shall describe her for you, but I might point out that she was a butcher's daughter." He gave Holmes an inquisitive look.

"Ah. So she was well fed. That does marvels for the appearance. Good skin and teeth, then?"

Tabernet laughed. "Indeed so! Very good, Monsieur Holmes. A fair complexion with a touch of rose at the cheeks when the lesser emotions were stirred, but deathly pale in her fury. Her small nose was slightly turned up, her mouth... well, the mouth of one, I fear to say, who was born to be a harlot, broad with thick sensual lips, made for kissing. Her hair was very blond, closer to white than yellow, and her eyebrows hardly stood out from her pale skin. Her eyes were a grayish blue with flecks of brown around the pupils. She had a small mole on her right cheekbone."

"The police report said she told you two stories: first, that two other women were involved with the crime, secondly, that it was a man who planned it all. Which do you believe?"

"The first one. As I said, she thought her accomplices had betrayed her, so she told me the truth. When she changed her story the next day, the man was too much a creature of melodrama, the stock villain who leads innocent young girls to ruin."

"Why do you think she changed her story?"

"Well, for one thing, the two women could not be found." Tabernet set down his empty coffee cup and its saucer. "We could never even verify that they existed. However, besides her beauty, the thing that most struck me about Dujardin was her intelligence. She was smart enough to realize that if she could convince a jury that some older man had seduced and tricked her, they would be far more likely to let her off than if she had been part of a female conspiracy. Despite her humble origins, she was shrewd and clever. We could not catch her in any of our usual little traps. I said she was a woman, not a girl, and she had the brains of someone beyond her years."

"Juvol said she had been to school."

"Yes, a convent school. She had been a model pupil. Despite her humble origins, her father had grand expectations for her. She had moved from nearby countryside to the city and was working at the perfume counter in the most exclusive of the *grands magasins*, the store Au Printemps. She had told them she was two years older than her actual age, when they hired her. She was a very successful sales girl. They had only praise for her." We had all finished our coffee. Tabernet rose slowly to his feet. "Would you gentlemen care for a cigar?"

"No thank you," I said.

I could see Holmes briefly weigh the decision. Although there was nothing he cherished more than a good cigar, he despised their more common, inferior brethren. "Yes, thank you," he said at last.

Tabernet went to the mantle over the fireplace, took down a thick cut-glass humidor and removed the metal top. He removed two cigars. He and Holmes went through the elaborate lighting ritual, first taking off the ends with cigar cutters, striking a match, inhaling, etc. Soon they were sitting back in their chairs, cigar in hand.

"A very good cigar," Holmes said. I could see he was relieved. "Tell me more about her first account with the two women."

"Well, the most striking thing was that the story did not involve the painting. Actually that was true for both stories. She always said they were only after money and jewels. When we found the frame atop the wardrobe, she wondered aloud where that old piece of wood had come from. When I told her about the painting, she stared at me as if I were mad, and when I told her it was worth thousands of francs, she did not at first believe me. She laughed and said I was trying to trick her. When I finally convinced her of the truth of the matter, her earlier fury returned.

"She claimed two other women were involved, Suzanne and Angélique. She had met the older woman, Suzanne, at the perfume counter, then later at a café, and they had struck up a friendship. Suzanne eventually admitted that she and her friend were courtesans who had been seeing a very wealthy man, a count. His wife was going to be away for a week or two, and he was interested in having a trio attend to his lustful desires at his home. She asked Dujardin if she would participate as the third. They were going to bind him—he was fond of tie-up games—then steal money and jewels. Supposedly Suzanne said nothing about murder." Tabernet's brief bitter smile made his opinion clear.

"You think that she knew murder was part of the plan?" I asked.

Tabernet shrugged. "Yes. I told you she was a woman not a girl, and a hard one at that. In my profession I saw many people murdered for a paltry sum. For the underworld of Paris, human life has no value. Perhaps as a doctor you see the better side of humanity, but I saw always the worst. No extreme of violence and brutality would surprise me."

Holmes drew in thoughtfully on his cigar, then exhaled the smoke. "But she knew nothing about the painting. She did not see either of the women take it from the house?"

"No, but she said that Angélique became ill, and she had to leave first with her. Suzanne was to follow after she had searched for jewels and further loot. The three were to meet the next day to divide the spoils. Dujardin asked how she could be certain that Suzanne would not just keep everything, so Suzanne let her take the count's diamond ring as proof she was willing to share the bounty."

"But you received an anonymous note about Dujardin, and you found the frame and the ring in her room."

"Yes. As I said, the frame was on top of the wardrobe, the ring hidden in a chink of the wall behind the bed. As I told you, the frame had her perplexed. The ring was a different matter. You could see her dismay."

The long fingers of Holmes's left hand drummed at the velvet chair arm. "It does appear that Dujardin was betrayed. Someone put a frame in her room knowing the police would find it. And Suzanne gave her the ring for the same reason. They also left a nightgown of Dujardin's size in the count's bedroom."

Tabernet nodded. "My thought exactly. One could not prove the frame was actually from the painting, unlike the diamond ring, which was clearly the count's. His valet and wife both recognized it and testified that he always wore it. However, despite all the efforts of my men and myself, we could never find a trace of the two women. We did ask at the café, and a waitress remembered Dujardin talking to another woman, but of course that is no real proof. Dujardin told us where they were supposed to live, but no one who fit their descriptions dwelt there."

"How did she describe them?"

"Suzanne was in her late twenties, tall with dark auburn hair and brown eyes, quite beautiful. Angélique was a little younger, of medium height, plump in a sensual way, with pale skin, blond hair and blue eyes."

"And later, when Dujardin changed her story, what was the man supposed to look like?"

"Tall, strong, with black hair and beard, black eyes, and a gruff voice."

Holmes laughed. "He does sound like a stage villain."

"Certainly there was not the same descriptive detail as with the two women. She claimed she did not even know where he lived. She gave us the name of Jean Martin, of which there must be dozens in Paris. However, she stuck to her story about Martin before the jury, and as I said, we could not find the two women. That was true of the man as well, but in that case, I was not surprised."

"Were you present for the entire trial?"

"Oh yes."

"And Dujardin was… skillful?"

Tabernet laughed. "She should have been on the stage! I said she was a woman, not a girl, but she knew how to feign innocence and remorse. Her tears were especially convincing. She could turn on the water faucets at will. I thought she might actually get off with a year or two, or even only a warning, because of her age and her unblemished background. She said she had been madly in love and had made up a desperate story about the two women to protect Martin. He had not revealed that he planned to murder the count. He knew the count's weakness for women, and she was to get into the house, then let him in. She claimed she was shocked when he stabbed the count and that he gave her the diamond ring to try to placate her before she fled in terror. Martin must have also planted the frame in advance to shift the blame to her.

"As I say, she was very good, but old Garmonte the prosecutor cross-examined her. He said the ring alone was enough to prove her guilt. Why had she kept it if she was so upset? Why had she not refused it, or thrown it aside, and why had she so carefully hidden it? True, she might look like an angel, but an angel would never have taken the ring from a dead man's hand. She was not prepared for such an attack. She lost her temper. The jury caught a mere glimpse of the imperious fury that I had seen, and it did not fit with her story. That, in the end, was why she got the twenty years. She was convicted for grand theft, but not for murder. In my opinion, she was lucky. She deserved the guillotine."

I stared at him. "Are you serious? An eighteen-year-old girl?"

Tabernet frowned. "Have you heard nothing I have said? *Woman*, not girl. True, the older woman may have struck the fatal blow, but they were all part of conspiracy to commit murder, and the penalty for that is death, regardless of one's sex. If anything, a woman is more deserving of such a fate, because such an act is so aberrant a betrayal of their gentler sex. All three should have gone to the guillotine."

I could see the logic of what he said, but the idea of a sharp blade slicing through a young woman's slender neck and lopping off her head was so repellant that I could not conceal my discomfort.

"It was as you said earlier, monsieur," Holmes said. "Henry is a doctor. His profession is saving lives, not taking them. His hesitation should not surprise you."

"It does not." Tabernet sighed. "I respect him for it. Even though I am retired, my forty years on the force have taken their toll. I often dream of crimes, of the villainous faces of men and women caught in their terrible acts, of the corpses of their victims, of the flash of the guillotine as it falls. Certain criminals appear again and again. Their crimes and their history are too familiar to me. I wish

I had worked in a bank, a store, the railroad, or anywhere else." He made a grimace of a smile. "I know some English, messieurs, and it is as Gilbert and Sullivan say in the operetta: 'a policeman's lot is not a happy one.'"

Holmes smiled. "Bravo, monsieur! All the same, I am sure Paris is a safer place because of your efforts."

"I am not so sure. Often it seemed futile. As fast as we could lock them up, new criminals sprang up from the dark fertile earth of Paris to commit robbery, rape or murder. The cycle of evil goes on. I am glad to be away from it."

Holmes looked grim. "I have often had similar reflections." He pressed the small stub left of his cigar into the big crystal ashtray. "Thank you for taking the time to discuss the case."

"It was my great pleasure. However, you have not said why you are interested in resurrecting this old business, Monsieur Holmes."

Holmes shrugged. "I believe Juvol told you we may have found the missing painting. It might also have some bearing on a current investigation."

Tabernet nodded. "*Ah.* Are you sure you would not care for another cigar?"

"No, no, we must be on our way." He stood up. "Perhaps you might fetch your wife. I really must thank her personally for so exquisite a meal."

After exchanging compliments with the old couple and shaking Tabernet's hand, we stepped outside. The sky showing over the roofs was a dull gray, but the rain had stopped for the moment. "I believe we can find a cab on the corner a couple of blocks away. I wish we could linger for a while and take a walk, but we cannot."

"What is the rush?"

"Can you have forgotten? We must find our Angèle, our

Angélique, Madame Anne-Marie Varin." He smiled grimly. "Someone with a sense of irony chose that name for her. No angels were a part of this black affair." His gray eyes stared thoughtfully at me from under the brim of his black top hat. "It is generous of you to accompany me. This was a disturbing crime—and a squalid one. Taking advantage of a man's sexual weaknesses to murder him…"

I sighed. "You are certain of that?"

"Yes, one way or another, I am certain. And you must not be too hard on old Tabernet. He spent his life working amidst the worst of human society. As he said, life is cheap in the underworld of Paris, and that attitude has had its effect on him. Little wonder he believes that convicted murderers deserve their fate."

"And you?—do you also believe they deserve their fate, whether the noose in England or the guillotine in France?"

"Some crimes are so monstrous, the victims so numerous, that the answer seems obvious. However, in general I am not certain, Henry—and I prefer it that way. I try not to think too much about their ultimate fate. Regardless of what they *deserve*, murderers and thieves should not generally be loose in society. They are too dangerous."

"But if someone made a mistake in their youth and has truly repented…?"

"How to be the judge of that, Henry? That is why we have courts of law and trial by jury."

We walked in silence for a while. The ferrule of Holmes's stick struck the pavement regularly. I felt restless and unsettled. We passed several small brick houses like Tabernet's, then went round a *boulangerie*. Ahead of us, the French of equivalent of a hansom—two large wheels, a single horse, driver up top—was parked alongside the street.

Soon we were in the carriage making our way downhill and south toward the Faubourg de Saint-Antoine. On the way, we passed the Père Lachaise Cemetery, the most famous in Paris. To our left was the old mottled stone wall, a good ten feet high, and behind it rose the small ornate roofs of the tombs and monuments, and the barren branches of the trees. Holmes stared silently at the wall.

"The cemetery is actually a rather pleasant place on a warm sunny day in June when the trees have leafed out," I said, "but it must certainly be cold and desolate now."

"I believe the Count de Laval is buried there. I wonder..." Holmes's laugh was bitter. "I'll wager Lupin ended up there as well. Perhaps they are even neighbors now." He laughed again, and I shook my head in dismay. I was glad when the long stretch of wall was behind us.

The Faubourg de Saint-Antoine was one of the older suburbs of Paris, far from the wide, grand boulevards of the city, forming something of a labyrinth of narrow cobbled streets and alleys, with various workshops and large dilapidated-looking buildings converted to apartments. We got out at the address Moullet had given us, and Holmes gave the driver a coin.

Holmes pulled open a tall wooden door which had not aged well and stepped into the dark interior. To the right was a door split horizontally, the top half swung open. Seated inside on a rickety chair where she could see anyone coming or going was an old woman knitting. Without a doubt she was the concierge, guardian of the domicile. One seeking a model for the sinister Madame Defarge from Dickens' *Tale of Two Cities* need look no further. This woman's dark eyes, her stringy white hair showing under an ancient bonnet, her thin lips set in a cruel hard line, her enormous bosom and rotund body (somehow thin concierges were a rare species), even her somber dress with a strange floral print, all made her a formidable presence indeed.

"Good day, madame," Holmes said. "We wish to see Madame Varin."

Taking in our appearance, she gave us a puzzled look. "Not the usual sort that comes calling. She's in room four on the second floor, but I think she is indisposed."

Holmes winced slightly. "How do you know that?"

"When I knocked at the door this morning to give her a letter, she didn't answer."

"And when was the last time she had visitors?"

"Yesterday afternoon."

"A woman?"

The old woman had piercing eyes which were fixed on Holmes. "Yes."

"Describe her."

You could see her debate whether to answer, but Holmes in his black top hat and black frock coat was also an imposing presence. "Short, red-headed, a plain sort of muslin dress. Hard to say if she was a lady or not."

Holmes drew in his breath slowly, then muttered, "*Damnation.*" He strode off toward the stairs, and I followed, a whisper of dread constricting my chest. The circular stairway was one of those classical old French ones spiraling around and upward: wrought-iron vertical bars, a worn oaken railing and steps. We went up two floors, and Holmes knocked at the door with its bronze four which was the first in the hallway. No one answered. He took his stick and hammered loudly at the door. "*Madame Varin—Madame Varin—ouvrez, s'il vous plaît!*" He shook his head. "It is as I feared. Come." He whirled about and started back down the stairs. I followed.

"Madame," he said to the concierge, "I must ask you to open

Madame Varin's door. I fear she is... unwell."

The woman gave him a wary look. "I can't just go opening the door for anyone."

Holmes took out his card and gave it to her, then withdrew the envelope with the letter from the prefect of police. The concierge put on some spectacles, balancing the lenses at the end of her long nose, then glanced down, first at the card, then at the letter. She gave a weary sigh. "No help for it, I suppose." She stood up, seized a big ring with keys on it and opened the bottom half of the door. She listed slightly to the left with each step, the effect more noticeable as we mounted the stairs. Her left hand clutched tightly at the railing, while the keys in her right jingled slightly.

She paused before the door. "Madame Varin!" she bellowed, the thunder of her voice a surprise. "Oh well." She selected a key and put it into the lock, while the other hand grasped the doorknob, turning it. She pushed opened the door. She stepped into the room, quickly turned and stepped out again. "*God protect us!*" she exclaimed.

Holmes slipped past her, and I followed. The curtains were drawn so the room was dim, but we could see the figure resembling that of a dummy hanging from the nearby bracket of a light fixture. "Lord!" I exclaimed. One glance of the grayish face and the protruding dark tongue was enough. I quickly looked away and seized Holmes's arm. "We must cut her down! We must—"

"No, Henry, it is far too late for that. Best to leave things as they are until the police arrive." He looked about, noticed a piece of paper lying on the floor and picked it up. He stepped out into the hall to read it, and I followed. "Oh very good," he muttered. Only three words were scrawled in block letters: LE *DIABLE GAGNE.*

"The Devil wins," I murmured in English.

The concierge made a quick sign of the cross, her big fingers touching forehead, belly, left shoulder, right.

"Madame, you must fetch the police. Get someone here as quickly as possible. I shall remain to watch over the body."

The concierge seemed resigned now that the initial shock was over. (I, on the other hand, felt my insides all in turmoil.) "I would not have expected it of her." She turned to leave, but Holmes grasped her arm.

"You would not?"

"*Pas de tout,*" she said: *not at all.* She lumbered off toward the stairway.

Holmes looked at me. "Stay out here if you prefer."

I drew in my breath deeply. "I've seen dead people before. Even hanging victims."

"But it is never an agreeable sight."

"No."

We went back into the room, and Holmes looked about. He noticed a lamp on a nearby table and struck a match to light it. I studiously avoided glancing at the body hanging near the wall. Holmes went nearer. I glanced at the lamp, and odd spots began to dance before the light. "I think I need to sit down," I muttered.

"Henry?" Holmes's thin fingers gripped my arm tightly, and he guided me to a large overstuffed velvet chair. I sank into its depths, drew in a deep breath, then leaned forward to get more blood into my head. "Are you all right?"

"Just a little dizzy."

He gave my arm a final squeeze. "Rest a moment." He turned and walked toward the wall where the body was hanging, pausing only to remove his top hat and toss it onto a chair.

Somehow I could not resist another quick look. She was wearing a blue dress which contrasted with the beige wallpaper with pink roses and green leaves. I repressed a shudder and looked down at the carpet. It ended about a foot from the wall. A chair lay on its side. Something caught my eye, and I blinked to see if it would go away. It did not. "What's that?" I asked, pointing. Holmes gave me a curious glance. "There, on the floor."

He bent over and picked up a black feather, turned it slowly in his hand. His lips had risen slightly, but his expression was glacial. "A crow or raven feather. If I had any doubts—which I do not—this would clinch it." He threw the feather aside angrily, but it only floated limply to the floor. "She was murdered in cold blood."

"Are you sure?"

"Of course I am sure! Look at her—or don't, as you will. There are no signs of a struggle—her hands are not even clenched. Without a clean break of the neck—impossible from the height of the chair—there is always a struggle. The mind may desire death, but not the body, and especially not from slow strangulation. She should have marred the wall kicking with her feet. That bracket looks none too strong. A person really battling for air might have even pulled it down, and yet it is not even bent, and the glass fixture on top is not out of place!"

"What a horrible way to kill someone."

"Yes, although…" He hesitated for a moment. "I think that, in the end, she may not have suffered much. It would have been very difficult to haul up a conscious person, especially if their hands were not bound." He reached out to grab one of her wrists and raised up her sleeve. "Which hers were not." He looked about, then strode to the small sink and stove. He held up one of the wine glasses sitting face down on the counter. "How convenient. They probably tidied up after themselves." He looked around. "Three clean wine glasses, but no open bottle of wine." He looked in the dustbin. "Nor any empty bottles. Our murderess probably put some chloral hydrate into the drink to sedate her, then hoisted her up."

"Could a woman do such a thing?"

Holmes shook his head, even as a frustrated laugh which was almost a snarl burst free. "Henry, will you never learn? Although... she could never do it alone. A man must have helped her. Perhaps he snuck in afterwards, or even at the same time, squatting below the bottom of the door where the concierge couldn't see him. They must have had a length of rope and hoisted her up, heaving and ho-ing."

"Good Lord," I groaned.

"They took a frightful risk. They could have pulled the gas bracket off the wall, but Varin is a fairly small woman—well preserved, actually—or *was*, not *is*. Plump but not exactly fat. They probably would have found some other object if the bracket hadn't held. Dujardin would have had a backup plan. She is clever this one, very clever. And that note with *le Diable gagne*, and the black feather. Oh yes, it is the same person without a doubt." I noticed his long slender hands were trembling slightly. "Henry, would you mind if I smoked?"

"Of course not! This is one time... I wish I smoked."

He smiled at that, then withdrew a cigarette, lit it, and inhaled deeply. "An interesting medical question for you there, Henry. Would a drugged person awaken if they were being choked to death, or would they remain mercifully unconscious?"

"Oh I hope so—I don't want to ponder it."

"Forgive me. My mind plays curious tricks on me in circumstances like this. I suppose it would depend upon the dosage." He exhaled a cloud of smoke, then began to pace, his left hand resting below the small of his back, palm outward. I sat wearily in the chair taking slow deep breaths.

After a few moments, he stopped next to the body and knelt down to examine one of her brown button boots. "No marks on the back, no sign she kicked at the wall, which would be impossible if she were awake. Perhaps she was indeed so deeply sedated she was unaware what was happening to her. And this rope... A person really committing suicide would have cut off a length and tied it to the bracket. This is looped around in a bizarre way and awkwardly secured. After they hoisted her up, they must have wrapped it around and tied it. Perhaps they even balanced her on the chair briefly, so they could knot it, then let her go slack again."

The sight of those two brown boots hanging there limply in the air two or three feet above the ground made my stomach feel queasy, and I had to look away. Holmes began to pace again. After finishing one cigarette, he lit another. When that was finished he shook his head impatiently. "It has been at least fifteen minutes. I would not think it would be so difficult to find a policeman." The door was ajar, and we heard footsteps on the stairs.

"Madame Varin?" It was a woman's voice, one with a slightly English accent which I could hear in her pronunciation of "madame." But the voice was oddly familiar. Holmes had turned toward the doorway, and he slowly raised both hands, as if it were a terrible effort. Then he opened his mouth, his face very pale, and seemed to briefly freeze.

Two women came through the door, one on the tall side of medium height, obviously the mistress, the other a veritable giant among women, stocky and broad-shouldered, probably a servant. For a second or two my mind seemed to whirl about, unable to comprehend what I was seeing. The shorter woman had black hair hidden under her scarlet hat, an aquiline nose, pale skin and fine features, her cheekbones prominent. She appeared as thunderstruck as Holmes and I. The silence lasted a few seconds, and neither the woman nor Holmes moved.

"*Mon Dieu*," the big woman murmured, staring at the corpse, but the other woman's eyes were fixed on us.

I moved first, rising slowly to my feet. "Violet?"

She smiled at me. "Henry." She turned toward Holmes, hesitated a fraction of a second. "Mr. Sherlock Holmes."

"*Violet.*" Holmes's mouth twitched into a brief extravagant smile. "You are not?—then you are not a nun?"

She smiled back. "No, I am not. Not yet at any rate."

Holmes frowned. "Have you actually considered it?"

"No, no, not really. I was never made for… obedience."

He gave a great sigh. "I see."

I glanced from him to Violet. "Well, I don't! Whatever are you two talking about?"

"I saw her in front of Notre Dame, Henry, that afternoon that I… when I behaved rather oddly. She was wearing a sister's habit."

"So that was the shock you had. Why on earth were you dressed as a nun, Violet?"

"It was a useful disguise for an inquiry I was pursuing." She smiled faintly. "Surely you must understand about disguises."

"Oh yes, so I do. How odd that I didn't notice you."

"You walked right past me," she said. "You were distracted. But I saw you. And Mr. Holmes."

Holmes nodded. "I know. I was certain…" He shrugged. "No matter, Mrs. Wheelwright."

Her face stiffened. "I do not go by that name any longer. It has too many painful associations. I am Mrs. Grace now."

Holmes smiled again. "Mrs. Rose Grace."

"How could you know that?"

"Madame Hardy told me about you."

"Madame Hardy? But she does not know Sherlock Holmes. She told me her husband wanted to hire you, but she would not have it. I suppose—he must have gone ahead and done it anyway. How like a man. But if you had come to her, she would surely have told me."

"Did she mention a visit from a clergyman, a friend of her husband?"

Violet laughed softly. "She did indeed. One of your disguises, I suppose. Very good." She was smiling, but her smile faded as she regarded the body hanging from the lamp bracket. "I am too late I see."

"You also came to warn her?"

Violet hesitated only an instant. "Yes."

"How ever did you find her?"

"I shall tell you if you, in turn, will tell me." When Holmes nodded, she went on. "Marguerite had not seen her for many years, but they had some acquaintances in common. I managed to find one who was still living in the same house in Paris. This person had lost contact with Madame Varin—who was originally Anne-Marie Darel. Anyway, it is rather complicated. I had to find a friend of a friend, who had moved to Lyon. She gave me Anne-Marie's current name and address. I returned from Lyon this morning, and I came straight away." She shook her head. "For all the good it did."

She and Holmes stared at one another, then looked away. Violet licked her lips, then bit at her lower lip. "And how did you find her?"

"Lupin's accountant had her address. Lupin was paying her two hundred francs a month."

"Lupin? Ah yes, and…"

I could restrain myself no longer. "Violet, where have you been all this time? And why did you not write to us? Michelle has been worried sick."

She sighed softly. "I meant to write her, Henry, I swear I did. I started several letters, then threw them away. I thought it was for the best."

I shook my head. "'For the best.'"

Holmes breathed in through his nostrils, almost a snort. "So you are a detective now, a female consulting detective?"

She smiled. "You know what they say: imitation is the sincerest form of flattery. I needed some outlet for my intellect and… my peculiar talents."

His expression grew grim, and then he jerked his head in the direction of the body. "This is a very dangerous business. You would do better to keep out of it."

"I can no more keep out of it than you could."

He eased out his breath. "I see. Why does that not surprise me?" He went to a small table and took the note he had found on the floor. "This will interest you."

Violet's dark brown eyes glanced down at the paper; I was struck again by how they contrasted so starkly with her pale white skin. She nodded. "*Le Diable gagne.* The same person who sent the first note. It was not suicide, was it?"

"No."

Violet frowned, then glanced sideways at her companion. "I am being rude. Berthe doesn't understand much English." We had been speaking English, but she switched to French. "Let me introduce my friend, Mademoiselle Berthe Lelou. Berthe, this is Mr. Sherlock Holmes and Dr. Henry Vernier. You have heard me speak of them."

"Yes, certainly. A great honor, messieurs."

She and Violet contrasted dramatically: Violet shorter, slender, fair-skinned with dark hair, impeccably dressed; Berthe, a good six feet tall, plump, broad-shouldered with massive arms and hands, blond, rosy-cheeked and blue-eyed. I could tell from the way she spoke that she was native-born French of a lower class, not someone raised as a lady, but it wasn't clear whether she was really Violet's friend or merely a servant. Berthe's practical blue muslin dress could have belonged to either. Holmes and I gave her a slight bow.

"You mentioned the first note," Holmes said, "so Mrs. Hardy must have told you about it."

Violet stared at him without speaking. "I cannot betray a confidence."

"In this case, you already have. But I understand. I do not expect you to reveal any intimate secrets. All the same, we share the same objective: to protect Madame Hardy." Again he nodded toward the body. "And there, if you require it, is drastic proof of the danger she faces. We should..." A certain wariness showed in his gray eyes. "We should pool our resources. We should work together."

She looked puzzled. "Do you think so?"

"Yes. Do you recall how the first note began?"

"*Quatre pour le Diable?*"

"Yes. Lupin was one, Angèle—Anne-Marie Varin—was two. Mrs. Hardy is three. And do you know who is four?"

She hesitated only an instant. "Simone Dujardin, I suspect. Marguerite gave me a name. I must find her. I was going to look for her next. Although... I think Marguerite is genuinely terrified of her."

"Again, we have the same objective. And do you know about the painting?"

"What painting?"

He smiled. "*La Madonna della Mela.* It is an interesting story."

Part Two,

Michelle

Chapter Six

As the train reached the drab outer suburbs of Paris in the evening, the rain outside my window poured down, obscuring the buildings and the intermittent gas lamps. Despite the gloom, I smiled in anticipation. Ours was an age when couples of the upper classes were often separated for long periods: men would go off with other men on hunting expeditions in Africa or treks in Switzerland, while the wives would vacation and shop in France or Italy. However, for Henry and me, a week apart seemed an eternity. Amidst the frenzied activity of my medical practice and volunteer work, he was my anchor. Although I was always surrounded by people, I felt lonely without him nearby. A glass of wine and supper together in the evening was always my favorite part of the day.

And for once, I had not received a desperate letter or telegram begging me to come at once because a ghastly body had been discovered! That had come to seem inevitable when he and Sherlock traveled together. More than anything, I was looking forward to some nights alone with him in a plush hotel room, nights when I would not be so exhausted that I fell asleep shortly after dinner and when I could truly devote myself to my conjugal duties.

We entered the north part of the city, and the train soon pulled into the busy Gare du Nord, one of the largest train stations in Europe. I said my farewells to the elderly French woman from Montparnasse who had been my seat companion, then sought out a porter in his blue uniform and hat to help me with my bags. I had traveled light, bringing only two large leather suitcases with some essentials.

I stepped out into the cavernous expanse of the station and looked about. High overhead were the iron girders and opaque glass of the peaked roof, while to the side were the huge arched windows. Men in their dark overcoats and hats and women in their colorful silken dresses and fancy coats thronged and buzzed about like some gaudy species of bee or wasp. Many were embracing. A whistle sounded, and then came the rumble of a departing train from a nearby track. I started toward the front of the train and the distant entrance to the station proper.

I went round a stout gentleman speaking French and saw a particularly tall handsome man wearing the usual black top hat and overcoat. He smiled at me. Soon we were embracing, and then his mouth and the faintly bristly hairs of his mustache touched my lips. The kiss threatened to prolong itself, but I drew away at last.

"How are you, my darling?" he asked.

"Very happy—and very excited."

"We shall just fetch a cab out front," he said to the porter, and we started forward, his gloved hand grasping mine lightly.

"I was just thinking," I said, "how nice it was not to have received an urgent telegram from you about the discovery of a body, especially one that has been partly devoured by some sea creature." He jerked to a halt and stared at me. "Oh dear. You cannot mean…? You do—you have found another body. But at least it was not partially eaten?"

We resumed walking. "No. But it was dreadful all the same. She had hanged herself."

"Dear Lord," I murmured. "Forgive me for being so flippant. And a woman? I didn't think women hanged themselves."

"Sherlock doesn't think it was suicide."

I slowly eased out my breath. "Of course he doesn't. Well, so much for the idea the usual pattern might have been broken. Who was she?"

"He thinks she was the second person mentioned in that 'four for the Devil' note I told you about—Angèle. There was a theft and a brutal murder about twenty years ago, and… But must we go into all that now?" His voice was plaintive.

"Of course not! It can wait. Tonight… I have other plans for tonight." I squeezed his hand.

"I think our plans for the night may coincide. The corpse is the unpleasant news, but I have some good news as well. At least I think it is good."

"What is that?"

"Let's wait until we get into the carriage, and then I shall tell you."

Henry had an umbrella, which he opened, and we darted out into the heavy rain and found a cab, the porter following us. Soon my suitcases were safely stowed, and Henry held the door open for me. "The Hotel Meurice!" he said, then climbed in and sat beside me. With a sort of shivery sway, the carriage was underway. The rain glistened on the dark street and obscured the bright yellow gas lamps.

Henry peeled off his gloves, then removed my left one so he could grasp my hand with his. He raised my hand, then kissed my fingers lightly. A more prolonged kiss followed, one which would not have been permissible in a public setting like the train station. When we were finished, I stroked his cheek lightly. "I missed you so."

"And I you." He kissed my knuckles again, and I sagged back into the carriage. "You must certainly be tired."

"It was a long day, but I am here now. And I am marshaling my energies."

"Very good."

I put my hand over my mouth, stifling a yawn. "Now what is this mysterious news of yours?"

The corners of his mouth rose up under his mustache. "Guess who has appeared?"

"I have no idea. I'm too tired for guessing games. Just tell me."

"Violet."

I sat up abruptly. "Violet? Here in Paris? You would not joke about such a thing. How on earth did you find her?"

"She found us. I'm afraid it has to do with the body we discovered. Violet arrived shortly after we did at the flat. She was also looking for the woman to warn her she was in danger."

"Good heavens, this is all too much. And Violet, why ever would she be looking for her in the first place?"

"She has become an informal consulting detective, a sort of female Sherlock Holmes."

An odd laugh slipped from my lips. "Oh now you must be joking!"

"Not at all."

"How is she?–is she well?"

"She seems in good health. She looks better than the last time we saw her, although she is still somewhat on the scrawny side. I prefer women with more curves. All the same, she is not so thin as before."

"And did she say why she has not written?"

"She said... she said she thought it was for the best."

"*The best.* What is that supposed to mean?" I felt both pain and anger.

Henry patted my leg gently. "You will have to ask her that. She wants to see you alone tomorrow. She suggested tea at about four, and then we shall all have dinner together in the evening."

"Tea? In France?"

"There is a nearby café which caters to the English and serves high tea in the afternoon."

"And she and Sherlock—how did they treat one another? Was there any acknowledgment that they might still care for one another?"

"No, not after their initial surprise at seeing each other. He was Mr. Holmes, and she was Mrs. Grace."

"Mrs. Grace? Why Mrs. Grace?"

"She is known in Paris as Mrs. Rose Grace, a widow. She told us the name Wheelwright was too painful for her, which I can certainly understand."

"Yes indeed."

"Obviously, too, she wants to keep her past a secret. She wants to put it behind her."

"But that needn't involve dismissing her old friends, I hope."

"She would be a fool indeed to dismiss a friend like you."

* * *

I came through a doorway and looked about the spacious lobby of the Meurice. Gaudy couches and chairs in the elaborate Second Empire style were scattered about, along with ferns and other plants in huge oriental pots, some small bronze statues, and a few dimly lit lamps. Overhead hung a large crystal and gold chandelier.

Violet sat at one end of a walnut and dark green velvet sofa decorated with small stars and two large patterned lyres, a third hidden by her figure. She was staring into the distance, obviously lost in her thoughts. I was relieved that her face was not so thin or pale, nor her dark eyes haunted with frightful energy, as in those dark times of the past. She looked much the same, but somehow her beauty was more mature, not so youthful as I remembered. Her nose was aquiline, the line of her jaw clear and distinct, her hair absolutely black, her skin pale, and her neck was still the longest and thinnest of any woman of my acquaintance. The simple, almost austere dress of dark purple silk emphasized her slenderness; it had no ribbons, lace, frills, flounces, elaborate patterns or contrasting colors.

I started forward. "*Violet.*" My voice was soft but carried in the mostly empty room.

She started slightly, saw me, and her face lit up. She stood. My eyes seemed to tear up all on their own, and I smiled. "Oh my dear, I am so glad to see you!" I took her slender hand between my two large ones and gripped it tightly.

"Michelle." She hesitated. "Perhaps *à la française*? *Les bisous, n'est-ce pas?*" We kissed one cheek, then the other, as French friends do, but then I could not restrain myself and hugged her tightly.

She laughed. "Strong as ever, I see! And still flourishing. You look well, Michelle, and about the same as ever."

"You look well, too." Still smiling, she gave my hand a quick squeeze, then leaned over to pick up her hat and umbrella. "Shall we have our tea? It's not far, ten minutes at most." She put on her hat, and we strode toward the doors. An attendant in a rather silly uniform complete with epaulets nodded and opened the door for us. Violet tucked her hair up under the hat, a sort of crimson derby with feathers on one side, then pulled on her gloves. The late afternoon carriage traffic on the Rue de Rivoli was brisk, and many people were out walking. We joined the throng.

Violet looked over at me and smiled again. "I too am glad to see you," she said. "It has been a long time." Her glance was faintly wary.

"Yes, it has." I strove to keep my voice neutral. I did not want to ruin our reunion with reproaches.

A weary smile pulled at her lips. "Of course, I have no one to blame for that but myself."

"Oh, Violet, you must not start by blaming yourself or apologizing!–not this time." My voice had a faint quaver.

"Oh, Michelle, can you...?" She broke off with a laugh. "Oh heavens, I was about to apologize! Forgive me. Old habits die hard. Yes, you're right. Let's not begin that way. You have a certain air of prosperity about you, you and Henry both. Your practice must be flourishing. You must have more patients than you know what to do with."

I laughed. "That is certainly the case! As much as possible, I try to direct them to Henry."

"Ah, so he shares in your success. And I am sure he charms them."

"So he does, especially the elderly ones."

We turned right onto a narrow side street, Rue Rouget de Lisle. "The restaurant just across the street there, Pierre's, serves afternoon tea between four and six. It is all very British, although the cucumber sandwiches are served on sliced baguettes."

I laughed. "To my way of thinking, that would be an improvement."

"They also have tiny foie-gras sandwiches."

"The best of both worlds."

We had crossed the street, and Violet pulled open the door for me. A tall pale man in a black suit, his dark hair thinning on top, nodded at us. "*Bonjour, Madame Grace.*"

"*Bonjour, Pierre.*"

"*Du thé, comme d'habitude?*"

"*Exactement.*"

He led us to a large room in back with several round tables covered with brilliant white tablecloths and furnished with sparkling silverware. The clientele was obviously English. Two portly middle-aged gentlemen in tweeds with flushed rosy cheeks, blue eyes, brown hair and bushy mustaches and their dour plump wives in plain silks could never be mistaken for French. Pierre pulled out a chair for Violet, then for me. His chin bobbed in a gracious nod, and then he swept away. Violet removed her hat and pulled off her gloves. She had such slender, graceful hands and long fingers. I remember how well she played the violin, the amazing dexterity of the fingers of her left hand as they danced along the strings.

She smiled at me, but again her brown eyes showed a faint uneasiness. "I know you don't want to hear it," a brief smiled flickered over her lips, "but I really must make one brief, heartfelt apology, and then we can go forward. I do not wish to begin with idle chitchat—not with you." She picked up the linen napkin next to her plate, unfolded it, then set it back down. Her eyes were fixed upon me. "I am sorry, Michelle. I did not mean to cause you pain.

I should have written you. Lord knows, I meant to. I started several letters, but always in the back of my mind I felt, somehow, that I had troubled you enough."

"We are friends, Violet. Helping a friend is a trouble one embraces."

"All the same, I felt—I still feel—that bad luck follows me about and that you—and Mr. Holmes as well—might be better off without me intruding in your lives."

"Why not let us be the judge of that? Even if what you say were true, I would be willing to put up with a little bad luck because you are my friend. And Sherlock…" I hesitated for a second or two. "Have you forgotten that time in the Alps when you each admitted that you cared for one another?"

Her mouth rose up on one side, even as a rosy flush appeared on her cheeks. "No, I could not forget that. But if I did care for him, I would want what is best for him, and I do not think that includes me."

I shook my head. "Again, let him be the judge of that."

"He is a great force for good in the world, Michelle. I don't want to sully his reputation. You hid the newspapers well from me when I was recovering from my long illness, but I saw some of them afterwards. 'Famed detective smitten,' one said." Her face grew stern. "Another called me a 'murderess.'"

"That is nonsense—sheer nonsense. It was self-defense. Donald had struck you several times, and he was choking Sherlock to death. He had slapped me and knocked Henry out. If you hadn't hit Donald with the poker, he would have killed Sherlock and possibly you as well."

She drew in her breath slowly. "Yes, but I hit him with the poker twice. It always comes back to that."

"You wanted to be sure, and little wonder, given all that violence and pandemonium–remember, I was there. I saw everything, and I most definitely did not see a murderess." I realized my voice had risen. The eyes of one of the English gentlemen in tweeds had grown wide, and the large freckled hand holding a fork was suspended in midair.

"Sherlock Holmes deserves someone better than me, someone far better."

"That is just nonsense!" My voice was a fierce whisper.

She leaned over and set her smaller hand over mine and gave it a squeeze. "We must agree to disagree, and now that I have made my apology, we can proceed to the trivialities. I promise you that in the future I shall write you a note at least every six months. For better or worse, we are friends, and–"

"For *better*."

She smiled. "Yes, I think so, too, and I understand now that I owe you that much at the very least. You saved my life, Michelle, and I shan't forget that again. You took the revolver away from me when I was ready to blow my brains out, and for that, I am forever in your debt." I opened my mouth, but she raised her hand, fingers outspread. "Enough reminiscing! Enough pontificating! On to the present and trivialities! We must bring each other up to date."

Two waiters in black approached us, one bearing a tray with a tea service, the other a tiered stand with various tea snacks. Both men set their offerings before us. The older waiter with a Van Dyke beard and mustache said, "*Ah, bonjour, Madame Grace.*" He placed a tea cup and saucer with a pattern of pink roses before each of us, then poured from the matching teapot. The brown liquid gave off a fragrant steam.

"*Bonjour, Jean.*" Violet gestured at the stand with its stacks of various pastries and small sandwiches. "*C'est formidable.*" She saw him pouring tea for me. "*Jean, c'est une vieille amie, Madame Michelle Vernier.*"

He glanced at me. "*Ah, vous êtes française, madame?*"

"*Je suis une créature de deux pays, demi-française, demi-anglaise. Ma mère était anglaise, et mon père était français.*"

"*Ah, mais vous parlez français parfaitement!*" He gestured at the food. "*Mangez bien.*"

Violet began to fill her plate. "You are indeed 'a creature of two countries, half English and half French.' Well said. Be sure to try the *baba au rhum.* They are extraordinary."

I smiled. "I've never had *baba au rhum* with afternoon tea."

"Well, once you do, you will understand that it should be a requisite part of the usual cast of characters."

"Ah, and an apricot tart. That is also not customary, but they are my particular favorite. And here are the cucumbers on the thin slices of baguette, and this must be…"

"Yes, *pâté de foie gras!* What could be more English than that? I had not exactly remarked it before, but that stand there with its tea offerings is also a creature of two countries, half English and half French. Try a crumpet. They are not half bad for France."

I started with a bite of the rum-soaked baba. I also took some of its cream and the cherry on top. "Oh, this is very good. It is a French concoction after all, and no one does it better than they do."

Violet also took a bite of the baba. "Shall we get on with it?– bringing each other up to date, that is."

"Well, it won't take long for me, because little has happened. My life is still much as it was when you last saw me. For you, on the other hand, much seems to have changed. Do you live alone or…?"

"No. Do you remember my maid Gertrude and the footman

Collins? They came with me to France. There is a new development: they have become man and wife."

"Really? But he is so tall, and she is so small."

Violet smiled slyly. "Somehow they manage. I am renting a house in the suburbs, in Auteuil, about half an hour by carriage. A French couple also lives with us, and they are the complete opposite of Gertrude and Collins. My friend Berthe is the largest woman I have ever known, a good six feet tall with brawny arms and shoulders. She makes you seem petite, Michelle."

I laughed. "That's hard to believe."

"You will see what I mean when you meet her. Her husband of some six months, Alphonse, is an inch or two over five feet and quite slender. His grand mustache is the biggest part about him. He looks almost emaciated, but he is wiry and strong."

I was alternating between the apricot tart and the baba; the baba was first to go. "They are servants, I take it?"

"No, no. Not at all."

"Then why are they living with you?"

"They help me with my work."

"What work? Oh, of course—your detecting, I suppose."

"Exactly. Both of them know French and all the various patois far better than I ever will, and they are also familiar with the dark underbelly of Paris. With them I can go places where I would never dare venture alone. Theirs is a checkered past, to put it mildly. I met Berthe during my first case. She obviously knew who had stolen the jewelry. I gave her the choice of telling me the truth or letting the police ask the questions. Strange as it may seem, in seeking out the actual thieves, we became friends. When it was over, I asked her if she wished to leave her service and come to work for me. She accepted eagerly. Alphonse came along during another case.

"Both Berthe and Alphonse are conundrums, their appearance completely misleading. Because of her size, her strength and a certain quiet shyness, people have always assumed something must be wrong with her. They think she is slow or stupid. I was guilty of that at first, but I soon discerned that she had brains. Alphonse understood that immediately. As for him, his diminutive stature is also misleading. He has the heart of a lion, and the confidence and feistiness of a giant. I have seen him take on men six inches taller and take them down. He is loyal and true, but woe to you if you antagonize him!"

"So you have your own little household in the country. A cook, too, I suppose?"

"Yes, a very good one. She also manages our poultry." A certain hesitance must have shown in my face. "What is it, Michelle? Say it."

"You must not lack for money. Donald must have left you… enough."

She sighed. "That is a long story, but I do not lack for anything. Donald was on a monthly allowance from his father, but he was given no huge sums. All the same, we were never extravagant, and I was in charge of investing the excess. I have a certain talent for finance." Again, a flicker of a smile. "As you may recall. That elaborate fraud involving the fake oil wells in England was my creation. Anyway, I did very well. As I told Donald…" A pained look came and went. "I made him a rich man. After his death, father Wheelwright, as you might expect, did not want to pass on anything meant for his son. I could certainly understand that. It felt wrong to me too."

I stared at her, uncertain. "Are you sure?"

"*Yes.* How could anyone expect the old man to give money to…" Now her smile was grim. "We won't say the M-word again."

I sighed. "But you have enough?"

"More than enough. I cannot keep a horse and carriage, or buy the latest fashions, but I do not miss either. If you don't give a fig about *la mode*, it takes a long time to actually wear out a silk dress. Besides, if I wanted to, I think I might make myself rich in my new occupation."

"Occupation?—being a consulting detective?"

She laughed. "As a woman doctor, you should certainly understand! Women feel more comfortable confiding their difficulties to one of their own sex. As I say, I could be rich, and when I assist those with great wealth, I do take their money. I think I can generally find a better use for it than they can. I give much of it to various charities. However, for those without the means to pay, I do not charge for my assistance."

"When did you take up this unusual trade of yours?"

"It has been almost two years. I stumbled into it when a French friend had her jewelry stolen. Do you remember the so-called 'Angels of the Lord,' that group of women, servants who stole from their masters and prostitutes who blackmailed their high-class customers? Because of my ties with them, I had far more experience and knowledge than any woman of my class. I knew at once that the theft must have been an inside job. Berthe was not exactly a participant but..."

"Not exactly?"

She smiled. "Suffice to say she knew more than she should. After it was all over, I realized I had found an outlet for my intelligence and my energy, as well as a way of atoning for my former crimes. I would help those women who were victims of various crimes."

"Only women?"

"For the most part, yes. And of course, the exemplar for my

efforts was Sherlock Holmes. I have sought out and read his monographs such as the ones on the shape of ears and on tobacco ash. His writings have been very helpful."

"Well, you could certainly have no better model. All the same…"

"What is it?"

I took a quick sip of tea, then shrugged my shoulders. "Detective work can be a dark and messy business. And dangerous."

"That might be a description of life in general: a dark, messy, dangerous business."

"Oh, Violet, you haven't exactly changed, I see."

She looked almost hurt. "But I have—my energies are directed toward good now, not evil."

I reached over to grip her hand. "Yes. That is a great difference. And you are right, as a woman doctor, I should understand. Women in distress would be much more comfortable turning to a woman for help than a man."

Her smile was radiant. "Exactly."

"And so you are trying to help this Mrs. Hardy?"

"I am." She sipped her tea, her dark brown eyes fixed on me. "Might you be willing to go see her, Michelle? She has declined so, even since I met her. I would like to be sure she is not physically ill. She is a haunted woman."

"Henry told me about the note. If one is superstitious… little wonder she is afraid."

"It is not just that. She… I know a sense of guilt when I see it, Michelle. And I know how it can eat at one."

"Perhaps you should be more careful about which cases you accept."

"I am careful." She paused for an instant. "I never accept cases where the husband is violent or abusive. But this is different—she needs my help. She has no one to turn to."

"What about her husband? Henry thinks he loves her and would forgive her almost anything."

"She does love him." She was frowning fiercely.

"Well, I can certainly have a look at her."

"Ah, I knew you would."

"Henry told me about this peculiar priest who came to see her— has he not been a comfort?"

"Not at all. He is... I have not met him, but I do not trust him."

"Perhaps... because you are not Roman Catholic..."

"Ah, but I am, Michelle."

"What? I thought you were Church of England."

"So I was raised, and I went every Sunday for many years, although I was never much of a believer."

"When did this happen?"

"My faith, precarious though it may be, is perhaps the best thing to come from my dark times, Michelle. It has also been almost two years. When I came to Paris, I felt drawn to the old churches and great cathedrals. I liked to sit quietly in their vast shadowy interiors. Somehow they seemed to calm my soul and ease all that agitated, useless churning inside my head. I met an old French sister at Notre Dame. She became my confidant and my spiritual guide. I formally joined the church last Easter."

I shook my head. "I cannot believe it."

Her old familiar mocking smile, one strangely akin to Sherlock's, appeared. "For such a reprobate?"

"No, of course not. You surprise me."

Her eyes suddenly went opaque, turned inward. "I... when I pray, sometimes I ask Donald for his forgiveness. We were like two savage animals sharing a cage. He was trapped, too, trapped by his father, bound by convention and duty, but ultimately I was not. I knew there was a way out. I could have simply opened the door and walked away. I could have left and started a new life far from London. Instead I stayed and tormented him." Her eyes came into focus again, as she eased out her breath. "My religion helps me live with myself, a difficult endeavor at best–that, and helping others caught in their own traps."

I stared thoughtfully at her.

"What is it? There must not be secrets between us this time."

I was thinking about what she had told Sherlock at that last meeting in the Alps, that she could not think of love until she had atoned for her crimes. "And have you redeemed yourself?"

Her smile softened. "I am still working on it."

The cork came loose with a resounding pop, and the waiter rushed to pour the foaming white liquid into Holmes's glass. Sherlock took the glass between his long fingers and thumb, raised it so the candlelight set the yellow liquid aglow. Tiny bubbles rose up toward the still-fizzing white surface. He took a sip, and then his dark brows came together over that beak of a nose as he pondered in judgment. At last he nodded. "*Excellent.*"

The waiter topped his glass, then went round the table filling first my glass, then Michelle's and finally Henry's. Holmes raised his glass, revealing an inch of white folded cuff above the black wool of his sleeve. He and Henry still wore their somber black frock coats, but I had put on an electric-blue evening dress which left my shoulders and sternum bare, a provocative garment which ensured that Henry would quickly begin kissing my neck and chest the moment we returned to our room. Violet still had on her simple purple dress.

"I had considered a toast to crime," Holmes said, "since that is what has again brought us together, but it does not seem exactly propitious. Let us drink instead to friendship, both old and new. Henry may be my relation by blood, but he is also an old and true friend. Through him, I have been gifted in turn with two friends of the female sex, first Michelle, and then..." He hesitated for a moment, then smiled. "...Violet Grace." His gray eyes were fixed on her. "I do hope you consider me a friend."

She smiled. "Of course I do."

"Your health, then." He clinked her glass, and then we all took turns doing the same.

The champagne was cold and wonderful, and it made me realize I had not had champagne in a very long time. "This is simply delightful," I said.

Henry gave my hand a squeeze. "I know your weaknesses. I'll have to watch out for you. I don't want to have to carry you up to our room, especially as we are up two flights."

Holmes smiled. "I hate to think what that might do to your back, Henry. Truly, rather than physician heal thyself, physician spare thyself!"

Violet was smiling, but she appeared pensive. "Propitious or not, it is true, you know: it does seem to be crime that always brings us together."

"Oh, Violet!" I exclaimed.

She was staring at Holmes. "But perhaps we can move beyond that. Eventually."

Holmes's mouth twitched into a brief lunatic sort of smile. "I should hope so. Our every meeting should not require a fresh corpse." Henry laughed sharply, but I shook my head with a half-serious, half-comic groan.

"Yes, we must move beyond crime to more elevated topics—music, the arts, the state of England and France, but first..." She was still smiling, but her dark eyes were serious. "Business before pleasure—there are a few details I want to go over." She turned to me. "No more than five minutes, Michelle, I swear it!"

I shrugged. Henry also looked wary.

"You told me about the painting, Mr. Holmes, and about the murder of the Count de Laval and the trial of Simone Dujardin. Clearly our 'four' were behind the crimes."

"Who are the four?" I asked. I looked at Holmes, but he gestured with his hand palm up toward Violet.

"They are Marguerite Hardy, Gaston Lupin, Anne-Marie, our Angèle, and Simone Dujardin," she said.

Henry shook his head. "Mrs. Hardy seems such a serious, decent woman. It is hard to believe."

Violet was staring at Holmes. "You said Lupin was an excellent copyist. He must have painted duplicates of *La Madonna della Mela* and sold them for a fortune. Across the continent there are those criminal dealers who specialize in selling stolen artwork. Italy would provide a ready market for a native son like Botticelli, and American millionaires might also be interested. The theft would have allowed each of the dupes to believe themselves the proud owner of a genuine masterpiece."

Holmes smiled. "Very good, madam. You do indeed have a calling in your new profession."

"That is a great compliment coming from you, Mr. Holmes. However, a central question remains. Which of the four actually killed the Count de Laval?"

My stomach seemed to twist, and I took a big swallow of champagne. "Could a woman possibly stab an unarmed, naked, completely vulnerable man?"

"Surely it must have been Lupin," Henry said. "One of the women must have let him in the house while the other two distracted the count."

Violet's smile was suddenly mirthless. She and Holmes stared at one another. He spoke at last. "There is little profit in speculating at this point. We must have more facts. And there are still two persons left who can answer that question should they choose to do so."

Henry put down his glass and folded his arms. "Then shouldn't we also have an open mind about Lupin? We don't know for certain that he had the stolen painting or that he even knew Mrs. Hardy. You said he had an incredible eye and memory. Perhaps he merely saw the original and painted a copy. Possibly even with the count's blessing."

Holmes stared at Henry, his eyes narrowing. "Lupin and Mrs. Hardy were *intimately* acquainted."

"How do you know that?" Henry asked.

"I shall tell you another time when the ladies are not present. For now, take it on faith. Besides, we must not use up more than the allotted five minutes."

I swallowed more champagne. "And have those five minutes passed?"

Violet glanced at me, then reached over and gave my arm a sympathetic squeeze. "Yes, it is close enough. Let us move on. Although..." Her eyes shifted again to Holmes. "I haven't told Marguerite yet about Anne-Marie's death. What should I do?"

"Tell her the truth. At this point, trying to hide things is not in her best interests."

"I suppose not. Oh, one last thing—Michelle has told me she will come with me tomorrow and have a look at Marguerite. She is distraught and looks unwell. I would like to make sure that she is not physically ill."

Holmes made almost a bow. "That seems very sensible indeed. There is the added benefit that Michelle is an excellent judge of character."

Henry's cheeks had begun to redden. "I can't say I much care for it. Must Michelle be dragged into this wretched business? She came to Paris to get away from work and toil, not to exchange one form of drudgery for another!"

Now it was my turn to squeeze Henry's wrist. "I do not mind, and if the poor woman is ill or suffering, I may be able to help her. That is my duty as a doctor."

Henry's mouth stiffened, opened partway, then closed briefly. "Well, I don't have to like it."

Holmes's eyes were serious, seeming to contradict the playful curve of his lips. "I understand your concern, Henry, but you must know by now the futility of trying to prohibit Michelle from anything. She always insists on rushing toward the front line of battle." This remark made Henry glower all the more.

"But as Madame Grace has remarked, the five minutes are up, and crime must be forgotten. We must give all our attention to the gastronomic and gustatory splendors which await us." He raised his glass again. "To *la France* and *la belle cuisine!*"

Chapter Seven

Sunday morning Violet and I went to an early Mass together at Notre Dame, then took a carriage to the Hardys' townhouse near the Champs-Élysées. Its magnificent door swung inward, revealing a short older man in a dark suit. He smiled at Violet. "Ah, Madame Grace, *bonjour. Entrez, entrez.*"

We followed him to the large well-furnished sitting room where a dark-haired woman in a beautifully cut purple silk dress sat upon the sofa. She rose. Marguerite Hardy's hair and eyes were that dark brown, not quite black, so typical of French women, but she was very pale, her mouth grim. Just over her forehead was a striking blaze of white hair. I saw the ripple along her throat as she swallowed. A rather tiny blond woman, obviously a maid, had also risen from her chair.

Violet had pulled off her gloves, and she raised one hand toward me. "Madame Hardy, this is an old and dear friend from England, Michelle Doudet Vernier. She also happens to be a medical doctor."

A sort of forced, stiff smile pulled at Marguerite's lips, but her eyes were puzzled. "Truly? I have never known a woman doctor." She nodded politely. "A pleasure."

"The pleasure is mine," I said.

Marguerite's dark eyes shifted again to Violet. She was a big boned, broad-shouldered woman built something like myself, but she appeared thin, her face almost gaunt with shadowy half-circles under her eyes. "You found Anne-Marie."

"Yes," Violet said. "But..."

"She is dead."

Violet drew in her breath slowly. "Yes, she is."

Marguerite closed her eyes, her mouth twisting to the side, then opened them. "I knew it. How?"

"Does it really matter?" Violet asked softly.

"Tell me. I must know."

"She... she was hanging from a bracket on the wall."

Marguerite would not have noticed the oddly passive construction—not the simple "she hanged herself"—but I did. Marguerite went paler still. One hand went awkwardly to her forehead perhaps to brush away her hair, but it was trembling so badly she quickly lowered it. Her jaw was thrust forward, her teeth clenched, and both hands and arms were quivering now. I stepped forward and grabbed her wrist. "Don't be afraid," I said. She stared at me, but could not seem to speak.

I turned to the maid who was quite alarmed. "Get me some brandy," I said, and she obeyed at once. "Sit down, Madame Hardy—please sit down." Her eyes were all swollen black pupils and she hardly seemed to register my words. I nudged her back toward the sofa, gently helped her down. Her hands and arms were still shaking. The maid had a glass of brandy, but I knew

Marguerite would never be able to hold it.

"Listen to me, madame—look at me—no, no, look at me. Yes, that's right." Her eyes focused at last on my face. "You have had a shock, but it will be all right. I want you to take a sip of brandy." I put the glass before her lips. "Take a sip, please. Yes, that's very good." The liquid made her shoulders quiver. "Now another. And another. Take a long slow breath. Very good—now let it out—slowly, though. Yes, now again. And another sip of brandy."

Gradually her breathing grew calmer, although it was very deliberate. Her big eyes were still fixed on mine. "Thank you, Doctor."

I smiled sadly. "You are quite welcome."

I glanced up at Violet. Her hands were clenched into fists, but as she drew in her breath, they relaxed and opened up. The small muscles about her mouth were taut, her expression stern.

Marguerite's eyes shifted often into the distance, even as her face gradually relaxed. "She was my friend such a long long time ago," she said. "We were girls together. We were so young. We were going to be friends forever. But it did not work out that way. It was my fault, all my fault."

"If it was long ago…" I began. "The past is done. If you were gone from her life, you cannot blame yourself for what happened to her. She led her own life apart from you."

Her eyes met mine, even as her lips rose into a brief bitter smile. "You do not know me, Doctor."

I put my hand over hers. She had finally stopped shaking. I held out the brandy glass. "Finish it. It will do you good." She took the glass, and I drew in my breath and sank back into the sofa next to her.

Marguerite sipped the brandy, then glanced at Violet. "I am better now, Madame Grace. Sit down, please."

Violet sat in a chair, and there was a brief silence. The maid was still standing and hovered nearby. "I think I could use a brandy myself," I said.

The maid bowed. "I shall just fetch you one, *madame la docteur*." She poured some from the carafe and brought it to me.

I took a quick sip, then touched my lips together and touched them with my tongue. "This is quite remarkable, hardly a medicinal concoction. What is it?"

"It is one of my husband's Armagnacs." She glanced at the maid. "You may leave us, Jeanne."

"Are you certain, madame?"

"Yes."

The maid curtsied and left. Marguerite was staring down at her hands, as if willing them not to misbehave again. Violet was watching her. "I brought the doctor because I wanted her to examine you."

Marguerite briefly raised her head. "There is nothing wrong with me." Violet laughed softly.

"I shall be the judge of that," I said. I took another sip of the Armagnac. I had never tasted anything like it before. "It won't take long."

Marguerite drew in her breath and eased it out slowly. "As you wish, then."

"Let's catch our breath first."

Violet was still staring at her. "One death out of four might be a coincidence, two in a row is definitely not. You wanted me to find Anne-Marie and warn her. I found her, but too late. You said Simone Dujardin might wish both ill. It's time you told me all you know about this woman."

"Not now. Later. *Please.*"

I stared at Violet and gave a quick shake of my head.

"She might take money," Marguerite murmured. "I would pay her whatever she wants, but it is probably too late for that."

Violet shook her head. "Once you start with a blackmailer, it never ends."

"Finish your brandy," I said, "and then I can do my examination."

I swallowed the last of my own, then took her glass and set them both on the sideboard. She started to rise, and I quickly returned to her side. She blinked a couple of times, and my hand seized her arm. I was an inch or two taller than her, but despite being rather thin, she felt quite solid, unlike Violet who was slightly built and rather delicate.

I picked up my black medical bag which I had left near the end of the sofa. "We shan't be long." Violet nodded, then turned to some magazines on a nearby table.

Marguerite led me to a stairway. "My bedroom is upstairs, but it is so cold. I suppose I must take my clothes off."

"You needn't take them all off, but is there a warm room, one with a door we could shut?"

"Yes, the study. This way."

The room had a wall of bookcases and a large walnut table with matching chairs, and a fireplace at the far end. I shut the door, and then, of one accord, we both approached the fire. The heat coming from the glowing coal was most welcome. Marguerite stretched out her hands, and I did the same. She had big hands like me, but her fingers were slender and graceful-looking alongside my more workaday digits. My hands were permanently reddened and rough from using carbolic acid as a disinfectant, while her skin was still smooth and unblemished, typical of a fine lady who never dirtied her hands in any actual work.

"I shall want to listen to your chest with my stethoscope. Let me undo your dress." I undid the hooks one by one; they were the type of tiny tedious fasteners I most abhorred. I pulled down her sleeves off her shoulders and stared at her tightly laced corset. I shook my head. "This will not do. You are not a woman of twenty seeking a husband. There is no reason to cinch yourself so tightly." I undid the laces and proceeded to loosen them.

"That does feel better," she said.

I laughed. "It is nice to be able to breathe."

I set my medical bag on the table and withdrew a stethoscope from its depths. I rubbed the bell with my hand, then blew on it twice to warm it. Goosebumps prickled the rounded skin of her shoulders, and I directed her back nearer to the fire. The outline of the top ribs of the sternum showed below her clavicle. Her dark eyes stared intently at me, the pupils great black pools beckoning you to their depths.

I frowned slightly, then set the bell against the thin cotton. As might be expected given the recent shock, her heartbeat was rapid. I noticed a skipped beat, then another. Ectopic beats were common enough after forty, but they could be disconcerting to the patient.

"Breathe deeply for me. Again. And once more. Your lungs sound excellent."

She gave a nod, and then came a sudden deep yawn. "Pardon me." Her eyes blinked dully.

I felt her throat and breasts for any abnormalities, then had her remove her corset entirely so I could check her belly. When we were finished, I helped get the corset back on, laced it up, then refastened the tiny hooks to her dress, a more difficult endeavor than undoing them.

I gestured at one of the sturdy wooden chairs by the table. "Sit down for a moment." She did so, then fought back another yawn. As she relaxed, she appeared more and more exhausted. "How is your sleep?"

Her mouth twisted into a smile. "What sleep?"

"As bad as that?"

"Yes."

"Do you have trouble falling asleep or staying asleep?"

"Both."

"Did you have problems even before you received the note?"

She blinked dully, her forehead creasing. "I have always had difficulties, but not nearly so bad."

"Have you anything to amuse you or distract you? Do you like to read or go to the museums?"

She shrugged. "I do like books, but I cannot seem to concentrate, and as for the museums... I used to enjoy wandering in the Louvre. One can never see it all. But now..."

"What is it?"

"I do not like to go out. I am afraid..." She seemed to lose her thought midway.

I shook my head. "Have you thought of sending for your husband?"

She jerked upward, her eyes widening in alarm. "*No.* I cannot!"

"Why? If you are afraid... you needn't face this alone."

She shook her head back and forth. "No–no."

"But if he loves you..."

"He does love me–and I love him."

"Then why don't you send for him?–or go to him?"

"I cannot drag him into this business–especially now. It is too dangerous. If anything were to happen to him... I don't care about myself–my life is coming to an end–but he must live."

"Coming to an end? What are you talking about? Such thoughts are not helpful."

"And if he were to find out... I could not bear the shame! He is a good man, a decent man, the best of men, but even he... Some sins cannot be forgiven."

I stared at her. "Aren't you a Catholic, madame? Well, then you must believe in forgiveness. That is a matter of doctrine, after all. God can forgive any sin."

She stared at me. "And do you believe that yourself?"

"I do."

Her mouth twitched into a brief smile. "You believe it because you are good, because you have never done anything truly wicked."

I stared back at her. "And you have?"

"Oh yes. And now... the Devil is after me."

"Again, if you are a Catholic, you must believe that God is stronger than the Devil. All this nonsense about curses and poisons and Satan... That is not the true church, but only superstition. This is not the Middle Ages, after all!"

"It is all the same to the Devil—evil never changes. Damnation never changes."

I opened my mouth but could not think what to say. I could see from her eyes and her face that she was becoming anxious again. I put my hand over hers. "Please. Calm yourself. We needn't talk about unpleasant things." She stared at me, her lips somehow pinched-looking. "I wish you would send for your husband."

"I cannot."

"Very well, then. There doesn't seem to be anything physically wrong with you. I suspect you notice your heartbeat, especially at night."

"I do. Sometimes it beats very fast, and sometimes... it seems to jump about."

"If these problems with sleep continue, I can give you something to take." She only shrugged. I reflected that if someone could ever truly create an effective non-problematic sleeping draft, they would become wealthier than old King Croesus. "Is there anything else you want to tell me?"

She stared at me, her mouth tightening, pain written in her face. I touched her hand. "Another time perhaps, when you are ready. Let us rejoin Violet."

"Why do you call her Violet? I thought her name was Rose."

I hesitated. "So it is. It is an old sort of play-name between us, another flower instead."

"I see." We both stood up. She managed a smile. "Thank you, Doctor."

"You're welcome. We must find something to occupy you. By the way, do you like music?"

"Oh yes, very much. John and I often go to the opera."

"There was... some talk of going to the opera." I realized I shouldn't mention anything about Sherlock to her. "They are doing Verdi's *Macbeth*, a rarity. I have never seen it before."

"I have not heard of it. *Macbeth*. What is this *Macbeth*?"

I recalled that only a few well-educated French knew Shakespeare, and even those few, mostly from French translations in rhyming couplets. "Macbeth was a Scottish king, a very wicked man."

"I like the operas of Verdi, especially *La traviata*. It is so sad, but beautiful."

We were in the hallway and stepped back into the sitting room. Violet set down a magazine and stood up. "There you are, at last."

"I'm sorry I kept you so long," I said.

"What is the verdict?" Violet had a characteristic mocking smile. "Will she live?"

"I believe so. I must leave soon. I need to get back to the hotel to—"

Marguerite gave me a startled look. "Hotel? You are staying in a hotel?"

"Yes. The Meurice. It's very nice."

"I thought you were staying with Madame Grace."

Violet watched her carefully. "Alas, I have not the room. My house is full."

"Ah, but, Doctor, why didn't you tell me? You could stay here with me while you are in Paris. You would be most welcome. Be the tourist during the day, but return here in the evening. We have a very nice guest bedroom."

She was staring at me, her back to Violet. I was about to say something about Henry, but Violet raised her hand and shook her head forcefully. I frowned. "That would be very kind of you, but I don't wish to impose."

"It is not good to stay all alone in a hotel, and I have a very good cook."

I chewed thoughtfully at my lower lip, my eyes fixed on Violet, who quickly jerked her chin down and then up. "I... I shall have to think about it."

"What is there to think about? Please, I would be happy to have you as my guest, and as you said, we could go to the opera. When is this Verdi Mac-whatever?"

"*Macbeth,*" Violet said. "I would like to go too. There is a performance the day after tomorrow on Tuesday evening."

"There is a box that John and I often use. I shall send someone to see if they can reserve it for us."

"Wonderful!" Violet exclaimed. "We can have a ladies' night out." Again, the mocking smile.

Marguerite smiled. "Yes, it is something to look forward to." Her face had some color at last, and I realized what a beautiful woman she must be when she was not weighed down by care. "And you will come to stay with me, yes?"

Again, Violet gave a furtive nod in my direction. "I… I shall have to think it over. Let me sleep on it, as they say. I shall tell you tomorrow." I knew exactly what Henry's reaction was likely to be. "Either way, we shall stop by in the morning."

She touched my shoulder lightly. "The answer must be yes."

"And we must have a serious chat soon," Violet said. Marguerite seemed to wither under her gaze. "I do not wish to upset you further, not today. One shock is enough. All the same, we must talk about how to proceed next. I want to help you, but you must confide in me. You must trust me. And I have… friends, who could be helpful as well."

Her dark eyebrows came together. "The abbé says that only a priest can help in cases such as this, that I must put my trust in him."

Violet shook her head. "Well, he would say that, would he not? There is an English expression, 'God helps those who help themselves.'"

Marguerite look faintly puzzled. "It is like the moral of the fable of La Fontaine," I said, "the one where the cart is stuck in the mud. '*Aide-toi, le Ciel t'aidera.*' Help yourself, and Heaven will help you."

She shrugged. "Perhaps. I hope so." She smiled. "*À demain.*"

"*À demain,*" Violet and I said: *until tomorrow.*

Marguerite rang the bell, and the tiny maid appeared and led us to the front door where our coats were hung. "You are a doctor, madam?" she asked me in heavily accented English.

"Yes, I am a doctor," I replied in French.

She stared at me in disbelief and switched to French. "And, madame, the mistress, she is not too sick, I hope? How I worry about her! She is the kindest of mistresses, and to see her always so sad. Ever since that terrible letter!"

"There is nothing much wrong with her physically. But her... her mind, her spirits, that is another matter entirely."

"But, *madame la docteur*, you have no accent whatsoever. How is this possible?"

"My father is French, and I lived in France most of my youth."

"Unbelievable." She helped me into my coat, which was certainly large enough to have swallowed her up entirely. "How wonderful that you may stay with us–and if I can do anything to help the mistress, you need but ask it of me. I would do anything to assist her." Her pale blue eyes had filled with tears. "I pray alongside her and the good abbé. I am sure he can keep the Devil at bay."

Violet's forehead had creased. "You are sure?–you do think he can help her?"

"I am certain of it. He is kind and good."

"How reassuring to know that."

I don't think the girl truly caught the sarcastic edge, but her enthusiasm seemed to falter. "*Bonne journée, mesdames.*"

We stepped out onto the sidewalk. The street was quiet, although the distant muted rumble of the Champs-Élysées could be heard. "That was a little snide," I said. "The poor girl doesn't know any better."

Violet stood very straight, her head held high. "You think not? I do not trust her. Those tears came a little too easily."

"They were heartfelt."

Her smile showed a certain contempt. "I have more experience with those in service than you do, Michelle. I have… an ear for them. I know when things are amiss—when they are slightly out of tune."

"Well, I think you might give her the benefit of the doubt."

Her smile softened. "That is the difference between us, Michelle. You are always ready to give someone the benefit of the doubt, while I…" She shrugged. "My consolation is that when you expect the worst of people, you are rarely disappointed."

"That sounds like something Sherlock might say on a bad day."

"And he is a very perceptive man." She slipped her hand about my arm. "Come, let us have some lunch. I am starving, and then we will see what activities the men have planned. By the way, you simply must stay with Mrs. Hardy, at least for a while. It will help Mr. Holmes and me immensely."

"Perhaps you would like to explain that to Henry."

She laughed. "That I shall leave to you, Michelle."

That afternoon Henry, Violet, Sherlock and I visited Napoleon's tomb at the Dôme des Invalides, and then, since the rain had ceased, we walked to the Champs de Mars and, at the northern end, Eiffel's recently constructed tower. Later we met again for dinner at the hotel. The day had gone well, and we were all in good spirits until during dessert when I mentioned Marguerite's offer for me to stay with her. Holmes thought that was a splendid idea, but Henry's face went red, his mouth stiffening. His gaze at me was icy, his restraint somehow more telling than an outburst. I suggested the two of us take an after-dinner stroll, and we left Violet and Sherlock watching us warily as they sipped their port.

We walked slowly through the Tuileries along a broad gravel path in the direction of the river. In a black opening in the clouds overhead a few stars twinkled feebly. I held his left arm loosely with my hand but said nothing, biding my time. We came to a park entrance, a gap in the long stone wall with its balustrade along the top. Carriages passed by before us, and we had to wait to cross the busy road. Before us was the Passerelle Solférino, a cast-iron bridge built midway through Napoleon III's roughly twenty-year reign. Gas lamps lit up the bridge, and also the banks of the Seine. We turned left and walked for a while along the river.

At last Henry turned, then leaned on the stone wall. Below us the black waters of the Seine touched another walkway, yellow highlights dancing along its surface. A paddlewheel boat went by, agitating the water, making it lap at the concrete. The trees planted along the river were bare of leaves now. Across from us we could see the long expanse of the brightly lit train station, the Gare d'Orsay, with its arching windows and its two pointed roofs and gigantic clocks. They each showed 9:50.

I still held Henry's arm loosely. "Don't be angry," I said at last.

He was silent for a few seconds. "I'm not exactly angry, not now, but... my feelings are hurt."

I squeezed his arm tightly. "I shall make it up to you, I promise."

"But more than my feelings... It could be dangerous. You are putting your life in peril." His voice shook slightly.

"No, no, it's not as bad as all that."

"You cannot know that—you cannot. You have not really thought this through."

"It is as I said. Mrs. Hardy is miserable and afraid, and she needs my help."

"Why can't Violet stay with her?"

"She did not invite Violet. She invited me."

"And you did not even tell her that you were married."

"I told you—she did not ask." I did not want to let him know that Violet had encouraged my silence.

"What has that to do with it! You could have volunteered the fact."

"Oh please, don't upset yourself again—I promise you I'll be careful. And it won't be for long, I promise, if for no other reason that I need to get back to London soon."

He was quiet for a moment, then let his breath out in a long sigh. "I was so looking forward to a few nights alone with you."

The tone of his voice made me feel terrible. "I promise you, Henry—I shall make it up to you. *I promise.*"

"Something will come up. You will always be too busy."

"Don't say that. You must know how much I love you. I shall be free much of the day—she's only expecting me in the evening— and I've already seen Paris, but not your hotel room. And... and I swear that in July we will go somewhere together alone for at least a week! My practice will be abandoned. Sherlock and all his dreadful cases will be forgotten. It will be just you and me. Perhaps... Yes! Let's go to Brittany again, Saint-Malo and Dinard. We can eat crepes and drink cider and spend our nights locked in each other's arms."

He laughed softly. "You are clever, Michelle."

"Cleverness has nothing to do with it. I promise we will go."

He was quiet again. "I shall hold you to that promise."

"Henry..."

He turned away at last from the wall. I touched his cheek with my gloved hand. His black top hat gleamed with a glistening stripe of yellow light, and the shadow of the brim hid his eyes. I tilted my head to kiss him and closed my eyes. At some point I felt his hat be knocked off by my own.

At last he drew back. With the hat gone, I could see his eyes more clearly and his flattened hair. He raised his hand and touched my face. "Promise me you will be careful, that you will take no foolish risks."

"I promise you."

He shook his head. "You must mean it. You must not just say it to placate me."

"Oh, Henry, I do mean it. Because I know what it would mean to me to lose you, I could not bear for such a thing to happen to you. I will be careful, I swear it."

He ran his forefinger along my cheekbone down to my jaw. "Now I believe you." He drew back, then bent over to pick up his hat.

I took his arm again. "Let's get back to the hotel. We have at least tonight alone together. Let's not waste it walking along the river!"

He laughed softly. "As you wish, madam."

Monday morning Violet and I returned to Marguerite's with my luggage. She was delighted to hear I was accepting her invitation, and we were served a wonderful lunch. Afterwards, as he had requested, Violet and I rejoined Holmes at the hotel. We took a cab to the police headquarters near Notre Dame, and just before two, we three strode down one of its grand marble corridors.

Holmes paused before the door to Commissaire Juvol's office and raised his right hand. "A caution, ladies. As you might well suspect, I have not said a word about Madame Hardy to the commissaire. As my client, her involvement in this business must remain a secret."

Violet nodded. "Of course. That goes without saying."

Holmes rapped twice, then opened the door for us. We stepped into the large spacious room with two tall windows. Somehow the room conveyed a sense of order, and the large mahogany desk had an immaculately clean surface. The man seated there rose and approached us. He was taller and more handsome than I would have expected, very well dressed in a smart navy suit, the arc of a gold chain showing across his waistcoat. He had big hands and brown hair with a reddish tint, not a typical-looking Frenchman at all. His mustache was even larger and more abundant than Henry's. He smiled at us, his eyes giving Violet and me that appreciative glance of the French male appraising females.

"Ah, my dear Holmes, and so these are the two formidable ladies you mentioned in your note!"

After a round of introductions, Commissaire Juvol approached his desk, where a circular object leaned against the wall hidden by a cloth. Juvol paused for an instant, then snatched away the covering and gestured with his big hand. "*Voila, mesdames! Je vous présente la* Madonna della Mela."

The painting was tilted such that the warm light from the window illuminated it. Somehow I had thought it would be larger. It was less than two feet across. The Virgin had the distinctive long slender face and hands of Botticelli's women. She had very full, rather sensuous lips. She wore a sort of gauzy veil and a blue robe with gold trim over a red-orange garment, all of which were highly idealized, not something the poor wife of a Jewish carpenter could ever have afforded. Her hand and the Baby Jesus's jointly held the shiny red apple, and with his other chubby hand, he seemed to bless us spectators. Both faces had nearly transparent golden halos hovering about them. The blue and orange tempera appeared slightly faded, especially alongside the elaborate gilt frame. I had seen the *Madonna of the Pomegranate* in the Uffizi in Florence, but I couldn't remember much besides it being considerably larger.

Violet stared thoughtfully. My eyes shifted from her face to the painting, then back again. Both women had the same long slender face, but like many Madonnas, this one had wavy blond hair. The eyes were a curious pale amber color, while Violet's were dark brown, and her mouth was much wider than the Madonna's, although both, oddly enough, had a certain sensuous fullness to the lips. Violet's face also had an intelligence lacking in the Madonna's countenance. I noticed that Sherlock, too, was staring at Violet rather than the painting. I could tell from his eyes that his feelings for her had not changed.

"Well, ladies, what is the verdict?" Juvol looked at Violet, but when she remained mute, his eyes shifted to me.

"I could not begin to say," I said. "It looks like Botticelli, but then I am certainly no expert. I would be easy to fool."

"And you, Madame Grace?" Both Juvol and Holmes were staring at Violet. She was still regarding the painting, the hint of a frown marring her smooth forehead.

At last she gave a partial shrug. "I am no expert either, but that mouth… There is something rather voluptuous about those lips, as if they owe more to Rossetti or one of the Pre-Raphaelites rather than to Botticelli."

"Do you think so?" Holmes set one hand on the desk and leaned forward to more closely examine the Madonna. "Perhaps…" he murmured, "I see." He reached out with his fingers, and they hovered over those painted lips, only an inch away, tracing the line of the mouth. He frowned, then stood upright and crossed his arms as he spoke to Juvol. "You have kept us in suspense for long enough. What is the verdict of your experts?"

Juvol smiled amiably. "The verdict is... a draw!"

"What do you mean?" Holmes asked.

"Just that—we cannot be sure if it is an original Botticelli or only a clever copy. There are no obvious anachronisms in the painting, so I had two of the leading Parisian experts on Renaissance Italian art examine it. One said it was a genuine Botticelli, a lost masterpiece, *un veritable chef-d'oeuvre* worth a fortune. The other said it was a clever fraud, the woman's face much too modern." He glanced at Violet. "Perhaps he noticed the same issue with the mouth as you did. Anyway, at this point the painting's status is indeterminate, and unfortunately it is likely to remain that way for a few years."

He had taken his left hand out of his pocket, and he gestured upward with both big hands. "Someday soon it will be different. There will be chemical tests to determine the exact nature of the pigments used, but our lab is not there yet. The skeptical expert thought, in fact, that the color of the robe appeared to be from cobalt blue, a paint only developed in this century. If that could be proven—which today it cannot—that would be conclusive. I must admit that I suspect that, given Lupin's skill as a copyist, it is only a fake, but we cannot say for sure."

Holmes shrugged. "A pity you cannot be certain. However, there may be other ways of resolving the question."

Juvol stared at him closely. "And what might they be?"

Holmes smiled faintly. "There may be some... old acquaintance of Lupin's who might know the truth."

"Well, if you find such an acquaintance, be sure to let me know."

"Certainly, Commissaire. By the way, has your investigation of Madame Varin turned up anything interesting?"

"No. She seems to have had no real friends, and her main

occupation was drink—with occasional male visitors added to the mix. Another rather wasted life."

"I assume you must have checked her bank account. Did she have much money?"

"Only a little. Her monthly payment from Lupin was her only source of income."

"Was there a will?"

"None that we can find."

"So the state will get that pittance of hers. Well, Commissaire, thank you for taking the time to show the ladies and me the painting."

Violet and I also thanked him. We were about to leave, but Holmes stopped abruptly before the door and turned again to Juvol. "I nearly forgot—that other matter, the bottle of morphine. I hope the results were more conclusive than in the case of the painting."

"They certainly were, *mon cher* Holmes! The dosage in the bottle was three times as strong as what was indicated on the label."

"Ah." Holmes nodded. "So if Lupin injected what he thought was his usual dose, whatever the amount, it would no doubt have been enough to kill him."

"Yes, indeed. Of course, the dosage could have always been off—it could have come from the chemist that way. They hardly manage to standardize these things, and dosages rarely match what the label says. Nevertheless, I think a plausible assumption would be that someone switched the bottles on him, thereby murdering him."

"You have, no doubt, questioned the servants. Barrault was probably the only one in the household who actually knew his master was using morphine, but he seems an unlikely suspect. For one thing, he would have disposed of the bottle afterward. I don't suppose you could find the petite red-headed Mademoiselle Labelle?"

"No. She vacated her lodgings the day after Lupin died."

Holmes's sardonic smile appeared. "What an odd coincidence."

"Exactly! *Au revoir, mes amis.* Oh, and one other thing..." His pleasant face briefly grew stern. "If you should find this Mademoiselle Labelle or Mademoiselle Dujardin, please let me know. Especially if they are one and the same person! I am counting on it."

"So I shall. *Au revoir.*"

We started down the corridor, passing two policemen in their blue uniforms with the neat blue brimmed caps and the short capes typical of the French police. I was on one side of Holmes, Violet on the other.

"That was most interesting, Mr. Holmes," Violet said.

"I thought you would find it so."

"It may also prove helpful for me in the future to have made the acquaintance of the commissaire."

"Without a doubt. He is very good. For a policeman."

Violet laughed softly.

"Are we going back to the hotel now?" I asked.

"If you have the time and the inclination, I would like to make another stop. It is distant enough we shall take a cab. Would you like to see the bedroom of Monsieur Lupin?"

"Ah!" Violet exclaimed. "I surely would."

"All right," I said with little enthusiasm.

We took a carriage across Paris to a neighborhood off the Champs-Élysées and stopped before a row of townhouses. A rather surly-looking butler let us in, but when the valet Barrault appeared, he smiled and greeted us enthusiastically. He was a small balding man with an enormous black mustache: we were all taller than him. However, when Holmes explained that we wanted to see Lupin's bedroom and the private study, he grew troubled. Holmes mentioned a letter from the prefect of police.

"But that did not say anything about any ladies," he said.

A faint smile pulled at Holmes's lips. "This lady..." he nodded toward Violet, "is also a consulting detective, and we are working together."

Barrault gave a great sigh. "Very well, Monsieur Holmes. You know best."

We went up the stairs, and he opened the door for us. Violet and I both stared in disbelief at the Gothic monstrosity of the bed, an enormous black wooden construction with its four black square wooden posts joined by arches, the canopy formed of miniature gables.

"Good heavens," Violet said. "Is that a bed or a chapel with a mattress?"

Holmes smiled, but his gray eyes were uneasy. "It is a unique piece of furniture."

Violet started toward it, but Holmes touched her arm lightly. "It does not merit further perusal. The artwork is of more interest."

Violet nodded. She was staring intently at the painting on the wall, a voluptuous nude of a red-headed woman with her back to the viewer.

Holmes glanced at Barrault. "Please open the study door for us, and then you may go."

With another mighty sigh, Barrault nodded. "Very well."

Holmes waited until he had left the room, then opened the door. "Ladies."

Violet turned away from the painting, stared intently at Holmes, then followed me into the study. It was a large airy room with a desk, the walls covered with paintings, most of them easily recognizable masterpieces.

"Good Lord," I murmured. "I see what you mean about him being a superb copyist. I went to the *Mona Lisa*. It certainly looks like the one in the Louvre. And this self-portrait of Rembrandt..." I stared at the various paintings in awe. I recognized the couple in Renoir's vibrant *Dance at Bougival.*"

Abruptly, I realized that neither Holmes nor Violet had spoken. I turned. She was standing with her back to me before a large painting, another nude of a voluptuous red-head, probably the same woman as in the other work in the bedroom. Holmes stood a few feet behind Violet. He seemed to have risen up slightly on his toes, and his long fingers were spread slightly apart. All in all, he resembled some cat about to pounce. I frowned slightly, then approached Violet.

The woman was seated, her body twisted slightly to the side, her head turning even further, just past profile, so that her ear and the bun of her hair were noticeable. One breast was only a rounded semi-circle, while you could see the shape of the other, the swooping curve down to the nipple, then the more rounded bottom. The rendering was very realistic, graphic rather than idealized, and it was clear that the red of her hair must have been colored, probably with henna, since her pubic hair was dark brown. All in all, her body had a certain sensual glow.

"I think he must have been in love with her," I murmured.

Violet turned to me. Her face had an odd smile, half playful, half ferocious, but her dark eyes were troubled. "You don't recognize her?" She glanced at Holmes.

"Even as a physician, I don't see many ladies displaying themselves thus!"

"But her face," Violet said.

I stared more closely. "She is turning away. You can hardly see her face. All the same..." There was something vaguely familiar about the curve of the jaw, the ear, the partly revealed nose and mouth, the long neck.

Violet stared at Holmes. "It is her, isn't it?"

"Yes."

"Who?" I asked.

Holmes nodded in Violet's direction, and she said, "Madame Hardy."

"Madame Hardy! I think not–I..." Something about the face suddenly seemed to come into focus. "Oh. I suppose... it might be her. But so much younger, and so carefree, so unafraid."

"Exactly," Violet said. "And it is her exact ear, is it not, Mr. Holmes?"

He smiled. "It is indeed."

"And her hand, as well," I murmured, recognizing the long graceful fingers and something about the way they turned. "But how could she be so imprudent?" I asked, "–to pose as his model and let him paint her this way! I cannot believe she would be so stupid."

"That does seem idiotic," Violet said.

Holmes stroked his chin lightly. "I have pondered that, and I think that she did not actually pose for Lupin. He had a very good memory, an eidetic sort of memory. She must have been intimate with him, and afterwards, he probably made sketches. He may have even done this painting sometime later as a kind of memento of their relationship. I would wager she does not even know this painting and the one in the other room exist."

I groaned softly. "How dreadful it would be to discover such a thing! To be paraded thus naked before the whole world." Violet said nothing, but I saw that she shared my sentiments.

"This is Lupin's private study," Holmes said. "He kept this

painting here for himself alone. It was not something he would have ever sold or put on display. He could always see her as he remembered her, in the full splendor of her youth."

Violet shook her head. "Remind me never to take up with an artist."

Holmes's dark brows rose in dismay, and he was at a loss for words, but I laughed. "I had never realized, before, the dangers of such a relationship!"

Violet was staring again at the painting. "You were right, Michelle. He must have been in love with her." She looked around the room. "Everything else is a copy, an imitation. Her image is the only original one kept here. This proves that they were connected, that he was part of the conspiracy."

Holmes nodded. "I believe it was Napoleon who said, '*Un bon croquis vaut mieux qu'un long discours.*'"

"What is a *croquis*?" Violet asked.

"A sketch," I replied. "'A good sketch is worth more than a long speech.'"

Violet drew in her breath and released it in a long slow sigh. "This painting must not be put on the market and sold to simply anyone. Madame Hardy does not deserve that. Can you and your friend the commissaire see to it, Mr. Holmes?"

Holmes looked equally grave. "Yes."

Chapter Eight

The following morning, I rose from the sofa to meet Monsieur l'Abbé Docre. He was three or four inches shorter than me, very slight and slender, and I felt like a robust giantess alongside him. To be fair, Henry was one of the few men who didn't make me feel that way. The priest's black eyebrows had come together in a sort of inquisitive frown. His eyes shifted from my face downward, quickly appraising me, then rose again. The pallor of his face contrasted strikingly with his curly black hair and the satiny black fabric of his soutane. His narrow mouth rose into a smile, and he gave a short bow from the waist. *"Enchanté, madame la docteur."*

"C'est aussi un grand plaisir pour moi," I replied, reflecting that I had never had a priest greet me with *enchanté* before.

"So you live in England, although you are French. I suppose…" The creases deepened. "Do you still follow the Catholic faith?"

"Yes." Although I was not a regular churchgoer, that was still more true than false.

His face lit up, his relief obvious, and again his eyes seemed to wander over me in a disconcerting manner. "Excellent! You are a true daughter of *la France*, after all."

Marguerite watched him impassively. We had been chatting amiably in her sitting room before his arrival, curses and the Devil forgotten, but now the small muscles about her mouth and eyes had tensed, a worn care showing in her eyes.

"And you actually are a medical doctor?"

My mouth tightened. "Yes."

"As such, then we have much in common."

"How so?"

"We both act as confessors. People tell us things they hide from others. And we often see the sordid side of life."

I shrugged, thinking of my work at the clinic for the poor. "That is true enough."

"Yes, it is a somewhat trite observation, but our occupations are indeed much alike."

"How so?"

"The care of others is our vocation. You labor to heal the body, while I treat the infirm soul."

An ironic thought made the flicker of a smile pull at my lips.

"What is it?" he asked.

"I was remembering that central precept for physicians: *primum non nocere*. First do no harm."

He seemed to rise up slightly, raising his chin. "That goes without saying. Unfortunately, sometimes, as with medicine, the cure for a cankered soul can be painful."

"They also say that sometimes the cure is worse than the disease."

"Not with the soul, *madame la docteur*–never with the soul.

And you, back in England, do you have a spiritual advisor and confessor to guide you?"

"No."

"No? That is a grave situation. We all require such a person. How long do you plan to remain in Paris?"

"I... I am not certain."

"Should you decide to remain any length of time, I would be happy to meet with you for an examination of conscience, absolution, and penance."

My smile felt stiff and forced. "How kind of you."

His eyes lingered a moment. They had a certain feverish energy. He turned to Marguerite. "The study, as usual, madame?"

She nodded, then glanced at me. "I suppose you will be going out to see the sights?"

"No. I shall wait until after lunch."

She tried to smile. "Good." She hesitated, then reached out and gave my wrist a quick squeeze.

Docre's eyes were still fixed on me. "A pleasure indeed. You are, I can tell, a woman of spirit, of wit, as well as being a treasure trove of precepts." He let her go first, then followed, pausing only briefly to give me a parting smile. They were an odd pair, she so tall in her spectacular green dress with its billowing silken skirts and puffy sleeves, he a short slight figure in his black soutane.

I stared rather grimly at the doorway.

"He is a holy man," Jeanne said, "a bright light shining in these dark times."

She was standing by a nearby chair where she had been doing some embroidery work. I stared at her closely. "Do you think so?"

"I know it. If anyone can help madame in her time of trial, it is him." Her chin bobbed emphatically, and then she sat again and took up her needles. She stared at the clock on the mantel. "Generally I go in after they have been together about half an hour and pray with them. Perhaps you would like to join us as well."

"I think not." The words had slipped out spontaneously.

She looked surprised. "As you wish, madame." A slight flush colored her cheeks. I reflected how hopelessly young and innocent she appeared, with her perfect pink and white complexion, her blond hair and delicate features. What could she know of terrible crimes or guilt?

I sat back down on the sofa, then picked up a copy of *The Lancet* I had brought with me. I tried to keep up with the journal, but I was hopelessly behind. I hesitated between an article on "A Spreading Variety of Nerve Dullness" and another on "Chlorobrom in Seasickness," and finally chose the former because it might be, of all things, less dull! It took me only a page or two to realize that my hopes were not to be realized. I stifled a yawn with my hand, then briefly closed my eyes. I had not slept well the night before in the unfamiliar bed without Henry near me.

I dozed briefly, then opened my eyes when I heard Jeanne rise from her chair. She smiled at me, then set down the circular hoop and left the room. I glanced at the clock, then drew in my breath resolutely and began a second try, this time with the chlorobrom article. I was finally immersed in it when I heard someone clearing his throat. Monsieur l'Abbé stood just past the doorway, a black prayer book clasped in his fine slender white hands. He nodded, staring at me as if we were old acquaintances.

"I have left Madame Hardy and Jeanne to their prayers. I must be going."

"Good day then, Monsieur l'Abbé."

"But first... it deeply troubles me that you have no spiritual advisor.

When was the last time you made the sacrament of Confession?"

"I... It has been a while."

"How long exactly?"

"As I said—a while."

His expression was grave. "I see. Might I suggest... Do you know Saint-Sulpice?"

"Yes, of course. I have lived in Paris before."

"But I suspect you have not climbed to the top of its towers and seen its hidden sights. I should be free tomorrow around four in the afternoon. You could confess yourself, and then I might show you the secret parts of the church."

I stared at him in disbelief. I wanted to simply exclaim *no*, but I realized that Holmes and Violet would leap at a chance like this. I stared more closely. I wasn't exactly afraid of him. I was certainly bigger and stronger than he! Clearly I could prevent him from physically abusing me. All the same, there was something disturbing about him.

"Will you come, *madame la docteur*?"

"I shall... I shall consider it. If I have time..."

"Make the time—it is very important. One should not go unconfessed for long periods of time, not when God is willing to offer us his forgiveness. After all, we are all sinners."

I smiled. "Indeed we are."

"*À demain*, then."

"*Au revoir, Monsieur l'Abbé.*"

Once he was gone, I sighed deeply. I should have just told him no. I would have to discuss this with Holmes and Violet. I knew what Henry would think. Oh, I did not want to upset him all over again! I tried to resume my reading, but I could not concentrate. Jeanne came back into the room, curtsied, then sat and took up her embroidery again. I was still thinking about Docre's offer.

Surely it could not be as I somehow suspected—he was a priest, after all!—and yet his behavior was not like that of any other priest I had met. Henry often told me how beautiful I was, but I had never been quite convinced. Not that it greatly mattered to me—I was no longer a big awkward girl pining after men. All the same, as a simple fact, could the abbé possibly be attracted to a woman so much larger than him? It seemed very unlikely in someone so aristocratic and haughty, completely against society's dictates. But was that perhaps part of my appeal? I felt my face suddenly heat, even as I laughed. *This is absurd,* I thought.

I stood up abruptly and started for the doorway. "I shall just look in on your mistress," I said to Jeanne.

I walked down the hall to the study door and grasped the knob. I could hear quite clearly a muted sobbing from within. I hesitated, wondering if she wanted to be left alone, then realized that she had already been left alone for far too long. I pulled open the door. Marguerite was kneeling on a prie-dieu before the window, her face buried in her arms which rested on the velvet cushioned top. She was weeping and hadn't even heard the door open.

"Marguerite?" Her crying stopped abruptly, but she did not raise her head. "Oh my dear, what is it? What is wrong?" I went over and set my hand on her shoulder.

She slowly rose upward, drawing in her breath. Tears smeared her face below her dark desolate eyes. Obviously unwilling to try to speak, she shook her head.

"Can I help you? Tell me."

She was trying to control her breathing. "No one can help me."

I frowned. "Obviously not a priest."

"Oh, he is trying. Truly I am grateful for his aid. It is only…"

An odd grimace pulled at her face, twisting and transforming it, but she quickly regained control. She tried to smile, and her lips trembled.

"You should send for your husband. Let me send for him."

Her eyes were suddenly stubborn. "*No.*"

"This is foolishness! You cannot face whatever this is alone. You have said you love one another. That is why people marry—so they can help one another in the dark times. I know... I could face anything with my husband—anything!—but alone I am nothing."

She tipped her head sideways. "Your husband?"

I realized my mistake too late, but I was not going to deliberately lie to her, not now. "Yes."

"But I thought you were not married. I thought a doctor could not marry."

I laughed. "Why ever would you think such a thing?"

"You are older, and it is a very demanding profession. And you said nothing."

"You did not ask. And celibacy is definitely not required of women physicians."

"But where is your husband?"

I bit briefly at my lower lip. "He is... away on business, all tied up, so to speak. I am hoping he can join me soon."

She stared up at me for the longest time. "He would be welcome to stay here, too."

I laughed softly and squeezed her shoulder. "You are very kind. Come now. I think you have prayed long enough." I helped her stand, and she staggered slightly. "What is it?"

"Nothing. I feel faint sometimes when I get up too quickly."

"Has anything in particular upset you?" She would not answer. "Was it because of him?—because of Monsieur l'Abbé?"

"No, not him, exactly. It was..." She grew paler. "It was my penance."

"Your penance? It is that difficult? One million Hail Marys, I suppose."

That made her smile briefly. "If only it were that simple."

"One million Hail Marys would take a long time to say. We could calculate it. I suspect it might take several months." That made her smile again. "Why don't we get our coats, and I shall take you out to lunch before I begin my sightseeing."

"Oh, but we are dining out this evening with Madame Grace before the opera."

"So much the better! There is no rule that one cannot dine out twice in one day. Come along now. I think some air will do you good." I had grasped her arm just above the elbow.

She nodded. She look relieved.

I hesitated, still holding her arm. "And promise me... at least think about sending for your husband."

She shrugged. "If only I could."

We dined that night at a small restaurant not far from the Palais Garnier, the opera house. Violet, Marguerite and I were all wearing our finery. Violet had on a spectacular burgundy silk I recalled from a long-ago dinner in London, while Marguerite wore green again, and I, the electric-blue gown Henry so loved.

As we launched into our *plats principaux*, our main courses, I happened to notice our bare arms. We had, of course, removed our gloves for dinner. Our arms reflected the differences in our general physiques. Mine were the sturdiest and most muscular of the lot; also the fairest, my skin nearly white; my wrists were thick and the span of my knuckles broad. Violet had much more slender arms, rather wiry, all the muscles and the bone of the elbow distinct. Marguerite's arms lay somewhere between the two of us. They were strong-looking, but thinner than mine and gracefully shaped, the fingers of her hands longer and somewhat delicate. Her skin was the darkest, a pale sort of café au lait. I reflected that had Henry been present, he would have enjoyed looking at the three of us! Knowing his faithful heart, I did not begrudge him the simple pleasure of staring at other women.

Marguerite had begun the meal rather pale and withdrawn, but the food and the wine had the desired effect. She grew more relaxed, more animated. I could easily see how her husband must have been smitten. In her late forties, she was still a lovely woman, a real Gallic beauty with her dark brown eyes and bound-up hair. A spectacular emerald necklace lay on her breast, matching earrings at her earlobes. Every so often the jewels caught the candlelight and made the green sparkle.

Violet was at her best. She was no longer the thin agitated woman that I had known before the catastrophe in England. Even back then, something of her ironic sense of humor had always survived; now I was aware just how amusing and charming she could be. She and I had always enjoyed joking with one another. Between us, we actually had Marguerite smiling a few times! Nothing was, of course, said of satanic curses or the Four. We discussed the French versus the English, a topic of general interest, and I, because of my dual heritage, was considered the ultimate expert and arbitrator.

As we finished our main courses, the subject changed to music, and soon to the opera in particular. Henry and I occasionally went to the opera, generally at Sherlock's urging, but Marguerite and

Violet were clearly passionate enthusiasts. They discussed some of the more memorable productions and singers of the last few seasons at both Covent Garden and the Palais Garnier.

The waiter placed a dish of crème brûlée before me, and with great relish I took up my spoon and drove the front edge through the sugary crust. The first taste, crunchy along with smooth and sweet, was always the best. "What is your favorite opera?" I asked Marguerite.

She had also ordered crème brûlée, and she paused, spoon in hand. "It is difficult to choose. I think it would be between Verdi's *La traviata* and Gounod's *Faust*."

Violet shook her head. "The two female extremes—a courtesan who reforms and an innocent maiden led astray, both of whom die tragically in the last act. I'm afraid I find both operas overly sentimental. Then, too, for a consumptive, Verdi's Violetta can certainly reach the high notes in that last act!"

"Come now," I said, "you are hardly being fair. Since when has verisimilitude been required for opera? And what would opera be without sentiment?"

"I suppose you are right, Michelle. Gounod rather outdoes himself at the end of *Faust*. That must be the only opera where the heroine, so to speak, ascends into heaven carried by angels. I recall a famous production where they had Marguerite on a hidden wire and actually hoisted her upward at the end. Somehow it was almost comical."

Marguerite was frowning. "I always find the ending most moving. It never fails to bring tears to my eyes."

Violet set her hand gently on Marguerite's forearm. "Forgive me—playing the cynic is a sort of habit for me. I must admit that despite that, the end of *Faust* often draws me in as well. The female choir and the organ can be quite overwhelming."

I swallowed another mouthful of crème brûlée. "Were you named after the character in *Faust*?" I asked Marguerite.

She shook her head. "Mama never went to the opera. She just liked the name. It is a common one nowadays for girls in France." Her lips formed a faintly bitter smile. "I have little in common with my namesake."

"I think Marguerite and Violetta are more alike than first appears," I said. "Violetta begins as a frivolous courtesan, while Marguerite is an innocent country girl. But Violetta's love for Alfredo transforms her, and although Marguerite is corrupted by Faust, by the end both women have redeemed themselves."

A sardonic smile pulled at Violet's mouth. "It would indeed be nice if angels could come down from the sky and carry us off into heaven."

Marguerite nodded emphatically. "Yes—it would. The end is my favorite part. For once the Devil loses, and Marguerite is saved. God has pity on her and forgives her sins."

"I hate to say it..." Violet hesitated.

"That is not like you," I said. "Go ahead—out with it."

"Well, the Devil—Mephistopheles—is my favorite character in *Faust*. He is so very French, so Gallic and charming. I have a bias toward bass-baritones. I much prefer them over tenors, and it takes a native French speaker like Marcel Journet to do the role justice. The Italians generally butcher the part."

"Yes," Marguerite said, "that is certainly true. They sing with a terrible accent. All the same, I find the scene in the church when Marguerite tries to pray and Mephistopheles mocks her very disturbing. He is not the *galant* then, but a true devil." Her face had paled slightly. "Of course, it is only... the theater. The Devil does not have an actual body."

"What?" Violet asked. "No goatee, mustache, horns and tail?"

"No. People have both a body and a soul, a spirit part akin to God, but angels and demons are pure spirit, like God Himself."

Violet nodded. "Ah, yes. That topic was covered in the theology book we studied."

Marguerite gave her a curious look. "Theology book? You are Catholic, then, Madame Grace?"

"Yes, a recent convert."

Marguerite raised her spoon, hesitated, then set it down. "I only wish the Devil were more like the one in the opera: if he had a body, one we could see... then you would know when he is *here*. As it is... his spirit is only a presence, something we can *feel* but not see. And who knows where that presence begins and ends?"

"He is not God, though," I said sternly. "He is not omnipresent—not everywhere at once."

Marguerite took a swallow of wine. "I hope not."

Violet had sat back and folded her arms; she had skipped dessert. "I was very disappointed to learn that angels do not have functioning wings like the ones in all the paintings. One wonders how they flit about. Do they just need to think it, and presto, they are somewhere else?"

I laughed. "One cannot think about any of these things too closely! You will lose yourself in a maze. Our brains and our senses are so limited. You simply have to believe in a power beyond us, something bigger and greater. In the end... perhaps it is heresy, but we tell ourselves stories to help ourselves to understand God better. We should not be too literal-minded."

Violet stared thoughtfully at me. "We have arrived at the same point, Michelle. I have stumbled upon a certain faith, but for me, it means I cannot accept all of Catholic theology as hard facts, but only as approximations, as stories, even as fables. I am not even certain that the Devil exists. Perhaps he is only a projection outward of all that is evil within the collective human soul, giving it form and substance."

I shrugged. "This has grown rather serious for an after-dinner conversation."

Marguerite still looked grave. "Oh, I believe in him. I believe in the Devil."

Violet and I exchanged a look. "Violet," I said, "you have not told us what your favorite opera is."

"It is a problem for me, because I prefer spunky heroines, and there are so few. I am rather fond of *Lucia di Lammermoor*. At least Lucia can rouse herself to stab Arturo, the bridegroom forced upon her by her brother. I also enjoy her mad scene, especially when they use the glass harmonica rather than the flute."

"Do you like *Lucia?*" I asked Marguerite.

"Not particularly."

"Actually, you would never guess one of my favorite operas," Violet said.

"If we would never guess, then you must tell us."

"It is Rossini's *Cinderella*."

I laughed. "You must be joking!"

"Perhaps it is a case of opposites attracting. Cinderella is the embodiment of goodness and doesn't have a spiteful bone in her body. I like the opera because, for once, goodness—*la bontà*—triumphs at the end. She marries her prince and forgives even her wretched stepsisters and stepfather. I like all the florid singing in the opera, too. Rossini's comedies are like an Italian version of Gilbert and Sullivan."

"This is a side of you I did not know," I said. "I have not seen that opera, but will be sure to go if Covent Garden ever performs it."

"And you, Michelle," Violet said, "what is your favorite?"

"I have not seen so many as the two of you, but I think perhaps... perhaps *The Magic Flute*."

Violet laughed. "Of course! I should have known someone with your sunny disposition would favor Mozart, and that is the most jubilant of all his operas. And you, like Pamina, have made it through the trials by fire and water with your prince, and now you live happily after!"

I smiled. "Well, I hope so." I had finished my dessert. Marguerite had left hers half-eaten. If she had been Henry, I would have offered to finish it for her. "I think we had better be going if we want to be on time."

Marguerite insisted on paying for the meal. We put on our coats and started down the pavement toward the Opera. It had recently been converted to electric lights, and the facade was brilliantly lit. There were those who found the Opera terribly overdone, but I liked the elaborate, almost rococo exterior with all the sculptures and friezes. Nearby, on either side of the green copper dome where Apollo stood at the summit with his lyre, were two golden statues, angelic female representations of Harmony and Poetry. As we drew nearer, I could make out the row of comic and tragic masks sculpted along the bottom of the roof. I had managed to somehow ignore them for many years, seeing only ornamentation, until Henry had pointed them out to me. He and Sherlock were both experts on the Palais Garnier because of a celebrated case involving the opera ghost which had taken place just before Henry and I were married.

Equal in spectacle to the exterior was the grand stairway indoors with its beautiful marbles and multitude of lights. A throng of people was gathered: we passed women in beautiful gowns and jewelry, men in their black formal wear or, occasionally, in the gaudy red and blue uniforms with gold epaulets of the French military. One soldier smelled strongly of cigar smoke, while his lady had on some overpowering perfume—a dreadful mélange! We passed the heroic bronze maidens holding their sculpted torches with multiple lamps as we went up the stairs.

Marguerite led the way, and soon we came to the box she had reserved. One of the nice parts about having a box was that you need not queue up to check and then later recover your coat. We draped ours over a chair, then went to the front and stared about the vast auditorium. Two colors dominated: much of the dome, the pillars and fronts of each stage of loges were gold, while the three-story-tall curtain, the seats, and much of the loges were red. We were on the first floor up, quite near the stage on the left side, a prime location. The steady drone of the spectators filled the hall. Above us was the grand chandelier of bronze and crystal, more dazzling than ever now that it was lit with electricity. A slight shiver went up my back as I recalled Henry describing how it had once come crashing down.

I looked right, left, then right again. Henry and Sherlock were sitting in a box on the second tier, about six over from our own box. Henry scratched at his chin, then smiled at me. Sherlock had been quite enthusiastic about attending the opera, and since he knew the management, he had little difficulty getting seats.

We all sat, Violet in the center, I to her left, Marguerite to her right. Violet had a bound libretto, and she set it on her lap. "I have done some research," she said. "*Macbeth* was originally composed in 1847, but he reworked it for a performance in French here in Paris in 1865 during the height of the Second Empire. It was not well received and has not been revived in Paris since then. They are performing the later version tonight, but since the main singers are all Italians, it will be sung in their language."

"A pity," Marguerite said. "I know little Italian. You must tell me what is happening. I do not know the story at all."

"It is simple enough," Violet said. "Macbeth wants to be king of Scotland, and he has an ambitious evil wife who drives him to murder. He becomes king, but everything goes badly from then on."

Marguerite was briefly silent, but nodded at last. "I see."

The conductor appeared in the pit, and the applause began. He took his bow, then raised his baton, and soon launched into the overture. It was very atmospheric, low notes, then dancing twittery noises in the strings with high piccolo accompaniment, suggestive of the witches flitting about. That faded into a sweeping but melancholy melody. Soon the curtain rose on the blasted heath, all gray and green and shadowy, with dark forms stretched out on stage. They rose up, revealing the female chorus of witches, even as a flash of light simulated lightning, accompanied by musical thunder. The witches all wore shredded black rags, and the three main ones had manes of wild red hair.

I glanced down at Violet's libretto. The women were singing a fairly literal translation of the witches' opening speeches from Shakespeare. The setting was bleak and cold, but I could not help but recall warm French summers spent with my mother and my older brother. Determined I must be truly bilingual, she had spoken English with us, but she had wanted her children to also understand the Bard's challenging archaic and poetic language, so we had started with *A Midsummer Night's Dream* during my summer holiday when I was only eight. *Macbeth* was another of the plays we had read together a few years later.

Soon Macbetto, as the witches had sung, and Banquo entered. Both men had red beards and hair, and wore armor and furs along with drapes of plaid cloth. Macbeth might be short and barrel-chested, but he had a beautiful commanding baritone voice. Banquo's cavernous bass matched his great size. The music varied between something truly dark and sinister, and something slightly lilting and dance-like.

I heard Violet whispering an explanation to Marguerite. I leaned forward slightly. Just past the slanted side partition of our box, I could follow the curve of our tier with the other loges, and a level up, I saw Holmes's pale eager face with his distinctive beak of a nose. He was blocking Henry, who must have been sitting further back. Normally Sherlock would completely immerse himself in music, but I saw him raise a pair of binoculars to look at us, rather than the stage.

The scene shifted to Macbeth's castle, which was hardly better lit than the heath. Lady Macbeth entered and read, rather than sang, a letter from Macbeth; then her high dramatic soprano voice filled the hall. It was always a mystery to me how opera singers could create such voluminous sound, and it was especially true for someone so petite and slight as this woman. She wore a red dress and had bounteous red hair, surely another wig. She called upon the infernal ministers to come to her aid in inciting her husband to commit murder. Soon Macbeth entered, and the two embraced.

Again I heard Violet's whispered voice: "*She wants him to kill the king, but he's unsure and worried. She tells him they will not fail if he does not tremble.*"

Soon Duncan, the old king, and his knights and courtiers arrived to be greeted by Macbeth and his lady. The woodwinds played a sort of little march. The nobles had hardly trooped on stage, when it was time for them to leave.

After they were gone the lights dimmed, leaving Macbeth surrounded by shadow. He spoke with his servant, who left him. Once he was alone, he started, then reached out with his right hand, singing, "*Mi si affaccia un pugnal? L'elsa a me volta? Se larva non sei tu, ch'io ti brandisca!*" I knew what the first part must be: *Is this a dagger which I see before me, the handle toward my hand?* I glanced down at the libretto. The second line was quite different from the English, *Come, let me clutch thee.*

"*He sees a dagger*," Violet whispered, "*but he is not sure if it is real or imagined. He is trying to grab it, and realizes it's only a vision.*"

Marguerite seemed to rise up in her seat, to stiffen. Her eyes were fixed on the stage, her jaw tightly clenched. Macbeth staggered about, trying to seize the imaginary dagger. Kettle drums punctuated the sinister music.

"*He's singing something about a horrible specter, about blood on the blade, about bloody thoughts.*"

"*No more!*" Marguerite whispered loudly. She set her gloved hand on Violet's wrist. "I... Thank you, but I understand."

Violet turned slightly, her eyes shifting briefly to mine.

A shimmery sound—either some type of gong or cymbals. I knew it was supposed to be the bell, and the bass strings accompanied Macbeth as he sang in Italian, *Hear it not, Duncan, for it is a knell, that summons thee to Heaven or to Hell.* Macbeth pulled the dagger from the sheath at his side and strode toward the portal to the king's bed chamber.

Lady Macbeth re-entered and sang two lines. Her earlier self-confidence was gone; she seemed afraid. Macbeth murmured something off stage, and she sang something about "*quel lamento.*" Macbeth staggered through the doorway, the blade of the dagger held upward. I wondered if the stage attendants had been carried away, if they had accidentally doused him with a bucket of fake blood. His face and garments were splattered, and the hand holding the dagger was bright red. The spotlight also revealed the bloody crimson along the narrow blade. He let the hand with the dagger fall, then sang softly, "*Tutto è finito!*" *All is finished.*

A sort of muffled bang nearby made me start, and the people in the nearby boxes turned toward us. The orchestra and the performers heard nothing; they played and sang on. Marguerite must have knocked over her chair getting to her feet. She had clenched her fists, and her mouth was open in distress. She turned and fled, leaving the door to the box ajar. I was the first to follow her, but Violet was right behind me.

I stepped outside and looked right, then left. An usher in formal wear appeared quite surprised. Marguerite's back was to me; she was striding toward the stairs, almost running, her green dress a sort of blazon against the red of the carpet and the gold of the friezes and decorations around the loge doors. I strode after her. Violet followed.

"Marguerite!" I could not bring myself to shout, but my voice was urgent and slightly hoarse.

We came to the grand stairway, passing two more surprised ushers along the way. Marguerite was taking the stairs at a frightful pace, without bothering to lift her dress. I had a horrible vision of her tripping, then rolling down along those hard white marble steps to land in a heap at the landing where the two stairways met. This time I did actually cry out her name. She made it to the landing, then started down the central staircase. When she reached the bottom, she actually began to run.

Violet was beside me, and she muttered something, even as she seemed to stumble slightly. I grabbed her arm quickly, felt her totter briefly, then catch her balance. Her mouth pulled into a pained smile. "Thank you!"

"We mustn't go too fast." I was holding up my skirts. "We don't want to fall and break our necks."

"No, indeed!" We were both rushing down the steps as quickly as we could.

We reached the bottom and started after Marguerite. An attendant in black by the door cried, "Madame!" but she ignored him and shoved open both tall doors with her hands.

Violet and I followed and stepped out into the chill night, prepared for a chase, but Marguerite had stopped at last. She stood at the edge of the pavement, staring out at the square. It had begun to rain in earnest and was very cold. We had all left our coats back in the box, and Marguerite was being drenched by the rain. I felt gooseflesh sprout along my bare upper arms. I walked up to her. "Marguerite?" I grasped her arm, wary that she might run off again. She was breathing hard, her fists clenched, and I felt a shudder quiver through her. She bared her teeth, then raised her head to glance up at the gray-white sky, letting the rain wash over her face, even as a sort of groan slipped free. Violet had taken her other arm.

"It is all right," I said. "You are not in danger."

She looked at me, her eyes wild, but they seemed to change as she recognized me. "Oh no," she murmured. "No, no."

"That blood was a trifle overdone," Violet said. "But it was most assuredly not the real thing."

"I cannot... I cannot..." Another shudder passed over her. "I cannot bear the sight of blood. It makes me... *sick.*"

"Come back inside," I said. "It is freezing out here."

"No, no—I will not go back!—I am done."

I considered trying to persuade her to give the opera another try, then remembered there was probably worse to come—Banquo stabbed to death, and later his bloody ghost appearing at the banquet. I shook my head. "Of course you need not go back. We shall get our coats and leave. Perhaps some strong drink at a bar will help calm your nerves."

"I just want to go home! Oh, this was a mistake—a dreadful mistake!"

"We shall certainly take you home, if that is what you wish, but first come inside while I fetch our coats. You needn't come with me to the box, but there is no reason to wait out here in the freezing rain. Come along now."

She drew in a long shuddery breath, then let it out in almost a gasp. She nodded, and Violet and I led her back through the doors. The attendant, an older man with bushy silvery eyebrows, stared at us, his concern obvious. "Is madame well?" he asked.

"She has taken ill. We shall just see her home. It is nothing grave. She will be fine."

He nodded. "I am glad to hear it."

"I'll just get the coats. Look after her, Violet."

Violet's black eyebrows had come together, her brown eyes grim, and she nodded. She led Marguerite toward a nearby bench while I started back for the stairs.

On the landing where the grand stairway split into two, stood two men in their black formal wear, white tie and waistcoats, one quite thin with a high forehead and slicked-back black hair, the other sturdier, with thick brown hair and mustache: Holmes and Henry. I slowed as I approached them.

Henry took a step forward. "Is she all right? We saw you run outside. We were about to follow when you all came back inside."

"I think so. I have to fetch our coats. We are leaving."

Henry shook his head. "I suppose you must, but it's a pity. The opera is very good."

"You might as well stay and watch the rest."

Holmes had said nothing, but his gray eyes stared intently at me, a slight mirthless smile pulling back his lips. I felt a sudden surge of anger. "You expected this, I suppose?"

"What?" Henry said.

Holmes was silent for a few seconds, then said, "'The play's the thing wherein I'll catch the conscience of the king.'"

"What?" Henry repeated dully, like an echo.

I glared at him. "It's a quote from *Hamlet.* He was going to try to trap Claudius into revealing his guilt by putting on a play which mimicked the murder of Hamlet's father. It worked, too. Claudius panicked and had to leave—*didn't he.*"

I was suddenly furious. "This is no play—this is not Shakespeare! You had no right to frighten her that way!"

Holmes drew back slightly. "*I* did not frighten her."

"Do not mince words with me, Sherlock Holmes. It was a cruel trick, and it was wrong of you to make me complicit in your dirty business!"

His lips parted, his eyes troubled. "I'm sorry, Michelle, but I had to know for certain. It *was* her."

I stared at him, then took half a step backward. Henry's hand grasped my arm. "I do not believe that," I said. "I cannot believe that."

"I was watching through the binoculars. I saw her face."

"You saw that she was afraid. Lady Macbeth didn't actually stab Duncan, but the horror of it still destroyed her."

Holmes shrugged. I could see that he thought the matter was settled. I stepped around him and started up the stairway. Henry was at my side. "Michelle," he said, "Michelle." We reached the top and started toward the hall with the box entrances. "I didn't know—I swear I didn't. I thought we were just going to the opera. Please slow down." I turned to give him a pained smile, and he touched my cheek with his white-gloved hand.

My eyes briefly filled with tears. "I hate this," I whispered.

"I know. Next time we shall go to the opera alone."

We went to the box, and he helped me gather the coats. They were all laid across my arms. "I must see you and Sherlock tomorrow. Tell him we shall all meet, Violet included, at noon in the lobby of the Meurice." He nodded.

Holmes was still standing on the landing. We did not speak as I passed him, but Henry gave my arm a parting squeeze before I started down the stairs.

Chapter Nine

When our carriage reached Marguerite's townhouse, Violet paid the coachman and asked him to wait for her, then came inside with us. Jeanne was surprised to see us so early, but I explained that her mistress had taken ill. "A pity!" she said.

"Why don't you help her get ready for bed," I said, then turned to Marguerite. "I shall join you shortly and give you something to help you sleep."

She frowned briefly, then nodded. She took a step toward the hallway, then turned back to Violet and me. "Thank you for being so considerate, Madame Grace, *madame la docteur*. I am sorry to have spoiled our night out."

"No matter," Violet said. "Unlike the good doctor, I don't much relish the sight of blood myself. Next time we shall choose one of those Rossini comedies!"

Once Marguerite was gone, Violet and I stared at one another, then sighed in perfect unison. That unexpected harmony made us both smile. Violet shook her head. "She certainly was terrified.

Sit down, Michelle, and if you wish, I shall bring you some of her husband's marvelous elixir from Armagnac."

"There is nothing I would like better." I sank into the depths of the sofa, pulled off my long white gloves, hesitated, then removed my fancy shoes. "I cannot bear anything with a higher heel. They always make my feet hurt."

Violet approached me with a glass of the amber brandy in either hand, then gave me one. "You have never been one to suffer for fashion's sake. You were not born with your allotted share of feminine vanity."

I sipped the liquid, felt it warm my throat as it slipped down. "Lord, what a day. This brandy is truly remarkable."

Violet sat beside me and raised the glass to her lips. In profile, I could see the slight curve of her nose and the length of her slender neck. She licked her lips, then shifted her eyes toward me, then away again. "I suspect you must have seen Mr. Holmes."

I felt my brow furrow. "I don't particularly wish to talk about it."

"Ah." The word merged with her sigh. She took another sip of brandy. "It was that dreadful?"

Somehow my mouth felt stiff, anger starting to manifest itself there. "He said... 'the play's the thing wherein I'll catch the conscience of the king.'"

"Oh yes," she murmured. "More Shakespeare–*Hamlet*. Rather apt."

I was still frowning. "Did you know what he was up to?"

She turned, and her brown eyes regarded me, her black brows coming together, a slight crease showing between them. "You did not?"

"No, I did not." I let my head fall back, then slowly turned it first left, then right. "I must be stupid–Henry and I must both be stupid. I could not conceive of such a thing." I could not keep my distress from my voice.

Violet put her hand over mine and squeezed gently. "You are not at all stupid. You simply are not... devious." Her smile was bitter. "You do not have the twisted mentality of Mr. Holmes and me."

"It *is* twisted. She so deserved a night of respite from all her cares. Did we have to put her through this?"

She was still staring at me. "I don't know, Michelle. I don't know. What is done, is done."

"Sherlock believes she did it—that she stabbed the count."

"Does he now? He actually said that?"

"Yes, words to that effect."

Her dark eyes were still fixed on me. In the dim room they were all great swollen black pupils, and her lips were pressed tightly together. She turned away and took a sip of brandy, let it linger in her mouth, savoring the taste. She was silent for a while, and I had not heart to make idle conversation. "He is wrong, you know. I was watching her, too."

Again I frowned. "Is he?"

"One can never be sure, not until someone actually speaks the truth. But yes, I think he is wrong. Above all else, he is a gentleman. Once upon a time, he... he did not want to think the worst of me, so now he is... overcompensating in the other direction."

"Oh, this is all giving me a headache—so it was Lupin, after all?"

She laughed softly. "Oh, Michelle." Again she sipped her brandy. "I am certain that one way or another, we shall soon know what happened. Do not fret about it now. Let us drink our brandy and relish it along with a quiet moment."

After that we did not speak again. The clock on the mantel ticked loudly. When we were finished, we sat with our glasses held between our hands on our laps. I was tired and discouraged, but somehow I was still happy to be with Violet, to have found someone again who I had thought might be lost to me forever.

At last she stirred. "I must be going."

"Oh, I told Henry that I must see him and Sherlock tomorrow at noon—and you as well. Can you be at the Meurice at that time?"

"Certainly. What is it about?"

I ran my hand slowly back through my hair. It felt tight and tangled at the back; it would be good to let it all down. "Monsieur l'Abbé Docre has invited me for confession and a tour of the secret parts of Saint-Sulpice tomorrow at four."

Violet frowned in earnest this time. "Are you joking?"

"Would I joke about such a thing?"

"You must not go alone," she said sternly. Her mouth twitched into a smile on one side. "I shall accompany you."

I stared back at her. "That would be something of a relief. He looked at me in such an odd way."

"I know you will not acknowledge it, but you tend to have that effect on men."

"Not so much as you."

She smiled in earnest. "We shall not argue the point." She gave my hand another squeeze, then took my glass. "I shall see you tomorrow." She rose and set both empty glasses on the sideboard near the decanter of Armagnac.

I drew in my breath. "And I must see to Mrs. Hardy." I rose resolutely from the comfortable sofa. "Until tomorrow, then."

I went to my room, found my bag and prepared a sleeping draft for Marguerite. Her room was next to mine. She was sitting on the bed in her nightclothes, a long lacy white gown and a matching robe. Her long dark hair hung about her face, spilling onto her breasts which were evident under the thin fabric. One lock was white. I had not seen her before with her hair down; it made her appear more vulnerable. She no longer looked so frightened, but only very weary.

"You may leave us," she said to Jeanne.

The maid curtsied, smiled at me, then left the room. I held out the glass. "Drink this. It will help you sleep."

Her forehead creased. "What is it?"

"A few drops of chloral hydrate and laudanum. It will help you sleep through the night."

"I took laudanum once. I took it for many months. It was difficult to stop, but I finally managed it. I do not wish to begin again."

"One night will not make an addict of you. Drink it down."

She sighed, then took the glass and swallowed it all at once. She returned the glass, and I set it on a nightstand.

"Go ahead and get under the covers."

She stood, raised the quilt and blankets, then swung her feet around. They were large and shapely like her hands, but not so big as mine. I tucked the covers round her. She stared up at me, a sort of dull aching misery showing in her eyes. Her arms rested on the quilt, and I gave her hand a squeeze. "You will feel better in the morning." She stared intently at me. "What is it?"

"I... I do not want to be alone."

I stared at her, then at last I walked round the bed. It was a wide one, made for two, with two sets of pillows. "I shall stay with you for a while. Do you mind if I lie down, too? I am tired. I have my shoes off, so I shall not soil the covers."

"Do not worry about that."

I hesitated for a moment. The room was cold. I pulled aside the covers, then lay down beside her, still in my evening gown. I had, however, already wrapped a shawl about my shoulders and arms to keep them warm. I pulled up the covers. "This is quite cozy."

"*Merçi,*" she murmured, "*merçi infiniment.*"

"*Pas de tout. Dormez bien.*"

I closed my eyes. *Merçi infiniment* was a phrase with no real English equivalent. *Thank you infinitely* was the closest translation. The Italians said *mille grazie, thanks a thousand times,* which was a much smaller number than infinity. I reflected that Henry and Sherlock were probably still at the opera, which must just be finishing up. I thought again of the trick Holmes had played, and I stirred slightly, drawing in my breath. I was too tired to be angry. He was rarely wrong, and if he thought Marguerite had... But Violet said he was mistaken. Oh, I didn't want to think about it anymore.

I remembered the opera, Macbeth and Banquo in what the French must consider Scottish dress—those plaid cloaks, draped over their armor, with some furs thrown in. They had not worn helmets, probably so you could see those red-hair wigs. And Lady Macbeth had a wig of such abundant red tresses. Where had I recently seen a red-headed woman? I stirred slightly, then the vision of a naked woman with red hair came to me. The painting—at Lupin's. A much younger, untroubled Marguerite, with her hair dyed, probably henna.

Macbeth was supposed to be bad luck, wasn't it? The Scottish play. People must have their superstitions. Obviously in a play with so much swordplay, accidents could happen. But this was Verdi, not Shakespeare. Would the curse still hold for a musical rendition in Italian? I was being silly. The music had been beautiful. It had a dark melancholy tone. Perfect for Marguerite.

I could hear Marguerite beside me breathing deeply, almost snoring. My own breathing had also slowed. I thought of getting up and going to my own bed, but I was far too comfortable. I thought of the painting again, and the image of the naked woman with the red hair was even more vivid. She turned toward me, and I could see that the dark eyes were truly Marguerite's. Odd that she had taken off her nightclothes.

She sighed wearily, almost a heartsick moan. *Yet who would have thought the fat count to have had so much blood in him?* No, no, I thought—it is supposed to be, *Yet who would have thought the old man to have had so much blood in him?*

She was still staring at me. *Thou canst not say I did it: never shake thy gory locks at me.*

That is wrong. It was Macbeth who said that to Banquo, not Lady Macbeth.

My mother stared at me. Everyone said I looked like her. She also had fair skin, freckled now in the summer, and blue eyes, a wide, rather sensuous mouth which formed the same playful smile. *It is rather horrible, but somehow beautiful too. Shakespeare loved metaphors. You remember what a metaphor is? We talked about them. Here is a good example, and it is beautiful but awful at the same time: "Will all great Neptune's ocean wash this blood clean from my hand? No, this my hand will rather the multitudinous seas incarnadine, making the green one red."*

We were sitting before the Mediterranean, and the vast blue-green sweep beneath the clear blue sky abruptly turned a sort of dirty gray, then began to pinken. *I don't like this—you don't need to show me.* The red waves lapped at the shore, making me shudder. *No, no, that is impossible!*

It's only a metaphor, Mother said, *only a metaphor.*

The naked red-headed woman clutched at her right wrist. Her long beautiful fingers were stained red. The red had also splattered her face and even her bare breasts, the color striking against her pale skin. She was mouthing something over and over again. I could only distinguish the word *out*.

Oh, I don't like this, I cried. *Let's read something else*. My mother looked faintly worried. *It's only a play, after all*.

Marguerite put her hands behind her back, slightly thrusting forward her bare bloody breasts. *Guess what I have?* I shook my head. *You won't guess? I suppose I must show you*. She brought her hands round, and in the right one was a knife. She held up the blade, making a drop of blood shimmy down the long silver blade.

My eyes opened wide, and I was aware of my breath coming and going. A candle still burned on a nearby table. Marguerite was fast asleep. The chloral hydrate would have worked quickly. *Only a dream*, I thought, *only a dream*. Henry would probably be back at the hotel by now. How I wished he were in the bed with me! When I had nightmares, I usually just felt for his body, his arm or his flank, and that calmed me. I still had on my evening gown; the dress was constricting me. I could not sleep in such a thing—and I did not belong here.

I threw the covers aside, swung my legs round and stood up. I stared down at Marguerite, frowning. She should be all right. The laudanum should keep her asleep through the night, especially since she was unaccustomed to it. I wondered if perhaps I should stay with her. I could put on my nightclothes, then come back. All the same... It was ridiculous to think—mere superstition—but somehow I did not want to be in the same bed with her—not now, not tonight.

I went to my own room, undressed, put on a simple nightshirt, then slipped between the icy sheets. I fell asleep almost at once, and my dreams, while not exactly peaceful, were free of Macbeth and bloody deeds.

* * *

Knowing what was to come, I had set my hand over Henry's. His lips beneath the neatly trimmed brown mustache were compressed and were turning white. His blue eyes had a frigid glare. The quiet before the storm, I reflected.

"Have you taken utter leave of your senses? I… I forbid it! You are not going to see that priest. It is absolutely out of the question."

Holmes ran the fingertips of his right hand slowly along the left side of his jaw. "It could prove useful."

"*Useful,*" Henry hissed in a hoarse whisper. He gave his head a fierce shake.

"She will not go alone," Violet said. "I shall accompany her." The suggestion made Holmes frown. He was seated in a big overstuffed armchair, while Violet, Henry and I were on a sofa. The corner of the Meurice lobby where we sat was deserted save for us four.

"Oh wonderful," Henry snarled, "that's just wonderful."

"If there was trouble, I think I could best him in a fair fight." I smiled wryly. "I'm bigger than Monsieur l'Abbé, after all."

Violet also smiled. "It would be two against one."

Henry shook his head. "And if he should have… have a knife or some other weapon, what then? He seemed unbalanced, and lunatics often have preternatural strength."

Holmes also looked uneasy. "Let us do this. The ladies shall meet the abbé at the designated time, but Henry and I shall also go to the church. We two shall sit in the pews. Should there be the least sign of trouble, you must leave at once. We will be waiting for you."

"No, no," Henry moaned.

"We shall take one further precaution," Holmes said. "Michelle, as I recall, you are proficient with a revolver."

"Yes, I am."

"I brought one with me from London. You shall take it with you in your handbag." He gave a resolute sigh. "That should provide adequate protection for any contingency."

Henry was still red in the face, and I felt his hand twitch under mine. "So help me, if I had any sense, I would pack up and leave at once–just go back to London and forget this whole ghastly business." His eyes shifted to me. "And I would drag you along with me, since you are completely incapable of behaving sensibly and looking after yourself."

"You needn't speak to me that way." My face felt warm.

Holmes leaned forward in his chair. "Do you think I would allow it if I thought they would truly be in danger?"

Violet's smile was bittersweet. "Michelle and I are not fragile damsels prone to the vapors and faints at the first sign of danger. We can take care of ourselves. The risk is low, and it is a calculated risk. Madame Hardy is in peril, and we must help her any way we can. It is as simple as that. Monsieur l'Abbé is a mystery. This meeting should help us determine whether he is a saint or a scoundrel. I'm inclined toward the latter, but I'll wager by dinnertime we shall have a definite answer." Her forehead creased in thought, and she raised her fingers to touch her chin, even as she smiled. "I wonder. I could wear my sister's habit again. That might be an interesting experiment."

Henry stared at her. "Why on earth were you dressed as a nun that night we saw you in front of Notre Dame?"

"Ah, I explained that to Mr. Holmes. Madame Hardy had told me of Docre's visit, and I asked my friend Sister Ann about the priest. She told me he was giving an inspirational talk to her order in a chapel at Notre Dame. I went with her that evening, and we knew I would blend in best if I came as a nun. Sister Ann knew a fellow sister about my size, and I decided to pay her for a spare habit. You never know when such a disguise may prove useful!

"Ann helped me get everything on. It is a more complicated wardrobe than you might imagine, especially all those wrappings round the head. I suppose, strictly speaking, it is sacrilegious to disguise oneself as a nun, but Ann thought of it as a grand sort of joke. She said a practice session would help me determine if I had any real aptitude for the religious life."

"I think you may go as an English lady this afternoon," Holmes said. "We need not put your soul at risk a second time."

"What did you think of Docre's talk?" I asked.

She frowned. "He is a compelling speaker with a piercing tenor voice, very dramatic, but his presentation was not clearly organized. It jumped about a great deal, and in the end, was often trite. It had to do with temptation and the struggle of the soul to choose between light and darkness, between good and evil. He also discussed the nature of angels and demons in a rather literal-minded way."

Holmes's gray eyes stared off into the distance. "I wonder who he really believes is stronger, God or the Devil." His gaze shifted to Violet. "Perhaps you will have the opportunity to find out."

Violet and I trudged round and round, ever upward, toward the summit of the bell tower of Saint-Sulpice. I held a candle on its holder which cast a feeble light. We paused occasionally to catch our breath. The great bronze bells were like some enormous creatures, perhaps whales, lurking in a shadowy sea, and we could hear the soft moan of the breeze coming through the sounding shutters.

"I cannot believe Henry made it up here," I said, "not with his vertigo. It must be improving, or perhaps it was simply too dark to see much."

"I wonder how many steps there actually are. Onward and upward, as they say." Violet resolutely drew in her breath and resumed the climb.

We came at last to a sort of circular rotunda up top, and I grasped a rusty iron rail. It moved some six inches. Startled, I let go even as I edged back against the wall.

"Careful," Violet murmured. "He must be on the roof."

We went through a trap door in the ceiling and stepped outside. Docre was leaning against the wall staring out to the west. The clouds had parted, leaving a swath of sky where the setting sun glowed red-yellow, casting a fiery light over us. We stepped closer into the strong wind, unblocked by any obstructions up this high. The sounds of the city formed a muted roar.

"Monsieur l'Abbé?" He didn't seem to hear. To the west in the distance we could see the brilliant golden dome of Les Invalides and the black skeleton of the Eiffel Tower.

I reached out my arm to touch his shoulder, hesitated, then let it drop. "Monsieur l'Abbé!" It was almost a shout.

He turned; a smile began at the sight of me, vanished as his eyes took in Violet behind me. His black eyebrows formed part of an inquisitive frown. "*Madame la docteur.* But who is this?"

"She is my friend," I said loudly, "an English woman. Madame Violet Bennet. She also was interested in Saint-Sulpice. And in spiritual advice."

He gave an appreciative nod, his eyes fixed on Violet. The wind had brought some color to her cheeks, and she looked quite stunning in the red hat with the feathers. His admiration of her beauty was clear enough in his eyes. "*Bienvenue,* Madame Bennet. And you, also, are Catholic?"

"Certainly, Monsieur l'Abbé Docre. *Seulement une fille humble de l'église.*"

My eyebrows came together. *Only a humble daughter of the church.* I thought that might be putting it on a bit thickly, but Docre was pleased with the response. "Your French is excellent, madame. I am glad we will be able to speak freely."

"No more than I," Violet replied.

He hesitated only an instant. "And your husband, madame, is he with you on your visit to our fair city?"

"No. I am a widow."

"Alas." He touched her lightly on the upper arm. "I hope the Church has provided you with some consolation?"

"Indeed it has."

Docre stepped back and swung his arm about in a great arc. "Behold the grand city of light, all of Paris spread out before you in its glory! There below teem the masses of our metropolis, most of them gone astray, their lives dominated by labor and petty sorts of sin."

We drew nearer to the wall and stared down at the square to the west, mostly empty now in November, the trees all bare, the fountain still. The buildings, the trees—all had a sort of golden glow because of the sun low in the sky. We took a few minutes to walk slowly round the wall, looking in all four directions. Docre provided a running commentary, even as he set one hand gently on my shoulder, then on Violet's. We could see the hill of Montmartre to the northwest with its partly constructed basilica there. To the east was Notre Dame, to the south the Jardin du Luxembourg. The sun sank behind a streak of gray cloud, the bottom half turning red and coloring all the cloud pinkish-orange. The light around us dimmed and lost color.

Violet was beside me, and she suddenly shivered. "What is it?" I asked.

"I'm rather cold."

"Ah, let us go inside then," Docre said.

It was a relief to get out of the cold air, and it was quieter, too, once the priest closed the trap door. He gestured toward the dark opening before us. "The rotunda here is nearly seventy meters up." He took a small torch and struck a match to light the wick. "I shall go first and guide the way." He slipped past us, brushing us closely. I reflected that either he was wary of heights, or he enjoyed being near to ladies. "Would you prefer the tour first, or should we descend for Confession?"

I glanced at Violet, whose face was largely hidden in shadow. "The tour, I think," I said.

"Very good, although perhaps we may occasionally touch upon matters of spirit." He started down the circular staircase. I took the candle, and we followed. "We shall pass our five shapely ladies: Thérèse, Caroline, Louise, Marie and Henriette."

"What ladies?" I asked.

He laughed. "Those are the names of the great bells of Saint-Sulpice." He paused and shone the light on a vast curving expanse of metal, the bronze worn and pitted. "This is Mademoiselle Henriette, and down there is Caroline. Caroline is the most grand of the bells. It takes four great strapping men to make her sing. You can see the metal footrest where they must stand, two on either side."

"It must be deafening up here when it rings," Violet said.

"Indeed it is, madame. Caroline is very loud in her cry."

The priest kept up further commentary as we descended,

pausing occasionally to point out some detail of the bells or the workings of the sounding shutters. The sun had set by then; already there was much less light coming through the shutters than when we had ascended. We came at last to the first landing where there were four doors. He shone the light on one of them.

"There are lodgings here. Behind this door is the dwelling of the old bell-ringer Carhaix and his wife. He has been at his work some thirty years. As you might guess, he is almost completely deaf. A pity, but the sacrifice was made for the greater glory of God." He pulled open one of the doors. "This leads to the great attic of the church and more chambers." He started forward, and we followed. It was a vast, dim, dusty sort of cavern, massive wooden beams on either side and overhead supporting the roof. My nose felt itchy, and I saw dust particles dancing in the beam of the torch.

"Here lies a sister of the five ladies, one who has unfortunately split herself." He traced the outline of the crack along the surface of the bell. It lay on its side like some beached whale or other great fish. "And we also have some statues of the saints which are broken, as well as an old baptismal font just there. The attic is like that of a grand old house, a storeroom for the broken-down and discarded. Just ahead there is the room which serves as my oratory. I come here to pray and meditate."

He swung open the door, and we immediately felt a welcome warmth. He stepped inside. Violet and I looked at one another, then followed. It was bare and austere, with only a small table and two chairs, the tiny black stove which warmed the room, a narrow spartan-looking bed, and of course, a prie-dieu, an antique with leather-covered kneeler and a velvet top to support one's arms. A small window let in the gray light of dusk. The priest gestured at the stove where a steaming kettle sat.

"I know you English are lost without your tea. May I prepare you some?"

I frowned slightly, but Violet smiled. "Only if you will join us, Monsieur l'Abbé."

"Gladly, madame, gladly." He poured the hot water from the kettle into a plain white tea pot. "We must give it a few minutes of course." He lit a small lamp on the table, extinguished the torch, then stepped back to gesture at the chairs. "Please sit down, *mesdames.*"

"But where will you sit?" Violet asked. "There are only two chairs."

"The bed is good enough for me." He pulled out a chair for each of us, then sat on the bed and leaned upon his right hand. The mattress had hardly any give. His sensual lips formed a polite smile, and his gaze shifted from Violet to me, then back to her. "Have you been in Paris long, Madame Bennet?"

"A few months. I wished to put my past behind me and begin anew."

He nodded. "A beneficial attitude." He smiled. "Your French really is excellent for an English woman. Not perfect like that of *madame la docteur*, who has no accent, but impressive all the same."

"Thank you, Monsieur l'Abbé. I have labored at it."

"And it has paid off indeed. You have been here several months, you say. Where do you go for Mass?"

"I rent a home near Auteuil, and a small church is nearby where I generally go. Sometimes I come into the city for the Mass at Notre Dame."

"Ah, you must visit us here at Saint-Sulpice! I often preach at the ten o'clock Mass."

"I shall make a point of coming!" She smiled enthusiastically.

"Excellent!" His smiled faded, his expression suddenly distasteful.

"I doubt that Auteuil would have a priest who could provide a clever lady such as yourself with proper spiritual instruction."

"No, I think not," Violet said. "And do you think such instruction is truly necessary?"

"But certainly! How is the female soul, weak as it is created by God, to progress without the firm guidance of a holy father?"

My mouth twitched slightly as I tried to keep my face neutral. Docre noticed it. "You do not agree, *madame la docteur?*"

"Oh yes, absolutely."

"I think our tea is ready." He stood, took down three cups and saucers from a shelf, then poured out tea. "I fear I have no sugar. It is an indulgence which I do not permit myself."

"I prefer mine without sugar," Violet said.

"Very good!" He pushed our cups toward us, then took a cup and saucer, sat back on the edge of the bed, and took a polite sip.

His eyes watched Violet as she pulled off first one glove, then the other: one did not eat or drink tea in gloves. Her fingers were so long and slender compared to mine, her hands like those of Botticelli's graceful ladies. I actually put my own hands under the table as I pulled off my gloves, but his eyes lingered on my fingers as I set them on the table.

I quickly took a sip of tea, then nodded. "It is very good." His dark brown eyes stared at me over the rim of his cup. *What on earth am I doing here?* I asked myself. Perhaps Henry had been right: I had taken leave of my senses.

"And do you have many ladies to whom you provide spiritual guidance?" Violet asked.

"A select few."

"And how do you choose them? I suspect they all may be under forty and rather pretty."

Docre seemed briefly disconcerted, then shrugged. "Come to think of it, they are under forty. And I must confess that I am not one of those narrow ministers who despises beauty. It is a gift from God which he gives only to a lucky few." He gave an appreciative nod at us both.

Violet glanced at me. "I think we are being complimented, my dear."

"So we are." I tried to keep my voice sprightly.

"And you might have time to meet with me on a regular basis, Monsieur l'Abbé?"

"I would absolutely make the time, madame." It seemed clear to me that Violet had made a conquest, that his interest, though divided, had shifted toward her.

"And what might you teach me, what tenants of the faith? You do not strike me as some narrow moralist who would focus only on the threat of damnation."

His smile faltered. "Damnation is not something to be mocked."

"Certainly not!" she exclaimed. "Forgive me if I gave the impression I was suggesting such a thing."

"All the same, there is a certain higher level of the soul that can be obtained, a meeting with God in the joining of human spirits. We are all islands apart, but in true union can come great joy. Men and women were not meant to always be so separate and distant, one from the other."

He did not remark it, but I recognized a certain sardonic quality to Violet's smile. I decided I wanted to change the subject.

"And do you truly think you can help Madame Hardy? She is in such spiritual distress."

"Ah." He shook his head gravely. "Indeed she is. The Devil has made great inroads. I fear that some great sin from her past hangs like a millstone about her neck, beckoning to Satan."

The metaphor seemed almost comical to me (I could see Marguerite with a millstone necklace round her neck), but I only nodded. "Is it Satan himself?" Violet asked. "Or only one of his minions?"

"Satan is everywhere. His minions never act alone."

"I thought only God was everywhere," I said. "Only god is omnipresent."

Docre shrugged. "Satan is not in Heaven, but he lurks everywhere in this world of ours."

"I suppose if he is almost everywhere, at least he cannot be seen," Violet said.

"Ah, but he can!" Docre spoke with utter certainty.

"How is that possible?" I asked.

"He manifests himself locally to inspire fear."

I could not restrain myself. "Does he have horns and a tail?"

"Horns, no. The tail... not exactly."

I laughed although I was not amused. "Does he look like a man?"

"Not at all. He is a great black shadowy being. He has no head, but two red whirlpools for eyes and a greater yellow-white one for a mouth."

Violet and I exchanged a glance. "And the angels, what are they like?" she asked.

"Luminous beings. But it can be hard to distinguish demons from angels. The demons are clever. They can assume almost the same form. They are, however, all much smaller than their great lord and master."

Violet hesitated an instant, then said, "'*Ô toi, le plus savant et le plus beau des Anges, dieu trahi par le sort et privé de louanges...*'"

I frowned in concentration. *Oh you, the wisest and most beautiful of angels, god betrayed by fate and denied praise...* That was from one of Charles Baudelaire's poems from *Les Fleurs du Mal–The Flowers of Evil.* As I recalled, the poem was a prayer to Satan.

The words struck Docre dumb. He stared at Violet, his eyes opening very wide, his jaw thrusting forward slightly. His face was so pale against the black of his soutane and his curly hair. His mouth twitched into a smile which came and went quickly. His voice was a sudden hoarse whisper: "'*Ô Satan, prends pitié de ma longue misère!*'" That was the refrain of the poem, which repeated itself every few lines: *Oh Satan, take pity on my long misery.*

Violet's brief smile was grim. "'*Toi qui sais tout, grand roi des choses souterraines, guérisseur familier des angoisses humaines...*'" *You who knows everything, great king of underground things, familiar healer of human agonies...*

Docre smiled again, then said, without much of a pause this time, "'*Ô Satan, prends pitié de ma longue misère!*'"

"Bravo, Monsieur l'Abbé," Violet said. "You know your Baudelaire. I would hardly have expected it."

Docre frowned, his eyes fixed on her, his indecision obvious. "I... I have an appreciation for poetry, for the grand beauty of his language. I do not, of course, condone its blasphemous content." Somehow the last sentence was rather equivocal. "And you, Madame Bennet, why would you choose a prayer to Satan to quote to me, a priest?"

She shrugged. "Oh, we were talking about the Devil, and it was just the first thing to come to mind. I'm afraid 'The Litanies of Satan' is a favorite. Of course, I don't condone all the blasphemy either, but my French teacher recommended I study the poems to assist in my learning."

Docre gave her a probing glance, then turned to me. "And you, *madame la docteur*, are you also familiar with Baudelaire?"

"Oh yes. My mother had a copy of the poems."

"Your mother!"

"Yes, she was English, you know, and she too was studying to perfect her French." I did not tell him I had started reading *Les Fleurs du Mal* during the long summer holiday when I was sixteen, mainly because one of the sisters at school had denounced the poems as blasphemous, degenerate and obscene. What respectable young woman could ignore them after that? I had taken the volume down from an upper shelf of the family library and read the poems furtively in my bedroom.

"And they please you?"

"Oh yes." That at least was mostly true.

He nodded. "Most interesting." He took a final sip of tea, then set the cup on the saucer and rose to put it on the table. "There is a poem I am particularly fond of, 'The Giantess.'" His eyes half-closed. "'*J'eusse aimé vivre auprès d'une jeune géante, comme aux pieds d'une reine un chat voluptueux.*'"

I would like to have lived near a young giantess, like a voluptuous cat at the feet of a queen. It took an effort of will to keep smiling, and I suspected my smile must have grown ferocious, because he drew back slightly. I had guessed right before: my height must be part of my appeal for him. I knew that particular poem very well because it was a joke between Henry and me; he often quoted it when we were in bed together, especially the later part about feeling the giantess's magnificent shape and slumbering in the shade of her breasts. He would kiss me, then murmur "*ma belle géante.*" I tried to reassure myself that the poem would not be permanently ruined for me, that the speaker had more to do with its effect than the actual content.

"I know it," I said.

"Ah," he murmured. My smile wavered.

Violet must have seen that I was faltering. "The language is certainly lush and voluptuous. Do you think that in itself is wicked, Monsieur l'Abbé?"

His smile broadened. "I do not. They are only words, after all. And... what is voluptuousness but the abundance of God's beauty, an invitation to the soul's delights?" His eyes watched us both carefully.

Violet laughed. "I could not agree more. If the body in all its grace and beauty was created by God, can it be wicked to appreciate that beauty?–to savor it? Certainly not!"

I could tell she was playacting, but Docre was quickly taken in. "I agree with you completely, madame. The joy in its beauty can take us to a mystical plane above this wretched earth of ours! And it is all so brief, so ephemeral–such beauty must be seized during the short instance when it exists."

Violet laughed again. Her cheeks were flushed, but unlike Docre, I knew it was not from passion. "Again, I could not agree more."

He nodded, then glanced at me. "And you?"

I told myself that if he actually touched me, I would slap him, and that resolution gave animation to my smile. "I am *la géante*, after all. I like a voluptuous cat at my feet. Or *à l'ombre de mes seins*." This last made Violet's smile falter, her eyes giving me a questioning look.

"Ah." He had lowered his eyes, but a smile still played about his mouth. "There are mysteries, grand mysteries of the flesh, voyages which take us beyond ourselves to another plane, to a land where there is no more division, where the soul cries out its joys at union, at the unimaginable meeting of two souls. How can true joy be wicked, heavenly bliss diabolical? Or perhaps…" For an instant his eyes turned inward. "It is all the same, all one—God and Satan, pleasure and pain, the celestial bed and the infernal sty!"

He leaped suddenly to his feet, making both Violet and me start. I clutched at my handbag, aware of the bulky shape of the revolver within it. "I have something to show you! Come with me. You should find this interesting." He seized the handle of the lamp and started for the door.

Violet and I stared at one another, and I half raised the handbag by way of reassurance. I took the candle, and we followed him further along the attic, which was nearly completely dark now, the light from some low openings mostly gone. He came to another door, withdrew a ring of keys, selected one and opened the door. "Wait only one minute." He darted inside with the lamp and closed the door.

"Henry was right," I said. "We have both taken leave of our senses."

"I think it is the abbé who has taken leave of his senses." She gave my hand a quick squeeze.

The door soon swung open. "*Entrez,*" he proclaimed. Violet went first, then me.

The chamber was quite a contrast with the other, lavishly furnished with a grand canopied bed, one with a sort of awning and a bedspread of the same heavy fabric, red with elaborate golden edging and fringe. He must have lit the silver candelabra which sat on a spectacular chest of drawers; both the dresser and the bed frame appeared to be from the time of Louis the Fourteenth. On the floor was a multi-colored Persian carpet of fantastical design straight from the Arabian Nights. On one side of the bed was a huge full-length mirror in a gold frame; on the other stood a grand-looking stove. Obviously it had not been started: the room was freezing.

"A chamber fit for a queen, is it not?" he proclaimed proudly.

"My, yes!" said Violet enthusiastically.

"Oh yes." Actually, to my taste, it seemed more like a chamber from an expensive brothel rather than that of a royal palace.

"This room is for our most special guests, those of the highest nobility who wish to lodge in the church itself. The bed there has one of the finest mattresses made in Paris, the work of an antique enterprise which has furnished all the most exclusive homes."

Violet glanced at me. I didn't quite know what to say, and my lips formed a sort of frozen, lunatic smile. She drew in her breath resolutely. "Charming—it is charming. If only we could stay and try it out briefly!—but alas, we have an early dinner appointment. There is no time."

I nodded eagerly. "No time at all."

Still smiling, Violet touched his arm gently. "We must return another day. Perhaps some evening. When we shall not be quite so rushed—when we can *linger* for a while."

He nodded. "I understand, madame. As you wish. Know that I shall be always at your disposal." He gave a formal bow more fitting for a courtier than a priest. "Let me take you back to the landing, then."

"You are *très galant*, Monsieur l'Abbé," Violet said.

"Truly," I murmured.

As he led us back down the dark cavern with its thick beams all about us, I felt myself gradually calming. I smiled grimly. I would not have to shoot him after all! I did wish I could have slapped him just once. We came to the landing at last, and the movement of air in the tower made my candle flame flicker.

"It is only one final flight of steps, and then you will be again in the church. I must, alas, leave you and return to my oratory for my evening prayers and meditation. It has been the greatest of pleasures! Rarely have I met *two* such fine ladies. You may be English, but you put our French women to shame! I only wish I knew your language so we might better understand one another. How you shame me! I understand not a word of your Shakespeare, but you know by heart the great Baudelaire! I shall doubtless see you soon at Madame Hardy's home, *madame la docteur*, and you, Madame Bennet, I hope you will not make yourself a stranger to me!"

"Oh no. I wish to continue our discussion. It was most enticing."

"Yes, was it not? *Au revoir, mesdames, et encore, quel grand plaisir!*"

Still smiling, we turned and started down the stairs. I was first, the candle thrust before me, and I went very quickly. I stumbled once, and Violet caught my arm. "Careful now!"

"Lord, I'm glad that is over with. I still cannot quite believe it. His intentions were clear enough, were they not?"

"Quite clear. A pity we have a dinner appointment."

"Violet! Don't joke about such things."

"I'm sorry." Her voice grew serious. "It is my way of dealing with such utter... perversity. To say the least, his tastes are quite unusual for a priest. How odd that he seemed to know Baudelaire's 'Litanies of Satan' by heart!"

"I was surprised that you could quote it."

"After I decided to come with you, I spent some time reviewing the poem. I never dreamed it would receive such an enthusiastic response. Clearly he has a secret life. I suppose that he, at least, does not force himself on women. I'll wager he finds many willing participants amidst French high society, women in search of mystical union under the bed sheets."

"It's a good thing he did not try to force himself on *me*."

She laughed softly. "I am certain that what you said earlier was correct: you could best him in a fair fight."

Chapter Ten

Violet and I went with Holmes and Henry to a nearby bar. Over wine, we described our "tour" with Monsieur l'Abbé. Holmes was not in the least surprised, while Henry was seething. Afterwards, the three went off together while I returned to Madame Hardy's house for dinner. The sleeping draft had done its work, and she had slept well the night before for the first time in many days. However, as the evening wore on, I could tell that she was growing apprehensive. I was exhausted from the day's activities and fell asleep lying on my bed while still dressed.

My dreams were full of Saint-Sulpice: winding staircases, shadowy bells, vast dim interiors, flickering candles, a spartan oratory and an overdone bedroom. The reds and golds of the bed were vivid, then the blotchy pitted bronze surface of a great cracked bell lying on its side, the opening like some enormous mouth. Dimly I heard bells ringing from the tower, and four men struggled with the largest bell, working to stir its massive bulk.

A red sea stretched out before me. Perhaps it was the Red Sea, but could it actually be *this* red? There were no waves, but the surface swayed and undulated. Even the gray sky had a pinkish tint. Something was wrong with the way the water moved: it was too sluggish, too thick. It was not water.

Will all great Neptune's ocean wash this blood clean from my hand? No; this my hand will rather the multitudinous seas incarnadine, making the green one red.

Oh, not *Macbeth* again! He was whispering the words, then singing them in his deep baritone voice. It was blood, a sea of blood, and even from a distance I could see something bobbing about out there. Somehow I managed to draw nearer. It was a face, Marguerite's face surrounded by her dark swaying hair, much of which was submerged in the bloody sea. Her hands struck at the water, keeping her up. I could see the terror in her dark eyes.

It's only a play, only an opera, only a metaphor. Take my hand. Take my hand. Perhaps I could pull her into the boat.

She stopped struggling, and her hands disappeared. Her face stared up at me, and I had never seen such despair. She was there for a moment, and then she slipped under and was gone, only the swaying red surface of the bloody sea remaining.

No, no, no. I might have plunged in, but Henry had grabbed hold of me. *Have you taken leave of your senses?* But she is drowning, she is drowning, she cannot breathe, her mouth and lungs are filling with blood, she cannot breathe. Even the sky is red now. She cannot breathe.

My eyes jerked open. "Lord," I whispered. Slowly I sat up. The clock near the bed showed that it was just after one. I had fallen asleep around ten. I hadn't even taken my shoes off. I reached down to unfasten them, then pulled them off. I stretched awkwardly and took a long deep breath. The nightmare had not yet left me. It had been even more vivid and disturbing than yesterday's. A candle on the nightstand flickered, casting a feeble light. I began to undo the buttons down the front of my dress, then hesitated.

There was no harm in checking to make sure she was all right. I opened the bedroom door and stepped into the hall. Marguerite's was the next room down. The door was ajar and cast light onto the carpet and the opposite wall. I came closer, then grasped the doorknob and pushed gently. The hinges wanted to squeak.

"Who is there?" Marguerite was sitting up in bed, a lamp lit nearby.

"Only me." I stepped into the room. She sighed, then sank back into the pillows. Her long dark hair hung loosely about her and spilled onto the white gown. "I had a nightmare."

She looked more closely at me. "Why are you still wearing your dress?"

"I meant to take it off, but I fell asleep first."

The black pupils of her dark eyes were swollen in the dim room. "What was your nightmare?"

"I... I don't quite remember. Some monster or something chasing me."

"I have dreams like that, dreams where some dark thing is chasing me, closing in on me."

I frowned. "I suppose you haven't slept."

She shook her head. "I hate the night. It lasts forever."

"All the same, it always ends, doesn't it? And day comes again." I drew in my breath resolutely. "Let us go downstairs and sit for a bit. Sometimes it helps to get up."

"Do you think so?"

"Yes. Come along."

She slipped out of the bed, put on some slippers and then a

white robe. I had a shawl over my shoulders. I took the candle on its holder next to the lamp. We went quietly down the hall. We passed another open door, and I heard someone snoring loudly.

"Who on earth is that?"

"Jeanne."

"Who would have thought such a tiny woman could snore like that."

We went down the stairs, then to the drawing room. It was dark, save for the dim red glow of some coal embers in the fireplace. I opened the grate and set down another chunk of coal, then took up the bellows and pumped until flames were going. Marguerite had sat on the sofa and drawn up her legs, so that they and her feet were covered by the robe. One elbow rested on the sofa arm.

"Would you care for brandy?" I asked.

"No." She smiled faintly. "I must admit... I can tell you this now, but you must promise that it will remain our secret."

"Certainly."

"I do not much care for brandy, even the most precious ones. It is wasted on me."

I laughed. "Surely your husband must suspect something!"

"He does not. I know what one is supposed to say, how you are supposed to act."

"And you have never been tempted to tell him?"

"No. Spirits are his great passion, both brandies and whiskeys, and he knows so much about them. I envy him, you know. I wish I had some such passion, or better yet, a passion like yours, *madame la docteur.*"

I frowned slightly. I had hardly spoken with her about Henry. "What do you mean?"

"Your profession. I can see that you are dedicated to medicine.

Madame Grace told me what an excellent doctor you are, and I have seen that first-hand. My husband's profession brings joy to people, I suppose, but it is not like yours. You help people."

"Well, I try to. However, it is with varying success." I thought of something Henry often said. "We doctors always lose in the end."

She shrugged. "Such is life. You do good with your passion. Others..." She stared forward at the fireplace. "They do great harm. They have evil passions."

"Have you never had a great passion?"

Her smile was brief and bitter. "Once, when I was young and foolish. There was a man, not so much wicked as... insipid. Then, too, I wanted to be a great lady. I did not understand then that wealth and position mean little, that they cannot make you truly happy."

"Doesn't your husband make you happy?"

She stared at me, her forehead creasing. "He tries. He tries so hard, and sometimes... he succeeds. He is a very good sort of man, unlike the other one." She was staring again at the fire. "I have done nothing with my life. It has been... at best, a waste."

"You talk as if it were over with—it is not. Many years may remain. Do something with them."

She turned to me. "But what? That has always been the question."

"Is there no charity that interests you, no unfortunates that you might aid?" Again she turned her gaze upon me. "Well?"

"I have given money to societies for fallen women, the prostitutes of Paris and London. At the beginning, I went to some of the homes to visit with them, but I could not bear it. *I could not.*"

I shrugged. "That is, perhaps, understandable."

"Their situation is so dreadful here in Paris. There are these... examinations."

"It is an abuse of the medical profession!" My voice was angry.

"Perhaps you should choose another cause, something more congenial. I work often at a charity medical clinic, but I admit it can be dispiriting. Perhaps you would enjoy working with children. They always need help at the orphanages."

She was silent a long while. "I wanted children, you know. They give a woman's life a purpose. But it was not meant to be. I am not certain... When I was younger, being around children was difficult because it reminded me I had none of my own. Perhaps now that I am older..."

"You are a devout Catholic, are you not?"

"Oh yes, I hope so. You must have realized that from the visits of Monsieur l'Abbé Docre."

His name made my lips compress tightly. "Through your parish church you might find some work with needy families and children."

She nodded. "Yes, you are right. I must try it. It is not enough to give only money and to always be fretting about what cannot be, what I cannot have."

I smiled. "That's better. And does your faith not help you?"

She let out a long sigh. "It did. It did before. I found our Lord during the darkest time of my life. I was in despair, I did not want to live, but I went to the church and sat for many hours. Finally I made my confession to the priest. When I left I felt... all hollowed out, but forgiven–redeemed, reborn. Something of the feeling from that day has sustained me, but now..." She looked at me again. "I worry so about the Devil. I worry about Hell. *He* will not leave me be–he pursues me always."

"Is that what the abbé has told you?" I could not keep the anger from my voice.

"The Devil is very strong," she whispered.

"But not so strong as God! That is doctrine, after all. He cannot beat God."

"No?" I could hear the uncertainty in her voice.

"*No.*" I leaned over to squeeze her hand. She started slightly. I stared at her, then let go and sat back.

She was silent a long while. "When I was younger, I committed a grave sin. Now I must pay for it."

"God can forgive any sin—that is also doctrine."

I could see the ripple along her throat as she swallowed. "If only I could believe that."

"You mustn't let anyone frighten you, especially not a priest. Try to remember that feeling you told me about after your confession."

She let out a rather jagged sigh. "He has given me a terrible penance."

"What penance? Tell me."

"I cannot. It is a secret from the confession. Tomorrow I must... tomorrow..." She stifled a sort of moan.

"Can I be of help? Whatever it is—you need not face it alone."

She turned toward me, her anguish apparent even in the dim light of the fire. "If only you could, but he said... only Jeanne, but perhaps if you were nearby..."

"What is it? Where are you going?" Her eyes shifted to mine, and I willed her to speak.

"Père Lachaise, the cemetery."

"What? What is there?"

"I must visit a grave."

"Whose grave?"

"I cannot tell you. I must go only with Jeanne, and I must be there exactly at 4:30. That is when Monsieur l'Abbé will begin his prayers in the church. Then we will find out for certain."

"Find out what!"

"I cannot tell you. I have already said too much. It is a secret—it is my penance, and it is my burden alone."

"Let me come with you."

I could see the struggle in her face. "If only you could, but I must face him myself alone."

"Face whom?"

She shook her head. "I cannot say. Only... perhaps you could come to the cemetery and wait for me—if you promise to obey me, to leave me and Jeanne alone for a few minutes. He did not forbid that, exactly. Can you promise me that?—that you will leave me alone for a few minutes?"

"I don't like to make any such promise."

"Then you must not come!"

"But if you insist, I shall promise it. But should you need me, you could always cry out—you could scream and I would come."

"Yes, yes, that is fair! A good idea, indeed. It would be good to know that I have a friend nearby. Someone I can count upon."

I nodded. "Yes."

She hesitated, then reached out and touched my hand. "Perhaps God has sent you as well—perhaps you are my guardian angel, after all."

I smiled. "I promise you I have no wings. I am no angel."

"But you are good," she whispered. "I know that." She stared intently at me. "I wish I had known you before all this... misery. I was not always like this—so weak, so afraid. I have never known any women like you and Madame Grace."

"How so?"

"You are both so strong, so brave. I wish I had a fraction of your courage." She yawned deeply, and it seemed to leave her relaxed, if exhausted. "I think I can sleep now. Would you like to come with me to Mass in the morning?"

"Gladly." Her yawn had done its work: I was doing the same. "Should we go back to bed?"

"Yes." We both stood, and I stretched out my arms.

"*Merçi*," she said. "*Merçi infiniment.*"

We went to a morning Mass at Saint-Roch, a late Baroque church in Paris which happened to be quite near the Meurice. As usual during the week, the participants were mostly women with only a few old men. Jeanne knelt to Marguerite's left, I to her right.

I must confess I gave the Mass little attention. I was trying to decide if I should tell Holmes about Marguerite's upcoming visit to Père Lachaise cemetery. She had spoken to me in confidence, and my inclination was to say nothing. All the same, since this penance was Docre's idea, I suspected some sort of trap. Then, too, she—and I—might be in danger.

I had returned Holmes his revolver. Perhaps it was foolish, but I didn't feel afraid. However, was it fair to Henry to put myself in danger without warning him? I suddenly recalled the time he had gone with Holmes into the foul and dangerous London rookery Underton without telling me first. I had been furious with him, upset and tearful. Didn't I owe him the same courtesy I had expected from him? I had arranged to meet Violet in the lobby of the Meurice at one PM. I could discuss the situation with her—although even that was betraying a confidence.

After Mass I had an early lunch with Marguerite, then set out again for the Meurice. Violet sat in the lobby, a newspaper spread out on her lap. She had pulled off her gloves, and one slender hand rested on the sofa arm. Her face and bearing were almost regal, and although hardly plump, she no longer had that thin desperate look I recalled from the past. She was a remarkably beautiful woman; it was hardly surprising she had fascinated the abbé. Her eyes shifted upward, and she smiled, even as she folded up the paper and set it aside.

She stood and said, "There you are. Have you eaten? Ah, well, will you keep me company during lunch? I can tell you about the morning's activities."

"What activities?"

"Mr. Holmes and I made a visit to Saint-Lazare." Her smile had vanished.

"The women's prison? What for?"

"I shall tell you soon enough. Let us go to Pierre's. They make an excellent croque-monsieur."

While we waited for her sandwich, she told me about their visit. Her face was pale and grim. The prison had been a leprosarium in the twelfth century, then was taken over by Saint Vincent de Paul and his mission in the seventeenth. It had served as a woman's prison since the beginning of the century. An order of nuns ran the prison and also acted as guardians. It housed a variety of women, many of them diseased prostitutes who were treated at its hospital, or young women who had gone astray. Some more serious offenders like Simone Dujardin also ended up there.

"It's a rather moldering old building of gray stone, horribly dreary, and there is no color: the nuns have their black habits, all the women their plain gray woolen dresses."

Holmes had presented his letter from the prefect of police to the mother superior. She had been most impressed and actually knew him by reputation. She called in a sister who had known Simone

Dujardin. The sister described her as a model prisoner, a hard worker who did not complain and was most devout. Dujardin had been released a year early. She had never had any visitors. Clearly she had been estranged from her parents and her sister.

The waiter set Violet's croque-monsieur before her. She smiled. "*Merçi bien, Jacques.*" The sandwich smelled delicious. She took a half between her hands. "We learned very little about Dujardin. We already knew, I think, that she was a great actress, who might have turned more fruitfully to the stage in her youth. However, we did find out something more significant. Mr. Holmes asked the mother superior if she knew a certain priest, Monsieur l'Abbé Docre."

"What?—and did she?"

"Oh yes. He had acted as a sort of chaplain for two or three years. He gave inspirational talks to the prisoners, and also acted as confessor."

I smiled, but my lips felt pinched. "A confessor."

"It is clear enough. He must have been attracted to Dujardin. Perhaps he even found a way in the prison to actually... He gave up his work in the chapel about a year ago, at about the same time she was released. Mr. Holmes thinks they must be lovers and are working together, or rather more likely, that he is only her tool."

"Given his behavior yesterday, he certainly doesn't believe in limiting himself to one woman!"

"No." She lifted her sandwich, took a bite and chewed slowly, but clearly her thoughts were elsewhere.

"What is wrong?"

"The prison—it was horrible. And I could not help but think..." She set down the sandwich, even as her face went paler still. "I might have ended up at such a place—or something even worse. Our English prisons are not run by sisters. The sisters at least have a certain compassion for the prisoners."

"Surely not for murder—we have talked about that. It was not murder."

Her smile was pained. "No, but the 'Angels of the Lord' were guilty of theft, extortion and blackmail. And of course, there was the great swindle involving the fake oil-well scheme."

"But…" I could not think what to say. At last I reached over and grasped her hand firmly. "But you are not in prison, thank God!"

"Thank God, indeed. All the same, I wonder…" She stroked her jaw, then pushed a curl of black hair off her forehead. "Do Marguerite and I both belong in prison? Does justice not demand it?"

My lips were compressed tightly together. "What purpose would that serve?"

"What purpose does it ever serve for the repentant? Why should we two be excepted?" She stared intently at me.

"I cannot truly speak for Marguerite. I hardly know her. All the same, it seems clear that her primary motive must have been greed. She wanted to be rich. You, on the other hand… You may have been misguided, but you were driven not by greed, but by a desire for justice. You wanted to right all the wrongs done to the poor and the miserable, to servants and prostitutes. You stole from the rich to give to the poor." I smiled faintly. "You wanted to be Robin Hood."

She thought about this. "Yes, I suppose that is true. I never wanted the money for myself."

"And there is another reason you should not be in prison. You can do much good in the world. Your new profession is helping women in trouble like Marguerite. No, I think most assuredly you do not belong in prison, but I must confess that I am not impartial, not in the least. Because I love you dearly I cannot bear even the thought."

Now it was her turn to clasp my hand tightly. "Oh, Michelle, I thank God for a friend such as you! If I had known you sooner, my life might have taken a different turn."

"Well, it has taken that different turn now. Life is full of continual twists and turns. Eat your sandwich. It will get cold."

She laughed. "Very well." She took another bite.

"And now I have something to ask you about." I told her about my talk with Marguerite the night before, her penance that afternoon at Père Lachaise cemetery, and my dilemma about telling Sherlock.

She finished her sandwich, then shook her head gravely. "I do not like this, not at all. You do not think you could talk her out of going?"

"No. She still thinks *l'abbé* wants to help her."

"I could come to the cemetery and join you." She tapped briefly at the table with her fingertips. "On the other hand... I shall speak to Mr. Holmes for you. This whole wretched business is far too dangerous for us to act on our own." A brief smile tugged at her lips. "After all, he is the master, and I am the pupil."

I stared incredulously. "Am I hearing right?"

"You must never tell him I said such a thing!"

"Certainly not."

"I had better get back to the hotel. He thought he would be back around three this afternoon. I shall wait for him, and if he does not return, be assured I shall certainly come on my own."

Marguerite, Jeanne and I got out of the carriage at the cemetery entrance. The afternoon was gray and overcast, and the cold misty drizzle made it seem as if the sky itself had sunk down, no longer distinct from the earth below. I had an umbrella, but it wasn't actually raining hard enough to justify opening it. On either side of the gate were tall rounded stones with Latin inscriptions and sculpted torches in relief. Ahead I could see the wide cobbled path with the bare black trees on either side.

I sighed softly. In summer Père Lachaise was actually inviting with all its trees and greenery providing welcome shade, and an occasional light breeze touching your face. Now this autumnal dreariness amplified its sorrowful nature as a necropolis. Marguerite glanced at me. Her face was pale, and the fear showed in her eyes and in the tension of her mouth. I gave her arm a quick squeeze. Even Jeanne's youthful face looked grim.

We started forward, and I couldn't help but think of Dante passing under the gate into Hell inscribed with, *Abandon all hope, ye who enter here.* Spread out before us was a vast grid of graves, tombstones, monuments, crosses, cenotaphs, statues, inscriptions— especially inscriptions: *to the memory of, beloved father, mother, son, daughter.* And dates, everywhere paired dates so that you could see who went first, how long a spouse must have lived on alone. The worst for me were always the graves of children, especially those who had not lived even a year—or only a few days, or a single day even. I shivered slightly. There was no use working myself into a state. Someone had to keep a level head.

The landscape was monochromatic, mostly devoid of color. A light mist and the drizzle obscured everything, and the tree trunks and branches were all mostly gray-black, the brown washed out of them, and the tombs and monuments and crosses all tended to be variations of gray or a light tan. Many were like curious little houses with iron grates across the doorways and pointed little roofs, distant cousins of the sheds one might find in a garden. Others resembled miniature churches complete with arched windows and doors, gables, and crosses on top. Statues of angels or bronzes of the deceased were also common. A few evergreen trees or bushes were a dark dull green, and a lone pot of red flowers in a bronze vase assailed the eye.

We passed a side path which curved off into the distance, lined with more trees and more graves, fading into gray obscurity. Again I thought of Dante, and then the idea of specters: spirits or souls wandering about. This did seem the perfect place for them. Thus far we had seen no one but ourselves.

We took a slight jog to the left, and ahead was another stone monument, this one about twelve feet high and six feet across, with a peaked roof. It had brown double doors, each with a grate, and on either side, sculpted torches of the same brown metal. On top in large letters was ROSSINI. I smiled and eased out my breath. "Oh look." I touched Marguerite's hand, and she flinched slightly. "Rossini may be dead, but his joyous music certainly lives on."

She nodded, trying to smile. She was wearing a heavy purple coat with a black sable collar and cuffs. Her hat was black with purple feathers and a brim which shielded her from the rain. Jeanne had on a plain modest black coat and hat. We came to another pair of side paths. Marguerite reached out and took my hand, gave it a fierce squeeze.

"Wait here now. We shouldn't be long." Her voice had an odd pitch, and her black eyes were fixed on me. She tried to swallow, but could not.

"If you need me, just call—I shall come at once."

She nodded, not trusting herself to speak. She started down the path to the left, and Jeanne followed her. I sighed and shook my head. The drizzle was getting worse. I stepped closer to a nearby fir tree, seeking shelter so I wouldn't have to open my umbrella.

Nearby came a chorus of squawking caws. The black splotches of the crows covered a nearby fir tree.

I heard an inquisitive meow before I saw the cat. It was a grayish brown tabby, one who would certainly blend into the background. His yellow eyes stared up at me, and his long thin tail had risen in a typical sort of cat greeting.

"Well, hello." I pulled off my glove, bent and petted his head. He butted against my hand, then rubbed his side against my leg. As he went by, I saw that he was indeed a he. "It's nice to have some company." I scratched at his throat, then behind his ears. That made him circle about, then rise up slightly and rub his whiskers against my dress. He made a gruff sort of sound related to a meow. I squatted down and stroked his back vigorously. We chatted for a bit, then I stood up, and he trotted off in the direction Marguerite had gone. "*Au revoir, Monsieur Chat.*"

A chill breeze stirred the nearby fir branches. The sun wouldn't set for a while yet, but you could tell that night was approaching. At that moment, it was hard to believe the sun even existed–it was totally hidden, lost somewhere behind all the layers of gray. I was not really afraid, but I was suddenly glad I had not kept this visit a secret from Sherlock Holmes.

I glanced down the side path and saw the dark form of the cat racing toward me. "*Monsieur?*" I murmured, but he bounded past and slipped between two monuments to vanish. His once thin tail had greatly puffed out. I was frowning when I heard a cry which was akin to a moan.

I turned and strode quickly in the direction Marguerite and Jeanne had taken. Again I wished it was summer, that there were green leaves and light to break up all the monochromatic monotony surrounding me–that, and all these geometrically straight or curved lines of the slabs, tombs, roofs, which seemed unending. "Marguerite!" I shouted.

"Madame!" Jeanne's voice was ahead to the right.

I went round a very tall mausoleum with FAMILLE BREUNET above it, and I saw Marguerite's dark figure bent over, one knee and one hand on the ground, Jeanne beside her. I rushed toward them. Rising over them was a monumental slab of reddish-pink granite flecked with black; in the gray it almost seemed aglow. Chiseled into the stone in huge letters was LAVAL.

"Good Lord," I murmured. No wonder she had been afraid. The count was buried here.

I seized her arm and helped get her to her feet. She staggered. Her eyes were completely wild, the white showing about the pupils. "I saw... I saw..." She gulped for air. "It was *him*—and his dog—his..." She turned and grasped Jeanne's arms so tightly that she winced. "Did you see him—did you?"

Jeanne stared at her. "See what, madame?"

"The man—the man in black—and that dog."

Jeanne bit at her lip. "I..."

"Did you?—did you?"

"I... I saw nothing, madame. Nothing."

Marguerite released her, then clawed at her throat, her eyes turning to me. "It was his ghost—his spirit. He will not forgive me—he will not let me rest—*never*."

Now I took her arms. "I don't believe that—I don't believe in ghosts."

"But I saw him!" she moaned.

"Tell me exactly what you saw."

"It was a man all dressed in black, short and stout, with a full beard and a top hat, a taller top hat like the kind they wore back then—and that black dog, his dog—the same terrible dog I saw before. It growled at me, and I was so afraid—I thought it would attack me again, tear my throat out!"

"If it was a ghost dog it couldn't tear your throat out, could it now?"

Her breath was a sort of pant. "Couldn't it?"

"Of course not."

"It was him, the count. If the penance worked and the abbé's prayers, he would have left me in peace, but now..."

"That is just nonsense! It's quite possible you saw just an ordinary man and his dog walking through the graveyards."

"But Jeanne saw nothing!"

I turned to her. "Is this true?"

She hesitated only an instant. "Yes, *madame la docteur.*"

"You see?" Marguerite groaned.

"I don't believe in ghosts, and I never will. Come on, let's get away from here—you have done your penance."

"He will never leave me alone—never, never!"

I squeezed her arm hard until I saw pain register in her eyes. "That is enough of that. You have had a shock, but it is over with. Let's go. We all need a warm fire and something to eat and drink."

I could feel her tremble. "I am afraid. I am so afraid."

"I won't let anyone hurt you, I promise. Come—let's go. Let's get away from this wretched place."

I still had her by the arm and led her at a brisk pace. She was still shaking. All the stone and concrete blocks and slabs were oppressive; truly it felt like a necropolis—a city of the dead, made up of this myriad of tiny houses and churches, the ground itself planted with unseen coffins of wood and metal, each holding the moldering shell of a person. I stared up at the sky. This was not all there was—the soul was free; it was not trapped in the ground, but hovered or soared in the air, more bird than worm.

We came to the entranceway. The drizzle was changing to real rain, further obscuring everything. An old woman dressed all in black leaned on her cane, all hunched over. Gray-white hair showed under her voluminous black hat. "Not feeling well?" she croaked. She had an ever so faint English accent. I stared more closely at her dark eyes. Somehow they did not appear old. Violet saw that I recognized her, and one corner of her mouth rose in a brief half-smile.

"We need help," I muttered.

"I'll tell my husband," she said softly in the croaking voice. Marguerite and Jeanne had taken little notice of our brief exchange.

We soon found a carriage, a four-wheeler. Jeanne sat on one side, Marguerite and I on the other. We were well on our way, when Marguerite suddenly tried to stand up. "I have to get away—I have to get away—he is after me!" She made to grab the door handle, but I pulled her back down.

"No one is after you." I took her by both shoulders, then touched her cheek with my right hand. "No one. You are safe now."

"Am I?" She could not seem to stop shaking.

"*Yes.*"

When we reached Marguerite's townhouse, I made her walk up and down the block twice. I could see she was full of nervous energy, and I wanted her to use up some of it. I told her to breathe deeply, and I made reassuring comments as we walked. She did finally stop trembling. We went inside at last. I had sent Jeanne in earlier, and she was waiting for us. She took her mistress's coat, and I marched Marguerite into the sitting room and went to the sideboard. I poured an Armagnac for her and one for myself.

She shook her head. "I hate brandy–*hate it*."

"Think of it as medicine." I guided her to one end of the sofa, then returned for my own glass and sat almost next to her. I took a big gulp, which warmed my esophagus on its way down.

Jeanne hovered close by. "Is there anything I can do, *madame la docteur?*"

"No. Let us rest for a few minutes."

"Very good." She turned, and just then we heard the front bell ring. "Who can that be?" She left to go to the door.

A minute or two later Violet swept into the room. With her was a tall thin man, his black hair swept back off his high forehead, his nose like a bird of prey's beak and his eyes with their predatory ferocity. He wore a long black frock coat which fell almost to his knees.

"I have brought some reinforcements," Violet said.

Marguerite stared up at them, then away. Her earlier terror had abated, but she seemed numb or dazed. Holmes stood before her, refusing to be ignored. I stood, and she did the same.

"My name is Sherlock Holmes, Madame Hardy. You have heard of me."

Her lips parted, and she stared up at him. She closed her mouth without speaking.

"Your husband has engaged my services. I know you did not want that, but he–and I–have your best interests at heart. This has gone on long enough."

An odd laugh slipped free, and then she clamped her lips tightly together.

Holmes glanced at me. "And who might you be, madame?"

I gave him a curious stare.

"What is your name?"

"I am Dr. Michelle Doudet Vernier."

"Ah, a physician. I take it the lady is in your care?"

"So to speak."

"And what has happened?"

I hesitated only an instant. "We were at the cemetery. She thought she saw a man and a dog, the ghost of Count de Laval and his animal." The name made her eyes widen and fill again with fear.

"I do not believe in ghosts, Madame Hardy. Why would you think a man and his dog were ghosts?"

"Easy..." I whispered to her, even as I gave her arm a squeeze.

"He looked exactly like the count, and they were near, but Jeanne could not see them."

"Ah. She could not?" Jeanne was hovering nearby, and Holmes turned and swept toward her. She took half a step back. "So, mademoiselle, you did not see this man and his dog?"

She licked her lips, looked away, then back. "I... I cannot be sure."

"You cannot? You either saw them or you did not. Did you see them?"

"If... if madame saw them, then they must have been there, I suppose."

"A curious answer. You are not sure if you saw them?"

"It was so rainy and misty. I do not wish to contradict my mistress. Oh, I am not certain!" Her eyes had filled with tears.

Holmes turned back to Marguerite. "So you see, madame, perhaps your ghosts were creatures of substance after all."

Marguerite was staring at Jeanne. She looked exhausted. "Jeanne?" The maid said nothing.

Holmes crossed his arms. "Madame Hardy, I would like you and Dr. Doudet Vernier to come with me to my hotel. We can speak briefly and then have a good supper together."

"I'm not hungry," she said.

"All the same, will you come?"

She stared at him. She appeared totally spent. "I don't know."

"Please." She nodded at last. Holmes turned again to Jeanne. "Fetch her coat, mademoiselle." He turned again toward us. His gray eyes almost glowed. "Yes, this has gone on far too long."

Part Three,

Henry

Chapter Eleven

Wednesday night I did not sleep well. Perhaps Michelle and Violet had been in no real danger from Docre, but Michelle's willingness—her eagerness—to take risks, worried me. I thought of the many terrible things that might happen to her.

Holmes had told me to meet him at eight in the morning should I wish to go to Saint-Lazare with him and Violet, but given my mood, visiting a gloomy women's prison was the last thing I wanted to do. I rolled over in bed around 7:30 and went back to sleep for a while. Holmes was back by mid-morning, and Violet had business to attend to, so I joined him on two other visits.

The first was to a Madame Lebrun, the older sister of Simone Dujardin. She might have been a beautiful woman at one time, but she had become rather fat. Her plump face showed a certain weary lassitude and disinterest, but her sister's name made her scowl. Neither she nor her parents had seen Simone since she had been sent to prison. Madame Lebrun knew of her sister's release, but she had made no effort to find her or meet with her. The two girls had attended the same Catholic girls' school, but Simone had "gone bad" early on.

Holmes stared intently at her, his black eyebrows coming together over his long nose, forming two creases. He only seemed to be half listening. She told us she had no idea where her sister might be, nor did she care.

"Tell me, madame," Holmes said. "Do you have any children?"

She gave him a puzzled look. "Yes."

"A daughter?"

She laughed. "A good guess, sir."

"And only the one? Well, thank you for your time, madame."

We started down the winding staircase of the apartment building. "That was an utter waste of time," I said.

Holmes laughed softly. "You are mistaken, Henry. Did Madame Lebrun look at all familiar to you?"

I frowned. "Now that you mention it, she did. But I cannot say to whom."

"Ponder it for a while. Eventually it may come to you."

Next we went to the Reverend Algernon Sumners's lodgings in the Marais. The stout oaken door swung open, and there, an orange tabby cat at his ankles, stood the reverend. As before, he was wearing a black soutane, and the golden pince-nez was perched on his bulbous nose just above the abundant salt-and-pepper mustache and goatee. The smell of pipe tobacco assailed our nostrils, partly masking a strong odor of cat excrement. Behind him we saw the large desk strewn with papers and books, as well as the tall bookcases filled with thick volumes.

"Ah, Holmes, Dr. Vernier! Do come in."

Holmes came quickly to the point and asked if he had discovered anything about upcoming Black Masses in Paris. Sumners had

had to do some probing, but one of his sources had finally come through. A Mass was scheduled at an abandoned former convent near Saint-Sulpice on Saturday evening. He was not certain who would be presiding.

"Could it be Monsieur l'Abbé Docre?" Holmes asked.

"Docre!" I exclaimed.

Sumners puffed thoughtfully at his pipe. "I cannot rule it out. My sources agree that Docre is an enigmatical figure with an interest in the ladies, but not about whether he is an actual Satanist."

"Wouldn't a priest who can quote from Baudelaire's 'Litanies of Satan' be a likely candidate?"

Sumners shrugged. "It is suspicious, indeed, although perhaps he simply wants to know the enemy, so to speak."

"I think Henry and I shall be attending that Black Mass on Saturday evening."

Sumners sat upright and smiled broadly. "Oh, might I come along as well? I haven't been to a Black Mass in simply ages! Unlike the genuine article, they are never boring, and I always seem to learn something. Not, of course, that I condone blasphemy and sacrilege! All the same, they are quite interesting in a bizarre way."

Holmes stared at him, a sardonic smile gradually appearing. "We would be delighted to have your company."

We returned to the hotel and found Violet waiting for us. She took Holmes aside to speak with him. I sank wearily into one of the plush chairs. Holmes gave me a quick look, then resumed his conversation with her. He nodded once. Afterwards, he told me they had further business to attend to, but he asked me to wait for him there in the lobby after six o'clock.

I went to the front desk, hoping there was a message from Michelle and that she might join me later on that afternoon, but there was nothing. The weather was so wretched I resolved to spend time in the Louvre. I wandered about the long galleries glancing at masterpieces. I wondered if anyone had actually ever counted the number of fat cherubs drawn, painted or sculpted in the museum. How I wished for Michelle's company! This had hardly been any sort of holiday for the two of us. I saw more of her back home in London than I had in Paris.

I was in the lobby of the Meurice reading a newspaper at the appointed time when Holmes entered accompanied by Violet, Marguerite and Michelle. My eyes widened, and I frowned as I stood up. Holmes gave me a grim smile.

"Come along, Henry. I shall explain soon enough."

We went upstairs to Holmes's room, a suite, which had a comfortable sitting room. Holmes turned to Marguerite. She appeared somehow both exhausted yet keyed up. "Madame Hardy, this is my cousin and friend Dr. Henry Vernier."

She looked faintly puzzled. "Vernier?"

"He is Dr. Doudet Vernier's husband."

She seemed even more confused, looked at Michelle, then again at me. "I don't understand."

"I did not want to explain at your home," Holmes said. "Not in front of your maid."

"Why not?"

"Because she is in the employ of Simone Dujardin."

She certainly reacted to that: she flinched, her eyes opening wide. Instinctively, Michelle put her hand round her upper arm. "No, no," Marguerite said.

"I'll wager anything she has been in your service a year or less. How long exactly?"

"I... I..." You could see her struggle to concentrate. "Seven or eight months."

"Dujardin probably gave your prior maid a substantial sum to quit. Jeanne is the daughter of Dujardin's sister. I'm certain her mother knows nothing about it, but the girl must have met up with her aunt. Dujardin is probably paying Jeanne to spy on you, and I suspect she has convinced Jeanne of the righteousness of revenging herself upon you."

Marguerite closed her eyes as she sighed. "Not Jeanne. Not her, too. Oh Lord, can I trust no one?"

"You can trust *me*, madame. First, and above all, you must believe it when I tell you that the Devil or ghosts or diabolical curses are not involved in this business. Only human maleficence is at work. You did not see the Count de Laval's specter today. That was only Docre's servant disguised with a false beard. They also have a hound which resembles the count's dog. It was the same animal who approached you in front of your home last week. On that occasion, it was, no doubt, called back by one of those high-pitched whistles which only dogs can hear."

"Docre's servant? But the abbé could not have known about it—he wants to help me. And he is a priest."

"Yes, but he is also the lover of Simone Dujardin."

She shook her head. "No, no—that cannot be—he has taken a vow of chastity! He is a priest!"

Michelle sighed softly. "That vow means little to him, believe me."

"She's telling the truth," Violet said. "Docre is a garden variety lecher, and he is Dujardin's creature. You must believe us. We only want to help you."

Marguerite stared at Holmes. "All the same, it might have been a ghost—you cannot be certain."

"Madame, I was there. I was watching. I saw the man and the

dog, and I saw you nearly faint. I followed the man. I even spoke with him. I complimented him upon his dog. That white blaze on the dog's head is only makeup."

"But... but I did not see you."

Holmes smiled. "That is because I did not wish you to see me."

Violet nodded. "I was there, too. There were no ghosts, only a flesh-and-blood man and dog."

Marguerite's gaze shifted from Violet to Holmes, then to me, then to Michelle. "You are all in on this together," she murmured.

"Yes," Holmes said, "all in it together to help you."

"How can I trust you?"

Michelle again touched her arm. "You trust me, don't you? You must know I would not harm you, that I want to assist you. It is the same with these others. We can save you from that monstrous woman."

Marguerite put her lower lip between her teeth and lowered her eyes. "No one can help me. She is the Devil."

Holmes shook his head impatiently. "You give her too much credit."

"You do not know her, monsieur. You do not know who she is, what she is capable of. The Devil works through her—she is his tool."

"Madame, that attitude is not helpful. She is only a mortal. She may be evil, but she has no diabolical powers. She can be bested."

Marguerite's forehead had creased. "Can she?"

"Yes, but you must be honest with me, madame. You must work with me. Why don't you...? Please sit down."

Marguerite sat in the sofa, and Michelle joined her. Violet and I sat in the chairs, but Holmes remained standing. He began to pace in a way which reminded me of the big cats in the Lion House at the London Zoo.

"I know nearly everything, madame. You were a courtesan, most likely a celebrated one, but when you reached your late twenties, you must have seen the writing on the wall. Perhaps, too, you had wearied of your occupation and the triviality of the high society life. Furtive meetings with the likes of the Count de Laval must have grown tiresome. You wanted to retire while in your prime. Your affair with Lupin was probably based on mutual attraction. Perhaps you saw the *Madonna of the Apple* at the count's home or heard about it, and then it came up in a conversation with Lupin. He was amused and could not hold his tongue. He told you that the painting was his own invention, only a clever fake he had created based on Botticelli's Madonna with the Pomegranate. He must have boasted of his skill and ingenuity."

She shrank back into the corner of the sofa. "How can you know all these things?"

"And so the two of you concocted a scheme to steal the painting. Or rather, given all that I have heard about Lupin who was not particularly clever, *you* concocted a scheme. Lupin could then paint copies of his fake and sell each for a fortune. An ironic twist, that! There is always an underground market for stolen masterpieces. In this case rich Italians would have been interested, and perhaps a few American millionaires. Each would buy their copy, hide it away, and savor it in secret. Those forged paintings made you and Lupin rich, didn't they?"

She looked at him a long while, then jerked her head downward in a brusque movement.

"You didn't want to take any chances. Dead men tell no tales, as they say. The safest thing was to eliminate the count."

A sort of dull anguish showed in her eyes, and her lips parted. Michelle's lips drew back even as she set her hand on her forearm.

"The count enjoyed women, and the more the merrier. You and your friend Anne-Marie had already entertained him, but he was interested in a trio at his home. It was arranged for a time when his wife was away traveling. He must have let you in secretly after the servants had retired. You had met Simone Dujardin at the perfume counter at Au Printemps. You saw something in her, something cold and calculating, as well as a formidable intelligence. She was a kindred spirit, a younger version of yourself. You knew she would serve for your purposes. You invited her to be the third member of the trio and to join in the conspiracy. But you didn't tell her the real objective was the painting, not money or jewels. She could help in the theft, but then be left to take the blame. Somehow you planted a picture frame in her apartment, and you gave her the count's diamond ring. Lupin must have sent the telegram alerting the police. She was… the sacrificial goat.

"And so that fateful night, you tied up the count and gagged him. He thought it was only a game. But then… you stabbed him—you stabbed him through the heart and left Dujardin to take the blame."

Marguerite drew back as if she had been struck, and I felt a sort of sick pain low in my belly. Michelle looked horrified, but Violet scowled. Marguerite suddenly sprang to her feet and shook her head wildly. "*No, no, no.*"

"That was your plan—that was the way it was supposed to be."

Marguerite held her two hands outward, palms upward in supplication. "Yes, but I could not do it, monsieur!—I could not! It was the plan, but when I held the knife and saw his white belly…" She made a choking sobbing sound.

"You deny it then?"

She wiped at her eyes. "Monsieur, I have committed many

grave sins, but I am not a liar–not now. I blame myself for the count's death, but... I have returned to the Church. It is my consolation. I am a Catholic, and I believe in God. I swear to you by His most holy name that I did not kill the count, that I did not strike the blow."

Holmes's mouth compressed tightly. "Then who did?"

"You know everything, monsieur–*everything*–I see that. Then you must know who."

He sighed. "Yes, I suppose I do. It was Simone Dujardin, after all." A cold smile flickered over his lips. "The butcher's daughter."

"Yes." Marguerite had begun to cry. "I tried to stop her. I told her that somehow it would be all right, that we needn't kill him. She laughed at me, and then she stuck him as if he were only a pig or some other animal..." She shuddered. "It was horrible, horrible. He could not cry out because of the gag. Anne-Marie and I were both sick, but not her. So much blood–blood everywhere! She was proud of what she had done. I knew then–and ever since–that I had made a mistake, a terrible mistake; that my life was over, that my life was ruined, that..." She could not go on.

Holmes and Violet were pale and stern-looking, while Michelle was clearly distressed. I felt slightly sick myself. There was no doubt in my mind that Marguerite had told us the truth.

Holmes sighed at last. "So you went ahead and took the painting–probably after the other two women had left. You gave it to Lupin and let him paint his copies. You let him make you both rich."

"May God forgive me–I followed the plan."

Michelle rose, put her arm about her, and gently helped her sit back down on the sofa. "Sherlock, isn't this enough?" Michelle's voice shook.

He shrugged. "For now, yes."

Violet folded her arms, then glanced about. "I think we all need something to drink." She stood up and walked toward the sideboard with its bottles and glasses.

"Heavens, yes," I groaned.

Michelle still had her arm around Marguerite. "It's done now, my dear." She looked at Violet. "She hates brandy. Give her anything but brandy." The two women sat on the sofa.

"She hates brandy?" I said dully.

Violet picked up a bottle and examined the label. Holmes stared down at Michelle and Marguerite. Michelle took out a handkerchief and offered it to the other woman. She wiped at her eyes and wept quietly. Violet poured some amber liquid from a decanter into one glass, then whiskey from a bottle into another. She used the gasogene to add soda water, then went to Michelle and Marguerite.

"Brandy for you." She gave a snifter to Michelle. "And whiskey and soda for you." Marguerite wiped at her eyes with the handkerchief, then took the glass. Violet stared at Holmes and me. "Gentlemen?"

"Whiskey and soda," Holmes said.

"Brandy," I mumbled. I thought of trying to help, but I felt somehow incapable of moving.

Violet brought us our drinks. I took a big swallow, felt the liquid smolder its way down. Violet and Holmes sat down. We all quietly sipped at our drinks. Marguerite was still crying, but she would pause to take an occasional swallow of the whiskey and soda. The clock on the mantle ticked loudly, and we could hear the sound of traffic on the Rue de Rivoli below.

Marguerite stopped crying at last, drew in a great shuddery breath, then let her head briefly fall back against the sofa. She downed the last of her drink. Her eyes were red, and she looked absolutely exhausted. She stared at Holmes. "What now, monsieur?"

"Will you be guided by me, Madame Hardy?"

"Yes. I am so tired of this all. Will it ever end?"

Holmes's mouth twisted. "I suspect Monsieur l'Abbé Docre told you that if your prayers at the tomb did not work, a special ceremony would be required, a sort of exorcism."

She frowned, a strange smile briefly appearing. "You do know everything."

"It is this Saturday evening, is it not? He plans a Black Mass."

The fear showed in her eyes. "Then the Devil..."

"The Devil has nothing to do with this! It is the two of them, Dujardin and the priest. You must play along with them and go. Of course, he won't tell you it is going to be a Black Mass." She looked alarmed, but he raised his hand. "But Henry and I shall be there, too."

Michelle set her hand on Marguerite's. "And I shall accompany you."

I clenched my teeth and slowly eased my breath out. "*Michelle.*" Her eyes were defiant. I felt the sudden fear in my chest. I knew it would be futile to argue with her.

Violet nodded. "And I shall also go with Mr. Holmes."

Holmes's gray eyes were troubled. "I wish there were another way. She has three lodgings that I know of in Paris, but she has disappeared, completely vanished. She is a wild animal stalking her prey, but she senses that she is being pursued. She knows I am on her trail. She is cautious, but she will not be able to resist this opportunity, especially since you and Michelle will say that Mr. Sherlock Holmes was suddenly called back to London on urgent business even before he could speak with you. You will mention that in front of Jeanne, who will doubtlessly tell her aunt."

"I shall do as you say." She stared intently at Holmes. "I would do anything to be free of her once and for all. I dream of it, dream of the time before... Do you think I might possibly be able to pay her to leave me alone?"

Holmes frowned fiercely. "No, I do not think so."

A wan smile pulled at her lips. "She wants me dead, doesn't she?"

Holmes stared at her. "I am not so sure. If that was all there was to it... I think she could have killed you by now if that was her primary objective. I think... I think she wants you to suffer."

Marguerite's mouth opened wide, and a second later she went, "*Ah.*" She drew in her breath, then laughed once. "Of course. Well, she has certainly succeeded in her objective." You could see the truth of that in her dark eyes.

Holmes still looked troubled. "I am hopeful... I..." His frown returned.

"They should both be locked up!" I exclaimed. "Or... if anyone deserves the guillotine, it is her! She has murdered three people, and that priest must have helped her kill Anne-Marie. She truly is like a savage beast, one not fit for human society!" Violet was staring oddly at me, an ironic smile pulling at her mouth. "Do you find this amusing, Violet?"

She shook her head. "No, Henry, not really. I envy you your moral fervor."

Marguerite's dark brows had come together, her eyes half-closed. "You are wrong, you know, Monsieur Holmes, when you say the Devil had nothing to do with it. The Devil has everything to do with it. She truly is his tool, his way of..." She shuddered. "I also was his tool once, and I did not even realize it. I was so proud, so proud of myself. I was a fool. I see that now. Pride is... pride is like an open doorway, an invitation to the Devil. If you leave that door open, you can be sure he will come in." Her eyes were desolate.

"Ah," Violet murmured softly.

Michelle gripped Marguerite's hand. "But in your case, you have closed that door. He cannot get at you now."

"I pray you are right."

Holmes had been listening, his face grim. "Madame Hardy, all these thoughts about the Devil—or curses, or supernatural poisons, or specters—only makes things worse. We are all poor weak creatures, but we have our reasons. That is what raises us above the animals. In a case like this, you must cling to your reason. You must not surrender to dark fantasies or to despair. That way lay only ruin."

Marguerite sighed softly. "I do not know if I believe in reason."

"It is all we have."

Michelle and Violet exchanged a look. Violet spoke first. "That is most certainly not all we have. There is God, after all."

"And there is love," Michelle said.

Violet smoothed a tendril of black hair off her face and drew in her breath. Holmes was staring at her. The corners of her mouth rose and fell. She stared down at the empty brandy snifter. "But we must not start philosophizing, not now—not when it is time for dinner."

Marguerite gave her an incredulous look. "I cannot eat."

"You could sit with us."

Marguerite shook her head. "I want to go home."

"As you wish," Holmes said. He swallowed the last of his drink and set down the glass.

"I shall keep her company," Michelle said. I eased my breath out slowly but said nothing.

"Why don't you have dinner with Henry and Mr. Holmes?" Violet said to Michelle. "I can go with her." Marguerite's expression made it clear she wanted Michelle to stay with her. "Or perhaps not. Instead... it shall be a ladies' night again! I assume you can feed us?" Marguerite nodded. "In that case, we shall leave the gentlemen to dine in peace." She stood up.

The rest of us rose. My feelings must have been evident from my expression. Violet touched my arm with her long slender fingers. "Cheer up, Henry. Tomorrow you can see your bride, I promise you! In fact..." She turned to face the others. "I would like you all to join me for a lunch in the country. We can forget this wretched business for an afternoon, and you can see my home in Auteuil and meet Berthe and Alphonse. Collins and Gertrude are eager to see everyone again." She glanced at Marguerite. "And you are welcome to come, too."

Marguerite still looked dazed. "I do not know."

"A change of scenery will do you good."

Holmes raised his hand. "One word, Madame Hardy. Your maid and the abbé must suspect nothing. You must try to act the same as ever with them. And as I said, you must mention in Jeanne's hearing that Sherlock Holmes was called away on important business—even before he could speak with you. Say, too, that he will return next week and will meet with you then. That should give matters a sense of urgency."

The ladies started for the door, while I stared at Holmes glumly and shook my head. Michelle hesitated at the door. "Go on down," she said to the two women, "I shall join you in a moment." She closed the door behind them, then turned to Holmes. "Sherlock, you must send for her husband. She has dealt with this on her own for long enough. She needs him by her side."

Holmes's brow furrowed. "Do you think so?"

"I am certain of it!"

"Very well, I shall telegraph him. He is still in Scotland, I believe, and it will take him at least two days to get here. Hopefully things will be resolved by then."

"You should have sent for him long ago."

"I had certainly thought of it. Believe me, I do not enjoy seeing Madame Hardy suffer. I would spare her if I could. All the same, if her husband were here, he would be one more target, one more way Dujardin would have to torment her."

Michelle paled slightly. "I had not thought of that. *Au revoir*, then." Her eyes still troubled, she turned toward the door, stopped, then walked over to me, smiling. She pulled off her glove and touched my cheek with her hand. "Poor darling." She kissed me lightly on the lips. "I shall see you tomorrow. A few hours' respite in the country does sound wonderful." I took her hand and kissed her knuckles. She smiled again, then turned and left.

I shook my head. "Well, Sherlock, time for another tête-à-tête dinner together in Paris, the great capitol of romance!"

Holmes laughed. "A good bottle of Bordeaux will help raise our spirits." He shook his head. "We have certainly earned it. What a day." His smile faded away.

"What is it?" I asked.

"I am glad Madame Hardy did not kill the count. That would have... complicated matters."

The sun had broken through long gray strips of cloud, setting the grass, the moss, the green bushes and a fir tree aglow with a wintry light. Yellow glistened off the black feathers of the chickens, and their red combs and wattles were radiant in the sun. They strutted about behind the wire fence, clucking and cooing as they pecked at the earth. Behind them was their sanctuary, a well-built coop where they could lay their eggs. Holmes and I had worn tweed suits for our Auteuil visit, and his battered woolen walking hat somehow softened his stark angular visage.

He gave an appreciative nod. "Magnificent birds. You must be regular consumers of omelets."

Violet laughed. "Indeed we are."

The cold had brought a flush to Michelle's fair skin, and she looked quite happy. Her right hand grasped my arm tightly. "I've always been curiously fond of chickens. A pity, Henry, that we cannot raise them in the city."

I stared in disbelief. "They are only rather dumb birds."

"They may not be as clever as crows," Holmes said, "but they are hardly stupid."

Violet clapped her gloved hands together. "Bravo, Mr. Holmes! I would not have thought you would be an admirer of our feathered friends."

"I grew up in the countryside, and someday I hope to retire there."

Violet cocked her head slightly, smiling. "You must certainly be joking!"

"Not in the least. London has its many attractions, not the least of which are all the musical events, but who could actually prefer the wretched air of a London winter? 'Air' is actually rather generous for the foul yellow fog. One can hardly breathe it. No, one of these days I shall weary of the detective business and flee to the country. I shall play my violin for an hour or two every day and write my memoirs to correct Watson's many falsehoods, and of course, I shall raise chickens."

Violet slipped her hand about his arm. "Bravo for you! It seems an enviable life, but I cannot really believe you."

Holmes glanced down at her. "No? And why not?"

She stared up at him, her head held high in a way which emphasized her long slender throat. In the sunlight her brown eyes were not so dark, had more color in them. "Because you enjoy the thrill of the chase, and the challenge of a worthy case. I think you would soon grow bored in the country and long for London, wretched fog and all."

He shrugged. "Perhaps. But a wise man knows when it is time to quit, when it is time to retreat from the battles of life."

Violet smiled. "You are not one to retreat—not you."

He stared closely at her, smiling in turn. "Neither are you."

Violet gazed again down at the earth where the hens pecked about searching for fragments of grain. "Some of us humans may have the pleasure of retiring, but for chickens, retirement—alas!—means one thing. My cook Madame Parigaux is quite strict. Once they stop laying, a twist of the neck and straight to the pot with them!

"Well, our little tour is almost finished. Last would be that row of espaliered apple trees." She raised her gloved hand to point at the stone wall with its series of trees wired together, thick trunks with the lateral branches interleaving like fingers. A few apples still remained, but the majority must have been harvested. "The French invented espaliered trees, and they are the masters. There are some splendid examples in the Jardin du Luxembourg. And now, our lunch must be nearly ready."

She and Holmes started back for the house, her hand still grasping his arm lightly, and Michelle and I followed. Violet had exchanged her fancy boots for a pair of wooden clogs. Michelle, Holmes and I wore sensible shoes, so the wet grass and stretches of mud were not a problem. Marguerite, on the other hand, had dressed more formally and had not wanted to dirty her fancy boots or twist an ankle. She was inside with the two couples: Collins and Gertrude, Alphonse and Berthe.

The old house was constructed of stone, but some of the trim was painted light blue, which rendered it more cheerful. A pathway of brick led to the back door, a row of rhododendron bushes to one side, the lawn to the other. Large trees grew about the property, their leaves gone by now—up ahead was a matted yellow-brown carpet under the barren branches. The dwelling was truly a refuge from the turmoil of Paris with its block after block of apartment buildings and shops.

Violet opened the door for us, stepped in last and slipped out of the muddy clogs. She sat down on a wooden bench to put on her shoes. We all hung up our coats, then went to the sitting room. Alphonse was leaning forward at his end of the sofa speaking French to Marguerite in an animated manner. Berthe listened quietly.

Being situated between the two women made Alphonse seem even smaller. His frame was slight and wiry; his thin wrists and gawky neck stuck out from the white shirt cuffs and collar. He was probably in his thirties, but his hair was already receding. No doubt by way of compensation, he sported an enormous black mustache which drooped to his jawline and dominated his face. Marguerite's wrists and hands were bigger than Alphonse's, her shoulders broader, too, but Berthe was truly colossal—her hands with the broad knuckles and huge fingers bested us all. As I had suspected, when we were all introduced, she was the only woman I had ever met who actually made Michelle appear small.

Collins and Gertrude sat on the nearby love seat. He was ruddy, blond and tall, while she was fair-skinned, dark-haired and short. They were frowning slightly, probably because they could not understand Alphonse. Violet had explained that the two couples had been trying to teach the other couple their own language. It was slow going, no doubt, and I had already noticed that Alphonse's French was not exactly up to the standard of *l'Académie Française!*

Madame Parigaux appeared. "*À table*," she cried, "*à table!*"

We all went to the dining room and sat around the large oval table, and then Madame Parigaux appeared with a china platter bearing a steaming leg of roast pork, the smell delectable. "Would you do the honors, Mr. Holmes?" Violet asked.

"Gladly, madam."

The platter was placed before him. He picked up the knife and a sharpening steel, made a few passes across the blade, then carefully touched the edge. "An excellent knife." He began to carve, while Madame Parigaux reappeared with a large bowl of potatoes and another with carrots and other vegetables.

"And, Henry, could you pour the wine?" Two open bottles of red were at my end of the table. I stood, and began to fill everyone's glass.

The meal was not the fancy cuisine of an expensive Parisian restaurant, but it was simple and delicious. Everyone seemed hungry, including Marguerite. I paused in my meal to occasionally refill the wine glasses, while Holmes was also eager to slice and pass out more meat. Surprisingly, although he was the smallest of us at the table except for Gertrude, Alphonse ate by far the most. The wine seemed to stimulate conversation. Madame Parigaux brought out two more bottles. Gertrude and Collins were talking with Michelle about how different Paris was from London. At the other end of the table, we were all speaking French. After the meat and vegetables, a salad course was served, then a cheese plate, and finally an apple tart made from the fruit of Violet's espaliered trees.

Afterwards Violet brought out a flask of apple brandy from Normandy, and we lingered a long while at the table. The light coming through the nearby window still had a welcome golden hue: the sun had not been out for an entire afternoon in many days. Michelle and Marguerite had been discussing the difficulties in finding gloves and boots for larger women like themselves, but Berthe had laughed and said they knew nothing! Her secret was to buy men's things. Holmes and Violet were discussing breeds of chickens, something I would not have believed if I had not actually heard it. I savored the brandy even as my eyes lingered on Michelle. She had a certain way of smiling, of curving her lips upward mostly at the corners.

I covered my mouth, stifling a yawn. "It's a good thing we are not going anywhere tonight," I said. "I'm far too sleepy." Too late, I realized my blunder: I must have reminded Marguerite of the Black Mass tomorrow night. Her mouth stiffened, her smile faltering. No doubt it was always at the back of her mind. She had told us that Docre had visited that morning and proudly claimed that his ceremony would block the Devil's curse once and for all, turning it back upon its perpetrator.

Violet had been watching Marguerite, too. She lowered her arms, stretching them downwards and spreading her fingers. "Perhaps we should adjourn to the sitting room. It is more comfortable. Moreover, I think some entertainment might be in order."

"Entertainment?" Holmes said.

"Musical entertainment."

He smiled. "No doubt you have your violin with you, that splendid Guarneri del Gesù. You must play for us."

"I had hoped *you* might play for us, Mr. Holmes."

"I am sorely out of practice, while you on the other hand... I suspect you must play every day."

"I try to, at least an hour."

"Then I would be hopelessly outmatched."

She laughed. "This is not a competition! It is music, after all, not chess or croquet."

Marguerite looked faintly puzzled. "This is not a joke? Do you both actually play the violin?"

Michelle leaned over and touched her forearm. "They both play very well indeed."

Alphonse pulled off his napkin and set it on the table, then folded his arms. "I can vouch for her. I like to listen to her practice. I did not know the violin before I came to live here. It is a wonderful thing."

Gertrude nodded enthusiastically. "She plays even better now than she did back in London."

Violet smiled and set her long slender hand on Holmes's wrist. He was smiling faintly, but something in his eyes changed. "So will you play for us?" she asked.

"I suggest we share the stage, and ladies must go first."

She laughed. "You know, of course, what we must play." He gave her a puzzled look. "Bach's First Partita." He gave a slight nod. It was the first thing they had heard the other play, and I knew it was a favorite of them both. "Very well—to the sitting room, then, which shall act as our auditorium!"

There were contented sighs or yawns as we rose and stretched briefly, then made our way into the next room. I collapsed into the corner of the sofa, and Michelle sank down beside me and grasped my hand. I smiled at her. "It is good to see you at last, stranger," I said. Marguerite had sat at the other end of the sofa, and she smiled wistfully at us.

Michelle touched my cheek with her fingers. "You know I shall make it up to you."

Violet came into the room with her violin in one hand, the bow in the other. Holmes was standing next to the fireplace. "I suggest," she said, "that we alternate movements as we play." She looked around at us all. "There are eight parts in the partita, four dance movements, and each has its so-called double, a faster variant."

Holmes frowned slightly. "A Bach partita is meant to be played through in its entirety, not divided up piecemeal."

"Yes, but this is not the Royal Albert Hall. No one will be reviewing us for *The Times.* That way our audience will hear each section twice in a row. It will be more familiar the second time, and they will also be able to hear the contrast in our playing."

"Yes, with my inferior version always coming second! Very well, but surely the movement and its double must be played together. They are, after all, related, a sort of theme and variation."

"Agreed. And are you certain you would not like to go first?"

He swept his long fingers about in a graceful arc, part of a mock bow. "Courtesy demands that the ladies take precedence."

"Very well. I should warn you all, the partita takes about half an hour, so with two of us, it will last an hour. However, if it becomes tiresome, simply let us know, and the ordeal will cease. Is everyone comfortable?"

Holmes raised one hand. "And by the way, unless you wish us to stop entirely, no applause, catcalls, or distracting comments between movements. We must maintain our concentration."

Violet gave an emphatic nod. "Well put." She raised the violin, played a short melody, then adjusted the tuning pegs. This went on until she played a long sustained note. "What do you think?" she asked Holmes.

"Excellently tuned, madam."

She had a handkerchief under the violin, and she tucked both under her chin. She slowly drew in her breath, raised the bow and closed her eyes, then drew the bow along the string. Her feet were planted firmly apart, and she swayed slightly from side to side in time with the music. The tone was warm, full and resonant in the small sitting room; the long line of Bach's music rose and fell like some soaring bird doing heavenly acrobatics. No energy was wasted on gratuitous movement; she was quite relaxed. Her eyes remained closed. Every so often her black brows would come slightly together, a brief hint of a frown which came and went, and occasionally a sort of pleased smile stirred her lips. Her dress was of a plain purple muslin, a rather austere cut that suited her playing. Her white face and hands stood out against the purple and against the black of her bound-up hair. You could sense that her entire body went into the music, that she played with more than her fingers, hands and arms. Holmes watched her, his face stern, but his gray eyes showed admiration and wonder.

The music itself was extraordinary. I could not read music or follow musical forms or variations in any intellectual manner. All the same, Bach's music was its own sort of language which spoke to the beauties and mysteries of life. At that level, it was irresistible. Occasionally I felt I understood, but that came and went—and always there was motion, that long line of profound melody sweeping ever forward. She paused briefly at the end of the first part, took a long slow breath, then began the double section. Again the music poured forth, the tempo faster than before.

Only after the last note had died away did she open her eyes. She drew in her breath again, then lowered the violin and the bow. Unable to exactly follow his own strictures, Holmes mouthed the silent word "bravo," then took the instrument from her and settled it under his own jaw. It was immediately apparent how much longer and leaner his face was than hers—and his tall lanky body, as well. He had a good half-foot on her. He raised the bow, frowned rather fiercely, then relaxed and began to play.

If playing was a sort of dance, you could see they both knew the moves, but each had their own unique style. His was not quite so relaxed as hers, and his motions were broader. At times there was almost a ferocity in his eyes, but the music was best when he was calmer. He played better as the piece went on. Once or twice he did briefly close his eyes. He seemed to be seeking something, searching for it in the music, something you could never quite find but the quest itself was the satisfaction. He played perhaps a trifle faster than her. One thing was certain: anyone who actually heard him play Bach like this could never subscribe to Watson's flawed portrayal of him as all brain with no heart or passion! The second section, the double, was a bit slower than hers, but very clean and precise.

When he finished, Michelle and I exchanged a look. We had heard them play before, but never quite like this. Clearly they inspired one another. It became more and more obvious as our concert progressed—that, and the obvious fact that they were playing to one another, nearly oblivious to the rest of us. If the music was a language, they were speaking it. Occasionally as he listened to her, Holmes would give his head a brief shake in disbelief and admiration. Violet, in turn, folded her arms and stared at him in rapt attention as he played. None of us looked bored, none of us said anything, and we hardly moved during the brief intervals while the violin was transferred.

Violet played her second double at an unbelievable speed, the bow rising and falling, the slender fingers of her left hand dancing along the string. Even if it had not produced such beautiful music, it would have been a phenomenal physical feat in and of itself. When he took the violin from her, Holmes shook his head, perhaps resigned to the fact he could never play that fast himself, and indeed, when his turn came, it was slower, but still at a breakneck speed, the line of the music itself somehow a bit more precarious, on edge. He looked greatly relieved when he finished, and she smiled as she took the violin.

They played on, and yellow-white shafts of light streamed from the two large windows, motes of dust swimming along to the music. I closed my eyes to listen more intently. Again, I had the feeling I could almost understand the language of Bach. Occasionally two or even three voices spoke at the same time; how amazing that a single violin could produce multiple melodies all at once. The minutes and seconds swept along with the notes, part of some vast universal music. But it was hard not to watch Violet and Holmes, hard to ignore two such artists completely and totally caught up in their work. Violet finished at last, a crescendo ending in a final downward swoop of the bow on a long low note.

Holmes eased out a long sigh, obviously trying to keep silent, then touched his hands together, the long fingers outspread, as he gave a slight bow in her direction. He took the violin and played his own rendition of the last movement and its double. It was curious that they could play the same notes on the same instrument, but it was different, the music reflecting each person's own spiritual and physical dimension, as well as the odd quirk of chance which made the notes come out a certain way at a certain point in time. When Holmes finished at last, he lowered the bow and the violin, then wiped at his forehead with the back of his left hand, smiling even as he finally allowed himself an audible sigh.

The silence of the room was something we all savored.

"Bravo," Violet murmured at last. "Bravo."

"Bravo indeed!" Michelle exclaimed, and we all began to clap.

Holmes hesitated an instant, then took Violet's hand. They both bowed deeply from the waist. Violet appeared simply radiant, whiles Holmes looked slightly exhausted but exuberant. They bowed again. No one clapped harder than Marguerite. At last we all stood up. Holmes took Violet's hand with both of his and pressed it tightly to his chest, his eyes staring down at her. A crooked smile pulled at her lips. If I had had any lingering doubts whether they still loved one another, they were certainly resolved.

Everyone had stood up except Marguerite. She had pulled a handkerchief from her pocket and dabbed at her eyes. Michelle went over and put her hand on her shoulder. Marguerite's dark eyes stared up at her, glistening faintly. "Are you all right?" Michelle asked.

"Oh yes. I have never heard such music." Her face was pale alongside her burgundy silk dress. "I have been to the symphony, of course, but never so close as this. I did not know such music was even possible." She stood at last, wiped again at her eyes and thrust the handkerchief back into a pocket.

Violet stepped closer. "Did you like it?"

"Oh yes! You... you made me forget everything for an hour. It was so lovely. I hope..." Her eyes had a familiar desolation. "I hope I can hear you both play again."

Violet smiled and gave her hand a squeeze. "I promise you shall."

Chapter Twelve

A cold hard rain fell on Saturday afternoon. By evening, it had ended, but the sky was a flat dark iron-gray, with only a faint pink or yellow showing from the city lights. We took a carriage to a nearby street and walked to our object. Sumners had explained that it had been an Ursuline convent until the Revolution, when it was abandoned and stripped of all its religious trappings. An eccentric old man had bought the buildings some twenty years ago and offered its chapel for Black Masses. Apparently this was a favorite spot in Paris for such ceremonies, one truly consecrated, over time, to Satan.

For once, Sumners had dispensed with his soutane, even as Holmes and I had set aside our frock coats. We three men all wore dark suits and black overcoats, while Holmes and I also had on bowler hats. However, Sumners still sported an incongruous black hat, often worn by French clergy, one with a wide brim which curved up slightly on either side. The hat emphasized the mass of graying bobbed and curling hair about his plump face. Violet also wore a black coat, along with a black veil loosely draped around her head; in the chapel she could lower it to hide her face so Docre would not recognize her.

The only one of us in particularly good spirits was Sumners. "How long it has been since I have attended a Black Mass!" he had exclaimed cheerfully.

Holmes and Violet were grim. I was terribly uneasy, worried sick about Michelle. I had tried—futilely, I knew in advance—to talk her out of going with Marguerite, but she was adamant that Marguerite could not go alone. Holmes had told us he planned to take along his revolver, and I had told him that at the first sign of trouble—at the first sign the two women were threatened in any way—he must shoot first and ask questions later. He had sternly said he would do so.

I had said something of my fears in the carriage, and Sumners tried, in a curious sort of way, to reassure me. "The majority of the participants are inevitably women, you know, just as with the regular Mass, and most are harmless hysterics of one variety or another. The few men are generally older or infirm."

But I was worried more about Docre than the congregation—even though, as Michelle had repeatedly and rather comically stated, she could probably best him in a fair fight. We left the main street and went down a dark narrow alleyway. At the end was a high stone wall, the leaves of some greenery rustling softly on the other side. Sumners stopped before a door with a metal grating and rang a bell. A few seconds later bright yellow-white light from a lantern shone through the bars. "*Oui?*" said a woman's voice.

"We are here for the ceremony," Sumners said in French.

"The password?"

"Astarté."

"*Entrez, messieurs.*" The door swung open, revealing a stooped old crone in tattered black holding the lantern. "Do you know the way?"

"Yes," Sumners said.

She retreated to a sort of tent nearby which served as her lodge and which would protect her from the rain. We followed a flagstone path through a small garden with ornate palms rising on either side, then went up three steps. Sumners pulled open one of the massive oaken doors, and we stepped into a vestibule illuminated only by the flickering candles of two small red lamps. Sumners opened another door, and we entered a dark cavernous chamber.

The noxious smell was the first thing you noticed—something close, warm, humid, burnt and acrid which assailed the nostrils. Looking about, I saw two braziers which gave off a foul dark smoke. "What a stench," I murmured.

"Satanic incense," Sumners said.

"Fittingly enough," Violet said. "It is certainly not heavenly."

"What on earth makes such a smell?" I asked.

"Asphalt from the street, leaves of henbane, dried nightshade and myrrh are a few of the preferred ingredients," said Sumners.

The big room had old beams overhead, its walls cracked and dingy, the windows hidden by heavy curtains. The pink glass pendants of brass chandeliers cast a feeble light. At the far end was an altar. An altar boy in white was lighting tall black candles. Behind the altar was an elaborate golden tabernacle, and over it, what must be a painting and a crucifix. Both were hidden by heavy canvas coverings. Chairs of every variety were lined up in informal rows, with a few divans near the doorway. We made our way down an aisle toward the altar.

Sumners had been right: most of the participants were women, both young and old. Some were obviously deranged, their eyes wild, their smiles lunatic and inappropriate. In a corner was an old man in a frock coat with an enormous graying goatee and mustache worthy of Louis-Napoleon. A few other men were scattered about, none of them young. Holmes guided Violet into the third row, and Sumners and I turned to follow him. She had wrapped her veil about the lower part of her face.

I sat down in an overstuffed chair which appeared comfortable, but turned out to have a loose spring which stuck into my lower back. I squirmed about. The altar boy finished lighting the black candles, then turned and smiled at us. I smiled back reflexively, but it faded as I realized this was no boy at all, but only a small, stooped old man, his wrinkled face covered with some garish makeup. With a nod, he passed us.

Sumners must have noticed my expression. "Everything is an inversion with the Black Mass. Instead of innocent boys as altar servers, we have debauched old sodomites."

"But he is wearing white," I said.

"Part of the masquerade to fool Madame Hardy. At some point he will cast off his garment, and the blasphemous objects behind the altar will also be revealed."

Violet spoke very softly, her voice almost a moan. "How filthy."

Holmes said nothing, but he looked forbidding indeed, and angry.

"This air in here is so dreadful," I said, "so stifling. I can hardly breathe."

I hoped we would not have to wait long. All about us were the low whispers and soft voices of the women, as well as an occasional strange-sounding laugh. At last, a murmur swept through the congregation, and people stood. Docre had appeared at the back of the church, and he was slowly advancing, his hands clasped before him, the two altar servers in white at his side. He wore a bulky white robe belted with a rope. Next came Marguerite, and behind her, Michelle.

A wave of fear began in my belly, washed through my chest, even as I clenched my teeth. This was all insanity–complete insanity! If I had any sense, I would take Michelle and drag her out of here immediately. Holmes's eyes were fixed on me, and he gave a slight nod. His hand was in his pocket, no doubt clasping the revolver handle. As they passed us, I could see that Marguerite was terrified. Michelle, on the other hand, gave me a defiant smile. Not for the first time, I wished she were slightly less courageous.

Docre stopped before the altar and turned to face the congregation. His youthful aristocratic beauty, the aquiline nose and fine cheekbones, the black curly hair, seemed curiously out of place, especially alongside his two grotesque aged acolytes. He raised his white graceful gentleman's hands.

"Welcome, brothers and sisters! We are gathered tonight to welcome a new member into our fold, a lost soul who has been found." He gestured toward Marguerite, who turned and looked uneasily about the room. She could not bring herself to smile. He set his hand on her shoulder, and she flinched. His smile was slightly lunatic, his eyes wild. I wondered if he had taken some drug or if this was only the euphoria of madness.

"You must forget all that you think you know if you are to be saved–in fact, to be saved, you must be damned! You must cast aside the old and embrace the new. You must forget the crucified fool and embrace our true Master!" There were cries of approval, and Marguerite took half a step backward.

"Oh no, no," she murmured, shaking her head.

Docre and the altar boys quickly removed and threw aside

their white robes. The two old men were wearing red cassocks. Docre wore a grotesque chasuble of fiery red with the figure of a black billy goat showing his horns—and, I realized suddenly, he wore nothing else save a pair of red silken slippers! I could see his bare legs, arms and flank under the chasuble. He gave an exultant laugh, which made Marguerite step back to Michelle who put her arm around her. One of the men gave Docre a hat, which he quickly put on, also bright red, with two long red cloth horns like those of a bull. Were the situation not so grave, I would have wanted to laugh—he looked frankly absurd, like some clown or burlesque figure from the *commedia dell'arte* rather than a priest.

The two acolytes went behind the altar and pulled away the coverings, revealing a large tapestry of a dragon-like Satan rising from the fires of Hell, and a huge deranged crucifix, a naked Christ with an enormous member protruding grotesquely like Pinocchio's nose, equally and ridiculously long. One did not have to be a devout Catholic to find the figure blasphemous and disturbing.

"You have been given a second chance, Madame Hardy—a chance to be born anew by dedicating yourself to Satan." He whirled about and raised his arms toward the leering figure on the tapestry. I was grateful the chasuble hid his backside. "Master of Slanders, dispenser of the benefits of crime, administrator of sumptuous sins and great vices, Satan, thee we adore, reasonable God, just God!

"Superadmirable legate of false trances, thou receivest our beseeching tears; thou savest the honor of families by aborting wombs impregnated in the forgetfulness of the good orgasm; thou dost suggest to the mother the hastening of untimely birth, and thine obstetrics spares the still-born children the anguish of maturity, the contamination of original sin. Mainstay of the despairing poor, cordial of the vanquished, it is thou who endowest them with hypocrisy and ingratitude that they may defend themselves against the children of God, the rich! Great suzerain of virility, thou dost not demand the futile offerings of chaste loins; thou alone receivest the carnal supplications of our divine lust! Thou who dost fertilize the brain of man whom injustice has crushed, who breathest into him the idea of vengeance, who incitest him to calumny, violence, theft and murder, to thee we pray, great God, king of the disinherited, son who art to overthrow the inexorable Father!"

He paused for a second, and Sumners murmured, "A nice Manichean touch, that."

Docre resumed his litany of praise to Satan and to sin. Marguerite stood silently before his jumbled incoherent stream of words, her face white. Michelle still had her arm around her. After finally finishing his paean to Satan, Docre swung an arm toward the horrible crucifix behind the altar: "Jesus, artisan of hoaxes, bandit of homage, robber of affection, hear!—fugitive god, mute god, shyster god!" Thus began a torrent of abuse directed toward Christ. Again, one need not be a devout Catholic to find Docre's cruel blasphemous ravings upsetting. He ended by proclaiming that he would drive deeper the nails into His hands and open another wound in His side with the spear!

He whirled about and grasped a golden chalice from the altar, then withdrew, of all things, a black host and held it up. "And soon we shall consume your foul and polluted body!" Many of the women had begun to shriek and groan, to sway back and forth.

I clenched my teeth tightly. The fetid atmosphere made me feel as if I was suffocating. I could not endure much more of this. Come what may, I was nearly ready to drag Michelle and Marguerite from this dreadful place.

Docre laughed gleefully. "Are you ready to join us in our

sacrament, Madame Hardy?" She could not speak, but she shook her head emphatically. "No? A pity, that." He put the black host back in the chalice and set the goblet upon the altar. "Perhaps you can be persuaded. Perhaps *she* can persuade you."

Marguerite stared at him, her eyes wary. He stepped back, then swung his arm round toward the right. He did look absurd in that funny hat with red horns and a red chasuble with a billy goat on it.

"Don't you understand? You are already one of us. You always have been. You simply refuse to acknowledge it." A woman in shadow near the wall had spoken, a woman in red robes cut like a monk's, with a hood and a rope for a belt. I hadn't noticed her before in the crowd.

She slowly came forward, then pulled back her hood with her small white hands, revealing a beautiful face with arching eyebrows and full narrow lips made for a seductive pout. Long blond hair hung on either side, curling down onto the scarlet fabric. Upon closer look, you could see her face was a trifle worn, creases at the corners of her eyes and lines on her forehead.

"Dear Lord," Marguerite moaned.

The woman laughed softly. "You recognize me, I see. It has been a long time, has it not, Marguerite? I hope you don't mind if I call you Marguerite. We used our first names before. I was always Simone, and you—you were Suzanne, back then."

Marguerite's mouth twitched. Her hand was trembling. "Are you going to kill me, too?"

"I certainly hope that will not be necessary. As I said—and as the good abbé demands—we simply want you to join us in our dedication to the one true Master." She gave a slight nod in the direction of the tapestry. "Satan."

The muscles of her throat rippled as Marguerite tried to swallow. "Is this some—some joke?"

Simone's smile vanished. "Hardly a joke. I only want you to acknowledge the truth, that you have committed the blackest of sins and that you are damned along with the rest of us."

Marguerite was silent for a moment, then whispered hoarsely, "*No.*"

"Do you deny you are a sinner?"

Marguerite bit fiercely at her lip, then shook her head. "We are all sinners."

"And all damned as well, perhaps! Surely you cannot believe that you can live off the fruits of your sin for twenty years—live off the blood, so to speak, of the Count de Laval—and that somehow God will forgive you!" She laughed. "No, no, that is not likely."

"God can forgive any sin," Michelle said sternly. I quickly shook my head, but she didn't even notice me.

"Ah, and this must be the lady doctor I have heard so much about. *Enchanté, madame.* Say what you will, but Marguerite and I know better. If ever a sin were mortal, it was ours—and it was one sin, one sin shared between the two of us. The count's blood is on us both."

"*No,*" Marguerite groaned.

"You conceived of the plan. It was your idea to murder him— your idea to stab him."

"But I did not—I could not."

"Ah, but you could and you did—I was only your tool. I was like the dagger itself to you, only a means to an end. You knew that if you could not do it, I could. You knew that from the first. That was why you chose me. So there could be no way out, so that he must die. You chose your blade well."

"I did not know that—I swear I did not. I did not dream you were such a monster."

"*Monster?* You call me a monster? If I am a monster, who else created me, but you? Come along now, say you will join us. Say you will consume the black host and acknowledge Satan as your lord and master. Say that you will let the good father take you here before the altar to consummate the bargain."

A strange laugh slipped from Marguerite. "No!"

"I shall go first with him, if that will make it easier for you."

Docre was watching the two women, and I could see in his eyes that he found the mere suggestion exciting. My right hand formed a fist. Before long, I would hit him. This whole terrible business—this ceremony and its tortured participants—all teetered between the comical and the horrible: one minute I wanted to laugh, the next to scream.

Simone took a step nearer, then another. She held out her small hand and touched Marguerite lightly on the cheek. Their eyes were locked. "We were always friends. Sisters, almost—there was a bond between us. I give you the chance again to be my friend."

"We were never friends. *Never.*"

"Ah." Simone let her hand drop. "Friendship, love, loyalty… all empty abstractions. The truth is we live for ourselves, only ourselves. The true Master reigns in solitude, a universal solitude we all share. In the end, there is no friendship amongst the damned, only an acknowledgment of the terrible banal nothingness of the universe. Accept it—accept Satan, or die. The choice is yours."

"You are a liar, like your Master." Marguerite's voice shook with emotion. "I will never join you—never."

"Then die, harlot!—die!" Docre screamed. He turned to snatch a knife which lay on the altar next to the chalice, then swung it around and raised the blade high. The chasuble flapped out, and you could see his thin white naked body.

Simone's small hands flew upward. "No, no!—stop!"

I started forward, even as Michelle grabbed Marguerite and hurtled them both to the floor. From behind me, a thundering bang filled the chamber, echoing off the roof overhead. Docre screamed, and the knife fell from his hand. A sort of red flower had blossomed on his upper arm, and he clutched at it with his left hand, blood seeping from between his fingers and running down to his forearm.

Still holding the revolver, Holmes knocked aside a chair and strode toward the altar. Simone backed away and joined the other participants. Holmes picked up the chalice and hurled its contents at the congregation, the black hosts scattering about like dirty hailstones. "Out!—all of you out!" he shouted. He raised the revolver and fired once at the ceiling, knocking loose some plaster. People fled noisily for the exit.

Holmes thrust the revolver into his jacket pocket, then strode around the altar. He took the large crucifix off the wall, then raised it with both hands and smashed it as hard as he could against the marble top of the altar. The head and outspread arms broke off with flying splinters. He hit it again, knocking off the ridiculous phallus, then let it drop. He turned once more and used both hands to tear down the tapestry of Satan. Once accomplished, he stomped on it twice for good measure. Finally he broke each of the black candles, and then hurled the brass holders out amidst the chairs of the chapel.

Sumners smiled broadly and actually clapped his hands. "Oh well done, Holmes! Very well done!" The portly cleric was the only one of us who seemed none the worse for wear.

Michelle had helped Marguerite up. Docre was moaning and whimpering, and she wrapped her scarf round his wounded arm, then cinched it tightly. I grabbed the ridiculous hat by one of the red horns and pulled it off his head. "Where are your trousers!" I demanded sternly. He did not answer. He looked even paler than usual, his forehead damp beneath his matted black hair.

Holmes was breathing hard, a wild light still showing in his eyes. "Violet—where is she?"

"She went out," Sumners said. "She was following that small woman in the red robe, I believe."

"Damnation!" Holmes snarled. His face pale beneath his black hair, he threw chairs aside with a single hand as he made his way to the aisle. Marguerite followed him, as did Michelle and I. As I walked, I awkwardly got on my overcoat, thrusting first one arm into the sleeve, then the other.

"No running for me!" Sumners called out from behind us. "I shall just give the altar a splash of holy water and a quick blessing, then look after our wounded celebrant."

We went out the big main doors, and the cool damp air of night was a profound relief after the stench of the chapel. I drew in great breaths, even as I tried to keep up with Holmes, who had just pushed open the gate in the stone wall. A few members of the congregation stood about looking dazed or lost, but they ignored us. I stepped through the entryway and saw Holmes at the end of the alleyway. My walk became almost a run. I looked back once and saw Michelle and Marguerite just behind me.

Holmes was halfway down the block, nearing the square before Saint-Sulpice. I wondered if he had Violet in sight, or was just guessing which way she might have gone. The wind picked up, cold, and now wet on my face. A few hard drops of rain had begun to fall. A carriage rumbled by in the opposite direction, its lamps lighting up the cobblestones. I reached the end of the street and saw Holmes running across the square and around the shut-off fountain dedicated to the four bishops. Clearly he was headed for the main entrance of the church.

I followed, but he was going at a frightful pace. It was hard to believe a small woman like Simone could have been so fleet of foot. I went round the fountain and saw the tall white pillars of the great church with the steps between them. Holmes bounded upward, taking two or three at a time. Something was heaped before me on the ground. Hard to judge color in such low light, but it had a hint of red. I suspected it must be Simone's robe.

Because of his tobacco usage, my wind was much better than Holmes's, and I was gaining on him. Violet and Simone must be veritable gazelles. I also took the steps several at a time, then turned and went to the big door which had just swung shut behind Holmes. Inside the vestibule a candle flickered beneath a lamp on a small table. A short stout man in a dark suit had risen from his chair and gave me an alarmed look. "Monsieur, monsieur—it is the house of God—one must not run in here!" I strode past him and pushed open the door to the church itself.

A great black cavern opened up before me, musty-smelling, with a faint hint of incense, and in the distance flickering candles lit up chapels or statues, and farthest away was the dim red lamp by the tabernacle of the main altar. I had a sick feeling about where they must have gone. I turned and found the doorway to the bell tower. I could hear someone above me on the stairs and then Holmes shouting, "Violet!"

"At least it's dark," I mumbled. One candle was lit, and others were on holders. I used the lit candle to light another.

Michelle and Marguerite came through the doorway. "There you are," Michelle said. "Have they gone up?"

"Yes. I don't suppose you would consider waiting here?"

"No, Henry."

Marguerite's mouth looked stiff, her great dark eyes filled with emotion. "I must finish this."

I shook my head, then started up the winding spiral. "Sherlock!" I cried. "Wait for us!"

We went round and round, then came out on the first landing by the doorways. Holmes stood holding a candle, a tall dark figure with a white face and hatchet nose, Violet smaller and slender, the color of her purple dress only showing in the halo of light round the candle flame. Both had left their overcoats behind in the chapel. She was smiling fiercely.

"She has gone up there—we have her now—she's trapped!" She whirled about and plunged upward into the darkness of the ascending stairway.

Holmes's long white fingers groped at the air. "Wait, Violet!— no!" But he might as well have tried to stop the wind. He followed her up the stairs.

I shook my head at Michelle and Marguerite. "Blast it! You should both stay here—you should go no further."

Michelle smiled faintly, but Marguerite glared at me, showing real anger for the first time I could recall. "You heard me—I have run from her for long enough!"

I shook my head again and started up the stairs, holding the candle before me to light the way. The two women followed. By an effort of will, I did not look to the side to remark the deepening abyss at the center of the tower as we climbed ever upward, but I was aware of the dark massive shapes of the bells. As we passed the sounding shutters, I felt air on my face and occasionally heard the wind whisper, a kind of high shuddery hum. At one point I recalled that Holmes had said the tower was over two hundred feet high, a fact which I would have preferred to forget!

We came at last to the upper rotunda of the tower. Simone was near the final stairway to the roof, while Holmes and Violet stood some six or seven feet back from her. A candle on its holder was set on a ledge, and it illuminated Simone's face and also her hands, one of which held some small firearm. Compared to the other women's, her free hand was small, yet white and perfectly shaped, quite delicate—a perfect lady's hand. No trouble finding gloves for her! She wore an azure blue silk, something very well cut and expensive, far from the red woolen robe. She smiled at us.

She might look a bit worn about the edges, so to speak, but she still had luminous skin and eyes, a pert nose and full rose-red lips. One could certainly understand how she had woven a spell around men like Lupin and Docre. But I knew her beauty and that aura of innocence were utterly false, only a snare set to trap the unwary in a noose of evil.

"Welcome, welcome," she said. "We are all together at last. No more lunatic priests or crazed worshipers. We can have a serious conversation in private." I had stopped, but Marguerite grasped the railing and slipped by me. "Do be careful, Marguerite. I fear the railing here is in a sorry state of repair. We do not want you to have an accident and fall. By the way, as I just explained to Mr. Holmes, this is an American derringer I am holding, a small gun which can fire two shots. Because of its diminutive size, it is a perfect lady's weapon, especially for a petite woman like myself. However, it is not a toy. Emptied into someone's chest at close range, it would no doubt prove fatal. You must keep your distance and come no closer than Mr. Holmes."

"You cannot shoot us all," Michelle muttered. It was, I reflected, an absurdly self-evident statement.

Simone laughed. "One of you should be quite enough, I suspect, to compel you to do as I say! However, I don't wish to shoot anyone. We are at a standoff, and it is time we talked business. It is time we talked about what comes next."

Her grating familiarity and joking tone infuriated me. "What comes next is that you go back to prison, and then to the guillotine!"

Michelle grasped my arm tightly. "*Henry.*"

Simone laughed again. "That, I am afraid, is not a viable option. Here is what I propose. We shall all descend the tower, and then go our separate ways. All that has happened will be forgotten, and Madame Hardy and I shall each lead our separate lives. She can have Paris and London, while the rest of the continent shall be at my disposal. Neither of us shall ever see one another or interfere in the other's life again."

Holmes gave a short bitter laugh. "And why on earth would we ever trust you to keep such a bargain?"

"Because you have no choice. If you turn me over to the police, I shall tell them the truth about the Count de Laval's murder and the theft of *La Madonna della Mela*. I shall reveal how Marguerite Hardy planned the whole thing and how she has lived off the wealth of her scheme for two decades. In short, if I go back to prison and then to the guillotine, I shall not go alone this time! She will accompany me."

"Why would anyone believe you!" Violet exclaimed.

"Because I shall have witnesses to testify on my behalf, the eminent detective Mr. Sherlock Holmes being the foremost! I will, of course, also invite each one of you to testify. You will have to take an oath before God to tell the truth. You all know that this woman was behind the scheme, that she was the true mastermind, and I do not think any of you would be willing to perjure yourself. The English sense of honor is simply too strong. And even Marguerite..."

Her smile was withering. "Could you take an oath before God and then lie? Could you tell them you knew nothing about the crime and were not involved? I doubt it. Your precious religion would forbid such a monstrous sin, would it not?" Her laugh was mocking. "So you see, you have no choice in the matter. You must let me go and hope for the best, and really, I promise I shall leave her alone. I have enjoyed her suffering, it is true, and I would have liked to have prolonged it. We could have enjoyed the delights of Satanism with the good abbé for years to come! All the same, I am willing to let it go. I can accept the inevitable. One must make compromises in life. You do understand, do you not, Mr. Holmes?"

"I am pondering it." His voice was gruff, angry.

She laughed again. "Take your time if you wish. We have all the time in the world."

"Perhaps you might answer a question or two for me, madame. One or two mysteries remain. How did you learn of Lupin's involvement in the crime? Obviously Marguerite would never have mentioned him. And how ever did you find him?"

She gave an appreciative nod. "Ah, an obvious question indeed. Yes, it was always supposed to be just we three women. No man was ever mentioned to me, but it slipped out that Suzanne had a lover. Anne-Marie couldn't keep her mouth shut. She liked to joke about him, and one time she asked Marguerite how the little rabbit was." Simone had been speaking French, and little rabbit was *le petit lapin.* "The words are very close, you know—'*lapin*' and '*Lupin.*' When I learned of the painting later, I knew a man must have been involved, probably a painter, so after I left the prison, I went to art dealers and asked if anyone knew of an artist or seller with a name like Lapin, especially one active nearly two decades ago. It was at about the third store that the patron told me of an artist named Gaston Lupin.

"I knew then that the gods were truly with me, that my vengeance was foreordained! It was easy enough to find him after that, and even easier to tease and tempt him. He was fond of the ladies—although not so insatiable as the good abbé!—and he was terribly indiscreet. He liked to brag. We had not been intimate for long when he showed me the painting of the *Madonna of the Apple.* He had kept the original for sentimental reasons—the original fake, that is! Soon after he told me about the other forgeries. The whole story gradually came out. He thought the scheme was so clever, but I knew that the credit really belonged to you, Marguerite."

"And how did you find *me*?" Marguerite asked.

"Your name was in his address book. He had an entry for you and for Anne-Marie. He spoke rather fondly of you. And he would stare so at his paintings of you. I think he was still half in love with you. He had seen you and your husband leaving the liquor shop on the Champs-Élysées. He went into the store and asked the clerk who the man and woman were who had just departed, claiming that the man was an old friend of his. The clerk told him it was Monsieur John Hardy, the owner, and his wife Madame Marguerite Hardy. He then gave him Mr. Hardy's business card which included his Paris and London addresses!" She laughed. "How accommodating! So there you have it, Mr. Holmes. Do you have further questions?"

"Did you switch the morphine bottles on Lupin?"

"Yes, that was easy enough."

"Why did you finally kill him?"

"For revenge, of course. He had been willing to make me the sacrificial goat in the scheme! And he was becoming quite tiresome. I had everything I needed from him, and he had given me some gifts of expensive jewels."

"And you also killed Anne-Marie. I suspect Docre assisted you."

"No, that was his servant Alain, who has been most helpful. Alain was his valet during his youth, and the abbé has kept him in his employ, although not openly. What would his parishioners think if they knew he had his own private servant! In a way I did Anne-Marie a favor. Her life was completely meaningless! She was always shallow and rather stupid. Lupin and Marguerite only gave her a pittance, of course—nothing like a full share, and that she squandered. She had vaguely threatened Lupin, but two hundred francs a month was nothing to him, a small sum to buy her silence."

"I have met Alain," Holmes said. "And his dog."

She laughed. "The dog was a superb touch! I was only at the count's home that one night, but I remember his huge slavering black beast well enough. The dog we found was a close match, especially with a white streak painted on his forehead."

"And you did all this just to frighten me?" Marguerite's voice shook.

"Certainly."

"I suppose Docre has also given you money," Holmes said.

"Yes, of course he has—a great deal. I wanted to be self-sufficient, and so I am. That is why you can trust me to leave her alone. I have more than enough to live well, and I am not so stupid as Anne-Marie. I shall not throw away my money."

"But you have nurtured your desire for revenge for twenty

years," Holmes said. "How can I believe that you will let that go, that you will simply let Madame Hardy walk away?"

"Again, you will believe it because you have no other choice." Her smile was fierce.

Holmes shrugged. "I think not."

Simone's eyes shifted to Marguerite. Her pupils were huge in the dim lantern light, but a pale icy ring circled them. A terrible tension showed in her face: the war between beauty and something sick and deranged in her soul. "They would put you in prison and bring you to trial. Is that what you want? Your husband would feel obliged to attend. He would sit there and listen while I told them everything."

I heard a muted groan from Marguerite, her anguish apparent. "Whatever happens, John must never know—please, Mr. Holmes—promise me!"

"You are a monster," Violet whispered to Simone.

Simone laughed. "At least I did not bludgeon my husband to death! You see, I know your secrets, too. It was not hard to find out who you really are, Madame Wheelwright. But enough of this nonsense. You must all see the necessity of what I demand. None of you would be any good at lying under oath. We must all make our little sacrifices. I will forego my vengeance—although at least I have the pleasure of knowing she has suffered the agonies of the damned for a few weeks, and she will never, I think, rest truly easily knowing that I am alive! But I digress. Let us all descend and go our separate ways. We shall agree never to meet again."

I opened my mouth, then closed it. Letting her go seemed terribly wrong—indefensible—but she was right. I could see no alternative. Holmes had not spoken.

"Well, Mr. Holmes?"

"I am still thinking."

"You have done enough thinking! *Decide!* And you, Marguerite, don't you understand? I am being easy on you. I am letting you escape. You let me rot in prison for years. You used me to commit murder. And yet I am willing to let you go."

"You will kill someone else. You will kill again."

"That should not be necessary, but I cannot rule it out."

"I cannot… I cannot let you hurt anyone else."

"Idiot!" Simone's mock good humor had vanished, her face reddening. "Don't you see that I am giving you a gift that you do not deserve? Go while you still can. I give you the freedom you denied me."

"*On doit payer,*" Marguerite murmured. "*On doit toujours payer.*" One must pay. One must always pay.

Her back was to me, but I saw that she had clenched her fist. She moved so quickly, it caught us all by surprise. She brushed past Holmes and Violet and flew at Simone. The other woman's face was incredulous; her mouth opened wide. The two shots came one after the other, but then Marguerite had her arms round the smaller woman, swung both of them round to crash into the metal railing. It gave way in an instant, the curved rusty steel pulling free from the wall where it was anchored nearby, arcing outward, and then the two women tottered over the side near the black gap.

Violet leaped forward and grabbed Marguerite's arm. Violet tried to dig in her heels, but she swung sideways, teetering on the edge. "Let go!" Holmes cried, even as he sprang forward and seized her free arm. Violet's hand was yanked away as the two women plunged into the darkness. Simone must have been the one screaming, a sound that dimmed as she fell. They must have hit the bells: one of the smaller ones gave off a dim shimmery *bong*, a long note that merged with another, the sounds reverberating like a deep shudder through the dark tower.

Michelle had lunged forward and grabbed Violet's other arm, while in a panic, I put both my hands round Michelle's waist and slammed myself back against the stone wall, determined to keep her from the abyss. I felt her stagger for a moment and start to lurch forward as Violet slipped over the side, but then she and Holmes pulled Violet back up onto the rotunda. Michelle's weight shifted again, and I loosened my grip slightly. The rusting black railing hung swaying toward the center, still attached on one side, but useless now.

Violet sobbed once. "Oh no, no." Michelle let go of her, and Holmes drew her to him, encircled her with his long arms in their black sleeves, his hands clutching at her back. She hid her face against his chest.

I shook my head, aware of my heart still racing. "You scared me to death!" I said to Michelle.

"I couldn't let her fall, not Violet, too."

"It was insane."

"Thanks for grabbing me."

"Let's get away from here! Let's go now."

She squeezed my hand. "Sherlock?" she murmured.

"Henry is right. The sooner we get down from here, the better. It is dangerous."

I took up a candle and began the long descent in the darkness. The bells were silent now, asleep once again, mute. When we reached the main floor, I was about to go through the doorway, but Holmes said, "Wait, Henry." I turned round and my candle lit up his pale thin face and that of Violet. Her dark eyes glistened. "I need to go down and make sure..." His eyes shifted to Michelle. "Will you come with me, Michelle? A physician should examine the bodies." He set his hand on my shoulder. "Wait for us in the church. We shan't be long."

I gave him the candle, then stepped into the vast interior of the church with its scattered islands of dim light. I was grateful that he had asked Michelle to accompany him; he knew how squeamish I was about corpses.

Violet followed me. I heard her sigh. "I wanted so to save her." Her voice quavered.

"I know. It was... At least she can no longer torture her. I don't think I have ever known anyone, man or woman, quite so evil as Simone Dujardin."

Violet shook her head. "Nor I, either."

We were quiet. There was nothing more to say. Violet's long black veil was wrapped loosely about her neck, and she raised it to cover her head, then used one end to wipe at her eyes. Soon I saw a pool of light spread outward before me, and I turned just as Holmes and Michelle came through the doorway. He blew out the candle, then set down the holder. "There were no surprises. Both are dead. It was a very long fall, although the two bullets must have already killed Madame Hardy before she struck the ground." He sighed. "We had better fetch the police. I can finally speak freely with Commissaire Juvol."

"You cannot let him blacken Marguerite's name!" Violet exclaimed.

Holmes wearily shook his head. "Certainly not. Juvol is an honorable man. He can keep a secret if need be. We can trust him. The details about her past will not go into his official report. And I owe him an explanation."

"I feel so dreadful." Again Violet wiped at her eyes with the end of the veil. "I was supposed to protect her, to help her. I failed her. I failed her utterly."

Holmes took in a long slow breath. "You must not blame yourself–there is more than enough blame to go around." His lips formed a brief bitter smile. "If you are going to be a consulting detective, you must be prepared to fail occasionally. One cannot always win."

Michelle looked very stern. "We all failed her. I was the one with her tonight. I was the one that was supposed to watch over her."

"There is no use castigating yourselves," I said. "That wretched woman, that devil incarnate, was the one who killed her. As I told Violet, at least she can no longer torture the poor creature. She is free of her–and of her crimes–at last."

Violet's brow creased. "Was it suicide or sacrifice, I wonder? Probably both. She died so that none of us could be hurt by Dujardin. Suicide is supposed to be a mortal sin, but I cannot believe Marguerite did anything wrong or that God would condemn her."

A faint bittersweet smile stirred Michelle's lips. "Remember how much she liked the end of *Faust*? Perhaps... We can only hope that it is so, as with her namesake: that the Devil has been defeated, that the angels descended and carried her up to God."

Violet laughed, even though she was crying. "Oh, I would like to believe that."

The reality of all that had happened that night suddenly seemed to hit me at once: I was very tired and near tears myself. A mere hour before Marguerite had been living and breathing, but now she was dead, lost forever, or at least for a lifetime. Holmes had said nothing, but his face was pale, his eyes pained. He opened his mouth, then closed it.

"What is wrong?" I asked. The evident stupidity of the question made me laugh.

Holmes sighed. "Mr. Hardy is arriving tomorrow. Someone has to tell him what has happened, and that someone, unfortunately, will be me."

Chapter Thirteen

When the police arrived, Holmes had them send immediately for Juvol. Violet, Michelle and I sat in a back pew while the two men talked for a long while in the vestibule. Occasionally the voices of the other policemen echoed faintly off the vault overhead, and the vast silence of the great cathedral was somehow consoling. Violet had stopped crying. Michelle sat next to her, with her right arm around her. I held Michelle's left hand tightly.

Footsteps approached us, and a tall dark figure appeared. Holmes leaned over and said softly, "We can go now."

We all slowly stood and stepped into the aisle. "What did you decide?" Michelle asked.

"There will be no mention of Madame Hardy's past. Juvol will say that Dujardin was trying to extort money from her and that Madame Hardy threw herself upon the other woman to save the rest of us."

"True enough," Violet murmured.

We went back to the Ursuline chapel to fetch Violet and Holmes's coats. Juvol's men had arrested Docre, and the police surgeon was examining him. His injury was not grave, and neither Michelle nor I wanted to care for him. Sumners had been waiting for us, and Holmes told him all that had happened. He was dismayed and parted after shaking hands with us all.

We took a carriage back to the Meurice. It was only about eleven, although it felt much later. Michelle convinced Violet to spend the night at the hotel rather than trying to return to Auteuil so late. The two women sat in the big green Second Empire sofa of the lobby. Both looked pale and exhausted.

Holmes glanced at me. "Henry, would you walk with me?"

"Certainly."

We still had on our black bowler hats and overcoats. The rain had let up, but a cold hard drizzle still fell. We crossed the Rue de Rivoli and entered the Tuileries Garden. On one side were the trunks and branches of the tall bare plane trees, ahead was a gray sward of grass. Holmes had his hands in his overcoat pockets. Neither of us spoke for several minutes. I felt a sort of cold dull ache in my chest, more an emotional sensation than a physical one, a certain emptiness.

At last he spoke. "Henry, did you try to dissuade Michelle and Madame Hardy from going up the stairs to the bell tower?"

"Of course I did! Michelle did not even deign to reply, while Madame Hardy... she was adamant. She wanted to face Dujardin once and for all."

"I knew you must have tried to stop them. It was a stupid question. If only they had stayed behind! But then... she might have shot Violet instead." His voice was pained, and he shook his head. "For the life of me, I cannot think what I could have done differently. That wretched woman had me completely over a barrel. I could not conceive of any possible way out."

"Remember what you told Violet? You mustn't blame yourself. Sometimes a consulting detective—even a master like yourself—must fail."

"But must he fail so spectacularly!" His voice was angry.

"Was it failure? Another metaphor may be more apt. You were dealt a bad hand."

He drew in his breath, even as he nodded. "I never did greatly care for card games. Unlike with chess, luck often counts for more than skill."

"There you have it."

"But in the end... it was no game. A woman is dead."

"I know." My legs had begun to ache, and I was cold. "I know."

He must have heard a faint shiver in my voice. "We can go back now."

Michelle and Violet were still talking on the sofa when we returned. Michelle stood and smiled at me. "There you are at last. There's no need for me to get my things from Marguerite's tonight." She took my hand, then turned to Holmes and Violet.

"Goodnight," they said.

Violet was staring at Holmes, her forehead creased. Her brown eyes had dark hollows under them, and tendrils of her black hair curled down over her forehead and about her ear. "Mr. Holmes, would you sit with me? I cannot sleep yet."

He gave her a curious look, as if this were the most incredible request he had ever heard. He nodded. "Gladly. I shall not sleep tonight." They sat on the sofa, a distance of about a foot separating them. Both of them were so long and slender, their faces pale and wan against their dark clothing, a restless energy illuminating their eyes. Violet looked royal in purple, her chin thrust forward resolutely.

Michelle and I went upstairs to my room. Her night clothes were back at Marguerite's, but once in bed, I held her tightly and warmed her. "I wish it had not had to happen this way," I said, "but it is wonderful to have you back alongside me."

She kissed me. "I have missed you."

It was a while before I felt the subtle changes in her body, in her breathing, as she fell asleep. I was still wide awake, troubled, but grateful to have her alongside me once again. I had a restless night. When I finally slept, Simone Dujardin lurked in my dreams, gloating. Her white face in its nimbus of blond hair was young and beautiful, but her blue eyes revealed her evil nature. She was like some splendid-looking fruit with worm-eaten rot at its core. I tried to keep Marguerite away from the stairs to the tower, but she would not listen to me.

Although I was late falling asleep, I woke up early. I went down for breakfast around eight, leaving Michelle still fast asleep. Holmes sat alone at a corner table, sipping coffee, half a pain au chocolat on a small saucer before him. He had shaved, put on clean linen and a black frock coat, and he had some color back in his face. I sat beside him and ordered the same thing.

He took another bite of his pastry. "I must leave soon. I told Juvol I would meet him first thing in the morning. We have a few things to discuss."

"But you said he would keep Madame Hardy's past a secret?"

"Yes. And early this afternoon I have my other task. I must meet Mr. Hardy at the Gare du Nord." His mouth briefly pulled outward, and then he sighed. "He will be expecting his wife as well."

I hesitated. "Would you like me to come with you?"

He shrugged. "It is not necessary. I am the one he hired to protect her."

"All the same, I'll come if you wish it."

He smiled faintly. "You and Michelle have tender hearts, Henry. I can take care of this alone."

"Very well." I was greatly relieved.

He sipped his coffee. "I shall be busy much of the day, in and out, but let us plan on dinner together here at the hotel at eight thirty. Violet will also join us. We agreed upon it last night."

"How late were the two of you up?"

"Until three."

"Three! What on earth were you talking about all that time?"

"Mostly about music. We began with Bach and ended with Wagner." He smiled. "Appropriate, chronologically."

I shook my head. "Wagner? Why Wagner?"

"It was a distraction, Henry, a long and pleasant one. She wanted to hear about Bayreuth. She has never been there. As you may remember, I last went there two years ago for a performance of *Parsifal.* She has heard a great deal about the opera and would like to hear it, but Wagner specified that it can only be done at Bayreuth. Someday she would like to make the musical pilgrimage there."

"As I recall, you had mixed feelings about the work."

He smiled. "It is very long, even for Wagner. Much of the music is sublime, but in its totality, the opera is somehow, ultimately, unconvincing. Wagner himself was, in many ways, a thoroughly odious man, and perhaps that explains why his grand story of redemption does not quite ring true in the end." His gray eyes peered closely at me. "Why are you smiling that way?"

"It is the idea of you and Violet discussing *Parsifal* in the wee hours of the morning. You two are a pair."

His smile was ironical. "That is not typical, I suppose." He swallowed the last of his coffee, then stood up. "I must be on my way."

"Good luck with Mr. Hardy."

All traces of good humor vanished. "Thank you, Henry."

I did not see Holmes again until just before dinner. I had gone down ahead of Michelle. Still wearing the black frock coat with the silken lapels, he was seated at one end of our familiar friend, the green sofa, the long fingers of his right hand clutching at his chin as he stared fiercely into the middle distance. When he saw me, he nodded, the tension in his face easing.

I sat down beside him. "How did it go?" Both of us knew exactly what I was talking about.

He drew in his breath, his face contorting. "Badly–very badly, as one would expect. He was devastated. You, I think, can well imagine how he must have felt. He loved her very much, and he was not expecting such news." A grim ironic smile flickered across his lips. "After all, Sherlock Holmes was on the case."

"You mustn't be so hard on yourself–there was nothing you could have done."

Along with bleakness, a faint anger showed in his gray eyes. "Let us not talk about it."

"And what were you doing all afternoon?"

"Walking. And thinking."

"The weather was certainly dreadful."

"It matched my mood. I went into the Louvre for a while, but I was too distracted to pay suitable attention to the masterpieces."

"There you are!" Michelle strode across the lobby. She had

retrieved her luggage from Marguerite's house, and she wore one of her electric-blue dresses, our favorite color. It had the popular gigot sleeves ballooning out from the shoulders, then tapering and tight round her forearms, her hands hidden by white gloves. She was one of those few "outrageous" women who did not wear a corset, at least in informal situations, and to my mind she did not need it. She had a perfect shape, a narrow waist and broad curving hips, pleasantly full—not scrawny, but not fat either. Her red hair was bound up, and silver earrings glistened at each ear. I smiled at her, incredibly grateful to be loved by such a woman and aware that nothing could be more terrible than to lose her.

Her eyes filled with sympathy when she saw Holmes. We went to the dining room together, Michelle in the center holding each of us by the arm. We were barely seated when Violet came in. She looked about, saw us, then smiled and started for our table. Her face was faintly flushed, and she looked much better than she had the night before. She wore a beautiful green silk which I vaguely recalled from a few years ago.

Michelle rose and kissed her on the cheek. "You look much better. You must have slept."

"I did, a good nap on the sofa. It is so quiet at home in the afternoon." She turned to Holmes. "And you?"

He shrugged. "Morpheus and I are intermittent acquaintances under the best of circumstances."

We ordered our dinners, and Holmes selected a white Bordeaux to start with. "Champagne will not do this evening," he murmured. After the waiter had arrived with the chilled bottle and filled our glasses, Holmes raised his. "To Madame Hardy, a woman who..." His eyes seemed briefly lost, words escaping him. "Would that she were here," he finally said. We all said her name and clinked glasses. The wine was delicious, but we were all thinking anew of Marguerite's death.

Holmes held up his wine glass, staring at the pale yellow wine, twisting it slightly, then sipped again. "I have made a resolution I had best tell you about, so that I can eat my dinner in peace." He paused, then squared his shoulders slightly. "I have decided to give up my work as a consulting detective and retire to some rustic dwelling in Yorkshire."

We all stared at him for a few seconds. Michelle was the first to speak. "Is this some sort of joke?" Violet was still looking at him, but the set of her lips showed that she had no such doubts.

"I would not joke about such a thing," Holmes said.

I shook my head incredulously. "But that is simply insane! You are only in your early forties, and at the height of your powers! How could you abandon your profession now? You are irreplaceable."

He shrugged. "I would have to give it up some day. Better sooner than later."

"All this because of Madame Hardy's death?" I asked.

His smile was bitter. "I don't want to ever again have a conversation like the one today with Mr. Hardy."

Violet's dark eyes were fixed on him. "You told me that a consulting detective cannot always win. Can you not see the wisdom of your own counsel?"

"I have done this work for slightly over twenty years, and I have failed more times than I care to remember. I have also seen nearly every variety of human evil and perversion. It wears on a man. You are just starting out. It is not the same."

"Isn't it?"

I stared at him and shook my head. "I cannot believe it—nor can I believe you have thought this through. I have seen the black moods you are prey to when you do not have an interesting case to occupy your mind. Nor do I think prolonged isolation will be good for you. You were made for the bustle and activity of London, for the great varied masses of humanity, for the thrill of the chase after criminals—and not for some bucolic setting with only cows and sheep for company!"

They all smiled at this, even Holmes. "My mind is made up, Henry. Let us enjoy our last meal together in Paris and not mar it with arguments."

"Last meal?" I said.

"Yes. I shall leave in the morning and be back in London in the afternoon. I shall take the express train to York the following morning, then go on to Whitby. And... I was hoping... I was hoping..."

I stared at him. "You want me to come along?"

"I know you do not approve, but—yes. Just for a day or two, until I am settled."

My eyes rolled upward. That was the last thing I wanted to do! More days and nights apart from Michelle. But how could I refuse him?—especially if he really followed through on his decision. I jerked my head downward in an angry nod, before I could follow my more selfish impulses and refuse. "Very well."

Michelle leaned forward and set her big white hand on his wrist. "Sherlock, you are making a mistake."

His mouth stiffened. "I expected these objections. However, I must ask you to respect my decision, and again, let us not ruin our parting meal in futile discussion which can only lead to hard feelings. My mind is made up." He shrugged. "Perhaps, after all, it is not irrevocable. I may reconsider in a few months, but you must not count on it. Let us move on to more pleasant topics, so that..." he gestured at the plate just set before him of snails in their shells, reeking of garlic and butter, "…I can truly relish my farewell plate of escargot!"

Violet stared at him thoughtfully. "No one knows the strength of your will better than I. If it is truly your wish, I shall not try to dissuade you. All the same…" She smiled wistfully. "Might you consider staying on a few days in Paris? We have all been so busy and so preoccupied with fears and worries. We have hardly had time to enjoy one another's company, and who knows when we may be together again? Why not take a few days' holiday in Paris before setting off on this expedition to the wilds of Yorkshire?"

Holmes looked at her, then lowered his eyes. "You tempt me, madam, but I must strike while the iron is hot. With the full Yorkshire winter coming on, I wish to be settled in as soon as possible."

She shook her head. "A pity. If Henry goes with you…" She turned to Michelle. "I know your practice calls to you, but perhaps you might stay a little longer, even if only two or three days?"

Michelle gave Holmes a brief hard stare, then smiled at Violet. "Gladly. You are right. We have spent hardly any time with one another."

Violet clapped her hands together. "Wonderful! And there is room for you at Auteuil. I wasn't exactly telling Marguerite the truth when I said my house was full."

Holmes paused with the tiny snail fork in his hand, his eyes sweeping warily round the table. "All is settled then. Henry and I depart for London tomorrow, then Yorkshire, while the ladies remain behind."

I nodded angrily, not trusting myself to speak without bitterness.

"Settled, yes," said Violet. "All the same… a pity you are not Roman Catholic, Mr. Holmes." Her smile was faintly ironic. "You could retreat for a while to some isolated monastery in the French countryside for prayer and meditation. That was what the knights in all the old tales did, especially after some moral crisis. Lancelot went to a monastery, and Guinevere to a convent." Her cheeks flushed slightly as she realized the implications of the comparison. "Not that it is the same. You are not Lancelot, and I... You are more like one of those knights who has slain the dragon in a fierce and bloody battle and suffered grievous wounds. Again, in the past you might have retired to the monastery or gone off to become a hermit." Her voice took on a lilting, mocking tone. "You do not, I hope, intend to live in a cave, eat only nuts and berries, and wear rough woolen robes?"

"I do not. My repasts will hardly be the equal of Parisian food, but I shall hire a decent cook who can keep a well-stocked larder and prepare simple but hardy meals." Holmes turned toward me; I was scowling. "Come, Henry, you must not give me such looks."

"It was not directed at you. I was thinking of Simone Dujardin, that tiny blond woman with her deceptive beauty and innocence. Despite her diminutive stature, she was certainly the equal of some monstrous dragon."

Violet nodded. "Dragons are often female in the stories. And they are frequently motivated by greed. It is an apt comparison."

Holmes scooped out the black gooey flesh from a third shell. "A pity no one else cares for escargot. I would gladly share these."

"I am feeling adventurous." Violet resolutely set her small plate nearer Holmes. "It has been many years since I last tasted one. I shall give it another try."

"It is best with bread, especially if you are new to the delicacy." He took a piece of baguette, set it on the dish, then removed another snail and set it on the bread. He used his spoon to take up some butter and parsley to drip onto the bread. "Try this."

Violet took a large bite and chewed thoughtfully. She swallowed, then her mouth twitched. She raised one shoulder.

"Well?" Holmes asked.

"It is, frankly, not so bad as I remembered. All the same, I am not a convert." She picked up the bread and took another bite. "But I shall finish what I started."

"Bravo!" Holmes exclaimed. "Well, more for myself, I suppose." He took up the green bottle and poured more of the wine into our glasses. "While I eat these, you can at least occupy yourself with this agreeable white Bordeaux."

The restaurant was warm, pleasant, and quiet, the well-dressed crowd chatting or eating politely, no loud clattering of silverware or sloshing of glasses, and the wine did help raise our spirits, or at least helped us to relax and enjoy our time together. As he had requested, no one spoke further of Holmes's decision, although I had resolved to work on him during our journey. While we were all saddened by the death of Marguerite, still there was relief that the uncertainty and violence of the case were finished, and that Dujardin was gone forever and could harm no one else. And in the end, too, if I had learned anything growing up in France, it was that few comforts in life can equal that combination of good food, good wine and good company.

I also appreciated beautiful women, and Michelle and Violet were each stunning in her own way. Each had such beautiful hands, although they were so different: Violet's long and slender, graceful, Michelle's larger and stronger-looking, her skin even paler. Holmes might have an austere, at times forbidding exterior, but I knew that he felt the same attraction toward female beauty. You could see it in his eyes, especially when he gazed at Violet. But it was far more than mere admiration: a much stronger emotion was at work.

Our *plats principaux* soon arrived. Michelle and I often ordered lamb shanks in France. Neither of us liked bloody meat, and they were generally well cooked; more tender and less gamey than what passed for lamb in London. The rich smell was incredible. Holmes had a seared steak with slabs of fried potatoes, and Violet half a roasted chicken covered with herbs. The waiter had already brought a second bottle, a very good red Bordeaux, the dark double of the white.

Holmes swirled the Bordeaux artistically in his glass, held it before the lamp at the center of our table, observing its brilliant scarlet glow, then took a lingering sip. He shook his head. "Wonderful! And now I think it is time for another toast, a happier one. It is trite perhaps, but why not end as we began a few nights ago? To friendship." We echoed his words and all clinked glasses.

"We must not wait again for three years before we see each other," Violet said. "I know I have no one to blame but myself, but I promise I shall not be remiss in the future."

We all set to decorously with our cutlery. Violet was almost as good at carving up a fowl with knife and fork as Holmes. "If you go into hiding again," Michelle said, "I shall drag Sherlock Holmes out of retirement and have him hunt you down!"

Holmes nodded. "An enviable task, one I would gladly accept."

Michelle was staring closely at Violet, and Violet gave her a curious look. "Don't you trust me? Why are you looking at me that way?"

Michelle hesitated, then shrugged her shoulders. "It is only... it is not exactly dinner conversation."

"Let me be the judge of that."

Michelle set down her knife and fork. "You once said that you needed to do something to atone for your crimes. You were not certain how long it might take. I wonder, have you… have you finally managed to balance the scales?"

Violet's lips formed a crooked ironic smile. "And you expect a serious answer?"

"Only if you wish."

Violet stared at her. Her eyes shifted to Holmes who was watching her closely, then back to Michelle. Some three years ago, Michelle had told me about the final meeting of Holmes and Violet in Switzerland. They had confessed their love, but Violet had asked him if he could wait for her until she had somehow made amends for her crimes.

"If you had only asked me a few days ago! Things were going so well. I had just saved a seventeen-year-old English girl from a fortune-hunting scoundrel." She smiled at Holmes. "It was nicely done, even if I do say so myself. I employed Gertrude in the scheme. She had been asking to help in my endeavors, and she is really a very good actress. Collins was not so sure, but we brought him around. We made Gertrude into a wealthy heiress and set her up as bait for the bounder. He was completely taken in, and dropped his pursuit of the girl to go after Gertrude. Better yet, he sent Gertrude a love letter that was practically a duplicate of his earlier love letter to the girl! The young lady was heartbroken, but that is far better than being ensnared at an early age by such a man.

"Yes, I felt I was so close, but all the same, it had seemed to me that somehow Mrs. Hardy was the key. If I could save her with her dark past, then surely I could save myself. But now… I simply do not know."

"When will you know?" Michelle asked.

"When I sprout a halo and angels appear dancing about me! Or…" Her smile faded. "Or when I must." Her eyes shifted briefly toward Holmes who seemed suddenly preoccupied with his meat.

Michelle's brow furrowed, then she smiled. "This is much too serious a topic for dinner conversation. Forgive me."

"I can see the advantages of having active assistants in the detective business, as you do, madam," Holmes said. "That would facilitate things." He smiled at me. "Of course, Henry occasionally acts as my assistant."

I shook my head. "A very clumsy one, however!"

"Nonsense. You have been quite helpful several times in the past. As has Michelle."

Michelle gave an emphatic nod. "Women's intuition does count for something, after all. Men can be so unbelievably stupid at times." This made us all smile. "No, no, I am serious." She gave Holmes another hard look.

"I cannot argue with that," Holmes said, "but it is a rare person indeed, of either sex, who has not at one time or another made some embarrassing blunder which he or she would prefer to forget."

I winced slightly. "That is certainly true."

Violet was frowning fiercely. "Yes, it is."

"Come now," Holmes said, "this is another subject far too grave for dinner conversation, unless it be to lament our choice of plates. My steak is very good, but ah, if only I had ordered the lamb!" His voice shook with mock grief. We all laughed. He took the wine bottle and emptied it refilling our glasses. "This is our parting feast—I shall order another bottle, perhaps a Burgundy this time." He raised his hand in the direction of the waiter.

"A third?" Violet sipped from her glass. "You are going to make me tipsy."

"We have earned it after the past few days," Michelle said.

Violet had not been to Whitby and asked us about the coastal town and that part of Yorkshire. Holmes told her briefly about our recent case there and evoked the solitary splendors of the moors and the rugged coastline. "I should like to see it," Violet murmured. The third bottle did serve to further relax us all and to engender a warm feeling of companionship. We finished off the last of it during our desserts.

Michelle was delighted to discover profiteroles on the menu for the evening, and we shared the dish, a favorite of us both. The sweet choux pastry was very good, and this version was filled with vanilla ice cream rather than whipped cream, then topped with a rich dark chocolate sauce. Violet had a slice of *gâteau au chocolat* and Holmes a classic cherry clafoutis. We sipped at the dark red wine, which went so well with chocolate.

We lingered a long while at the table, but at last Holmes withdrew his watch. It was nearing eleven, and he wanted to get an early start the next morning. Michelle smiled and gave me a knowing look. Michelle asked Violet if she might stay another night at the hotel, but she said she would take a cab and return to Auteuil. "I shall say my goodbyes to you, Henry, and Mr. Holmes tonight. No sad farewells, but only an *au revoir.*"

We all stood up. I stretched my arms and looked about, feeling slightly woozy. I had drunk more wine than usual, not quite enough to approach drunkenness, but enough to notice a difference. We left the dining hall, said goodbye again, and then Holmes and Violet headed for the lobby, while Michelle and I started for the stairs. She held my arm loosely.

"Those two," she murmured, shaking her head. "So wise and worldly, and yet with each other they are still like shy children. You must work on Sherlock tomorrow while I do my best with Violet."

We were halfway up to the next floor, hand in hand, when I stopped suddenly. "Drat," I murmured.

"What is it?"

"I had better find out exactly when Holmes wants to leave in the morning. I hope it is not the crack of dawn."

She gave my hand a squeeze. "Well, don't be long. The wine may have made Violet tipsy, but it has made me amorous! We must make the best of our last night together."

I gave her hand a squeeze. "So we shall."

I turned and quickly went back down the steps. The corridor was dim, almost dark at the end, the doorway into the lobby a brightly lit rectangle. I passed through it and stopped by a large potted palm. In the far corner of the room Holmes and Violet were standing staring at each other. Behind them was another palm in an ornate oriental vase, the plant's great green fronds forming almost a canopy. "Goodbye then," she murmured.

I took half a step back, unsure whether to retreat or just step out and make my presence known. Violet turned and took a few steps, her gaze lowered, then suddenly whirled about and strode back to him. She did not hesitate, but raised both her hands and set them alongside his long thin face. She rose up on her toes to kiss him. His arms encircled her, and their embrace grew more passionate. I took half a step back, embarrassed to be intruding. My business had best wait until morning. Still, I had a certain nagging curiosity about how long this might last.

I was about to leave when she finally drew away, and his hands slipped down to the small of her back. "Heavens," I heard her murmur softly, and then after a pause, "I shall miss you so, Sherlock Holmes."

"And I you." He hesitated, then raised a hand to stroke the bun of black hair at the back of her head.

"I suppose this is hardly the place..." she said, looking about, and I quickly stepped back through the doorway. "Tell me, might I visit you sometime in Yorkshire?"

"You would be most welcome anytime."

"Thank you, and again, *au revoir*."

"*Au revoir*, Violet."

I took a few silent steps backwards, then began to whistle more and more loudly. I came again into the lobby. Violet was halfway to the front door, while Holmes was still standing in the corner. His cheeks were flushed.

"There you are!" I exclaimed. "What time are we leaving in the morning?"

"Around eight o'clock. Perhaps you might join me for breakfast at seven thirty."

"Very well." I stared at him closely. "I don't suppose you have changed your mind?"

The flush at his cheek deepened. "No, Henry, I have not."

The journey to London typically took about eight hours: some four hours by train from the Gare du Nord to Calais, another hour or two by ferry to Dover, then another two by train back to London's Charing Cross Station. Holmes and I went directly to the Gare du Nord after breakfast, and were on a train departing around 8:30. Once the locomotive pulled out of the station, the rain spattered our window and left liquid trails down the glass, and soon we passed through the dingy desolate suburbs of Paris beyond the central arrondissements.

I had pulled out some back issues of *The Lancet*, but they were to serve as camouflage. I now had some four hours to badger my cousin! However, his gray eyes stared severely at me from beneath his furrowed brow. "Henry, let us make an agreement for our journey in order to assure good relations. I suspect you are determined to try to change my mind about retiring to Yorkshire. I assure you, you would be wasting your time, and the probability is high that you will only succeed in annoying me. Hence, the subject is to be a forbidden one. Agreed?"

I frowned, glanced out the window, then back at him. His eyes had not wavered. I shrugged. "If you insist."

"I do." He had pulled out a book and opened it upon his lap.

"But let me just say one final thing, and then I shall keep silent. Very few people can truly claim to be irreplaceable, but you are just that—irreplaceable. You have saved many lives, and your absence from society will have grave consequences. Very well, I have had my say, and now I shall hold my tongue."

He stared sternly at me, but said nothing. He was probably right—there was no use us arguing and becoming angry. With a sigh I started reading an article on the medical curriculum in France. By the time I had finished, the train was passing through rolling countryside with huge black oaks, a few yellowish-orange leaves still clinging to the gnarled branches. Holmes's book lay open on his lap, but he was leaning against the windowsill and staring out at the landscape which swept by.

We made the trip mostly in silence, then stopped briefly in Calais for an excellent final French lunch, and afterwards boarded the ferry. Holmes wanted to go out on deck, and I accompanied him. We were near the bow of the ship as it cut its way forward into the water. I had made the trip a few times on perfect days, the Channel smooth and dark blue, the sky above a brilliant azure, and the cliffs of Dover a thin white strip in the distance which grew larger and larger, until one could make out the rocky surface and the variations in color, and see the green grass on top along with an occasional building or a lighthouse. Today was not such a day!

Instead, all was a universal gray. At least the waters were not too stormy, although the surface rose and fell, foaming white showing amidst the dark rough waters, and the sky overhead was a vast all-encompassing gray which had swallowed up the horizon, hiding the Dover cliffs, and merging into a blurry band over the sea. Thankfully, there was not much of a real wind, but our forward motion created a breeze against our faces. The fine rain was cold and stung, and my gloved hands clutched tightly at the metal railing.

"Do you really want to stay out here?" I asked loudly.

Holmes turned to me. His black bowler hat was jammed down tightly, hiding his pale forehead and emphasizing his pale thin face and beak-like nose. A black scarf was wrapped round his neck, up over the hat, and one end dangled down onto his black overcoat. He gave a brusque nod. "*Yes.*"

"Very well—I'm going back in."

I thought he might reconsider, but he remained outside until the very end. I joined him as we came alongside the quay, and soon we were descending the iron stairway, umbrellas in hand, since a major downpour greeted us upon our return to British earth.

Holmes was equally taciturn on the train back to London. I managed to catch up on the back issues, but by the time we arrived at Charing Cross, I was thoroughly tired of *The Lancet*. That morning Holmes had asked if I would join him for dinner at Baker Street—he had then wired Mrs. Hudson to let her know we were coming—and he had also suggested that I spend the night in his spare room, so we could set out together for York early the next morning. I had acquiesced, somewhat grudgingly. I could not understand his misplaced sense of urgency.

However, I first returned home to check on our mail and to bring our housekeeper up to date. I looked forward to sitting in my favorite chair with our black and white cat Victoria and stroking her long fur. I had missed her, and it turned out that the feeling was mutual! She meowed repeatedly at the sight of me, then clamored up onto my lap, purring loudly. I sat contentedly with her and stared out at the falling rain through our tall bow window, the sky growing dark so very early as December approached, and I wished Michelle were with me and that we might sleep together in our own bed that night.

Instead, I said my farewells to Victoria, promising I would return very soon, then set off for Baker Street. Mrs. Hudson greeted me warmly, and we went up the stairs together. All the lamps were lit, and Holmes sat in his armchair wearing his faded purple dressing gown, the bowl of his old clay pipe nestled in the palm of his right hand. Even though we had spent the day traveling together, he seemed genuinely glad to see me. He bade Mrs. Hudson open a bottle of claret and serve us each a glass as an aperitif.

He extinguished his pipe, set it aside, then took a sip of the wine. His black brows scrunched together, and he nodded. "There is nothing wrong with a good claret!—even if it does not have the pedigree of its more expensive French brethren which we have lately consumed."

"It does have its own virtues," I said. I looked round the familiar room and savored the warmth of the coal fire. "Perhaps I shall propose a toast of my own."

"Indeed?"

I smiled faintly and raised my glass. "To the ladies."

"I shall gladly drink to that." I was in the armchair opposite his, and we each leaned forward to clink our glasses together.

"I wish they were here," I said.

A smile flickered briefly at his lips. "Yes."

"And what book is this I see open before you? Good heavens, is that a Bible?"

"Yes, Henry. I was trying to refresh my memory. Despite my Anglican upbringing, I am not one who can quote scripture at will. Everyone, I suspect, knows this first line from Ecclesiastes, but not all that follows. 'To every thing there is a season, and a time to every purpose under the heaven.'"

I frowned slightly. "'A time to be born, and a time to die.' I can't go much further than that. I know the Catholic Bible in French far better than the King James version."

He opened up the book to a place marked by a red ribbon. "It continues on in the same vein. 'A time to plant, and a time to pluck up that which is planted; a time to kill, and a time to heal; a time to break down, and a time to build up; a time to weep, and a time to laugh; a time to mourn, and a time to dance; a time to cast away stones, and a time to gather stones together; a time to embrace, and a time to refrain from embracing; a time to get, and a time to lose; a time to keep, and a time to cast away; a time to rend, and a time to sew; a time to keep silence, and a time to speak; a time to love, and a time to hate; a time of war, and a time of peace.'"

"I can see why that passage might interest you." I smiled. "And what is the season for you? Which is the time?"

His gray eyes were faintly troubled. "I wish I knew, Henry. Ah, but here is Mrs. Hudson with our supper. We must give our full attention to a hearty cut of good English roast beef!"

Holmes had clearly resolved to be sociable, perhaps to atone for his gruff silence during our journey, and we ended up talking about our younger days and some of his recent cases I had assisted with. I could not refrain from pointing out that several of the participants owed their well-being and their very lives to him. Although he only shrugged, my observation seemed to relieve him. His thin face lost some of its intensity, and I could see weariness in his eyes and in the set of the muscles about his thin lips.

"It is curious," I said, stretching my arms. "Traveling often consists mostly of waiting, yet all the same it is quite tiring. It is only a little after ten, but I am ready for my bed." I stood up. "And you look rather exhausted. How long has it been since you had a good night's sleep?"

He frowned in concentration. "I am not sure."

"Will you not retire too?"

He shook his head, then set the stem of his pipe between his lips. The sleeve of his purple dressing gown had slipped down halfway to his elbow, and its breadth emphasized his thin bony wrist. The slipper filled with pipe tobacco sat next to him. "I shall sit up and smoke for a while."

"Goodnight then."

I went upstairs, got ready for bed, and fell asleep almost at once. First, however, various land and seascapes paraded through my mind, images from the day's journey, but they were interspersed with fragments of medical jargon from *The Lancet.*

I rose early, soon trudged downstairs, and found Holmes slumped to the side and asleep in the armchair. The room stank of tobacco, and the clay pipe sat on the nearby end table, a thin tendril of smoke rising from its bowl. The slipper had lost most of its contents. Reluctantly I woke Holmes. He needed to be up if we were to catch the 8:45 to York. We fortified ourselves with a hearty breakfast, Mrs. Hudson providing ham and scrambled eggs for me and curried fowl for my cousin, a favorite dish of his which I could not abide at any time of day!

And so began a new day of travel: yet another cavernous and busy train station, another first-class compartment; and the dreary gray outskirts of London soon gave way to green rolling countryside. We reached York by early afternoon and caught the next train for Whitby. The railway wound alongside a river between mountains, the sides covered with shaggy firs and stunted trees. The clouds and rain had followed us, but as we approached Whitby a wan sort of sunshine cast yellow highlights on the dark wood and the plush velvet upholstery of our compartment, and welcome light streamed through the large windows. It was not far from the station to our hotel, but we took a cab because of our luggage. Holmes signed the registry and asked for our bags to be taken to our room.

"Are we going somewhere?" I asked.

"Yes—up to Whitby Abbey, if you will join me. We have just time before dusk and darkness set in. I need some exercise after our two days of travel, and as you may recall, the view of the town and the sea, as well as the ruins of the abbey, are spectacular."

"An excellent idea, although it is likely to be freezing cold up there, what with the usual icy wind. At least the rain has stopped for now."

"We are well prepared for the cold, I think."

And indeed, we both had on rough home-spun walking hats, heavy woolen overcoats and tweed suits complete with waistcoats, as well as scarves. Holmes had also brought along a sturdy blackthorn, something far more suitable than his usual formal walking stick.

We made our way through the narrow cobbled streets of Whitby and came to the famed 199 steps which led uphill to the Church of

Saint Mary and the abbey beyond it. Halfway up, Holmes paused to catch his breath, which came out in steamy clouds. His face was pale and wan under the brim of the black bowler, and he looked almost ill.

"Are you sure you feel well enough for this?" I asked.

"It is only fatigue, I believe." He smiled at me. "As well as lungs corrupted by tobacco smoke! Let us resume."

I glanced back behind us at Whitby divided in two by the River Esk which flowed into the sea, then resumed the steep climb. The stone steps wound round and upward. I vaguely remember hearing how coffins were carried up this way in the past for burial in the churchyard. What an unenviable task that would be! We reached the summit at last and turned away from the church to stare out at the sea. I felt the frigid pressure of the brisk incoming wind on my face. Great swaths of gray and yellow clouds washed over the sky, but the hidden, faintly glowing orb of the sun hung over the horizon. To the south, the sky was much darker, ominously so. The sea itself was a dark gray-green, flat but frigid-looking. Anyone who fell into those waters would be lost in minutes. A few small solitary fishing boats were headed back to port.

"I don't like those clouds," I said. "It is certainly cold enough for snow."

It was a relief to turn away from the cold wind. We trudged around the left side of the church, which had a square crenellated tower with gaps more suitable for a castle and a squad of bowmen, and through the graveyard. Many of the tall tombstones thrust up above the sparse green grass had ornate curving tops, but their surfaces were stained black, so weathered and pitted by the elements, that one could not make out the names or dates.

Beyond, along a rise, stood the ruins of Whitby Abbey, curiously lit by that vast fading sky and masked sun. The sandstone, with all its hues of white, tan and brown, seemed faintly pinkish against the stark gray of the inland sky, and the long expanse of green lawn almost glowed. It was the various shades of the individual stones that made the structure so beautiful, the subtle mixtures of harmonious color, and it took decent light like this to distinguish them. Much later, and all would merge into a shadowy dirty gray. Tall columns topped with perfect Gothic arches marked the long nave, and on the left side of the structure, at the inverted V of one summit, was the stone framework of a circular rose window, its stained glass long gone.

Holmes raised his stick, pointing. "England has many ruined abbeys, but none I think is as splendid as this one."

"I agree," I said.

"There have been settlements here for centuries. The Romans had an outpost. The first monastery was in the sixth century. This one was built in the eleventh, but the beginning of the end was in the seventeenth century when Henry began his war against the Catholic Church. Now this magnificent structure has been left to ruin for a good two centuries." He shook his head. "It is far easier to destroy than to create."

"All the same," I said, "think of how it stood in its full beauty for four or five hundred years. Generations of monks lived, labored, and died here. I wish I could have seen it then in all its splendor."

Holmes nodded. "I, too. Let's have a closer look."

We wandered round the outskirts, then entered through one of the arches and walked along the nave, out of the biting wind. The roof overhead was mostly gone, the gray sky above framed by stone, and green turf had sprouted up inside. Only a sort of hallway off to the side still had a stone floor.

I shook my head. "These arches and columns always amaze me. It is hard to believe medieval men had the skill to create such intricate structures."

"Yes." He raised his stick. "Look at the layers in that arch there, and the columns within the columns, so to speak, building it outward from smaller units." He glanced upward. "It's getting darker."

I shivered slightly. "I'm ready to sit by a warm fire and drink some of the local ale."

We wandered back out onto the lawn and paused to look out at the sea. The dark bank of clouds had swept in from the south, casting a sort of sinister shadow out on the waters. Overhead the sky still had faint hints of color, yellow and perhaps pink. I blinked my eyes in disbelief, then felt an icy ping on my cheek. A few solitary white flakes came slowly tumbling down from that vast sky.

"Good Lord," I said, "it's starting to snow."

Holmes stared upward, then out at the sea. I could not see his forehead, but I could tell he was frowning. His pale lips looked faintly pinched, his eyes uneasy, and the bowler somehow seemed to emphasize his beak of a nose.

I turned impatiently. "Shall we go?–*please?*"

He was still frowning. "It will not do, Henry. It will not do."

"What will not do?"

"Winter comes soon enough. And you were right, I was right. A consulting detective must sometimes fail. All the same, I cannot simply abandon all those who may require my help. I have enjoyed my retirement while it lasted, but now it must come to an end."

I smiled at him. "Are you serious?"

"Never more so." His lips formed a characteristic sardonic smile. "After all, we cannot let *le Diable gagne*, can we?"

"Certainly not!" I exclaimed.

"Come, let's get back to the inn." We both started walking. The white flakes danced in the air all about us. "But first we must buy more train tickets."

"To return to London, you mean?"

"Yes, and then on to Paris."

"Paris?"

"Yes. We shall accept Violet's suggestion of a few days' holiday in Paris. Besides, I need to speak with her."

"Speak with Violet? But you already had several days to speak with her."

"I was preoccupied, as you may recall."

And so, the next day, we began the same journey in reverse: an early train back to York amidst falling snow, then the express to London, followed by another train to Dover. We took an evening ferry to Calais, spent the night there, and were on the first train the next morning to Paris. We pulled into the Gare du Nord around one PM. We hailed a cab from among the throng of vehicles and people at the station and headed straight for Auteuil. I asked Holmes if we shouldn't leave our luggage at the hotel, but he said that could wait. His face was faintly flushed, and I could tell that his spirits had completely altered.

Soon we reached the cobbled country lane leading to Violet's house, the bustle, noise and crowds of the city left far behind. The carriage came to a stop. Holmes smiled at me, then quickly got out. "*Attendez nous, monsieur, s'il vous plaît,*" he said to the driver. He strode down the stone path to the front door, and I followed. The sun had broken through the clouds, and yellow light shone on the lush green grass. He rang the bell, waited a few seconds, then rang it again.

The door finally swung open, revealing Berthe. It was always something of a surprise to see a woman almost at my eye level. She smiled at us. "*Ah, Monsieur Holmes, Dr. Vernier, bienvenue! Entrez, entrez.*" He stepped inside, and I followed.

"*Bonjour, madame. Est-ce que nous pouvons voir Madame Grace and Dr. Doudet Vernier?*"

"*Hélas, monsieur, elles ne sont pas içi. Elles sont parties en voyage.*"

I frowned. "On a trip?" I muttered.

"*J'ai quelque chose pour vous,*" she said, "*une télégramme. Attendez-moi une minute.*"

I shook my head. "Where on earth can they have gone?"

Holmes appeared amused. "I have a premonition."

"*La voiçi.*" Berthe handed him an envelope.

Holmes quickly tore it open, scanned the paper, gave a loud sharp laugh even as he let the hand holding the paper drop.

"What does it say?" I asked.

"It's from Michelle. She and Violet are in Yorkshire, at the hotel in Whitby. She wants to know where we are. She sent a telegram here, to the Meurice, and to Baker Street. 'Please advise,' she concludes." He folded the paper, put it back into the envelope and thrust it in his jacket pocket. "*Merçi, madame, et au revoir,*" he said to Berthe. "*À la prochaine.*" He whirled about and went back outside.

I followed, blinking briefly at the unaccustomed sunlight. "Where are we going?" I asked.

"To a telegraph office to send them a reply."

"Saying what?"

He paused on the path and turned to me. His blue-gray eyes were aglow under the brim of his top hat, flecks of amber showing near the black pupils, and he smiled. "To meet us in London tomorrow evening—at 221B Baker Street."

About the Author

Sam Siciliano is the author of several novels, including the Sherlock Holmes titles *The Angel of the Opera*, *The Web Weaver*, *The Grimswell Curse*, *The White Worm* and *The Moonstone's Curse*. He lives in Vancouver, Washington.

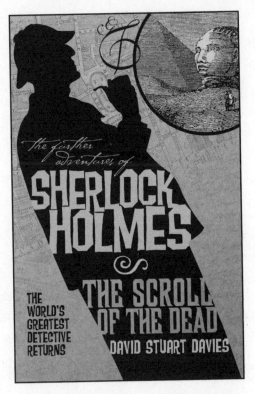

THE FURTHER ADVENTURES
OF SHERLOCK HOLMES

THE SCROLL OF THE DEAD

David Stuart Davies

In this fast-paced adventure, Sherlock Holmes attends a seance to unmask an impostor posing as a medium. His foe, Sebastian Melmoth is a man hell-bent on discovering a mysterious Egyptian papyrus that may hold the key to immortality. It is up to Holmes and Watson to use their deductive skills to stop him or face disaster.

ISBN: 9781848564930

AVAILABLE NOW!

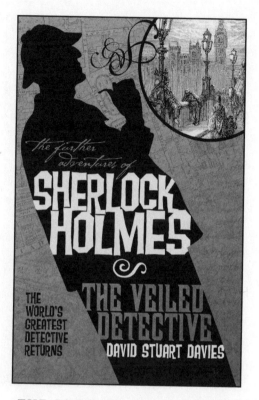

THE FURTHER ADVENTURES
OF SHERLOCK HOLMES
THE VEILED DETECTIVE

David Stuart Davies

It is 1880, and a young Sherlock Holmes arrives in London to pursue a career as a private detective. He soon attracts the attention of criminal mastermind Professor James Moriarty, who is driven by his desire to control this fledgling genius. Enter Dr John H. Watson, soon to make history as Holmes' famous companion.

ISBN: 9781848564909

AVAILABLE NOW!

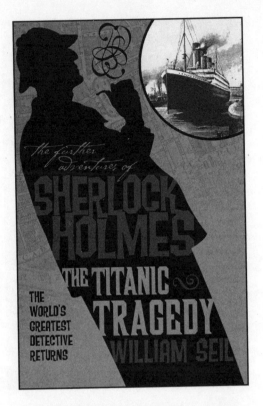

THE FURTHER ADVENTURES
OF SHERLOCK HOLMES

THE TITANIC TRAGEDY

William Seil

Holmes and Watson board the Titanic in 1912, where Holmes is to carry
out a secret government mission. Soon after departure, highly important
submarine plans for the U.S. navy are stolen. Holmes and Watson work
through a list of suspects which includes Colonel James Moriarty, brother to
the late Professor Moriarty—will they find the culprit before tragedy strikes?

ISBN: 9780857687104

AVAILABLE NOW!

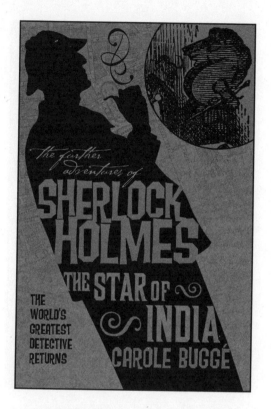

THE FURTHER ADVENTURES
OF SHERLOCK HOLMES
THE STAR OF INDIA

Carole Buggé

Holmes and Watson find themselves caught up in a complex chessboard
of a problem, involving a clandestine love affair and the disappearance
of a priceless sapphire. Professor James Moriarty is back to tease and
torment, leading the duo on a chase through the dark and dangerous
back streets of London and beyond.

ISBN: 9780857681218

AVAILABLE NOW!

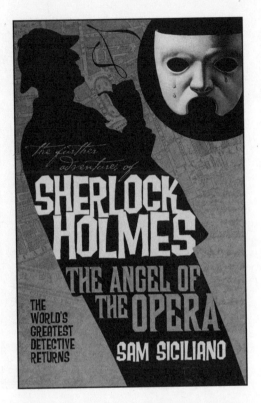

THE FURTHER ADVENTURES
OF SHERLOCK HOLMES
THE ANGEL OF THE OPERA

Sam Siciliano

Paris 1890. Sherlock Holmes is summoned across the English Channel
to the famous Opera House. Once there, he is challenged to discover
the true motivations and secrets of the notorious phantom, who rules its
depths with passion and defiance.

ISBN: 9781848568617

AVAILABLE NOW!